CAMILEON

CAMILEON

A Novel

Shykia Bell

To Lisa
Warm Regards!
Shykia Bell

iUniverse, Inc.
New York Bloomington Shanghai

Camileon

iUniverse books may be ordered through booksellers or by contacting:

iUniverse
1663 Liberty Drive
Bloomington, IN 47403
www.iuniverse.com
1-800-Authors (1-800-288-4677)

Because of the dynamic nature of the Internet, any Web addresses or links contained in this book may have changed since publication and may no longer be valid.

This is a work of fiction. All of the characters, names, incidents, organizations, and dialogue in this novel are either the products of the author's imagination or are used fictitiously.

ISBN: 978-0-595-48607-6 (pbk)
ISBN: 978-0-595-49338-8 (cloth)
ISBN: 978-0-595-60701-3 (ebk)

Printed in the United States of America

This book is dedicated to my devoted parents, Mildred & William, my family and my loving soul mate, Max.

It is also dedicated to the dreamers, who persevere through dark, perilous roads in order to find light.

Last, but certainly not least, I thank God for all of the above.

—Shykia Bell

Contents

CHAPTER 1

▼

QUESTIONS

Searing, unbearable pain ripped through Camile Leon's skull as she sat in her homeroom class. The sensation was so intense, all sense of perception seemed to fade into the recesses of her consciousness. All that remained was a high-pitched shriek which penetrated her eardrums and radiated throughout her brain. Relief was brief and fleeting, allowing her only a moment to inquire about the sound before it returned. However, no one else could hear it. She was ridiculed with sneers and snickers as her peers doubted her sanity. Ms. Hawkins, her teacher, even seemed uncertain of Camile's mental faculties. Before long, Camile identi- fied the source of her torment, a dog whistle being blown by her rambunctious classmate, Barry Collins. Once he realized he'd been found out, he and his goons laughed mercilessly in the face of their victim. They even called her *Teen Wolf* in hushed chants, inaudible to the teacher. At first, she said nothing, not wanting to cause a scene, but by the time class had been dismissed she could no longer hold her tongue. Her anger had reached its peak. Rising from her seat, she intercepted Barry just as he approached her desk on his way to the exit. He was nearly a full head taller than Camile, who shook in the shadow of his intimidating frame.

"Get out of my way!" He sneered.

"One of these days you're gonna mess with the wrong person." Camile said through gritted teeth, glaring into his eyes.

"Really?" Barry asked rhetorically. "And I guess *you're* the wrong person, huh? So whatcha gonna do, Teen Wolf? Howl at me?" He snickered.

"Just leave me alone! I'm sick of you! Just do the world a favor and disappear!" Camile lashed out before grabbing her bag and storming out of the classroom.

As she made her way towards the exit, Ms. Hawkins fixed her with a curious gaze and opened her mouth to say something. However, Camile left before her teacher could address her.

The ominous clouds in the dark afternoon sky seemed to rupture, unleashing a torrential downpour. It didn't take long for the gusting wind to snap the canopy of Camile's umbrella, causing it to collapse into an inverted fold. She tried in vain to fix it, but like her ego, it seemed beyond repair. Nevertheless, she clung to the broken apparatus as she jogged home, her feet sloshing in the water that had collected in her sneakers. Vibrant ribbons of lightning streamed across the sky followed by a violent clap of thunder just as Camile reached the building.

She stormed into the apartment, throwing her broken umbrella onto the floor as she entered. Her hair was plastered to her face, which was drenched with a mixture of fresh rain and salty tears. Her grey eyes flashed with intense anger as she kicked off her shoes. Although she was only sixteen, she already matched her mother's 5' 7" stature. Another trait she shared with her mother was her beautiful golden caramel complexion.

Although Camile was reeling from the latest round of insults from her classmates, it didn't compare to the devastation she felt when they made derogatory remarks about her mixed race. She'd been called such names as 'Oreo', 'Half-breed' and 'Ethnically confused'. As painful as those comments were, Camile didn't speak to her mother about them since she feared it would only exacerbate the situation. At one time, Camile had an ally, Rhonda Jones, but sadly she had gotten caught in a cross-fire between rival gangs on her way home from school one day. Until her death, Rhonda had been Camile's only friend and often kept bullies at bay. With Rhonda gone, it seemed Camile's intimidators were making up for lost time.

Her mother, Kylie, met her in the corridor upon hearing the commotion. Camile noticed she seemed a bit somber, but was too engrossed in her own distress to pay full attention. She wasted no time in voicing her grievances of the day's torment to her mother.

"Camile, I know it's been really tough for you lately." Kylie replied tenderly as she embraced her. "Your teen years will be some of the most challenging years of your life. Believe me I know. I also know you have the strength to push through them. Like life, kids can be so cruel, but you have to remember that all people aren't the same and that hate isn't the answer. It only begets more hate and will only do you damage in the long run."

"Right now, I only care about the short run! Why do I always have to go through all this pain? Why am I always so weak? I'm constantly being picked on. I'm never able to defend myself and I'm sick of it! I just want them to know what it feels like to hurt this much! I hope Barry takes my advice and disappears so he can just leave me alone!" Camile sobbed.

"Baby, is that what you told him? You didn't threaten to *make* him disappear did you?" Kylie asked gingerly, an uneasy look crossing her face.

"No. I didn't threaten him. I should've!"

"Camile, just be careful about what you say to people. Saying the wrong things can get you in a whole lot of trouble. Even thinking the wrong things can cause a lot of damage, not necessarily to others, but to ourselves. Look, I know how unfairly you're being treated. Karma will make sure your bullies will get theirs, but you can't let anger get the best of you. I know you don't want to hear this right now, but don't take revenge into your own hands. It's a slippery slope to devastation. As I've told you many times before, I would be fine with going up to your school so I can talk to—"

"No!" Camile interrupted.

Her already large eyes grew even wider as she calculated the potential horrors that would follow such a visit.

"Mom, please don't do that. It would only feed the jerks more ammunition. It's my junior year in high school and all I have to do is get through this year … and the next." She said with a hopeless sigh.

For the most part, the weekend was average and uneventful. On Saturday, Camile spent most of her time doing homework. Camile was an average student but would often find math to be the most challenging. Therefore, she usually dreaded math homework, but her interest piqued when it came to Geometry. As a result, she was able to solve most problems with ease. After storing her books in her backpack, she helped her mother with chores. Camile began clearing the wall unit shelves before wiping them down. Stashed in the rear of the top shelf, she spotted a leather bound book. Upon inspection, she noticed an old photo attached to its cover. In the photo, Camile and her father, Zephyr, were posed in front of a very large tree. Its bark was pure white and its bountiful branches bloomed with unusual red petals. Zephyr, a handsome man in his late 20's, was shown crouching beside Camile, who was then a chubby cheeked toddler.

Camile's auburn, shoulder-length hair was in curls. Her large piercing grey eyes were a trait she shared with her father—a tall, fair-skinned, medium built man with a megawatt smile. His glossy hair appeared to be jet-black and was neatly combed, except for a small, loose tuft that dangled above his brow. Camile wore a white dress which complimented her rich skin tone. Her outfit was accessorized with a blue satin sash and a silver necklace. Hanging from the chain was a beautiful stone, about the diameter of a silver dollar—which had various shades of blue. The stone was framed with intricate, leaf-like accents.

Camile removed the photo from the book and regarded it for a moment before approaching her mother.

"I thought you said there were no pictures of Dad." Camile remarked with great curiosity.

Kylie seemed genuinely surprised at Camile's discovery and stared at the photo with great perplexity.

"I didn't realize it was there." She answered softly. "All these years and it's been here all along."

With a heavy heart, Camile watched as her mother stared at the photo with tearful eyes.

"I thought this was lost in the move along with all the other pictures." Kylie sighed. "I'm sorry it took all these years before you could finally see what your father looks like. If I knew that picture was there, I would've shown it to you a long time ago."

"It's weird. Even though I don't remember him, I still miss him." Camile said quietly after gawking at the photo a few moments longer.

"You don't remember him because you were very little when ... Well, when he ..."

"*Died?*" Camile interrupted. "Mom, why can't you just say it?"

"Camile, don't start. There's no proof that he's dead!" Kylie snapped angrily before calming her voice. "I—I'm sorry. I just miss him too."

"I know, but there's no proof that he's alive either. He's been out of our lives for *thirteen years* now. If he's still alive, he would've had some kind of contact with us by now. I just can't standby and watch you hurt yourself by holding on to false hope."

Kylie took the photo from Camile and sank into the tan sofa. As she gazed at the picture, tears trickled down her cheeks. Camile, feeling terribly about causing her mother grief, sat beside her.

"Please don't cry." Camile said as she wrapped an arm around her mother's shoulders.

"Camile, I have to tell you ..." Her mother's voice trailed off as she drifted into a trance-like state.

"Tell me what? Mom?"

Kylie was non-responsive as she continued to stare at the photo with her dark eyes. Camile panicked.

"Mom!" She exclaimed.

"Oh!" Kylie gasped and she placed one hand over her chest as she forced out a nervous chuckle. "I was in my own little world there, huh?"

"What were you thinking about?"

"I forgot." Kylie answered abruptly as she made a motion to stand, but Camile gently took hold of her arm.

"Wait. You said you had to tell me something."

Kylie nodded with a soft smile as she placed her hand on Camile's shoulder.

"Camile, I just want you to know that right now—aside from you—hope is all I have left. It helps keep me going. I understand that you've given up on ever seeing your father again, but I believe he's out there somewhere. He loves us both so very much and I truly believe that we'll see him again someday."

"But Mom, if he's still alive … how come he didn't come back to us by now? Why didn't he at least try to contact us? So many years have gone by without a word from him. If he's not dead, then maybe he forgot all about us. Maybe he already moved on and—"

"Camile, that's enough!" Kylie said sternly before reducing her voice to a bitter whisper. "You're really testing my patience today aren't you? All I ask is that you let me hold on to my 'false hope'. Let me have at least that much."

Camile felt uneasy about her mother's volatile reaction to her questions. Nevertheless, she wanted answers.

"Mom, I didn't mean to make you mad. I just have so many questions. I just think it's weird that as much as we both miss Dad, we never talk about him. After all these years, I barely know anything about him. I don't know how or why he disappeared, what kind of job he had or how you met him. There's a lot I don't remember about my childhood. There are so many gaps in my life. Every time I try to ask questions about any of these things you always change the subject. Why?" Camile asked softly.

Kylie sighed as she wiped the tears from her eyes. She leaned back against the sofa and smiled faintly before responding.

"Camile, it might not have been right for me to do it, but I thought it would've made things easier for you if I didn't talk about him. I thought I was protecting you and that the less you knew about him, the less you would suffer. Evidently, I was wrong about that. I'm sorry if it made things worse for you, but please believe me when I tell you that I had your best interest at heart."

"I know." Camile said as she rested her head on Kylie's shoulder. "But there are so many things I want to know about him. It's not too late."

Camile looked into Kylie's eyes and smiled tenderly before pointing to the necklace she was wearing in the photo.

"Let's start with this. It's very unusual."

"Yes … it was custom made just for you." Kylie answered slowly as she stared at the photograph.

"Where's it now?" Camile asked.

Kylie frowned. There was a brief pause before she answered the question.

"You lost it at the swimming pool when you were very little. The clasp must've broken while you were swimming. The pool workers tried to help us look for it, but it was too late. Someone must've found it and taken it. It's such a shame. It was such a beautiful necklace."

"Why was I swimming with it in the first place?"

"You loved that necklace so much you refused to ever take it off. I tried to get you to give it to me but you made a big scene and eventually got your way. You thought it was your only connection to your father and you were afraid that it would disappear just like he did."

"It looks like I was right about that." Camile replied glumly as she hung her head. "Dad would've been devastated if he knew that I lost it. I bet it meant a lot to him."

"Oh baby, don't worry about it." Kylie said while hugging Camile gently. "It really wasn't your fault. You were only a child and I know you didn't lose it on purpose. Material things aren't the most important things in the world. They're just symbols that represent much greater things. Losing that necklace doesn't change the fact that your father loves you very, very much."

Camile took a moment to regain her composure before asking her next question.

"Where'd you meet him?" She asked.

"Before you and I moved to New York, I used to work at *Arizona General Hospital.*"

"Yeah, I remember that. You told me you worked there for a while before we moved here when I was three."

"Well, that's where I met your father."

"Really? Did he work at the hospital too?"

"Nah, he was a patient. He was in a terrible crash. It was a miracle he survived! The stubborn man didn't take the necessary precautions when he was traveling. Amazingly, he walked thirty miles to get to the hospital! It took him two days just to get to there. The poor man was a mess! He suffered dehydration, cuts, bruises, a mild concussion, and a dislocated shoulder that he managed to pop back into place on his own."

"Ugh! Sounds like he was a pretty tough guy." Camile replied. Kylie nodded with a slight chortle.

"He recovered nicely, but he insisted he still wasn't feeling quite right and requested additional care. I later realized it was just an excuse to get me to spend more time with him. Eventually, he worked up the nerve to ask me out."

Camile smiled as she continued to listen with rapt attention.

"Some of the other nurses would've killed to trade places with me. But I didn't accept his invitation. At least not right away." Kylie added.

"Why not?"

"I was getting over a pretty bad breakup at the time and wasn't ready to jump into a new relationship. What kind of girl do you think I was anyway?"

Camile and Kylie shared a hearty laugh.

"But your father wouldn't take no for an answer." Kylie continued. "Eventually, he wore me down and we started dating. He was very charming, kind and loving. He seemed too good to be true and I was always secretly waiting for the other shoe to drop."

"Did it?" Camile asked.

Her mother chuckled uncomfortably and avoided the question.

As Camile continued her discussion with her mother, she learned that Zephyr was an officer. Her mother finally seemed ready to reveal everything to Camile. However, she clammed up when it came to the particulars surrounding Zephyr's mysterious disappearance. Kylie also refused to discuss the reason she decided to move to New York.

"That, my dear, is a *very* long story. I'll have to explain that another time. I'm just so tired all of a sudden." Kylie said.

"Aw, can't you just tell me now?"

"Patience, Camile. I'll tell you in due time, but right now I'm very tired and really need to take a nap. Don't forget, you still have to mop the kitchen floor."

Little did Camile know, the answers to her many questions would elude her for years to come. Kylie stood up and proceeded to walk to her room. Camile noticed that subtle signs of her mother's age were beginning to emerge, particularly around the eyes. She also noticed that lately, Kylie seemed to grow tired more easily than usual. Camile felt uneasy about the realization that her mother was getting older. Camile's sudden recognition of this particular metamorphosis weighed on her mind as she began to contemplate time and mortality.

CHAPTER 2

▼

BORDERLINE ACCUSATORY

Camile dreaded the prospect of attending classes on Monday. Not because of the tough lessons and endless note taking, but due to the constant ridicule and torment she knew she would endure from her classmates. After she showered and dressed, she stared at her reflection in the mirror. She almost seemed hypnotized by her own gloomy eyes. They possessed the ominous intensity of a storm cloud, threatening torrential precipitation at any moment. Camile rubbed her hands over her face, which was flawless—much to the vexation of her female peers who were often plagued with pimples. As usual, she wore her thick, but semi-tamed shoulder-length hair back in a ponytail.

"Camile! Come get your breakfast, you don't want to be late for school!" Kylie called from the kitchen.

"Yes I do. If it were up to me, I wouldn't have to go at all!" Camile glumly muttered to herself.

She grabbed her school books and stuffed them into her bag as she headed off to join her mother in the kitchen. As she ate her breakfast, Camile noticed that Kylie looked much better than she did over the weekend. Her silky hair flowed freely and caught the morning sunlight. The silver streak in the front gleamed.

"Mom, you make the best pancakes in the world!" Camile said between bites.

"I guess the old lady's still got it!" Kylie joked as she flipped her hair.

"Mom, you're not old! You'll never be old!"

"Well, I wouldn't go *that* far, Camile. Anyway, getting old sure beats the alternative." Kylie chuckled. "Alright, enough stalling. Off you go! You're already running late."

"Do I *really* have to—?"

"Yes, you really have to go. Don't let a few bullies get in the way of your education. You're stronger than you give yourself credit for, so stop being your own worse enemy. You can handle anything that comes your way. You just have to believe it in here and here." Kylie said as she pointed to Camile's head and heart respectively.

"Alright, alright." Camile sighed. "Love you, Mom."

"Love you too, baby."

Kylie kissed her on the cheek and saw her out the door.

When Camile arrived at school, she noticed something seemed different, but wasn't exactly sure what. Usually when she went to her homeroom class the other students would point, laugh and even throw paper at her. That day was the complete opposite of the norm. There wasn't a peep out of anyone in the room once she entered. Camile received terrified glances from some of her classmates as she walked to her seat. Others avoided eye contact altogether as they nervously gazed into their books, out the window or at the empty blackboard in front of the room.

Camile grew increasingly curious about the strange behavior they were exhibiting. After getting settled at her desk she noticed that her teacher, Ms. Hawkins, was not yet in class. It was very unusual since Ms. Hawkins always had perfect attendance. Even more unusual was the fact that Barry Collins—who also had perfect attendance—was also absent. Although it was highly unusual, Camile was not concerned. In fact, she looked forward to a day without having to deal with Barry's antics.

Ms. Hawkins suddenly entered the room. She was accompanied by the principal, a police chief and a police officer. The quartet looked comically mismatched. Ms. Hawkins was a short, dark-skinned, petite woman. Her looks were average, but she was often mistaken for a student. She appeared to be quite young and had a trendy sense of style. Many of the students would often tell her that she was much too cool to be a teacher. Some of the girls even tried to duplicate her layered, shoulder-length haircut—without much success—and in many cases, the results were downright dreadful.

Principal Turner—who stood next to Ms. Hawkins—was a well-dressed, short, stocky fellow with classic male pattern baldness. The students often joked that the only thing shinier than his shoes was the top of his head. His eyes and cheeks had a permanent droopy appearance, which caused him to bear an uncanny resemblance to a bulldog. He always wore a grim, serious expression which never seemed to change—not even when he laughed! It really freaked the students out since it was impossible to gauge his mood.

After Ms. Hawkins placed her bag on the desk, Principal Turner nodded, prompting her to begin. She adjusted her glasses and cleared her throat before she spoke.

"Good morning." She greeted in a harried voice. "As you may already know there's an urgent matter at hand. Therefore, your full cooperation will be appreciated. For those of you who are unaware of the situation, Barry Collins never made it home on Friday. He's been reported missing. Chief Roberts and Officer Harris are here to interview all of his classmates, friends …" Her glance shifted to Camile before saying the words: "… and acquaintances."

Something in the way Ms. Hawkins looked at Camile seemed to cast an air of suspicion. This made Camile extremely uncomfortable. The fleeting look was borderline accusatory, but no one else took notice. Instead, the entire class stared at the chief as he stepped forward. He was a burly man—apparently in his early-forties—who stood 6' 2". His weight was approximately two-hundred sixty pounds. He wore a crisp white shirt, which was a stark contrast to his deep pink complexion. His hair and thick mustache were red as flame which intensified his vibrant blue eyes. The color alone made it seem as if they were capable of burning a hole into one's thoughts. Chief Robert's overall appearance was very intimidating to say the least.

"I am confident that the participation of everyone in the school will help the investigators find Barry as soon as possible." Ms. Hawkins continued as she turned to the chief. "Mr. Roberts, how would you like to proceed?"

"Well, we can simply talk to the students in the same order as they're listed on your roster." His deep voice boomed.

His voice startled some of the students and caused them to sit up at attention. Under alternative circumstances, Camile might have found it amusing.

As the names were announced in alphabetical order, the students were individually summoned for inquiry. Ms. Hawkins routed the students to the office to be interviewed. Camile's heart pounded, but she didn't understand why she felt so nervous. She knew she had nothing to do with Barry's disappearance. However, her awareness of that fact couldn't tame the uneasy feeling that gripped her. She felt the eyes of her fellow classmates burning into her back, which didn't help matters much. It wasn't long before over half the students were done with questioning. However, they didn't return to the classroom. In order to maintain the integrity of the investigation, they were separated until all students had been examined.

In the meantime, Officer Harris was left to supervise the students. He was a tall, handsome lean man with a chiseled jaw line, dazzling bright green eyes and strong features. His dark hair was smoothed back and his fair skin contrasted against his crisp blue-black uniform. The boys in the classroom were annoyed to see the girls all but swoon over the officer, who told funny stories in an attempt to lighten the serious mood.

"… so that's when I said 'I think you fellas need to pick a new spot to hang out.'" He joked.

The girls broke out in hysterical laughter. The boys groaned and sucked their teeth, clearly expressing their jealousy.

"Oh please! That's so corny!" One boy disgustedly muttered under his breath.

When Ms. Hawkins reentered the room, everything grew silent.

"Camile, you're up next." She announced.

Camile stood up and realized that her legs felt about as stable as rubber bands. She met Ms. Hawkins at the door and was escorted out of the classroom. As they stepped out into the hall, Camile heard voices coming from inside the classroom.

"She's a witch! She made him disappear!" Someone shouted.

"Shh!" Another voice hissed. "Do you want that freak to get you next?"

Other voices joined in and immediately built up to an unintelligible rumble.

"Alright, that's quite enough!" Officer Harris scolded.

The voices grew faint as Camile and Ms. Hawkins made their way down the hall. However, the painful words resonated in Camile's head as she sighed. The stinging sensation in her eyes felt all too familiar.

No! She thought angrily to herself. *Stop it! Stop being so weak all the time!*

Much to Camile's amazement, she successfully fought back the tears.

"Camile, I need to ask you something." Ms. Hawkins said as she suddenly came to a halt.

"Yeah?" Camile asked nervously as she stopped and turned to face her.

"I know that you and Barry weren't on the best of terms. In fact, I know that he was downright cruel to you—"

"That's putting it mildly!" Camile interrupted before she realized how rude it was. "Sorry."

"I just need to know, when you told him to disappear on Friday, what exactly did you—?"

"Camile you don't have to answer that!" A voice urgently called from the main staircase.

Camile and Ms. Hawkins turned around to see Kylie approaching them.

"Mom?!" Camile asked in horror. "What are you doing here?!"

Kylie walked over and put an arm around her shoulders.

"I found out about Barry. It was on the news. I just knew that you would be subject to questioning, which will be fine in the presence of our lawyer." Kylie said as she looked at Ms. Hawkins.

"Ms. Leon," Ms. Hawkins said quietly with an easy smile. "I think you're overreacting. No one in this school is being formally accused of anything at this point. This process is just to gather information that may lead to Barry's whereabouts. My duty is to—"

"Think what you must Ms. Hawkins." Kylie sternly interrupted. "With all due respect, I understand that your duty is to the school and I know you'll do what you must. But I'm sure you'll understand that my duty is to my daughter and I'll do everything in my power to protect her. I won't stand by while you prepare her to go before a lynch mob." She said as she stared Ms. Hawkins in the eye.

At that moment, Kylie was joined by a middle-aged man, carrying a small black briefcase. He wore a sharply pressed, navy blue pinstriped suit that flattered his medium-built frame. His hair was somewhat spiky and silver in color. It enhanced the intensity of his electric blue eyes, which sparkled like Topaz gems.

"This is my lawyer, Travis D'Arby." Kylie introduced. A note of defiance was present in her voice.

"Mom, you already have a lawyer?! Won't this make me look guilty?" Camile whispered in Kylie's ear, but the question went ignored.

Ms. Hawkins' face wore an odd expression that gave the impression that she already knew the lawyer. However, her words contradicted the possibility of that theory.

"Uh, pleased to meet you sir." Ms. Hawkins said as she nervously shook his hand. "Well, I guess we should get started. The chief is waiting in the principal's office."

Once the questioning was over, Camile and her mother were told to contact the chief's office if they heard, saw or remembered anything that might be helpful to the case. Kylie then offered to take Camile straight home but she declined.

"Mom, if I leave school early there'll just be rumors that I got arrested or that I felt guilty or something. It's tempting for me to go home right now, but if staying means I'll have a chance to get through this with at least a little dignity, I'm going to try." Camile said. Her mother regarded her with pride and amazement before tightly embracing her.

"I hope someday you'll see just how truly special and powerful you really are. Camile, I love you so much. No matter what happens, always remember that I love you." Kylie softly whispered.

"Mom, you're starting to scare me." Camile replied with concern. Ignoring the comment, Kylie continued hugging her.

During the entire week of school, the other students continued to ostracize Camile even more than usual. No one dared look in her direction much less speak to her. However, some were brazen enough to call her names like 'murderer' and 'witch' behind her back. Oddly enough, the thing that bothered her the most wasn't the behavior of her fellow students, but the behavior of her teachers, especially that of Ms. Hawkins. Ever since Barry's disappearance, Ms. Hawkins would stare at Camile in the most peculiar way. It was almost hauntingly disturbing.

The case of Barry's disappearance progressed with very few developments and several students—including Camile—were contacted for second and third rounds of questioning. By the end of the week, Camile was exhausted and sick of being called dastardly names by her peers. As much as she couldn't stand him, she wanted Barry to be found more than anything. She could cope with another two years of being bullied, but not a lifetime of being called a murderer when she knew she wasn't one.

Camile was in the middle of a boring chapter about the industrial revolution in her history book when she heard a series of gasps throughout the classroom. She raised her head to see none other than Barry standing in the doorway.

"Barry! Oh my God! Are you alright?" Ms. Hawkins asked as she ran over to him.

Looking dazed as he staggered into the room, Barry nodded in response to the question. He was wearing the same sweater and jeans he wore a week earlier. However, they were torn, tattered and scorched in some areas. His hair was disheveled and dirty. A crowd instantly gathered around him, erupting with jubilant cheers. Once they caught a whiff of the stench that wafted from his body, they immediately backed away.

"Phew! He smells like dog shit!" One girl exclaimed.

"Everyone, quiet!" Ms. Hawkins ordered. "Barry, where have you been? Were you kidnapped? What happened to you?"

As if on cue, everyone looked at Camile, who remained at her desk.

"It was ... it was—" Barry said slowly, clearly disoriented.

"Rebecca, get the nurse! Tell her we need an ambulance!" Ms. Hawkins urgently instructed one of the girls.

"It was beautiful! That's all I can remember!" Barry said before he fainted. Everyone in the classroom looked at one another with puzzlement.

It was later discovered that Barry had apparently been struck by lightning during the rainstorm a week earlier. He recalled cutting across the school's football field on his way home. He also remembered playing with his ball, repeatedly tossing it in the air and catching it. According to Barry, he had nearly cleared the field when an intense flash of light streamed down upon him from the sky. The next thing he knew, he was back in class with no recollection of any events that had taken place after he'd been struck. After a thorough series of tests, he was granted a clean bill of health and released from the hospital within days. Although everyone was happy about his return, many questions remained. Where had he been for a whole week and how did he survive? Investigators desperately tried to find answers, but without Barry's memory or sufficient clues, the investigation reached an impasse.

CHAPTER 3

▼

DISAPPEARING ACTS

Seven years later

Camile's struggle to belong continued into her twenty-third year. Up to that point, she threw herself into her studies and worked hard to achieve a Bachelors Degree in Interior Design. During her college years, she managed to make a few friends. However, each friendship failed, fading almost as quickly as they began. The same was true for Camile's romantic relationships. In nearly all her interpersonal encounters—whether social or professional—she was often ignored. On many occasions, people wouldn't even notice whether or not she was present until she was practically in their face. The fact that she had a diminutive voice didn't help matters much since people were prone to speak over her.

She also faced adversity in many of the jobs she held, none of which made her happy or quenched her desire to make a significant contribution to society. Camile was also bitter that she had spent four years in college to obtain a degree for a career that seemed unattainable. She worked insane hours as a sales clerk in a department store, a job she worked full-time since her early college years. At times, it was an extremely demanding job, carrying with it unwarranted stress levels. She contemplated quitting, but she needed the job in order to pay her rent and to keep up with her student loans.

Deep in her heart, she felt that there was more to life than stressing over things that in her opinion—other than financially—would make little or no difference in the end. As she witnessed people younger than her advancing in their lives and careers, she couldn't help but feel envious. Especially since she felt that her own life was being squandered. She often worried about the path on which her life was headed. What did it all mean? What was the point to her existence if no one knew she was even there? Was she more than the sum of her rare, fleeting friendships and failed relationships? Was there anything more for her than unresolved questions about her family and the endless string of unfulfilling, unsuccessful jobs? Her life's purpose was something she always looked for and yet it constantly eluded her. Camile hungered for stability and thirsted to belong. She desired that someday the overwhelming emptiness she felt inside would finally be filled.

Camile lived in a small Brooklyn apartment, approximately seven miles away from her mother. It was located in a relatively boisterous neighborhood. Everything from small bodegas to public transportation was easily accessible. For the most part, the area was fairly tame, but in recent months there had been a rise in crime. The most recent offenses included a couple of robberies and vandalism inspired by racial intolerance.

Her apartment was modest in size, but she used her interior design skills to make it a home. The style of her furniture was functional and elegant. Since her salary was meager, she purchased most of the furnishings at bargain prices from warehouse-type stores. The entire apartment—excluding the kitchen—was painted in a flat shade of pale green. She found the color soothing and relaxing. In the short corridor just inside the entrance there was an oval pewter mirror hanging on the wall. It was about a foot and a half in size and was framed with intricate floral scrollwork. There was a matching shelf just below it on which she usually tossed her keys and mail.

To the right of the corridor was one of her favorite rooms, the kitchen. She loved to cook, whenever she had the time and energy. Her culinary skills contributed to the few extra pounds recently added to her frame. The kitchen housed refurbished stainless steel appliances, which contrasted with the white Formica tiled floor. The cabinets were off-white with stainless steel handles.

The living room was to the left of the corridor and had slightly more personality than the kitchen. Medium plush grey carpet complimented the jade-colored walls. In one of the corners was a black, four panel screen that separated Camile's computer workstation from the rest of the room. She enjoyed the freedom of having a lot of space in her living quarters. It eliminated the feeling of disorderliness and chaos—at least at home.

The seating arrangement consisted of a comfortable black sofa and matching loveseat, both of which had simple contours. A rectangular coffee table added a modern accent to the room. It had a clear glass surface with a beveled edge that glistened when it caught the light. The table's glass base had a smoky grey color which almost matched the carpet perfectly. It gave the table's surface the illusion of floating at knee level. There were also two small matching side tables that were located on each side of the loveseat. Each side table supported an eccentric lamp. A medium flat screen TV was mounted to the wall at a point where it was visible from nearly every angle of the room.

Camile didn't find it necessary to decorate her place with many elaborate accessories since she spent most of her time alone or working. However, prior to moving into her own place, she made herself a copy of the photo Kylie kept of her and her father, Zephyr. It was framed and prominently displayed on the coffee table. She often looked at the photo during times of despair or when she contemplated her life. It seemed a form of meditation for her. She felt strangely at peace whenever she looked at the unusual tree in the photo's backdrop. She had seen many trees with pretty flowers and leaves, but not to that extreme. The petals were deep red in color and glistened with a lively iridescence.

Seven years had elapsed since the strange situation occurred with Barry. Throughout those years, her mother continually dodged Camile's many questions regarding Zephyr and her childhood. It was an evasion that angered and frightened Camile. She wondered why her mother was so determined to keep things so secret. As she prepared herself for her next visit with Kylie, she realized that she'd been too passive about the situation over the years. That day, Camile decided not to relent until she finally got some answers.

The late afternoon train was overcrowded as usual. A slightly nauseating and pungent smell wafted through the air. A group of rowdy teenagers pushed their way up and down the packed cars. A few of them were using some of the foulest language Camile had ever heard. It was clear that most of the passengers were annoyed with being subjected to such verbal pollution. However, they kept their opinions to themselves since they'd likely run the risk of getting knifed if they did otherwise. Camile's heart sank when she realized that she had eight remaining stops before she would reach her mother's neighborhood. When the train pulled into the next station, a group of holiday shoppers bustled onto the train, overstuffed bags in tow.

There was a sudden rush of commotion after a woman screamed. An elderly woman sitting across from Camile was being mugged by two large teen thugs. They each held a gun and demanded that the woman give them her money and jewelry. All the other passengers fled except for Camile and a businessman, presumably in his late forties. He took a shaky step toward the assailants, but ran off after one of the gangsters growled while waving the gun at him. Fearfully, Camile watched as the terrified woman tried to remove her necklace. However, the woman's hands trembled, hindering her attempt to undo the clasp.

"Come on! You're takin' too long, you ol' fart!" One of the muggers shouted as he ripped the necklace from the woman's neck.

At that moment, Camile had a sudden, inexplicable impulse to rise from her seat. Both thugs nearly jumped out of their skin, evidently surprised at the abrupt movement.

"Where the hell did *she* come from?!" One thug yelled to the other. His face contorted with intense fear and confusion.

"I dunno!" The other replied. "All the other punks ran away except for this ol' prune!"

He quickly pointed the gun at Camile and before she could react, he repeatedly pulled the trigger. Her heart skipped a beat before she realized that the gun hadn't gone off. The other thug also tried to shoot, but with the same result. Terrified, Camile could barely breathe as she stared at the thugs with wide eyes. Suddenly, their guns shifted to take aim at their own faces. Stricken with immense horror, they dropped their weapons to the ground.

"Yo, son! How da hell did she do that? This is some freaky shit! Let's roll up outta here!" one of them yelled.

The thugs ran out the car and directly into the path of two police officers who were called to the scene. Camile retrieved the necklace one of the hoodlums had dropped while fleeing. She proceeded to hand it to the old woman, but paused when she felt something brush against her right shoulder. Still agitated from all the excitement, she flinched before whipping her head around to see who was there. However, she saw no one else in the subway car other than the elderly woman. Camile stared at the empty space beside her and thought she was hallucinating, but couldn't shake the feeling of how real the sensation was.

"Miss, here's your necklace." Camile said tremulously while returning the item to its owner.

The old woman's eyes widened with immense fear as she sank deeper into her seat.

"Who are you? Where did you come from?" The woman asked faintly as she trained her teary gaze on Camile.

"I'm Camile. I was here the whole time. Didn't you see me sitting across from you?"

The old woman shook her head vigorously while regarding Camile with a fearful expression.

"No. You ... you just came out of nowhere, right after they snatched my necklace! Are you an angel or something? Is it ... my time to go?" The woman asked nervously.

All sound seemed to fade as Camile tried her best to make sense of what had just occurred. She figured she was very lucky the guns had malfunctioned, but couldn't understand why the assailants suddenly turned the guns on themselves. Even more bizarre was the fact that they thought she had something to do with it. By the time she arrived at her mother's house, she convinced herself that the woman was senile and that the brutes were on some serious drugs. It was the only rational explanation she could devise for all of them thinking that she had materialized out of thin air.

CHAPTER 4

▼

PRESSING THE ISSUE

Camile used the spare key to enter her mother's apartment and called to her upon arriving. As she took a deep breath, she smelled the sweet fragrance of chocolate cake baking in the oven. The aroma was so rich and inviting she could almost taste it. Kylie emerged from the kitchen wearing black jeans and a floral print shirt.

"You hungry?" She asked.

"Yeah. Especially after smelling that cake! A nice big slice should hit the spot." Camile answered with a broad grin.

"Oh, no you don't." Kylie sang. "Well at least not until you've had some real food."

"Alright, but just a little. Gotta leave room for the cake."

As they ate, Camile became less concerned about saving room for anything. She had two full helpings of spaghetti. It was the best she had ever eaten and could not recall it ever being so good. After the hearty meal and a helping of chocolate cake, she joined her mother for iced tea in the living room. Then she explained what happened on the train.

"Oh my goodness! Really?"

"Yeah. Everyone was too scared to help since the dudes had guns, so they ran off the train. I just sat there frozen with fear and shock. It was terrible. It felt like it was a dream or something, like it wasn't really happening."

"Is she alright?"

"Yeah, she's fine. She was really scared though. But something very weird happened."

"Weird? Like what?"

"When one of the guys snatched her necklace, I felt a strong urge to stand up."

"Camile, you didn't do anything stupid did you?" Kylie asked nervously.

"No. Of course not!" Camile exclaimed. "I was sitting straight across from the lady the whole time, but when I stood up it really freaked the guys out and terrified the old woman even more. I thought she was going to have a heart attack!"

Camile decided to leave out the details about the men trying to shoot her since the look on her mother's face already exhibited intense worry.

"Camile, what do you think scared all of them so badly?"

"Well, apparently they didn't even see me there until I stood up. They all swore that I just appeared out of nowhere. Isn't that ridiculous?" Camile chuckled.

The statement caused her mother to choke on her tea and she grabbed a napkin to wipe her mouth.

"Are you okay?" Camile asked urgently.

"I'm fine." Kylie said between coughs.

She forced out a quiet laugh as a few tears trickled down her face in result of her choking.

"It's just hilarious that's all!" She said as she regained her composure. "Who did they think you were? Casper the ghost or something?"

"It's weird, but the same sort of thing used to happen to me in school. Remember when the teachers used to always mark me absent when I was right there in front of them? I guess I was Casper in training back then huh?"

Camile joined her mother in laughter, but noticed that there seemed to be lurking concern behind her amusement. There were a few awkward moments of silence before Camile asked a poignant question.

"Mom, do you ever wonder if I'll make it in this world?" She asked at which time Kylie sat up straight and looked at her with great unease.

"Camile, that question makes me concerned. Why would you ask such a thing? I know you'll make it!"

"How can you be so sure? I mean, sometimes … I just don't know. Sometimes it just doesn't seem like I'm cut out for this world. It seems like I'm constantly trying to fit myself into different molds."

"Camile, that's a very dangerous thing to do. You can't please everybody. Believe me I've tried and with much failure. The only thing you're liable to get out of trying to squeeze into everyone else's mold is bent out of shape. Just be yourself and be confident that it'll be enough."

"But what if I don't know who I am? What do I do then?"

"You'll just have to try your best to find out who you are."

"Mom, I'm glad you feel that way. I would love to find out more about myself. How about we start with the past? Let's start with Dad."

There was a pregnant pause as Kylie pursed her lips and stared at her. For the first time in years, Camile detected a hint of anger in her mother's eyes.

"You set me up for this didn't you?" Kylie asked quietly.

Camile felt a wave of guilt build up inside her before she gave her response.

"I won't lie to you. I came here with the intention of learning more about my childhood. I know it must be painful for you to discuss, but it's been killing me over the years not knowing exactly what my roots are. Do we really have no other family members? Where did Dad go and was I the reason he left?" Camile asked.

Kylie sighed and there was a 'here we go again' look on her face.

"The answer to your first question is yes. There really are no other family members other than the two of us … and your father of course. I never knew my parents. I was an orphan and bounced between different orphanages when I was a child, but was never adopted. When I was a teenager, I ran away and made a life of my own. I sometimes held as many as three jobs, mostly retail and waitress jobs to make enough money for college. How cliché, huh?" She explained with a halfhearted chuckle.

"How come you never told me about all this before?" Camile asked.

"I have many reasons, vanity being one of them. But the biggest reason is that I was worried about how it would affect you if you ever found out. I was afraid that you wouldn't look at me the same way and that you would … be ashamed of me."

"Ashamed?" Camile asked. "How can I be ashamed of you? You did the best you could with the cards life dealt you. If anything, it makes me even prouder of you for what you've accomplished. It must've been very hard for you."

"You have no idea, but I know it's been really hard for you too. All of those years of not knowing the full story of your origins. That's why now, I'm finally going to tell you everything you want to know. It's long overdue." Kylie said in voice that was becoming progressively faint.

Camile didn't notice the transformation of her mother's voice. Her heart pounded with unbridled excitement as she sat up with a broad smile on her face. She had been waiting for this moment for so many years. Her mother took held her hand and looked deeply into her eyes.

"The reason why I never really spoke much about your father is because he—" She began.

She suddenly grimaced, shaking her head in confusion before continuing.

"The reason I never … The reason … is because he …" She repeated.

Suddenly, her head twitched violently and her hands trembled briefly before she fainted in her seat. Camile instantly became hysterical.

"Mom! Mom, wake up!" She yelled as she vigorously tapped her mother's face in an attempt to revive her.

"Mom, please wake up!" Camile screamed through her terrified tears. She quickly called for an ambulance.

Upon their arrival at the hospital, there was an endless flow of questions from the doctor as he and the nurse began to care for Kylie. Camile answered questions about her mother's allergies, medical history, etc. The nurses hooked Kylie up to an IV and her vitals were checked by a short, chubby, red-headed nurse with bright blue eyes. The nurse's white uniform included a slick silver badge with the name 'Nancy Miller' engraved on it. Nancy checked Kylie's vital signs—all of which were normal—before she finally regained consciousness.

"Mom!" Camile exclaimed with relief. "Are you alright?"

"I think so." Kylie answered while attempting to sit up. "I still feel a little woozy though."

"Kylie, it's best that you take it easy. At least until we figure out what's going on." Nancy said gently.

"Okay, okay," Kylie replied as she sank back against the pillow. "I'll try not to feed the stereotype of medical personnel being the worst patients."

"Now *that's* the Kylie I know. Always cracking jokes." Nancy replied with a comforting smile.

"Wait a minute. You two know each other?" Camile inquired.

"Of course." Her mother answered. "Nancy was like my right hand in Arizona. She just transferred here. You've met her once or twice, but you probably don't remember since you were very little."

"Camile, you've grown to become such a beautiful young woman." Nancy remarked with a smile.

"Of course! What did you expect? She gets most of her looks from me." Kylie said proudly.

Camile and Nancy both laughed in response. They were happy to see that her mother's pride, vanity and sense of humor were still intact.

"I'm fine. I'm just tired." She sighed. "It's late as it is and I really should be getting home. Camile and I have so much to talk about."

"Kylie," Nancy replied urgently, "you know as well as I that you'll need to remain here for observation, just to be on the safe side. Trust me. It's for your own good."

Camile resisted the temptation to be selfish. She desperately wanted to know more about her father, her childhood and her mother's past. However, she wasn't willing to sacrifice her mother's health in order to gain that knowledge.

"Mom, I guess if I've waited this long I can wait a little longer. Just focus on getting some rest." Camile said quietly as she tried to mask her disappointment.

Kylie regarded her with a smile when the doctor re-entered the room.

"Kylie, good you're awake. As you already know, I'm Dr. Kline." He said a bit playfully in a deep voice, smiling gently.

"Yes, doctor. I remember you." She replied through a faint chortle. "It must feel weird for you to treat your most brilliant colleague."

"It does indeed." He answered. "The good news is that everything seems to be perfectly normal so far. However, I would like to schedule you for a CT scan as a precaution. Dizziness can occur for several reasons; dehydration, malnutrition, lack of oxygen, etcetera … but it isn't the dizziness that has me concerned at this point."

Camile looked at her mother, a wave of concern crossing her features. Nancy tried her best to give them a comforting smile, but also seemed to have worry in her eyes.

"Your daughter mentioned that at the time of your fainting spell your head and hands trembled." Dr. Kline continued. "A CT scan may help us to determine the cause of that reaction and—"

"Dr. Kline, I know the drill." Kylie interrupted in an almost bored voice. However, Camile could no longer suppress her concern.

"Doctor, what could this mean? Do you think there's something seriously wrong with my mother?" She asked in a shaky voice.

"That's what we're hoping to find out from the scan. Right now it's impossible to know for sure. It may very well turn out to be nothing at all. I've seen it turn out that way with some of my other patients." He replied hopefully to which Kylie giggled nervously.

"Well, Dr. Kline, let's just hope that when you scan my head you'll find *nothing at all.*" She joked before she turned to Nancy, but when no one laughed along with her, she said: "You guys really need to work on understanding my humor."

Camile sighed as she glanced at Kylie before returning her attention to the doctor.

"How does the procedure work and how long will it take?" Camile asked.

"Oh, Camile. Don't worry about it." Kylie casually replied. "It's like an x-ray, but more advanced. It's not a painful procedure and it only takes about fifteen minutes to complete. But the annoying part is that the patient has to be completely still the entire time."

"Or what?" Camile asked nervously.

"Or the image will be blurry and they'll need to start the process all over again. That's all, baby." Kylie explained.

"That's funny. Usually when I describe the procedure it isn't so well received. Should I be afraid for my job, Kylie?" Dr. Kline asked jokingly, raising an eyebrow.

"No." She replied with a smile. "I work long enough hours just by being a nurse."

After Kylie got settled in for the night, she practically threw Camile out of the hospital and insisted that she would be fine. Camile reluctantly took the subway home, knowing how dangerous it could be at night with the increasing violence in the city. She was becoming increasingly uncomfortable around large groups of people. When Camile boarded the train she immediately sat in a corner seat and was relieved that the car was only at half capacity. As she slouched slightly in her seat, she thought about the photo of her and her father, Zephyr.

She found it to be relaxing to think about the unusual tree that served as a backdrop in the picture. Her hectic mind became quiet and her heartbeat regulated. Just as Camile started to relax, she saw something strange at the far end of the subway car. There were four people—two of whom were male college students, making use of their commute by studying together. There was also a handsome young man with a smooth, chocolate complexion. The length of his silky, raven hair was twisted in intricate cornrows that ran halfway down his back. He appeared to be in his early twenties. Next to him, was an older gentleman—apparently in his late sixties. He and the younger man wore clothes that had long since been out of fashion. The oddly dressed pair were sitting directly across from the college students. The students laughed with each other as they joked about their professor and talked about girls before struggling to return to their studies. The two appeared to be very good friends.

The older man walked over and sat next to one of the students and—to Camile's surprise—there was no response as the student continued to read his notes. The man then placed an arm around the boy's shoulder and there was still no reaction. Camile watched intently as the man leaned over and whispered something into the boy's ear. The boy suddenly jumped up, knocking over all of the books he and his friend had been studying from.

"Derek! What's the matter with you?!" His friend yelled.

"Chris! I don't ... Did you—?" Derek exclaimed, his eyes wide with fear as he turned in the direction of the older man who stood before him.

"Did I what?" Chris asked, but Derek failed to respond as he continued to look around frantically. "Derek! Dude, you're scaring me! What's up?"

The other passengers looked at them for a moment before ignoring the commotion. The older man turned to the young gentleman traveling with him and smiled.

"You see how easy it is, don't you, son?" Camile faintly heard him say. "Now you try it with the other one. It's good practice."

"I've been trying for weeks and I *still* can't get through." The younger man groused.

"Don't worry, you're making progress. It should be easier for you this time." The older man encouraged.

The younger man slowly approached Chris—who was picking up books and paper from the dingy floor. The man knelt down and whispered into Chris' ear, but to no avail. Chris continued picking up his things.

"You see? It's *still* not working for me!" The young man shrieked angrily as he stamped his foot, punctuating his vexation.

"Patience, son. You have to find your own method. My technique might not be the right one for you."

Camile sat up at attention, puzzled that none of the other passengers were paying any attention to the unfolding scene. The train pulled into the next station. Half the passengers exited the before the train resumed its course. Chris suddenly began cursing to express his frustration.

"This is stupid! If it weren't for you I wouldn't have missed my stop!" He yelled at Derek.

"It's working!" The young man exclaimed joyfully.

The father smiled slyly as he whispered something else into Derek's ear.

"No!" Derek shrieked as he fell to his knees and clasped his hands over his ears.

The son continued to do nothing as he simply stared blankly at Chris—who suddenly threw a book, hitting Derek on the head. Derek cried out in pain as he held his bleeding forehead—much to the amusement of the strange young man and his father.

"Why did you do that?!" Derek bellowed painfully as he held his head.

"So, that's what you think of me, huh?" Chris hissed. "It all makes sense now! At least you've finally grown a backbone to come out and tell me to my face!"

"Chris, I never said anything! What the hell are you talkin' about bro?!"

"Derek, don't play stupid with me man ... and I'm *not* your bro!"

"Don't you see what they're doing to you?" Camile asked, shocked at herself for doing so.

"Keep your big nose out of this, babe!" Derek snapped.

"Yeah. If you want to keep your pretty teeth, mind your own damn business!" Chris agreed.

The peculiar young man and his father looked at one another and then at Camile with horrified eyes.

"How come *she* can see us?" The young man nervously asked his father.

"That doesn't matter now! They're coming and we have to leave now!" The older man exclaimed urgently.

The father and son duo jumped into the floor of the subway car and vanished, leaving the two college boys entangled in a vicious brawl. Camile couldn't believe her eyes.

Ghosts? She thought.

"Come on, didn't you see them?! They were right there!" She exclaimed, but the boys were too busy fighting with one another. However, the other passengers chuckled amongst themselves as they made blatant gestures indicating their doubts about her sanity.

The train entered a dark tunnel and all the lights blacked out for a few seconds, leaving the entire car in complete darkness. When the train exited the tunnel, Chris and Derek were sitting next to each other studying and laughing as if nothing had happened. Camile looked at Derek's head and noticed that there was no wound and no evidence that a fight had ever taken place.

Did I dream all that? She thought to herself.

Derek blew a kiss to her. That's when she realized that she'd been staring at him a little too long. She quickly turned her attention to the window as the two boys laughed hysterically, much to her embarrassment.

Camile returned to her apartment just before midnight. She showered, changed into a sleepshirt and tried in vain to get some sleep. She tossed and turned, thinking about all the events that had taken place that evening. The worry she felt for Kylie had steadily increased and she felt guilty about her ending up in the hospital. She thought that if she hadn't pushed so hard for information, her mother wouldn't have ended up there.

Camile's thoughts began to run away with her. She felt so lonely and pondered the possibility of something terrible happening to her mother. What if it turned out to be serious and she lost her? What would she do without her? Tears streamed down her face as she sat up, surrendering to her insomnia. She went into the living room, sat on the sofa and stared at the photo of her and Zephyr.

"What was she going to tell me about you?" Camile asked sadly. "Why doesn't she like speaking about you? What have you done?"

CHAPTER 5

▼

UNEXPECTED CHARITY

Burning tears escaped Camile's eyes as she opened them at the sound of her phone ringing. Much to her surprise, the morning sunlight streamed through her living room window. She had apparently cried herself to sleep on the sofa while clutching the photograph. Wiping the sleep from her eyes, she sat up to answer the phone. Her ears were greeted by a woman on the other end with a shrill, nasal sounding voice. Camile instantly recognized the caller. It was Becky Bauer, her manager from her job at a retail company located in Midtown Manhattan.

"Hi, Camile. It's Becky. I know today's supposed to be your day off, but something's come up and we need you to come in. How soon can you get here?"

"I'm sorry Becky, but I really don't think I can make it today. My mother was admitted to the hospital last night."

"Oh, really? Uh … I'm sorry to hear that." Becky said unconvincingly with a faint hint of skepticism.

"Hopefully it's nothing serious. I'll know more after I check in with the hospital to see how she's doing."

"Yes, of course." Becky replied, failing at her attempt to conceal her disappointment.

"If everything's okay, I might be able to make it. I'll call to let you know either way."

"Alright." Becky sighed. "I hope everything works out, Camile."

For you or for me? Camile thought glumly as she hung up the phone.

She sat quietly for a moment as if to build up strength before calling the hospital. When Kylie didn't answer, Camile tried the nurse's station. Nancy answered. Her voice sounded low and tired, but was quickly energized when she heard Camile's voice.

"Camile, how are you?" Nancy asked.

"I'm okay, under the circumstances. How's my mother?"

"Oh, she's doing just fine. It's not official, but I think she might be able to go home tomorrow."

"But what about the CT scan? Aren't they supposed to do that this afternoon?"

"Your mother was so … enthused to get it over with that she convinced them to do it shortly after you left last night." Nancy answered.

"Why didn't she tell me she was going to do that? I would've stayed!" Camile exclaimed.

"She knew you would've, but she didn't want you to worry—"

"Well it's a little late for that isn't it?!" Camile interrupted before remembering Nancy had nothing to do with her mother's decision. "Sorry Nancy, I know it's not your fault. I shouldn't have snapped at you like that."

"Please! Don't worry about it. A little snap is nothing compared to some of the tempers I've had to deal with around here. I know you want to be there for your mother, but I think she had a valid reason for wanting to go through with the CT scan on her own. If there *were* something wrong, she probably would want to find out for herself first. That way she would have some time to process what was happening. She wouldn't be able to do that with you there. She knows you would be very distraught. This is all hypothetically speaking of course. Besides, you wouldn't have been permitted in the room during the scan anyway, it's standard procedure. I hope I explained that right." Nancy said.

"Yeah. I guess so. Where is she anyway?"

"She decided to take a walk to stretch her legs. I hope she doesn't start bothering the nurses again. She already lectured two of them on proper procedures on handling paperwork. I had to remind her that she's not here on the job. She's not exactly used to taking orders from me." Nancy chuckled. "Oh wait, here she comes now. I'll transfer you to her room." There was a click followed by four seconds of silence.

"Camile?"

"Hi, Mom. How do you feel?"

"Ready to go home! I hope I didn't scare you too much."

"You did, but I know it wasn't intentional. So, how did the scan go?"

"Oh, Nancy told you about that huh?" Kylie answered with a slight tone of guilt in her voice. "I know you would've wanted to be there with me, but I figured you've been through enough. I haven't really gotten the official results yet. Doctor Kline took a first glance at them and mentioned that so far everything looks good, but he still needs to analyze it a bit more closely just to make sure he hasn't missed anything. You know, standard procedure and all that. But, I'm going home one way or the other. I don't enjoy being in the hospital as a patient at all."

"I'll bring you some clothes to wear home. It'll take me a little while, but I can bring them to you this afternoon."

"No, you can bring them tomorrow. If you bring them today it'll only increase the temptation for me to breakout earlier." Kylie chortled. "Besides, I'm sure you must have all sorts of things you need to get done."

"Mom, you're more important than anything on my 'to do' list, you know that."

"Camile, you're so sweet. You make it so easy to see why I love you so much. I'll see you tomorrow okay?"

"Mom, are you sure you don't want me to come today? It's really no trouble."

"Yeah, I'm sure."

"Okay, Mom. I won't argue with you, but don't argue with me tomorrow when I tell you to take it easy when you get home."

"You've got a deal!" Kylie exclaimed happily. "I love you baby."

Camile returned the sentiment before ending the conversation. She then reluctantly returned Becky's call.

Now that Camile was wide awake, she realized that Becky's voice was comparable to fingernails screeching against a chalk board. Camile cleared her throat before speaking.

"Becky, it's Camile. I—"

"Yes." Becky enthusiastically interrupted. "How did everything go? Will you be able to come in?"

"Yeah, I can make it." Camile answered. She was a bit upset that Becky didn't care enough to ask if her mother was alright—if not out of concern, at least out of courtesy.

"Great! I'll see you soon."

Before Camile could say anything else, Becky hung up. Annoyed, Camile ironed one of her suits—a double-breasted navy blue blazer with silver buttons down the front, and on the cuffs. It came with a coordinating mid-length pencil skirt. Before she knew it, she found herself deep in thought about the bizarre waking dream she had of the strange men on the subway the night before. Although she couldn't deny how real it seemed, she still managed to chalk it all up to her weary mind and overactive imagination. After showering and brushing her teeth, she looked at the time and was shocked to see that nearly an hour had passed since she spoke to her boss. She wondered how time was moving so fast.

As she dressed, she watched the news. She couldn't even get past the overview of the top stories which included: a serial killer on the loose, a false terror threat, a huge bank robbery, a kidnapped three-year old girl who was later found murdered and a teenage gang on a brutal crime spree. Camile shook her head and shut off the television since the stories were putting a damper on her already somber mood. It seemed as if the whole world was imploding with violence and devastation—at least that's how the news reports seemed to illustrate it.

Camile exhaled hopelessly as she fastened the last button on her outfit. As she looked at her reflection to pull her long thick tresses into a ponytail, she wondered why such events took place. She applied lip gloss to her mouth before grabbing her bag and heading out the door.

As soon as Camile made it to work, she was attacked at all angles with things to do. Almost immediately upon arriving, she regretted it. Her boss was constantly on her back—which was nothing new. Becky reacted as if Camile could do nothing right. By the end of the day, Camile was exhausted. When she left the large building, she noticed a homeless woman with blisters on her bare feet. The woman looked very fragile and begged for money to buy food. Camile looked in her purse to see how much she would be able to spare. Just then, a tall, slender, pretty young woman exited the building and stood just outside the entrance. She wore an expensive designer dress under a stylish warm coat. Her hair was the color of toasted wheat and her green eyes emphasized her delicate features.

The woman pulled a compact mirror from her bag and arrogantly pouted her lips as she checked her make-up and tossed her shoulder-length hair. Camile gave the homeless woman one dollar at which time the vain woman giggled while rolling her eyes at the unfortunate woman. Infuriated, Camile shot a very disgusted look at the young woman, who reacted in shock—perhaps even horror.

The young woman placed her compact back into her bag, pulled out her wallet and took out no less than four hundred dollars—all of which she handed to the homeless woman. Camile was thoroughly stunned, but the young woman wasn't done with her unexpected charity. After removing all of her gold and diamond jewelry, she placed it in the hands of the homeless woman on top of the pile of money she'd already given her. She then removed her coat and placed it around the homeless woman's shivering shoulders. The young woman had tears in her eyes as she looked at Camile and then at the homeless woman.

"I'm so sorry! I didn't know! I just didn't know!" The young woman sobbed before running off.

"Wait!" Camile called after her. "What made you—?"

Before Camile could finish her question, the shivering woman had already darted around a corner. The only person that seemed more confused about the situation than Camile, was the amazed homeless woman.

"Miss!" She called to Camile. "How did you get her to do that? I've seen that lady everyday for at least a month and she never gave me anything but a hard time!"

"I have no idea." Camile replied, still shocked about what had happened.

CHAPTER 6

▼

HIDDEN SECRET

Camile arrived at her mother's apartment at around 8:00 P.M. that evening. She half expected her mother to greet her in the corridor as usual. The only thing that welcomed her was silence. As she slowly made her way into the apartment, she noticed that it seemed hollow and strange without Kylie there. She switched on the hallway light. It provided her with enough illumination to guide her towards Kylie's bedroom. The room was decorated with small trinkets and paintings. There were two fluffy mid-sized pillows neatly arranged at the head of the bed. The headboard was black and had a strong interlaced design. On her way toward the dresser, Camile couldn't resist touching the velvety, dark blue comforter that was neatly draped over the queen-sized bed.

She smiled as she recalled the memories of the many conversations she and her mother had in that very room. Camile also remembered playing dress up when she was around seven years old and how she often 'borrowed' some of her mother's makeup and jewelry for the occasion. She chuckled at the memory of Kylie's attempt to scold her for getting the makeup on everything. Camile also recalled that Kylie was unable to keep a straight face because she looked like a miniature clown. It seemed to take forever for Camile to help Kylie to clean up the mess she made—a result of overzealously dusting powder on her face.

Camile carefully opened several drawers and located Kylie's favorite red sweater. She also found a comfortable pair of black trousers and placed the neatly folded clothes into a tote bag. She smiled when she saw a bottle of her mother's favorite perfume. Camile couldn't help but dab a little on. As she relished the delicate scent of soft gardenia and vanilla, she couldn't help but feel that Kylie would walk in and catch her doing so. Chuckling softly to herself, she decided that she would bring the perfume to Kylie as well. However, just as she put the bottle into the bag, the top slid off and rolled underneath the dresser.

"Ugh!" She exclaimed. "I don't have time for this!"

Camile got on her hands and knees to look for the top, but couldn't see anything. The space beneath the dresser was pitch-black. Camile reached her arm underneath the dresser to feel around—all the while hoping her hand wouldn't touch anything unpleasant. However, she felt nothing but the plush carpet on which she was kneeling.

"Oh come on, it couldn't have disappeared!" She muttered under her breath.

She peeked underneath the dresser once more and just when she was ready to give up she saw a faint reflection. No, it wasn't a reflection, but a faint blue glow radiating from the far left corner underneath the dresser—opposite of where the perfume top had fallen. Camile became increasingly curious and quickly ran to get a flashlight so she could take a better look. When she returned, it became evident that she didn't require a flashlight at all. The strange object gleamed even brighter and revealed the location of the perfume bottle top on the opposite side.

However, Camile was more interested in the mysterious glowing object. She stretched her hand out to grab hold of it but her reach fell short. She utilized the back of the flashlight for assistance. As she tried once more, she finally made contact with the object, which then flickered and ceased glowing after she nudged it.

Camile hoped she didn't break whatever the mysterious object was, but figured it was too late to stop nudging it. She guided the object out from the bottom of the dresser. It was an old dirty piece of white cloth wrapped around something lightweight, small and tied with a blue satin ribbon. Camile was slightly apprehensive about unwrapping it, but her curiosity had gotten the best of her. She slowly undid the ribbon. As the cloth revealed the contents, she gasped and collapsed onto Kylie's bed behind her. Her jaw dropped, causing her mouth to open wide with disbelief. She covered her mouth and shut her eyes as if to erase the image she had just seen.

After taking a few deep breaths, she looked in her hand and saw a gleaming silver chain. Attached to the chain was a breathtakingly beautiful stone medallion with multiple shades of blue in it. Looking at the stone was like looking into the ocean, up into the sky and into the depths of space all at once. The medallion was about the size and shape of a silver dollar. It was the same necklace Camile's mother had led her to believe she lost as a child!

Camile was in total shock and began sobbing so uncontrollably, her entire body quivered. What was the necklace doing hidden underneath her mother's dresser? Why did her mother lead her to believe that she had lost the necklace so many years earlier? These were questions Camile knew she would inevitably have to ask.

That night, Camile returned to her apartment shortly after 10:00 P.M. She was so shocked about her recent discovery, she could barely recall how she got home. After placing the tote bag—containing her mother's clothes—on the shelf, she retreated into the living room and plopped on the sofa. She stared at the necklace as if she were hypnotized by it. Her thoughts were running rampant and she needed to distract herself, so she turned on the television.

It was still tuned to the news station she had been watching before she left that morning. There was a report on a string of hate crimes in Queens followed by a story about a political scandal. The program was interrupted by a breaking news bulletin.

"We interrupt this story with tragic breaking news." The female announcer began. *"Delilah Carabello, the daughter of famed computer software tycoon, Tyrone Carabello, has been found dead outside of her Park Avenue condo."*

Camile briefly shifted her gaze from the necklace to the television and back again. She saw a photo on the screen which made her do a double-take. The photo was of a woman, shown posing with her hand on her hip as she stared seductively at the camera. She had hair like toasted wheat and eyes as green as jade. It was the same woman who vainly preened herself while giggling at the homeless woman earlier that day. Now she was dead! Camile sat up in her seat as she increased the volume.

"Witnesses have stated that shortly after 5:00 P.M. this afternoon, the socialite leapt from her eighth floor condo and plummeted to her death." The reporter continued. *"A full investigation is underway at this time. However, officials have stated that this will most likely be ruled a suicide since there are no signs of foul play."*

"Oh my God!" Camile whispered to herself. "But I just *saw* her!"

The news coverage continued with fans pouring out their support to Delilah's family and friends who called into the station. One friend in particular was sobbing so uncontrollably, her words were nearly incomprehensible.

"I—I'm Natalie … Delilah was my best friend. She was like my sister!" The woman sobbed.

"Natalie, we are very sorry for your loss. We understand that this is a very difficult time for you. We appreciate you sharing your thoughts and memories with us." The reporter replied.

"D—Delilah was a kind and caring person." Natalie stammered.

Yeah, right! She didn't seem very kind or caring with that homeless lady today. Camile thought, but then immediately felt regret for thinking ill of the dead.

"She sent me a message shortly before … she died and …" Natalie's voice trailed off as she burst into sobs.

The sound alone made Camile's heart swell with overwhelming emotion. She somehow seemed to feel Natalie's sorrow and deeply sympathized with her misery.

"Natalie, what sort of message did she leave you? Do you think you'll be able to share it with us now?" The reporter asked.

"Yes. I think she would've wanted that." Natalie answered. Her was voice a bit more calm, but still shaken with grief.

"Please don't be angry at me for what I've done." Natalie read. *"I just can't take the pain anymore. Today, for the first time, I realized that I've become obsessed with my own beauty and well being that I've disregarded all others. There was this defenseless homeless woman who would always ask for help but I, like most other people, ignored her. I even had her removed from the front of the building a few times not caring where she would go, or if she'd survive.*

"Today I saw her again and was going about my usual routine, but something was different this time. I know it sounds weird, but when I looked into her eyes I realized that she could be someone's mother or grandmother. She had no one to depend on and she was too weak to do it for herself. She looked to us for help and we ignored her. Today, I finally helped her out, but the pain is still too much for me to live with. I don't know how many other people I've hurt out there and I can't stand to live with that. I can't bear to face that kind of pain again. I'm truly sorry. Love, Delilah."

As Natalie finished reading the letter, the news crew sat quietly at their desks—some with their mouths ajar. They, like most people, knew Delilah to be selfish, spoiled and arrogant. It was so strange to hear that her mentality had changed so drastically in the span of a single day. Camile was also shocked. She had no clue that the woman whom she had stared darts at just hours earlier was the famous Delilah Carabello. She was even more stunned that the homeless woman had such a profound impact on Delilah.

Then suddenly, Camile began having disturbing thoughts. *What made today so different than all those other days when Delilah ignored that lady? Is there a possibility that Delilah would still be alive if I hadn't bumped into her today? She probably wouldn't have even noticed the woman and would have gone about her business as usual.*

Camile pondered these disturbing thoughts until she found herself struggling to remain awake. Her eyes were getting heavier by the second and sleep was lingering near. She suddenly felt as though all her energy had been drained. After turning off the television, she gathered just enough strength to drag herself to bed. She fell asleep almost as soon as her head hit the pillow.

As she drifted off, Camile experienced the sensation of falling backward. She tossed and turned to resist the feeling as she descended into a dream. At first, there was total darkness. When it faded, she was in a circular mirrored room, desperately trying to find her way out. The room was very dimly lit and every move she made was mimicked by her reflections.

Hoarse, menacing laugher echoed all around her. The eerie voice was neither male nor female. *"You're not as noble as you think you are, Camile!"* The strange voice hissed. The surrounding mirrors began to rotate slowly at first and then progressively faster. The dizzying rapid rotation of the mirrors caused her to stagger around almost drunkenly.

"You're not as perfect as you think you are. That's why you're gonna die! That's why I'm gonna kill you!" The voice taunted.

Suddenly, the mirrors shattered one by one. Camile tried her best to shield her body from the flying shards but still ended up getting sliced by several pieces of glass. She cried out as sharp searing pain tore through her flesh. After all the mirrors had broken, Camile was left with cuts all over her body—especially her arms and legs. She lifted her right hand to nurse the cuts on her face. That's when she noticed the gaping wound on her inner left forearm. Upon further inspection, she realized there was a two inch piece of mirror lodged in her flesh. Wincing, she pulled it out and a stream of warm blood coursed its way down her arm.

Suddenly, she no longer felt pain, but still saw the disturbing sight of blood staining the shredded white nightgown she wore. Her bare feet were on a weird combination of blood, broken mirror and soil. However, the broken mirror melted into the ground as it opened up beneath her. Camile fell rapidly, flailing her arms to try to grab hold onto something. The scene blackened for a moment, shrouding Camile in temporary blindness. Fearful thoughts dominated her mind as she struggled in vain to wake from the nightmare. When the darkness lifted, she found herself standing in some sort of tunnel. Much to her relief, she noticed she was no longer injured.

Camile was grateful to have been relieved of the disturbing sight of her injured flesh. Her nightgown was also no longer damaged. As she looked at the ground, she noticed a rock with a bizarre design etched into it. There were a series of stacked, curved L-shaped carvings. They were intertwined with a zigzagged line.

Camile traced her fingers over the design before walking through the tunnel. Overwhelmed with a creepy feeling she was being watched, she whipped around only to see the empty path behind her. Continuing her walk, she hoped she would soon find a way out. However, the further she walked, the colder, damper and longer the tunnel seemed to become.

With each step, her bare feet grew increasingly dirty from constant exposure to the cold, moist soil that coated the tunnel. There was a faint illumination in the distance. Seeing this, Camile received a new wave of optimism. She increased the speed of her stride towards the apparent exit. Out of nowhere, a thick heavy stone wall slammed down just inches in front of her. The tunnel vibrated from the impact, causing the loose soil to rain down on her from above. After falling to the ground, she looked up and saw a recessed handprint in the left tunnel wall.

Camile awoke in a cold sweat. Breathing heavily, she placed a hand on her chest as if to prevent her heart from bursting out. After taking several deep breaths, she closed her eyes for a brief moment as she returned her hands to her sides. She reopened her eyes and was astonished by what she saw. The necklace projected images onto the ceiling above her as it glowed serenely. Camile watched with wide-eyed wonder and amazement.

The images faded in and out so quickly, she was barely able to make them out. Among the imagery was an hourglass running out of sand, a half moon, several road signs—all of which were too fuzzy to see in detail—and an image of the Verrazano Bridge. After the last image, the necklace abruptly stopped glowing. Once again the ceiling was quiet—as if nothing had happened.

Camile's mind began to spin as she quickly sat up in bed. She switched the light on so she could thoroughly inspect the necklace. She desperately searched for some logical explanation for the light show the necklace had just displayed. Camile checked to see if there were some small compartment that could house a battery, but there was none. If there was no electronic mechanism in the necklace, how could it possibly produce such a spectacular visual display? Did it really happen or was it just another delusion? Those questions and many others bombarded her brain for the remainder of the night, robbing her of sleep.

CHAPTER 7

▼

IMPROMPTU CONFRONTATION

The next morning, Camile dreaded her pending encounter with her mother. As she dressed, she attempted to think of the most delicate way to ask: *'Mom, how could you lie to me all those years?'* Conversely, she decided it was best to wait until her mother got settled at home before asking such intense questions. The last thing Camile wanted to do was to make a scene in public.

Shortly after arriving at the hospital, Camile announced herself at the nurse's station. She was directed to walk down the same sterile white hallway she had traveled the night of her mother's admittance. However, this time her journey down the corridor seemed much longer. It was due in large part to the burden of her recent discovery and the weight of the questions that plagued her mind. As Camile entered the room, she noticed an empty bed adjacent to her mother's.

The absentee patient's bed was closest to the door. Sitting at the foot of it was a strikingly beautiful female visitor with a creamy ivory complexion. She appeared to be slightly younger than Camile. The woman wore a red v-neck cashmere sweater and black slacks. Her straight, chin-length hair was golden bronze in color with shimmering highlights. The shade of her immaculate coif complimented her golden brown eyes.

"Hi, I'm Akalina." The woman said with a warm smile. "You must be Kylie's daughter. She said that you'd be showing up with her things soon. She's still in the shower though."

"Yeah. Thank God she's going home today." Camile replied.

"Lucky for her. I'm not sure when they're gonna let my mother out of this place." Akalina said glumly. "I'm sorry, your mother mentioned your name earlier, but I can't remember it."

"Oh, sorry for being rude. I'm Camile." She responded, shaking Akalina's hand before sitting in a chair by the window.

"Well, Camile." Akalina replied with a faint chuckle. "For someone who's getting their mother back you don't seem to be happy."

Camile couldn't help but envy Akalina's perfect hourglass figure—a stark contrast to her own, which was slightly out of shape. For as long as she could remember, Camile desired a narrower waist and a more defined feminine appearance. She also noticed that Akalina's appearance was similar to what she dreamed of having, but could never achieve. She would regularly complain of her 'inadequacies' to her mother—who often responded by telling Camile she had a distorted vision of herself and that her appearance was far from insufficient. However, she always suspected that her mother's opinion was biased. Eventually, Camile learned to accept her looks, although she often considered getting a makeover to enhance them.

"I'm really happy she's okay. I just have a lot on my mind right now that's all." Camile sighed.

"Oh, I know how that is. Life can be uncertain and downright scary. Our current situations are proof of that. On top of everything, the world is getting to be so damn cold." Akalina complained before regarding Camile with slight abashment. "Oh, brother! There I go rambling as usual! Just ignore it."

"No, you're right. Sometimes it seems like no one really gives a damn about anything anymore." Camile responded. "Don't get me wrong, I know *all* people aren't bad, but sometimes I look at the level of cruelty some people are capable of and it seems like they've set themselves back centuries! I mean … there *has* to be a better way to live than this. It's sick how everyone's walking all over each other. You know, basic sympathy doesn't even seem to exist anymore. My boss actually called me into work yesterday knowing my mother was in the hospital!"

Akalina's eyes narrowed in response.

"What? You've gotta be shitting me." She chuckled with disbelief, rolling her eyes. "That's when you told your boss to kiss your ass, right?"

"It's not that simple. I'm behind on some of my bills and can't afford to quit or get fired right now." Camile sighed. "Thankfully, my mother's condition wasn't serious. If it was, I certainly wouldn't have gone to that stupid job."

"*Stupid* job, huh?"

"Well, I'm stuck in retail. Believe it or not, I have a degree, but the job market sucks. I can't find anything in my field. Everything is so competitive. It seems like life is just one big race from the corporate world to the grave. Seriously, the age of retirement is getting so high that soon, people will be having their retirement parties at their grave plots."

"Camile, I couldn't agree with you more." Akalina responded after a hearty laugh. "The whole world's turned ass-backwards. Usually when I try to talk about these things, people shrug me off, thinking I'm too young to know what I'm talking about. They say I'm just overly pessimistic. I think they're just too scared to face the facts. I'm glad I finally met someone I could see eye to eye with."

"Me too." Camile said with a faint smile.

"It would be nice to continue this conversation under better circumstances. If you want, you can call me if you ever feel the need to vent." Akalina offered.

"Sure. I might take you up on that offer, but I'm sure you already have so much to deal with. I wouldn't want to bother you with my problems." Camile replied.

"To be honest, my offer isn't exactly selfless. I could benefit from some venting as well—in moderation of course. I guess what I mean is … I could really use a friend I can relate to." Akalina explained. There seemed to be a sense of pain, loneliness and longing in her eyes.

"I know what you mean." Camile replied with a gentle smile as Akalina handed her a card. "You're a hairstylist?" She asked after reading it.

"Yep. I guess it's my feeble attempt at making the world less repulsive." Akalina joked with a wink.

"Well, if you can do that, maybe you can help me find a new look sometime."

"Camile, you hardly need any help! You're a natural beauty."

"Well my 'natural beauty' doesn't seem to get me noticed. Guys don't even know I'm alive. At least not the right ones. Not that I'm looking at the moment." Camile sighed as she briefly recalled her failed relationships. "That's probably more than you needed to know."

"Oh, don't worry about it. If that's the case, by the time I'm done with you, you'll be fighting them off with a stick!" Akalina replied with a broad smile.

After an awkward pause, Camile decided to inquire about Akalina's mother.

"You mentioned that you're not sure when your mother would be going home. It's nothing too serious I hope."

Akalina shrugged her shoulders before elaborating her disappointment.

"I don't know. Apparently the doctors don't either. They can't seem to find out what's wrong with her! All they do is take blood, run tests, take x-rays and when they're done with that, they do it all again! Why can't they just admit there's nothing wrong and let her go? They're so fucking incompetent." Akalina hissed angrily.

"The doctors couldn't seem to find out what was wrong with my mom either." Camile glumly responded. "She jokes that the reason why they take so many blood tests is so they can feed the vampires that secretly work here."

"Well, I always thought they were suckers." Akalina quipped.

Camile and Akalina laughed aloud for a moment before quickly adjusting the volume of their mirth so as not to disturb the other patients.

"It's been too long since I was able to laugh like that." Akalina replied.

"I just wish it were under better circumstances."

"Yeah, me too. It's been really nice talking with you, Camile. Hopefully, we can do it again sometime soon." Akalina said as she stood up and shook Camile's hand.

"Hey, aren't you going to wait for your mother?" Camile asked.

"She's been out for tests since before I got here. I've been waiting forever for them to bring her here. I'm gonna check with the nurses to see what the hell's taking so long. Gotta protect her from those vampires you know." Akalina said with a wink.

At that moment, a tall nurse with short, black spiky hair entered the room. Her radiant, mocha colored skin complimented her light brown eyes. They seemed too perfect and Camile suspected she was wearing contacts.

"Vampires?" The nurse asked.

Akalina's face flushed with mild embarrassment.

"Oh, it was just a joke, Nurse ..." She explained before taking a moment to read the nurse's nametag. "Nurse Vela."

"Jokes are fine, Akalina. Just as long as I'm not the butt of them." Nurse Vela replied with a raised eyebrow. "There was a slight delay with your mother's procedure due to mechanical issues, but everything's been resolved. She's undergoing her x-ray now and should be done in about five minutes. She wanted me to come get you since she wants you to join her for lunch in the cafeteria today."

"Alright. I was actually just on my way to see what was taking so long, but you beat me to the punch." Akalina replied before turning to Camile. "Good luck

with everything. It was nice meeting you and I hope to hear from you soon."
Akalina said with a warm smile before grabbing her jacket and leaving the room
with the nurse.

Camile couldn't believe how easy it was to speak to Akalina. She hadn't been
able to communicate with anyone so easily—aside from Kylie—since Rhonda
had been killed. She often found it difficult to connect with people out of fear she
would once again suffer the pain of losing them. Her conversation with Akalina
distracted her from the weight of the situation that would eventually unfold
regarding the necklace and her mother's deception. Before Camile knew it, the
weight of her thoughts and questions returned with a vengeance when the bathroom door creaked open.

"Hi, honey! You're a sight for sore eyes!" Her mother exclaimed. She emerged
from the bathroom wearing a plush violet-colored robe, greeting Camile with a
hug.

Camile greeted her mother quietly while handing over the bag of clothes. She
reminded herself that she had no intention of immediately raising the subject of
the necklace. Kylie was just recovering from an unknown condition and Camile
didn't want to agitate her. She knew her mother would likely need time to recu-
perate.

"Oh, nice! You brought my favorite perfume." Camile's mother acknowledged while removing the bottle from the bag. She briefly relished the scent
before placing the bottle on the table. That's when she noticed the glum look on
her daughter's face.

"Camile, are you okay?"

"I'm alright. You just really scared me with this whole hospital business, that's
all. Let's hurry up and get you home. You've been here so long they probably
think you're on the clock or something." Camile said nervously through a forced
smile.

"Ah, there we go! The sun rises again!" Her mother exclaimed before laughing
nervously. "Okay, okay. I guess you're right. I can't wait to get out of here either.
Being a patient is no fun. I must admit that I made *myself* a little nervous by ending up here. But so far my scan results appear to be normal—despite what my
odd sense of humor may have led people to believe." She chuckled.

"I'm so happy to hear that. Apparently my prayers worked." Camile replied
with another forced smile.

Her mother averted her gaze for a moment. Briefly returning her attention to
Camile, Kylie smiled awkwardly then went into the bathroom to get dressed.
While Camile waited for her mother to get ready, she stared out the window.

Dark clouds rolled by, reflecting her somber mood. She wondered how her mother was able to act so 'normal' all of those years knowing that she had lied to her own daughter. She shook the thought away and turned on the television, sitting on the bed to watch. After a few minutes, she heard her mother call from the bathroom.

"Camile, did I put my perfume back in the bag? I can't see it in here." She inquired.

Camile spotted the perfume bottle on the tray table, retrieved it and brought it to the bathroom.

"You left it on the table." Camile said after knocking on the door, which Kylie opened promptly.

She looked down to take the bottle, but suddenly froze. Her face seemed to lose color and her hazel eyes enlarged with shock.

"Oh my God! You found it!" She said in a quiet, fearful voice.

"Mom, of course I found it. It was right there on the table." Camile answered, but there was no response from her mother. It frightened her. "Mom, what's wrong? Say something. You're scaring me!"

Her mother's eyes filled with tears as she pointed a trembling finger at Camile's chest.

"You've found it! It's starting!" She said in barely a whisper as tears fell from her eyes.

Camile was confused until she glanced down and realized her mother wasn't referring to the perfume bottle at all. The necklace had somehow slipped from behind the collar of Camile's shirt when she turned on the television. She quickly tucked it back in her shirt, but it was too late. The damage had already been done.

"Mom! Please calm down, it's gonna be okay." Camile said as she tried to lead her mother to the bed. Before she could reach it, Kylie collapsed to the floor.

"No! Mom, please wake up!" Camile screamed through panicked sobs. "Somebody, please help! Something's happening to my mother!" She yelled as she cradled Kylie's limp body in her arms.

Nancy entered the room and helped Camile lift her mother onto the bed. Camile was hysterical and frantically begged Nancy to help her mother.

"Camile, I know this is hard for you, but try to stay calm. We'll figure out what's happening okay?" Nancy said calmly.

"I can't! I can't!" Camile sobbed. "She's all I've got! I can't lose her!"

Nancy noticed the necklace, which had once again peaked out from beneath the neckline of Camile's sweater. Nancy appeared to be frozen in shock, but Camile only noticed the expression on her face—not the direction of her gaze.

"What is it?!" Camile shrieked hysterically. "What's wrong with her?! Why are you looking like that?"

Nancy quickly snapped out of it and continued to check Kylie's vital signs. Camile wept silently as Nancy worked for a few moments.

"That's strange. I can't detect anything wrong with her. Other than her fainting spell, she seems to be fine." Nancy replied.

"But that's what you said last time! People who are fine don't just faint like that! What if you missed something? What if I lose my mother on the count of your mistakes?" Camile asked sharply, but before Nancy could answer one question, she would interrupt with another.

"Camile, stop it!" Nancy exclaimed before calming her voice. "Your mother will be fine. She's my best friend and I don't want to lose her anymore than you do, alright?"

Camile wiped her eyes and nodded, hiccupping while trying to control her sobs.

"Right now, even though she's unconscious, she can still sense you. Your panic won't do her any good. She can use up a considerable amount of energy worrying about you when she really should be using that energy to get well. You need to be strong for your mother right now, understand?" Nancy asked gently and Camile nodded, stifling her sobs.

In the days that followed, Kylie lapsed into a coma, but remained in stable condition. The holidays came and went, magnifying Camile's somber mood. It was the first time she wasn't able to celebrate them with her mother. She was beyond devastated, but heeded Nancy's advice to remain calm and strong. Camile visited her mother daily after work. She recited some poems she'd written, played her mother's favorite music, but most of all expressed her love. Camile desperately hoped it would be enough to help bring her back.

During that difficult time, Nancy was supportive beyond the call of being a nurse. She told Camile that if she needed anything, she could call anytime. However, as nice as Nancy was, Camile didn't feel entirely comfortable with her. Camile knew that she wouldn't be able to speak to Nancy freely about certain things since they would likely get back to her mother—if or when she would wake up. Therefore, she remained cordial with Nancy, but only to the extent of discussing her mother's mysterious condition.

Camile often met Akalina for lunch in the hospital's cafeteria. The two would vent about their situations. Doing so felt therapeutic for Camile and she really enjoyed Akalina's company. One late afternoon, Camile went to the hospital for her usual visit with Kylie. It was her second week in a coma and the doctors still had no clue of what they were dealing with. Camile sat by her mother's side, holding her hand in silence. Dr. Kline suddenly entered the room.

"Oh! Camile, it's good to see you. You're here a bit later than usual aren't you?" He asked. Camile's presence clearly surprised him.

"Hi, Dr. Kline. Yeah, the trains were running *way* behind schedule." She answered, rolling her eyes as she recalled the commute.

"Have you seen Nancy by any chance?" He asked.

Camile noticed the beads of sweat on his brow when he removed his glasses to mop it with a handkerchief.

"Not so far." She answered, noticing a medical slide in his hand. "Is that my mother's?"

Dr. Kline made a brief movement as if to hide the slide behind his back, but he realized that it was hopeless.

"Yes," he replied as he cleared his throat, "but I was hoping to discuss this with Nancy before speaking to you about it."

"Well, why don't you speak to both of us about it?" Camile asked suspiciously as Nancy entered the room and stood next to the doctor.

"Speak to both of us about what?" Nancy asked curiously.

"Kylie's CT scan." Dr. Kline replied. "Nancy, you were there when I initially reviewed it."

"Yes, and?" Nancy asked, arching an eyebrow.

"It was clear, pristine and perfect for the lack of a better word." He answered.

"Yes, I agree. So what's the problem?" Nancy asked.

Dr. Kline held the slide up to the light. Then he vigorously pointed to the areas of the scan that displayed the frontal and temporal lobes of the brain.

"These!" He exclaimed. "They weren't there before. Something like this would stick out like a sore thumb!"

Camile and Nancy leaned in closely and saw two oddly shaped objects on the slide. Each object was about the size of a pencil eraser. They were almost perfectly circular and had tiny capillary-like extensions.

"What the hell are those things and why didn't you see them in the first place?!" Camile exclaimed nervously.

"At the moment we're not sure what they are. We didn't see them until now because they just weren't there before. This sort of thing would instantly raise red flags and is very unlikely to be missed by our staff and certainly not by me." Dr. Kline answered.

"So you're telling me these things just *magically* appeared out of nowhere?" Camile asked with angry sarcasm.

"No. That's not what I'm saying at all. I'm saying that someone must've made a really bad mistake. There must have been some sort of mix-up." He explained. "But the possibility of that puzzles me since we have extremely tight protocols for handling such sensitive information."

"Apparently your so-called protocols aren't as tight as you think they are!" Camile hissed.

The doctor frowned apologetically before turning to Nancy.

"Nancy, did you notice anything weird on the day of Kylie's scan?" He asked.

"No. Not at all. As far as I saw, it was a routine procedure." Nancy replied, clearly upset. "I just don't understand. How could this happen?!"

"I don't know, but I sure as hell intend to find out." Dr. Kline sternly replied, "There will be a full investigation. This level of incompetence will not be tolerated, not when there are lives on the line!"

Dr. Kline took a moment to center his thoughts and calm his voice.

"Camile," he said softly, "the next course of action we usually take when we discover something like this in a patient, is to perform a biopsy to determine if it's a benign tumor or something more serious. But, we'll need your permission before we can begin the procedure."

Camile expelled a deep breath and shook her head. She was very confused, angry and didn't want to make a hasty decision.

"I need to think about this." She stated. "I'm not feeling very confident in this hospital right now. I don't want to take the chance of my mother going in for a biopsy and coming out with a lobotomy instead!"

"I understand your doubts. Just keep in mind that we'll need your decision as soon as possible in order to expeditiously determine what kind of growths are in your mother's brain. The sooner we figure out what they are, the sooner we can initiate the appropriate treatment." Dr. Kline urged.

Nancy briefly hung her head before returning her gaze to Camile.

"Camile, I'm so sorry about this. We'll do our best to find out how this happened." Nancy said softly.

Camile was too stunned for words and only nodded as Dr. Kline and Nancy left the room. She returned to her mother's side and sat in silence. Her mind was bombarded with morbid thoughts and she felt like the room was closing in on her. Deciding to cut her visit short, Camile kissed her mother's forehead and left briefly thereafter in order to avoid breaking down. As she waited for the elevator, a familiar voice called to her. It was Akalina. Camile desperately wanted to be alone with her thoughts and didn't feel much like company since she knew she was just seconds away from crying buckets of tears.

"Camile, I thought that was you." Akalina greeted with a faint smile. "Well, I'm so glad that I won't have to come back to this place anymore." She sighed. "I've been here all day trying to sort out paperwork and stuff. I swear these people move slower than crippled turtles in peanut butter! Anyway, how's your mother?"

As if on cue, Camile burst into tears. Akalina instinctively wrapped her arm around her.

"Hey. Hey … I understand." Akalina said gently. "It's gonna be alright, Camile."

"I don't know." Camile said while crying on Akalina's shoulder. "I'm not sure if it will be!"

Camile forced herself to regain her composure, remembering that Akalina had issues of her own.

"I'm sorry." She said as she wiped her eyes. "I know you have your own problems to deal with."

"Oh, don't worry about it." Akalina said as her own eyes watered slightly.

"I haven't seen you in a few days. How's your mother? Was she released?" Camile asked.

Akalina regarded Camile with a very faint smile. She shook her head and dropped her gaze to the floor for a brief moment. She sighed and looked at Camile once again.

"No, not quite." Akalina answered as a tear rolled down her cheek. "She didn't make it, Camile."

Her voice cracked as the words came out in barely a whisper.

"Oh my God." Camile whispered sadly as she hugged Akalina. "I'm so sorry. I feel terrible. I'm crying my eyes out to you when you have your own sorrow to deal with."

"Like I said; *'don't worry about it'*." Akalina replied. "Besides we can cry together. Do you have any plans right now?"

"I haven't exactly been in the planning mood lately." Camile answered glumly.

"I have an idea." Akalina replied as she wiped the tears from her eyes. "Why don't we go drown our sorrows in a couple of drinks? Not much, just enough to take the edge off."

"Um … I don't know, I—"

"Gotta work tomorrow?"

"No. It's my day off, but—"

"Then come on. We don't have to stay there for very long. I just … really don't want to be by myself right now and I could use a drink. From the looks of things, so can you." Akalina said.

Camile thought about it for a moment before finally deciding.

"Alright, but only for a little while." She reluctantly answered.

"Thank you." Akalina replied, briefly closing her eyes. Apparently Camile's company really meant a lot to her.

CHAPTER 8

▼

DROWNING SORROWS

They arrived at the bar, called *The Laboratory*. It was crowded and the air was filled with loud conversations and trance music. The environment was hip and trendy, which explained its popularity. As soon as Akalina walked in, all eyes were on her. A throng of guys all but shoved Camile out the way as they approached Akalina—offering to buy her drinks. Most of the women stared darts at her and tried their best to ignore her. No one in the crowd seemed to even notice Camile's presence. They proceeded to bump into her and step on her toes. She began to reevaluate her acceptance of Akalina's offer. Akalina finally managed to break away from her admirers after graciously declining several advances. She grabbed Camile by the arm and moved further into the bar.

"Let's go to the back! It's much quieter there!" Akalina yelled to Camile over the loud music and boisterous crowd.

The noise was muffled dramatically once they turned the corner. It was also less crowded except for a few couples—some of which appeared to be glued at the lips.

The bar was very well designed. The floor was black with gleaming fragments, which made it look as though the patrons were walking above the stars. The dance floor had the same effect but with simulated fog to intensify the illusion. There were a series of round tables with brushed metal finishes. Each table was trimmed with a thin, continuous line of cool blue light and had an electronic menu embedded in the surface. There was also a stream of blue lighting around the floor's perimeter. The serving station was consistent with the brushed metal theme of the tables. Bartenders, dressed in lab coats, served drinks in beakers. All the walls were mirrored and gave Camile an eerie flashback to her dream.

"Camile, what do you want?" Akalina asked.

Jolted out of her daydream, Camile realized that Akalina and the waiter were staring at her. She was more than slightly embarrassed.

"Oh ... uh, I don't know. Something light, I guess." Camile answered.

"If you like light and fruity drinks, you'll love *Truth Serum!*" Akalina suggested.

"Truth Serum?" Camile inquired.

"Hey, lady! Are you tryin' to kill the poor girl or what? *Truth Serum* may be fruity, but it ain't no light drink."

"Well, it is to me, Ralph!" Akalina snapped.

"Easy, easy ... I was just givin' my opinion, that's all." Ralph said smoothly, a smile spreading across his deeply tanned face—accentuated by his tousled platinum-blonde hair.

"Well, if we wanted your opinion, we would've asked for it!" Akalina said with slight irritation, then thought for a moment before apologizing. "Ralph, I'm sorry. I'm just going through a lot right now."

"I see that. In that case, the first round's on me. So what'll it be? Don't go crazy though. I've been low on tips lately." He said with a smile and a wink.

"In that case, I'll have the *Synergy.*" Akalina replied.

"Oh! Baby, you're killin' me!" Ralph joked as he grabbed his chest before turning to Camile. "What about you, darlin'?"

Camile was a bit nervous about ordering anything from the drink menu. She didn't drink very often and when she did, she stuck to wine. However, the menu only listed what appeared to be considerably potent mixed drinks. Everything seemed so foreign and she wasn't quite sure what she would get herself into. Finally, she made a decision.

"I think I'll have the *Aphelion.*" Camile replied.

"Nice choice!" Ralph commended as he entered the order in a handheld electronic device. Apparently, it sent the order directly to the bar while he tended the other customers.

"Ralph is something else." Akalina remarked while shaking her head. "I'm really sorry you had to see me go off like that."

"Don't worry. Like you said, you really are going through a lot." Camile replied.

After a brief pause, Camile inquired about the death of Akalina's mother.

"So, when did your mother … pass away? If you don't mind me asking."

"No, I don't mind. She died three days ago, I would've called you but I didn't want to depress you any further. I know you have your own problems." Akalina said somberly.

"Don't be crazy. You're my friend!"

"I guess you're right." Akalina sighed. "I think I've been in denial about the whole thing until today. It's really starting to sink in. You know, I really thought she was gonna be fine. Even all the doctors were fooled, but at the last minute she did a complete 180 turn. No one saw it coming."

"Did they ever figure out what was wrong with her?" Camile asked.

"Yeah, but only *after* they realized it was too late. There was nothing they could do." Akalina said bitterly. "It turns out that she had some sort of strange, advanced form of inoperable cancer. *'A text book case'* the doctors called it. There were absolutely no signs until shortly before …" Akalina's voice trailed off. She sighed and looked down at the table.

"I'm so sorry Akal—"

"Hey, it's not your fault." Akalina interrupted. "But you know what's strange? At the end, they wanted to analyze her for research purposes, but of course I wouldn't let them. As bad as things were between me and my mother, I wasn't about to let them turn her into a post-mortem guinea pig. Not after all the shit she already went through."

"Is your family helping you to make the arrangements?" Camile asked.

"There's very little left of the family—at least on my mother's side." Akalina chuckled bitterly. "It was mainly just me, my mother, her sister and my grandmother. My aunt stopped all communication with us just after my grandmother died. She took it really hard, but she shouldn't have left my mother to deal with it all on her own. I mean, I did as much as I could to help my mother, but I was barely a teenager at the time. What she really needed was her sister. As for my father's side of the family, they totally shunned us. You see, my mother couldn't have children and my father desperately wanted a family. They tried all kinds of fertility treatments, but nothing worked, so they adopted me … as a *last* resort.

Akalina went on to describe her childhood. She was raised by her reluctant adoptive father who didn't acknowledge her as his daughter. As Akalina described it, he loathed her since she was a constant reminder of her parent's inability to conceive children of their own. Her adoptive mother, Holly, tried her best to provide love for her, but appeared to value her husband more. To appease him, Holly suggested they adopt a boy to raise as their son. He became furious since he didn't want to play father to another 'rejected child'. Akalina described her adoptive paternal aunts, Elana and Louise, as being abusive—using any excuse to physically 'punish' her. That is until something went terribly wrong one day. Her aunts had been pelting young Akalina with balls of clay from her play set. Akalina, only six at the time, decided she would finally defend herself somehow. However, before she could do anything, her aunts got into a vicious brawl.

"So you sat there and watched the whole thing?" Camile asked.

"You're damn right I did! I was in no position to break it up since I was just a kid. Besides, I wouldn't have broken it up even if I could since I was enjoying it way too much. After all the shit they put me through, that was my reward—watching them while they gave each other a dose of their own foul-tasting medicine. Camile, you should've seen it. They clawed at each other like the rabid dogs they were. By the time my parents came home the living room was trashed! There were even chunks of hair on the floor! Finally, there was something they couldn't blame on me. Man, I should've kept a lock of my aunt's hair as a souvenir!"

Akalina laughed aloud. Camile was shocked at the disturbing turn the conversation had taken.

"It must've been terrible!" Camile exclaimed, not knowing what else to say.

"Yeah. The place was completely destroyed! There was broken glass everywhere from the vases and stuff my aunts threw at each other. Oh, what I would give to have seen the destruction from my father's eyes! The place in shambles, glass everywhere, broken furniture and me calmly playing with my clay set in the middle of the aftermath. Imagine a photo of *that* on the family's holiday cards!" Akalina replied through hysterical laughter.

Camile was a surprised that she too was slightly amused by the images Akalina described.

"So were your aunts finally held accountable for what they did to you?"

Akalina shook her head while regaining her composure.

"No, they killed each other before my parents could fully investigate the matter."

Thinking Akalina was joking, Camile giggled nervously.

"Camile, that wasn't a joke. They really *did* kill each other. Not that I miss them or anything."

At that point, Camile felt extremely stupid and attempted to explain her misconception.

"Oh, I'm sorry. I didn't realize—"

"Nah, it's alright. I've been told that sometimes it's hard to tell when I'm being serious."

"How did they manage to kill each other? Did the fight really get that out of hand?"

"The place was wrecked! I'd say that's evident of a fight that got *way* out of hand!" Akalina exclaimed almost condescendingly.

Camile felt another wave of embarrassment as Akalina continued to elaborate.

"My parents confronted them to discuss what happened. Seeing the awkward expressions on their faces was priceless. It was almost as good as watching them fight. You see, Aunt Elana couldn't exactly say: *'We were just torturing your daughter. Then things got out of hand after the clay ball I was throwing at her hit Louise by accident.'* Instead, they looked at me like they expected me to squeal on them or something, but I just sat there smiling at them. Then out of nowhere, they started fighting all over again. They ended up taking the fight out to the terrace. My father went after them to try to break it up. By the time he got there, they tumbled off the tenth floor balcony."

Camile grimaced, imagining how gruesome such a death would be.

"Oh my God! That's horrible!" She exclaimed.

"Is it really?" Akalina asked, no longer smiling. "Think about it. If they didn't torture me in the first place, the fight would never have started. You know what they say about Karma, Camile."

"Yeah, I know."

"In spite of everything my father put my mother through, she stuck by him while he was grieving for his sisters. He thanked her by not giving a damn when she was sick. I strongly doubt he'll pay final respects to her now that she's gone since he didn't respect her when she was alive. After all, he's moved on with some young bitch. The girl's probably *my* age! She's already given him the son he's always wanted. That skanky ho obviously doesn't waste any time!" Akalina said angrily before glancing over at the bar to see if the drinks were coming. She impatiently exhaled and resumed her story. "Now he's too preoccupied with his 'new family' to even bother honoring my mother's memory. Even if for some reason he decided to show his sorry face at the memorial, it would be meaningless! He doesn't give a damn about me or my mother, he never did!"

Akalina suddenly realized her voice was too loud when people stopped what they were doing to gawk at her for a brief moment.

"You know what the worst part is?" She asked. Her voice significantly lowered in volume.

"What?" Camile asked cautiously.

"It turns out that he cheated on my mother with that slut! That conniving, no good, son of a—"

"Here are your drinks ladies!" Ralph exclaimed.

Camile felt relieved that the conversation had been interrupted. It was becoming too tense for comfort. She glanced at the tray which held two drinks that Ralph promptly removed and placed on the table.

"*Synergy* for you, Akalina and the *Aphelion* for your friend ..." His voice trailed off, prompting Camile to introduce herself.

"Camile." She replied bashfully.

"Camile, huh? That's a beautiful name." He replied smoothly.

Akalina cleared her throat and looked at Ralph with mild disapproval.

"Oh, right." He replied with an easy smile. "Would you ladies like to order somethin' to eat? The *Jalarockets* are to die for!"

Jalarockets were breaded Jalapeño peppers stuffed with cheese and wrapped in bacon. The women decided to split an order since the portion was enough to satiate two to three people. Upon making their selection, Ralph energetically zipped away to tend to the other patrons.

Camile studied her drink with amazement. She hadn't seen anything quite like it before. It was in a beaker, which had a wide base and narrow neck. The colors of the drink gradated from blue at the bottom to bright pink at the top. The mixture joined in the middle to create a violet hue.

"It's so pretty. I almost don't wanna drink it." She replied.

As if on cue, Akalina extended her hand towards Camile's drink.

"I said *almost*." Camile giggled, pulling her drink away from Akalina's eager grasp.

Akalina's concoction was vibrant with colors nearly neon in appearance. There were intense red, orange and yellow hues intermixing with one another. The visual effect was comparable to a lava lamp. Suddenly, there was a bright flash of orange light in the background. It reflected throughout the entire club by way of the mirrored walls. The brief illumination was followed by vigorous cheers and whistles. At first, Camile was concerned until she heard the roaring applause of the crowd.

"What was that?!" She asked curiously.

"The *Flamethrower*." Akalina knowingly answered with a smirk.

"*Flamethrower*? Is that some sort of drink?"

"*Sort of.* If you really want to know what it is, you'll have to try one for yourself. It's kind of a mystery drink. You're not supposed to know what it is until you order it ... and it's too late to back out." Akalina explained, still smirking mischievously.

Camile noticed Akalina's facial expression, a clear indication that she had an idea. This made Camile very nervous.

"I'll tell you what, you finish your drink … and I'll treat you to one."

"Oh no, no, no, no, no." Camile sang with profuse refusal. "I have every intention of *walking* out of here, thank you very much."

Akalina chuckled at Camile's response.

"You don't get out much, do you Camile?" She coolly replied before taking a generous swig of her drink.

"Not really. I don't really have a need to." Camile answered.

"Oh, yes you do. You just don't know it yet."

Camile shrugged before sipping her drink. She noticed that her necklace had caught Akalina's eye. Camile was becoming increasingly annoyed with the fact that it refused to stay tucked behind her shirt.

"It's from my father. I never really knew him though." Camile glumly explained.

"At least he left you something meaningful. My father left me with nothing more than bad memories." Akalina said bitterly.

Akalina attempted to reach out and touch the medallion, but Camile quickly tucked it back into her shirt as if by reflex. A brief wave of disappointment crossed Akalina's face. She quickly replaced the expression with a faint smile.

"Forgive me." She said in almost a whisper. "I just envy you, that's all. Your father at least left you something to show he acknowledged your existence. Mine probably wishes I was never born."

Akalina slumped in her seat, taking another swig of her drink and lowering her gaze to the table.

"Sometimes *I* wish I was never born." She muttered. The comment caused Camile to feel concerned for her friend.

"Akalina, you can't mean—"

"Hey, ladies! Here are your rockets. Enjoy!" Ralph exclaimed loudly, jolting Camile and Akalina out of their conversation. He placed a large platter of stuffed peppers on the table. As he turned to leave, Akalina caught his arm, stood up and whispered something in his ear.

"Yeah! That's what I'm talkin' about!" He shouted before entering something in his electronic device.

"Akalina, what did—?" Camile began to ask.

"Don't worry about it." Akalina quickly interrupted with a slight smile on her face. "So, you're very lucky to have a father that actually thought about you long enough to give you something."

"Yeah, he gave me a mystery." Camile replied almost bitterly. "I barely know anything about him and my mother constantly dodges my questions about him. Well, she was actually going to tell me before she ended up in the hospital."

"Well, maybe it wasn't meant to be. Maybe you're not supposed to know about him. Have you considered that possibility?" Akalina asked.

"Yeah, I have, but this whole thing is such a big mystery and I'm curious." Camile answered, "She refuses to say much about him. All I have is a picture of me and my father. Other than that, he's been a ghost in my life."

"What?" Akalina asked. "So you actually met him, yet still know almost nothing about him?"

"I was very small when the photo was taken, but I can't seem to remember *anything* about him or that part of my childhood. Everything I know was told to me by my mother."

"Camile that may be a blessing in disguise. If I had to do it all again, I wouldn't want to know a damn thing about my father or those witches he had for sisters. Not knowing about all of that would've spared me a lot of heartache and misery. Maybe there was something terrible that happened when you were younger and it caused your mind to block it out. I've heard that's what happens to people who've experienced severe emotional trauma. It's their mind's way of protecting them." Akalina stated.

"I'm not so sure, there's a big part of me that still wants to find out more about him and my early childhood. Still, I think it was a mistake for me to push my mother so hard. Now she's suffering and it's all my fault. If anything happens to her, it will be because of me." Camile said, tears filling her eyes.

"Camile, we all make mistakes. Don't be so hard on yourself." Akalina said gently while touching her hand. The sensation felt oddly familiar.

"I just don't know what to do." Camile said hopelessly. "If my mother never comes out of the coma—"

"Your mother seems like a strong woman. I'm sure she'll come out of it." Akalina said tenderly. "If and when she does, I suggest you never bring up anything about your father or your childhood. If that's what triggered her coma, it's apparently doing your mother more harm than good. Sometimes we have to make sacrifices in order to ensure the safety of the ones we love. Maybe you have to sacrifice your desire to learn more about your father and that missing time in your life. It shouldn't be that hard. I mean if your father really cared that much about you, surely he would've had some contact by now if he were still alive."

"What's that supposed to mean?" Camile asked sharply.

"I'm sorry. That didn't come out quite right. But from what you described, your father was a decent person. Decent people like that usually try to have at least some contact with their families, don't they? At least when they're able to." Akalina explained.

At that point, the women had finished their drinks and most of the pepper platter. Camile was feeling a little fuzzy, but otherwise alright. Although she was clearly irritated by Akalina's comments, deep inside she agreed with her. She remembered back when she was a teenager, she herself had doubted her father was still alive. Maybe that was the reason why her mother always found it so diffi-cult to talk about him. Camile thought maybe she had been right all those years and that her father was no longer living. She was beginning to feel overwhelmed with sorrow and felt the need to change the subject.

"Akalina, you mentioned earlier that you learned to defend yourself against your aunts, but they fought and killed each other. I'm curious. How exactly did you defend yourself?" She asked.

"Camile, something tells me that you wouldn't believe me if I told you." Akalina replied, brushing her golden locks from her pale face.

"I'm not narrow-minded you know."

"I know now." Akalina joked with a wink. "We haven't known each other long, but we've covered a lot of ground. It feels like we're old friends or some-thing."

"I know. It's strange. I never make friends so quickly. Come to think of it … I've never made any real friends at all."

Akalina sighed, thinking for a long moment.

"Alright, I'll tell you, but please don't think I'm some kind of a weirdo. Cam-ile, just before my aunts started fighting that day, I—"

Akalina was interrupted by Ralph as he returned to their table. Camile was more than slightly irritated. It seemed like every time she was on the verge of finding out something she really wanted to know, someone or something would always interrupt. Ralph was carrying two sets of tubes in separate gleaming stain-less steel holders. Each set contained two tubes—one long and one short. The short tubes contained a clear liquid and the long tubes contained a cobalt blue fluid. Camile didn't notice at first, but a crowd of spectators gathered around the table to witness the occasion. She was confused about what was happening until someone from the crowd yelled aloud.

"*Flamethrower!* Yeah, baby!" A drunken man bellowed.

Camile stared at a smirking Akalina.

"No, you didn't!" Camile exclaimed with mild shock.

"Oh, yes I did!" Akalina said with a defiant wink. "I'm gonna be the one to break you out of your shell, Camile."

The crowd was now chanting *'Flamethrower! Flamethrower! Flamethrower!'*

Camile looked around nervously as she clung to her reputation of being socially awkward.

"Don't worry, Camile!" Akalina shouted above the noise of the clamoring crowd while grabbing the short tube. "I'll give you a tutorial, but you'd better pay attention!"

The noise of the crowd escalated as Akalina chugged the contents and immediately followed it with the blue liquid in the longer tube. She didn't swallow the blue liquid, but held it in her mouth until Ralph held a lighter at arms length away from himself and in front of her face. Akalina blew a steady, controlled stream of the blue liquid upwards into the flame. It instantly intensified and flashed with an extremely bright orange light. The crowd cheered hysterically. Suddenly, all eyes turned to Camile.

"That's all there is to it. Your turn, Camile!" Akalina exclaimed, wiping the residual liquid from her mouth.

Camile just stood there with her eyes and mouth wide open for a brief moment before she replied.

"You expect *me* to do *that?*" She asked. The crowd answered for Akalina.

"Yeah! Do it! Do it!" People randomly shouted from the crowd.

Surrendering to peer pressure, Camile took the short tube and raised it to her lips, all the while thinking *Why am I doing this?* She quickly drank the clear liquid—which promptly warmed her inside—and set the tube down before immediately pouring the contents of the larger tube into her mouth. When Camile blew the liquid into the flame of the lighter, an intensely bright light flooded her entire range of vision. It took a moment for her eyes to adjust after the light faded, but once it did, she noticed that the crowd was significantly further away and was staring in silence. All eyes were staring at her with surprise.

"Whoa! That was a big one! Yeah!" A drunken woman cheered and the rest of the crowd joined in.

Ralph checked his reflection in a tray to make sure his eyebrows were still intact.

"That *was* a big one!" Akalina exclaimed as she chuckled. "Next time try to control the stream of the accelerant to go up, not out. The flames were all over the place. I'm surprised you didn't set people on fire!"

"Next time? I don't plan on trying that again!" Camile replied.

"Sure, that's what they all say," Akalina said with a smirk, "but it's too cool not to try again. Come on, you can't say it wasn't fun!"

Camile gave a slight smile and nodded. However, she felt a bit guilty about having any kind of fun while her mother was in the hospital. She looked at the time and realized that it was already 11:00 P.M.

"Akalina, thanks for inviting me here, but I really have to get going." She replied.

"Already? But it's only—" Akalina glanced at her watch. "Wow! Is it that late already? It feels like we just got here! Well, I guess all good things must come to an end."

She pushed a button on the table and within minutes, Ralph arrived with the check.

"Hey, how you girls feelin'?" He asked.

"Much better than when I first got here that's for damn sure!" Akalina exclaimed.

"Fine. Thanks." Camile said to Ralph. In actuality, she felt quite dizzy. The *Flamethrower* was really kicking in and she was apprehensive about standing up.

"Don't worry about the check. I got it." Akalina replied with a chuckle when she saw Camile go for her purse. "Seeing you take that *Flamethrower* is money well spent."

Camile didn't argue. Instead, she sat back in her chair and focused on breathing, closing her eyes for a few moments. The next thing Camile knew, she was in the tunnel from her dream. She walked towards the point where the wall had slammed down in her previous nightmare. She made her best attempt to stop walking, but had absolutely no control of her legs as she continued to move forward. She braced herself for the slamming of the descending wall.

With a loud bang, the heavy wall crashed down just inches in front of her. Although she already knew it was going to happen, it still caused her heart to jump violently in her chest. She looked at the upper portion of the left side of the cold, dim tunnel and saw a recessed handprint. She traced her own fingers along the heavily soiled, fossil-like print before placing her hand into it. Much to her amazement, it fit the contour perfectly and she instinctively pushed it. The mold acted as a button and moved deeper into the side of the tunnel. The wall in front of her rumbled loudly as it started to lift.

Camile's eyes opened abruptly and she was startled to find herself lying in her own bed, staring up at the images her necklace projected on the ceiling. But how did she get there? The last thing she remembered—aside from her recent dream—was talking to Akalina about the bill. Camile got out of bed and made her way to her dark, empty living room. She looked at the clock and saw that it was 1:15 A.M. She knew it was late, but she needed answers. She dialed Akalina's number and it rang two times before she picked up.

"Hello?"

"Akalina. It's Camile. Sorry to bother you, but—"

"Hey, it's no bother! I'm still up watching TV. What's up?"

"I don't remember anything after the check. How did I get home?"

Akalina laughed so hard at the other end, she started coughing. Camile failed to see the amusement.

"You really are a lightweight aren't you? I would've felt really guilty about letting you get on the train in your condition." Akalina explained. "So I split a cab with you to make sure you made it home okay. I watched you walk … well, *barely* walk into your apartment!"

Akalina continued laughing at the other end. Camile found it to be annoying. She was still very tired and struggling to connect pieces of what happened during the latter part of the evening. She realized she would have more energy and possibly better luck if she tried to sort things out in the morning. After ending the conversation, Camile drank a glass of cold water before returning to bed. Her mind raced with thoughts of everything that had transpired—including her most recent unusual dream. She wondered the eerie tunnel and slamming wall. She also pondered the images that were generated by her necklace. As usual, nothing made any sense. She contemplated the decision she had to make about her mother's medical treatment and became disheartened.

Camile tried her best to think positively. She forced herself to think that bringing up the subject of her father led to the detection of her mother's abnormal growths and would eventually save her life. Camile tried very hard to rationalize things in order to alleviate her self-blame. However, the lingering weight of her guilt continued to bear down on her mind. As much as she wanted to sleep, her thoughts ran wild with the 'what ifs' and 'whys'. Before she knew it, insomnia had taken over.

CHAPTER 9

▼

RECLAIMING REPRESSED MEMORIES

The next morning, Camile's red, puffy eyes were evidence of the sleepless night she'd endured. It was 8:00 A.M. and she figured she would get an early start and head off to see her mother right away. Her aching head pounded in time with the pulsing of her heart. As she took a couple of aspirin, she thanked God for its inventor. She showered, brushed her teeth and dressed in a pair of jeans and her favorite turtleneck sweater. She pulled her hair back into a ponytail as usual. Looking in the mirror, she had a brief thought about changing her appearance. She thought herself to be a bit on the plain side. In addition, she noticed she was beginning to look a few years older than her true age. She attributed this to her recent onslaught of stress.

For breakfast, Camile made eggs, toast and coffee. As she enjoyed her meal in the living room, she turned on the television to check the weather. Several times, she had an overwhelming feeling that she wasn't alone in the room. Occasionally, she even swore she saw something moving out of the corner of her eye. Camile was on edge and countless thoughts raided her mind at once. It took her a minute to convince herself that she was just overtired and imagining things. After all, it wasn't the first time it's happened. She recalled the hallucinations she had during her intense study sessions late in her college career. It was something that always followed her whenever she didn't get enough sleep or was gripped with apprehension.

There was rain in the day's forecast. The weatherman spoke about an approaching storm in excessively verbose technical details. Camile sighed and rolled her eyes. She loathed the fact that she had to listen to all of the technical mumbo-jumbo before getting the information she needed. Following the weather report were several stories—all of which were tragic. The coverage included a few missing person reports, an animal attack, a string of hate crimes and a prison break. Camile shook her head and wondered what the world was coming to. The stories made her feel that hope was nonexistent. She wondered what was left to look forward to. As she gulped down the rest of her coffee, a story came on about a criminal defense lawyer who apparently went insane.

According to the report, he tracked down eight of his previous clients and shot them dead before attempting to take his own life. All eight of his clients, at some point or another, were on trial for murders, rapes, pedophilia, kidnappings and/ or assaults. Thanks to his services, they were all acquitted.

"Although Mr. Shelton was seriously injured during his suicide attempt, he was still conscious and had this to say ..." The reporter announced.

There was footage of a visibly distraught man being wheeled towards an ambulance on a gurney. His bloody head was wrapped with gauze bandages and his eyes were only partially open.

"I just couldn't live with it anymore!" He exclaimed almost drunkenly, his body quivering. *"But I couldn't go without making things right first. I just had to make things right! That's what they told me!"*

After his last statement he was quickly lifted into the ambulance and rushed to the hospital. Camile suddenly felt an unbearable wave of depression and felt compelled to shut the television off.

Oh, I've gotta stop watching this shit! She thought to herself.

When she arrived at the hospital, Dr. Kline and Nancy were already in the room. She greeted them upon entering.

"Well, I've made my decision about the biopsy and—" Camile began, but stopped short when she saw the concerned expressions on their faces. "What is it now?" She asked, her voice laden with panic.

"Camile, why are you talking about a biopsy? As far as we can tell, there's nothing wrong with your mother's brain. The result of her CT scan has confirmed that there are no tumors, hemorrhages or any other abnormalities. I thought we already discussed all this." Dr. Kline replied, furrowing his brow. Nancy subtly nodded her acquiescence.

Camile couldn't believe what she was hearing. Her face contorted with disbelief. She wondered if she had too much to drink the previous night, but shook the thought when she remembered speaking to Dr. Kline prior to the drinks.

"What?!" Camile exclaimed in confused frustration. "Yesterday you told me about … no, you *showed me* the scan and I distinctly remember seeing two small tumors on it! You said I had to make a decision about whether or not I would let you do a biopsy. So … so don't stand there and tell me that you don't remember!"

"Camile," Dr. Kline said with concern. "I'm sorry. It's not that I don't remember. That conversation didn't happen. There was never anything unusual on the scan. As I recall, you were delighted to hear it. However, we were—and still are—puzzled and concerned about why your mother's in a coma. All of her medical statistics indicate she's in perfect health. We—"

"No!" Camile yelled as she snatched the medical chart from the doctor's hand. She quickly removed the slide from the file. Her heart sank after she analyzed the charts and the slide itself. There were absolutely no indications of anything unusual. The small tumors were nowhere to be seen! Camile shook her head, struggling to comprehend what was happening.

"No. I—I don't understand. I *saw* them! They were here. They were *both* here." Camile said faintly as helpless tears trickled from her eyes. Nancy walked over to her and put an arm around her shoulders.

"Camile, I can see that this is really tearing you apart. Have you gotten any sleep at all since your mother's been here?" She asked gently.

Camile pondered the question and realized that she had in fact been sleep deprived for the most part. But could the lack of sleep really lead to such extreme hallucinations? Then Camile thought back to the strange incident that happened on the train the night her mother was admitted. In her mind, she felt she was in the process of becoming mentally and emotionally unhinged.

"Not much." Camile finally answered, handing the charts back to the doctor. "I'm really sorry about freaking out like that. It's—it's just that it seemed so … *real!* I could've sworn that …" Her voice trailed off with a sigh. "Well, apparently I don't know what's real anymore."

"Camile, lack of sleep can lead to serious functional impairments. If you'd like, I can prescribe a mild sedative to help you get the rest you need." Dr. Kline offered, his face wearing a very concerned expression. Camile declined.

"Camile, just remember that we care about your mother very much. She's like the sister I never had. I will do everything in my power to make sure she'll be okay. That much I can promise you, but you have to take care of yourself. She wouldn't want you to suffer like this." Nancy replied.

Camile could see how much Nancy cared about her mother and it calmed her down some. However, intense melancholy was still simmering beneath the surface. She requested to be alone with her mother for a while. After Dr. Kline and Nancy left the room, she lay next to her mother and held her hand. At that moment, she knew that she could no longer rationalize anything. She could no longer use the excuse of it being a good thing that she pressed her mother for information about her past. It turned out that doing so didn't help lead to the early detection of the tumors since there were none. Camile felt that the only thing she had accomplished was making her ill. She was also terrified that her mind had presented the illusion of a problem that didn't exist, simply to make herself feel less guilty.

"Mom, I'm so sorry. Please forgive me." Camile whispered. "I—I don't know what else to say. I don't know what else to do."

She leaned her head gently against Kylie's and wept silently through closed eyes. Her trembling voice hummed a tune her mother used to sing. Humming the song triggered a distant memory of her childhood that, until that moment, she never knew existed. In the memory, she sat in the waiting area of a hospital, waiting for her mother—who was making her final rounds for the day. Little Camile was sitting on a chair, swinging her legs.

There were other children sitting in the waiting area playing games with one another. Their laughter was occasionally shushed by their parents who were watching soap operas. Camile sat quietly alone. A nurse approached her and handed her a small doll. The nurse had long, curly red hair, bright blue eyes and a curvy figure. It didn't take Camile long to realize that the woman in the memory was a younger Nancy. She wore a white uniform adorned with a silver badge inscribed with her name. The badge was also imprinted with the name 'Arizona General Hospital'.

"Hi, Camile!" Nancy said cheerfully. "You've been waiting so patiently for your mother. She's assisting a doctor with one last patient. She'll be out very soon. I've told her what a good girl you've been!"

Little Camile smiled as she blissfully hugged her new doll.

"Thanks, Nancy!" Young Camile happily exclaimed.

"You're welcome sweetie!" Nancy replied with a smile. "Now, I have to get back to my station to finish up some paperwork, but you just call me if you need anything alright? I'll be sitting right over there at that desk, okay?"

Nancy pointed to the nurse's station approximately fifteen feet across from the brightly lit waiting area. Camile smiled while nodding and waved to Nancy when she got to the desk. Nancy waved back before working on her mountain of papers and files. Camile noticed that the four other kids were staring at her, but would always turn away to laugh whenever she looked in their direction. They were clearly talking about her because they would whisper to one another, look at her and laugh anew. Their parents didn't notice because they were either too engrossed in the television program or were deep into some gossipy conversation.

"I dare you!" One of the girls whispered to the only boy in the group. The boy, who was around seven years old, stood up and approached young Camile.

"Hi." He greeted flatly.

"Hi." Camile replied cautiously.

"If you let us see your doll, you can play with us." He said.

"Really?" Camile replied, unable to hide her enthusiasm.

At that point, the girls giggled. The boy shushed them before returning his attention to Camile.

"Yeah, really." He quickly answered with a sly smile.

As much as Camile wanted to play with the other kids, something didn't feel quite right.

"Sorry, but you can't hold my doll." Camile answered quietly.

The boy thought for a moment before snatching the doll out of her hands, twisting the head off.

"No! What are you doing?!" Camile screamed through angry tears.

The boy proceeded to rip the hair off of the severed doll's head and threw the loose tufts around like confetti.

"Stop breaking my doll! Stop it!" Camile shrieked in despair.

The boy and the three girls laughed viciously as she retrieved parts of her doll from the floor. Nancy ran from the nurse's station to see what was happening. The boy's mother also approached.

"What's going on?" Nancy asked.

Camile was crying so hard she could barely speak.

"H—he broke m—my doll!" She cried.

"Why'd you do that?!" Nancy sternly asked the boy.

But before the boy could answer, his mother was already in attack mode.

"What do you mean 'why'd *he* do it'?! He *didn't* do it! This five year old brat was probably combing the doll's hair too hard when it broke! The woman snapped viciously, pointing at Camile for a brief moment. "She just wants somebody to blame, but she picked the wrong kid to pin this on!"

"It's amazing how you can stand there and tell a lie against a little girl! How dare you?!" Nancy retorted.

They were so busy arguing that they didn't notice the boy until the three girls began screaming hysterically. Nancy and the boy's mother turned to see the boy crying while ripping his hair from his scalp. One of the other parents gasped with horror.

"He needs help! Somebody stop him!" The woman exclaimed.

Nancy and the boy's mother struggled to hold his bloodied hands away from his head. Meanwhile, the girls continued screaming bloody murder.

"Don't worry, he's going to be—" Nancy began to say, but stopped short when she saw something even more horrifying.

One of the girls was also ripping out her hair and the other two were sitting on the floor banging their heads hard against the wall.

"Oh my God! What's happening to the kids?!" One of the other parents screamed.

All of the parents were desperately trying to restrain their children, except for the boy's mother—who was biting her tongue so hard that her mouth was full of blood. She grimaced painfully while releasing an insane, gurgling scream as her tongue fell onto the floor like a discarded piece of meat. Doctors and nurses swarmed the area in an attempt to restore order. A terrified Kylie arrived on the scene and assisted in controlling the situation before looking at Camile. She was calmly sitting in a chair, cradling her headless doll as she watched the chaotic situation unfold. She was in a trance-like state. Her face was expressionless, but she took great pleasure in watching the pandemonium.

"Camile!" Her mother yelled. "Please, stop it! Camile!"

"Camile?"

She opened her eyes as she quickly sat up and turned to her mother.

"Mom? Did you call me?" Camile asked as she looked at her face, but saw that she was still unconscious.

She looked toward the foot of the hospital bed and saw Akalina standing there.

"Sorry, Camile. That was me calling you. It looked like you were having some sort of nightmare." Akalina said.

"I didn't expect to fall asleep, but I guess it's only natural since I couldn't sleep much last night … or any other night for that matter." Camile said, rubbing her eyes as she sat up. "The funny thing is, it didn't seem like I was having a nightmare. It was more like re-living something that happened years ago. It was really strange."

"Really? What was it about?" Akalina asked curiously.

"It was …" Camile hesitated before answering. "On second thoughts, maybe I shouldn't discuss it until I understand more about it. Besides, I don't want to get into it right now it was way too creepy!"

Camile didn't want to scare off the only friend she had. She didn't want Akalina to think something was wrong with her. It wouldn't exactly strengthen a friendship by telling someone that you caused major chaos and somehow caused at least five people to inflict serious harm on themselves.

"No problem. Just remember, whenever you wanna talk, I'm your girl! So, how are you doing? How bad is your hangover? Not too bad I hope."

"Ugh! You just *had* to remind me!" Camile exclaimed, lying back down for a moment before getting out of the bed. "My head was *pounding* this morning! Just what do they put in those drinks anyway?!"

"Sorry, Camile. I should've taken it easy on you. But you have to admit it was a lot of fun though."

"Yeah. Well I think I may have had too much of a good thing!" Camile replied with a slight smile.

Akalina returned the smile before glancing at Kylie, then back at Camile.

"You know, I can see the resemblance." Akalina said softly.

"I used to hear that a lot. I have my father's eyes though. My mother's eyes are hazel. I wish she would finally open them already."

"Has there been *any* change in her condition?"

Camile expelled a frustrated sigh while rolling her eyes.

"I didn't mention this earlier, but yesterday they found what appeared to be … abnormal growths in my mother's brain. They claimed they hadn't seen it earlier because her scan results were accidentally switched with another patient's." Camile explained.

"What!" Akalina exclaimed. "That's completely irresponsible! How could they screw up something so important? What if they never caught the mistake? That could've been catastrophic!"

"Wait. It gets worse."

"*Worse?*"

"Today I found out that I imagined the whole thing. There never were any tumors. The slides were normal all along and there never was a mix up. I think my mind made the whole thing up so I wouldn't have to feel guilty about her ending up this way. Akalina, I'm scared. I really think I'm starting to lose it. My mother is the one person who would always help me to hold it together. Everything seems to be spinning out of control and nobody seems to know what's going on with her. I honestly think I should look into getting a second opinion. Maybe another doctor will be able to figure out what's happening to her."

"I think that's a great idea. Maybe if I'd done that, my mother would still be alive right now. I wouldn't want to see you go through the same thing I did." Akalina replied tearfully and then wiped her eyes. "I'm sorry, Camile. The last thing you need is for me to scare you about things like this."

"No, I understand where you're coming from. You don't need to apologize."

Akalina sat in the chair by the window and watched the snow flurries fall. She appeared to be deep in thought. There was an awkward silence as Camile walked over and sat in the chair across from her.

"Akalina, are you okay?" Camile asked.

"Yeah, I'm alright." She answered with a faint smile. "I just remembered how much my mother loved the snow."

There was another slight pause as Akalina continued gazing out the window. Camile felt obliged to say something, but before she could, Akalina had already filled the silence.

"She was cremated this morning." Akalina explained. "I would've told you yesterday, but the conversation was already a bit heavy-handed at times.

"Oh. Uh, I ..." Camile struggled to find words of comfort.

"Camile, you don't have to say anything. Things just are the way they are. I know it may seem strange that I went out drinking with you yesterday, but I would've gone crazy just sitting at home anticipating today's events."

Akalina pulled out her keys and stared somberly at one of the key rings. After exhaling a tremulous breath, she handed the key ring to Camile.

"Camile, I just realized that you never got to meet my mother since she always seemed to be out for tests and shit like that. I guess this picture is all I have left of her now." She said as she fought back tears.

Camile glanced at the photo and saw Akalina posed with a tall, middle-aged woman with beautiful blue eyes and long, straight, platinum blonde hair. The woman's pale skin appeared slightly worn. Her face had a few freckles and wrinkles. Despite that fact, the woman was very attractive for her age. Standing beside the woman was Akalina—whose golden copper hair was drastically lighter in the photo.

"Your mother was really pretty." Camile said.

"Thanks."

"You look a bit different though."

"I guess the truth is out." Akalina replied with a forced chuckle. "I used to lighten my hair to make myself look more like her. I even wore blue contacts for awhile. It's silly, but I thought that if I changed my appearance, she would accept me even more as her daughter. Besides, I was tired of having to explain to people why we didn't look at all alike."

"It's not silly. I understand why you would do something like that. If I were in that situation, I'd probably do the same thing. But platinum blonde hair and blue contacts would clash with my skin color." Camile quipped, resulting in a faint chuckle from her friend.

She handed the key ring back to Akalina. They continued watching the snow fall onto the busy streets below. Pedestrians hastily shuffled about as they shopped, ran for buses and commuted to work.

"Hmph! You see how busy they all are?" Akalina asked quietly. "They're all in a big damn rush to get nowhere. I wonder … if they knew death was right around the corner waiting for them, would they still run so fast?"

Camile was unnerved by the chilling comment and the menacing undertone in Akalina's voice.

"Did your aunt go to the memorial?" Camile asked, quickly rerouting the conversation.

"Yeah, but it was too little too late if you ask me. I guess she felt an urgent need to make peace so my mother won't haunt her." Akalina replied with a bitter chortle.

Camile stopped herself from asking Akalina if her father also attended the memorial. She knew it would likely trigger an angry tirade. Then she remembered the conversation about Akalina's 'evil' aunts and that Akalina was about to describe how she finally defended herself against them.

"Akalina, can I ask you a question about something you mentioned last night?"

"Sure, but I might not remember everything." She joked.

"After describing what your aunts put you through, you mentioned that you defended yourself. Then you said that they attacked each other. I was just wondering—"

"Exactly *how* did I defend myself?"

"Well … yeah."

"Okay, I never actually told this to anyone because they would probably think I was nuts. For some reason, there's something about you that I trust, but please don't tell anyone else okay?" Akalina asked and Camile nodded in response.

"Through my anger, I think I was somehow able to … appeal to my aunts without actually realizing it." Akalina carefully explained. "In the end, I think they genuinely felt guilty for what they did to me, but somehow they blamed and attacked each other for it."

Under ordinary circumstances Camile would have thought Akalina was completely nuts and would have made a beeline for the door. However, due to the strange happenings taking place in her own life, Camile was able to relate and identify with Akalina to a certain degree. She couldn't help but stare with disbelief and comfort that she wasn't alone in her eccentricities.

"I knew it! You think I'm nuts don't you?" Akalina asked in response to Camile staring at her.

"No, that's not it." Camile quickly replied before whispering. "Believe it or not, I've had similar things happen to me. I just thought they were just strange, random coincidences."

"Camile, the word 'coincidence' is usually a word people use to rationalize or block out what they're afraid of or are too feeble-minded to understand. You shouldn't confine yourself to that category. So, what sort of things have happened to you?"

"Well, do you remember Delilah Carabello?"

"The rich little snob that killed herself? Yeah. I saw the story on the news."

"I saw her outside of the building I work in. There was a homeless woman on the street asking for money. If Delilah would've just ignored her like everyone else, it wouldn't have gotten me very upset. But instead she primped and flaunted herself while laughing at her. Well, I got mad and before I knew it, she gave the homeless woman all of her money and jewelry along with her coat!"

"Wow! Then she went home and killed herself … out of guilt?" Akalina asked, furrowing her brow.

"Apparently so. I thought it was just a coincidence until you told me your story." Camile replied.

"Well, you already know my take on coincidence." Akalina sighed.

"I feel terrible. She would probably still be alive if it wasn't for me. Lately it seems like I'm ruining so many lives." Camile said sadly and turned when she heard Nancy enter the room.

"Good, you're still here. I was just—" Nancy stopped talking when she realized that Camile wasn't alone. "Oh, I'm sorry. I didn't realize you had company."

"Hi, Nancy. This is my friend, Akalina." Camile introduced.

"Hi, Nancy." Akalina greeted and then noticed that Nancy was staring at her. Arching an eyebrow, she asked: "Is there a problem?"

"No, not at all. Your hair just looks incredible. I was just wondering who your stylist is." Nancy replied.

"I am." Akalina replied almost boastfully as she smoothed her locks. "Actually, I was hoping that Camile would trust me enough to upgrade *her* hairstyle today. I know she's been under a lot of stress and thought she might enjoy some pampering for a change."

"Really?" Camile couldn't hide her enthusiasm since she often contemplated changing her appearance.

"Sure, if you're up for it of course. You've been such a good friend to me and I just want to pay you back." Akalina replied with a soft smile.

"Camile, can I talk to you outside for a moment? It's about your mother. Nothing's wrong, but it's confidential information. It won't take long."

"Okay. There's actually something I want to ask you." Camile replied before excusing herself and following Nancy into the hall.

Camile noticed that Nancy was paler than usual and had beads of sweat on her forehead. The two walked down the hall and entered an empty room. Nancy was quick to close the door behind them.

"Nancy, what's going on? Why do you look so … panicky?" Camile asked.

"Panicky? No, I'm just having a very busy day, that's all. I'm also really tired." Nancy said quickly and rather unconvincingly.

"Actually, before you start, there's something I need to ask you. Just a few minutes ago, I remembered something from my childhood. It was about the hospital in Arizona. Something terrible happened there and I think I caused it."

"What? Camile, it probably was just a dream. I saw you fall asleep in your mother's room earlier. From the looks of it, you were having one doozy of a nightmare. I would've waked you up, but I didn't want to take the risk of scaring you and I know you really need the rest." Nancy explained.

"No, Nancy. I don't think it was a dream at all. It was too real. I *felt* it. Nancy, you were there too. You gave me a doll and some boy broke it. After that, I got really upset and then all hell broke loose. You were begging me to stop and … well … that's all I remember. What happened? How did I cause all that chaos?"

"Camile, you poor thing. I can see that you're exhausted. You really need to get some rest. I'm really starting to worry about—"

"Nancy, please!" Camile was becoming increasingly frustrated and demonstrated the fact by throwing her hands in the air. "Don't tell me I'm tired, crazy or anything like that. Something's wrong with me. Something strange is happening to me and I have a feeling that's why my mother's in the hospital. She can't come to terms with the horrible things I've done!"

Tears began streaming from Nancy's eyes. It appeared that she was desperately and internally struggling with something.

"Camile, I—I'm so sorry that this is happening to you. I know it's hard for you to cope with your mother's unknown condition and you're internalizing it. I can clearly see that you're blaming yourself for all this, but you're only doing more damage to yourself. You really need to rest. Dr. Kline could prescribe a mild sedative to help you sleep—"

"Okay, Nancy. I give up. Now it's *obvious* that you're hiding something!" Camile said furiously.

"Shh, Camile ..." Nancy hushed as she touched Camile's arm.

"No, don't touch me!" Camile snapped, snatching her arm away. "This whole thing is some sort of a conspiracy and you're in on it, aren't you? Well screw this! I'm having my mother moved to another hospital so she can get the proper treatment she deserves!"

"Camile, I'm afraid I can't allow you to do that." Nancy replied quickly.

"What? Are you serious?" Camile snapped angrily. "In case you've forgotten she's *my* mother and I'm the one responsible for making these decisions since she's not able to do it herself! I *will* have her relocated to a different hospital and nothing you can say or do is going to stop me!"

"Actually, there is. Camile, I was hoping to discuss this with you calmly ... I'm your mother's Medical Power of Attorney. That's what I wanted to talk to you about."

Camile couldn't believe her ears. Her anger and confusion were beginning to mount.

"No! You're lying!"

"I'm afraid not, Camile. I have all of the paperwork to prove it." Nancy replied, handing over a bundle of papers that were among some folders she had been carrying. "I'll be more than willing to make copies for your records."

Feeling faint, Camile collapsed into a chair and flipped through the papers. Everything had the proper seals and it was clear that her mother had signed all the necessary forms. She tried desperately to figure out why her mother would choose Nancy to make such vital decisions. Camile was beginning to think she didn't know her anymore. Did Kylie not trust her at all? After thoroughly review- ing the documentation, Camile had but one question.

"Why?" She asked faintly, staring tearfully into Nancy's eyes.

"Your mother thought you might have that question. So she asked me to give you this if the time ever came." Nancy held up a violet envelope and handed it to Camile. "Apparently the time is now."

Camile took the envelope and placed it in her pocket. She couldn't bear to read it at that moment since she already felt as though her heart was about to explode with emotion.

"I'll read this later … in private. One way or the other, I'm going to get my mother the help she needs. There's gotta be a loophole in this 'Medical Power of Attorney' stuff and I'm gonna find it. Even if there isn't one, I'll wheel my mother out of here myself if necessary!" She exclaimed with quiet resolve. She stood up and shoved the papers back into Nancy's hands. Camile stormed towards the door when Nancy urgently called for her to stop, but she ignored her.

"Camile please, if she goes to any other hospital she'll die!" Nancy blurted out.

Freezing at the door, she turned to face Nancy. Her face was contorted with disbelief and horror.

"*What?!* What do you mean 'she'll die'?!" She asked, but Nancy said nothing as she continued crying and shaking her head.

"You know what's wrong with her don't you?" Camile whispered with angry disbelief as she began to pry. "You've known all along! How long have you known?!"

There was no response as Nancy continued sobbing.

"Have you been intentionally keeping her sick here? Huh? Answer me damn it!" Camile pressed.

"Camile, please … it's not what you think!" Nancy sobbed.

"If you'd just tell me what's really going on, I wouldn't have to jump to con- clusions!"

"Camile, I would tell you if I could, but your mother—" Nancy's head jerked suddenly.

"Oh my God! You twitched just like my mother did before she …" Camile's voice trailed off.

She somehow knew that if she continued to push for answers, Nancy would probably end up like her mother.

"Now do you see, Camile? I can't tell you anything. Not because I don't want to, but because I can't." Nancy said quietly with helpless sadness.

Camile couldn't explain it, but at that moment she somehow *felt* that Nancy genuinely cared about her mother. It was a mind-boggling moment of clarity. She couldn't explain it, but she believed deep in her heart that Nancy was on Kylie's side. However, her newly established trust in Nancy didn't change the fact that she was extremely frightened and confused about everything that was happening.

"I don't understand. How can I help my mother if I don't know what's going on?" Camile sobbed. "Nancy this is getting scary and it's really freaking me out! Why can't anyone just tell me what the hell is going on?!"

Nancy approached Camile with open arms and the two embraced. They sobbed for a short while in each other's arms. Suddenly, Nancy looked up into Camile's eyes after thinking for a moment.

"You said you remembered something from your childhood, right?" Nancy asked, to which Camile nodded. "Start there. I'm afraid that's all I can tell you, Camile."

"So the memory *was* real after all?" Camile asked.

"I'm afraid I can't say. Just be careful that you tell no one else about this." Nancy said as she walked to the door and opened it.

Camile was more perplexed than ever. She felt in her gut that Nancy was telling the truth about looking out for her mother's best interest. However, she couldn't understand what could be so bad that neither her own mother nor Nancy were able to tell her what was going on. The situation was becoming increasingly unnerving for Camile. She took a moment to collect herself before returning to her mother's room, where Akalina was patiently waiting.

"Is everything okay?" She asked.

Camile wanted to scream: '*NOTHING'S OKAY!*', but thought better of it since it would only prompt questions that she knew she couldn't answer.

"Yeah, everything's fine. Just something to do with paperwork and stuff. No big deal compared to everything else." Camile lied.

Akalina looked at her with doubtful eyes.

"Somehow I don't believe that, but whatever. It's your business." She said with a smile. "So, are you ready for your makeover?"

"What? You mean *now?*"

"Well yeah. You seemed pretty excited about the idea a few minutes ago." Akalina replied with an eager smile. "Come on, you deserve it. Besides, I owe it to you after yesterday's *Flamethrower*."

"Akalina, I don't know. It's not exactly the best time and I have some things I really need to take care of today."

"What and I don't?" Akalina asked, failing to hide her slight irritation.

"No, that's not what I meant. I just—"

"Do you always put your foot in your mouth like this?"

"Way too often." Camile replied. "What I meant to say is: 'we *both* have things to do.' I mean, you just got back from your mother's memorial after all. Maybe I can get a rain check on your offer?"

"Rain check? You can't put a rain check on beauty. All jokes aside, I really need to keep myself busy or else I'll break down! Anyway, when your mother finally wakes up, she'll be so proud to see that you've been taking care of yourself while dealing with this whole situation. Come on, how often do you get an offer for a fantastic makeover at no charge? Well, technically it's not free. You already paid for it with your hangover. Seriously you need to give yourself some breathing room before *you* break down." Akalina suggested with a half smile.

Camile thought it over for a moment and realized that Akalina was extremely persuasive. Still, she proceeded to resist—somewhat.

"Um, I still don't know, Akalina. How long do you think it'll take?" Camile was surprised at herself for even considering the idea given what had just happened.

"Probably less time than we've wasted debating this. Honestly, we could've been done already! The day's still young. You'll be done in time to take care of whatever it is you need to do. I know you're my friend and all, but you look like you've been run ragged. You're only going on twenty-four, but you look a bit older than your age. We have to fix that."

"Alright! No need for insults. I'll do it." Camile replied with slight irritation in her voice.

Camile gave in to the offer mainly to avoid the prying questions she knew Akalina would ask had she declined. At the same time, she was absolutely astonished that she agreed to Akalina's offer during such a hectic time. Especially after the bombshell Nancy had just revealed. However, there was a part of Camile that looked forward to getting a new look. In addition, she welcomed a distraction from all of the fearful chaos that was unfolding in her life.

"Sorry. I didn't mean to be so brutal with my comments." Akalina said apologetically.

"No, it's true. Just a little hard to hear. Then again, it's never easy to hear the truth, is it?"

Akalina nodded with a soft smile before standing up.

"I'll wait for you in the main lobby while you finish your visit." She said.

After Akalina exited, Camile approached Kylie and took her hand.

"Mom, I'm not sure if you can hear me, but I don't know what's going on here. I'm getting really scared. It would really help if you woke up and explained everything. The whole thing about Nancy being in charge of your medical decisions really threw me for a loop. I wish you would've discussed it with me so I wouldn't have had to find out this way. After all, *I'm your daughter.* Is there something about me that you don't trust? Why have you told me so many lies? Just what is real about my life? I know you can't answer these questions now, but I just needed to get them off my chest. Anyway, I still love you. I just hope your love for me wasn't just another lie." Camile said tearfully, gently kissing her mother's forehead before leaving.

CHAPTER 10

▼

METAMORPHOSIS

Akalina worked in a small, chic Manhattan salon called *Mane and Talons* located on Spring Street. It took nearly an hour to get there from the hospital in Brooklyn. When they entered, Camile admired the abstract décor among the plush leather sofa and matching chairs in the waiting area. Beautiful paintings and floor plants in decorative vases added to the ambience.

Camile followed Akalina to her styling station—which had huge mirrors and was stocked with the latest supplies and equipment. She felt somewhat lost since she had never been to a salon before. The salon was busy, but not overly crowded. Camile could feel the eyes of the other customers following her, which made her feel very self-conscious. *Of all times to get a makeover!* She thought. It made no sense for her to be there at that time, but she figured it was a little late to reconsider. She was also becoming a bit disturbed at how easily Akalina seemed to talk her into things. Akalina indicated for Camile to hang her coat before sitting in the styling chair. Once Camile was seated, Akalina casually leaned against the counter and wasted no time in getting down to business. She began by trying to convince Camile to shorten her locks.

"How much shorter?" Camile asked cautiously as she held her hair as if for dear life.

"*A lot* shorter. Maybe about my length. A similar style should look great with the shape of your face."

"No, I don't think so. I'm not ready for such a drastic change." Camile answered.

She had no intention of offsetting her recent traumatic events with a potentially devastating haircut. Nor did she desire to become a Bobbsey twin.

"If you're this strict about your hair, I'd hate to see how rigid you are when it comes to relationships." Akalina joked.

Camile gave a very faint smile. It was quite clear that she wasn't amused.

"Oops, I guess I hit a nerve. Now *I'm* the one with the foot in the mouth." Akalina said apologetically.

"Want some salt and pepper to go with it?" Camile quipped.

"Very funny." Akalina replied sarcastically. "But seriously, I never heard you mention a boyfriend. Is there a man in your life?"

"A new relationship is something I'm not ready for. It's another complication that I don't need in my life right now. I'm sure the right guy's out there somewhere, but—"

"So far you haven't met *Mr. Right?*"

"Exactly, but I've met many *Mr. Wrongs.*"

"I hear ya! That's why I'm just playing the field for now. I have no intention of getting into a serious relationship ... not right now anyway. It just leaves you wide open for hurt and rejection. I guess I just got sick and tired of being used." Akalina replied as she rolled her eyes.

"Usually people would dump me because I just 'wasn't there' in the relationship, whatever that's supposed to mean. I've lost a couple really good guys on the count of my 'failure to connect'. My last relationship was the worst though. It ended pretty badly. He basically left me after he got what he wanted out of me. I guess it left me so scarred that I've avoided getting into another relationship ever since."

"Ah! The ol' hump and dump technique. I remember when that happened to me, but I was not about to go quietly." Akalina said with a snicker.

"What did you do?"

"Well, one day while he was at work, I decided to pick up my things from his apartment. Before I left, I stopped up the bathtub, the kitchen and bathroom sinks and left the water running." Akalina explained through her mirth.

"Whoa, remind me not to get on *your* bad side." Camile said. "The place must've been a mess!"

"Oh, it was a mess alright!" Akalina chuckled proudly. "Ruined just about everything the sorry bastard owned. The place was completely flooded and his poor downstairs neighbors were more than pissed about it. But hey, the jackass had it coming after the rotten way he treated me. I eventually got over it, but not before I got even first. Little did he know, he messed with the wrong bitch! I still think I let him off easy though."

"Did he ever find out that you're the one who did it?"

"Yeah, but there was no way he could prove it. You see, I'm not the only one he's screwed over. The jerk had lots of enemies. Well, enough about him. I refuse to let a few bad apples spoil the bunch. There are some really cool men out there. I happen to know a few. Just so happens that they only see me as one of the guys. Go figure!" Akalina shrugged before coming up with an idea. "Hey, maybe I could hook you up with one of them!"

"That's nice of you, but no thanks. Now's *really* not a good time for that sort of thing with everything going on with my mother and all." Camile replied, feeling all the more guilty for beautifying herself during such a traumatic time.

"Sorry. I get carried away sometimes." Akalina replied. "Well, let's get down to business. Would you at least consider layers and maybe a bang?"

"I'm not against layers but bangs are out of the question. I have to be able to pull everything back easily."

"Camile, you're defeating the whole point of a 'makeover'. But you're the boss, no bangs."

When Camile saw a woman leave the salon with long, sophisticated side swept bangs, she instantly changed her mind.

"On second thought, I wouldn't mind having bangs like hers, just don't cut the rest of my hair that short."

"Uh-huh, I knew you'd come around. Now, how about a new hair color?"

"No. I like my natural color."

"Okay." Akalina sang as she rolled her eyes. "I guess we can get started then."

Akalina led Camile to the sink and began washing her hair. Camile started to unwind as Akalina massaged her scalp to work in the shampoo. The lather had a relaxing scent of tropical coconut and was immediately followed by a mint conditioner.

"Man that feels good!" Camile replied.

"See? And to think I almost had to drag you here!"

Camile closed her eyes and sighed quietly. She felt as though she were drifting away. When she reopened them, she was beneath the tree from her photo. She was lying on a bed of shimmering red petals, looking up at the sky—which was tinted pale orange by either a sunset or sunrise. Additional petals fell from the tree, drizzling around her. Camile was overwhelmed by feelings of peace, contentment and belonging. Suddenly, a light wind carried dust particles into her eyes, prompting her to snap them shut.

"Camile, I know it feels good, but your hair is all washed out. My hands are getting numb here!" Akalina joked.

"What? Already? But ..." Camile blinked her eyes a few times as though to snap herself back to reality.

"Camile, you were sleeping through the whole thing. I've been washing your hair for like twenty minutes."

"Really? Boy, I must be more exhausted than I thought!"

Akalina led Camile to the styling chair and began combing her wet hair. Once she finished combing, she picked up her scissors, stood in front of Camile, holding her head up.

"Now, I'm about to start cutting, so *don't* fall asleep unless you wanna bring A-symmetrical haircuts back in style!" She exclaimed.

Akalina's statement got Camile's undivided attention. She sat up straight in the chair and kept her eyes wide open. Akalina laughed aloud.

"Ha! That one always gets my sleepy clients. Wakes 'em up better than black coffee!"

"Thanks for the wake up call, but excuse me if I don't find it very funny." Camile replied.

"Most of my victims—uh, clients don't." Akalina joked. "Now, hold still."

Akalina began cutting. Camile watched nervously while watching chunks of freshly cut hair fall into her lap. She strained her eyes as much as she could to glance at the mirror without moving her head.

"Nah uh-uh." Akalina sang. "No peeking. Don't worry. I'm not taking too much off."

Before long, Akalina was done cutting and began to blow dry. Camile could already feel that the weight of her hair had decreased. She was beginning to worry if in fact too much hair had been cut. When Akalina finished blow-drying, she applied light makeup to Camile's eyes and lips. After the makeup application was complete, she spun the chair around so Camile could view the results in the mirror. Camile hesitated for a moment before looking, but when she finally opened her eyes, she was blown away.

"Oh my God!" She exclaimed. "I can't believe this!"

Her reflection revealed that her hair was sleek, shiny and had body to it. It was a far cry from the thick, frizzy mess she had grown to loathe over the years. The overall length ended a few inches below her shoulders. Long, sweeping bangs framed her face. Her eyes had a subtle dusting of shimmering eye shadow on the lids and were lined with dark brown eyeliner. Her lashes were enhanced with mascara and her lips glistened with a sheer berry-colored gloss. Tears welled up in Camile's eyes.

"Oh, don't cry. You'll ruin all my hard work." Akalina smiled.

"I know, but it's just that … for the first time ever, I actually feel pretty. I didn't think I could ever look like this!" Camile exclaimed.

"What can I say? You thought wrong."

"Oh, I have to give you something for this." Camile replied as she removed her wallet from her purse.

"No, don't mention it. Just remember this if I ever need a favor." Akalina said with a wave of her hand and a soft smile.

Camile couldn't help but feel a twinge of discomfort at the notion.

On her way home, Camile noticed—and couldn't believe—that she was the object of nearly everyone's attention. Normally, people would pass her by without giving her a second look—or even a first glance for that matter. However, this time was different. Women jealously glared at her as men approached her and made advances. Camile politely declined as she hurried to get home. In contradictory fashion, some cursed at her upon being rejected whereas others wished her well. Though she felt that her newfound popularity was strange and even slightly uncomfortable, she couldn't help but enjoy it. When she got to her building, three men practically tripped over each other to hold the door for her.

"Good afternoon!" Two of them greeted simultaneously.

"Hey, gorgeous! Did you just move in?" Asked the third man.

"Hi." Camile responded. "No, I've been living here for years."

"Now why the hell didn't we see this fine lady before today?" One man asked the other with a broad smile.

Camile thought the situation was comical since all three men had seen her in passing at least a hundred times during the course of the past few years. On more than one occasion, they had even let the door slam in her face and neglected hold the elevator for her. As she entered the elevator, she noticed all three men arching their necks to get another glimpse of her before the door closed. Shaking her head, Camile laughed at how fickle the trio were. Upon entering her apartment, she caught a glimpse of her new look in the mirror. She felt Akalina had worked a miracle and called to thank her again.

"Camile, I'm really flattered." Akalina replied. "I've never had a more gratified client, but believe me, the pleasure was all mine. Oh! I have to go now. My four o'clock just walked in and she's a real handful. I'll speak to you later. Maybe we could pay another visit to *The Laboratory* to celebrate your metamorphosis."

Before Camile could decline, Akalina ended the conversation. Tension crept back into Camile's mind as she remembered the emergence of her disturbing childhood memory. She walked to her computer and sat in front of the blank screen. Taking a deep breath, she thought about what Nancy told her earlier. *'… you remembered something from your childhood? Start there. I'm afraid that's all I can tell you, Camile.'* Nancy's voice resounded in her head. Camile tried to focus on several aspects of the memory such as the hospital, the children, Nancy and the incident that took place, but nothing made any sense. She listed everything and tried to make some sort of connection, but it seemed impossible. The frustration began to set in.

"What am I missing?" She asked herself after thinking for a moment.

Suddenly, she realized that she overlooked the fact that the incident had taken place in Arizona—the same place where her mother and father supposedly met one another. Camile searched through the online archives of old news clippings. She browsed for all articles relating to incidents that occurred at *Arizona General Hospital* when she was five. She found nothing other than the birth of sextuplets, a few law suits and a number of remarkable surgeries.

Camile seemed to search for hours before hopelessly sinking back into her chair. Submerged in deep thoughts, she peered out of the window into the darkening sky. She began to think that maybe the so-called memory wasn't real at all. She also wondered if Nancy had sent her on a wild goose chase in order to prevent her from looking for the real story. Camile paced around her living room and found herself gazing at the photo of her and her father, Zephyr. As she stared at it for a moment, her medallion began glowing steadily. Upon inspecting the stone, she saw that it displayed the number six. It only remained for a few seconds before it vanished. The stone ceased glowing immediately thereafter.

"Six? What's that supposed to …?" She asked herself. Suddenly, her heart raced with excitement when she realized what it meant. "Maybe I was six years old—not five!" She exclaimed.

Camile returned to her computer and revised her search parameters. She came across several articles—some of which conflicted—about a wild incident that took place at *Arizona General Hospital.* Most of the stories described a madman entering the hospital and attacking several people in the waiting area. The article continued to describe the gruesome incident in great detail and mentioned that most of the victims survived. However, there were two fatalities. According to the articles, the culprit was never apprehended.

This baffled Camile immensely. If a madman had done all that, why did *she* possess the memory of the event, but didn't remember the man at all? She searched article after article and all the stories seemed consistent. Just when she was about to give up, she clicked on one more link and came across the headline: *Little Girl Triggers Mass Hysteria at Arizona General.* It instantly piqued her attention. The story went on to describe how a six year old girl went on a rampage, severely injuring nearly an entire waiting room full of people. It was also reported that two young girls later died from severe head trauma.

According to that particular article, the motive and method of the attacks were unknown. However, the attack itself was detailed as being extremely brutal and merciless. The girl who caused the attack was to undergo a complete physical and psychiatric evaluation. The assessment would have determined whether or not the girl was to be committed to a psychiatric hospital. However, the girl's mother fled town with her before the appointment. According to other sources, the article was later declared unreliable. Nevertheless, Camile couldn't deny how remarkably consistent it was with her memory. Gasping, she clamped her hand over her mouth while shaking her head.

"Oh my God! It really *is* my fault!" She whispered. "Mom was trying to protect me. Now she's in the hospital because of me!"

Camile's heart was heavy and she was in tremendous shock. As she reflected on all the events that led to that moment, she began to plummet into a state of depression.

"How could I do those things? How could I be a *murderer?*" She asked herself, knowing she didn't have the answer.

She shuddered as she recalled the victims' screams from her memory, somehow feeling their emotional pain. She also remembered the immense pleasure she felt as she watched them suffer. She couldn't forget the resonating sound of her mother desperately pleading for her to stop. As much as Camile wanted the memory to go away, she was still bombarded by the blood-curdling screams of the victims and was filled with a disturbing mixture of satisfaction, anger, sorrow and remorse.

"No!" Camile shrieked through hysterical sobs. "I don't want to remember anymore! Please!"

CHAPTER 11

▼

TO END IT ALL

Camile continued sobbing while sitting on the sofa in her dimly lit living room. She drank several glasses of the wine she received as a holiday gift from a co-worker. She then hugged herself into a tight ball, gasping for air between sobs. In all her life, she never felt more helpless, distraught or lonesome than she did at that very moment. Her emerging past seemed to be tearing her life apart from the inside out. Above all, she still felt guilty about her mother ending up in the hospital, battling some sort of mysterious illness. Camile thought that had she never attacked those people in the first place, the recent chain of events would never have happened.

Camile realized that all her life, Kylie stuck by her and defended her even though she knew she was a murderer. How did she repay her mother? By making her lose her mind and ending up in a coma. Camile hated herself for the way things turned out. She grabbed a pillow and punched it in a failed attempt to release her anger. It was an action that was followed by more intense sobbing.

"Mom, I'm so sorry!" She said in a voice she didn't quite recognize.

Staring at the kitchen knife next to the phone on the coffee table, her bottom lip quivered slightly. There was frantic pounding noise in the background, but she was too distracted by her sorrow to pay full attention. She suddenly thought of Akalina. She thought maybe it would help if she spoke to her. Camile dialed the number and got a busy signal. Still sobbing, she tried again and got her voicemail. What was she to say? '*Hi Akalina, it's Camile. I just called to tell you that I'm about to kill myself, but thanks for the makeover.*'?

Frustrated, Camile violently slammed down the receiver. After rolling up her left sleeve, she took the knife in her shaky right hand. She squeezed her eyes shut as if summoning strength before slowly lowering the blade towards her arm. *If you go hard and fast, maybe it won't hurt as much. Then it'll be all over.* She thought while breathing deeply. Suddenly, she felt a tight grasp around the wrist of her knife-wielding hand. Startled, she opened her eyes and saw a dark skinned, older woman in a bathrobe. Her salt and pepper hair was in large curlers about the size of tin food cans, an indication of lengthy tresses. The woman's skin was in relatively good condition, but the wrinkles and puffiness under her eyes told tales of her age—which Camile guessed to be in the early sixties range.

"What the hell are you trying to do to yourself, girl?!" The woman asked sharply. There was a hint of a southern drawl in her voice.

"How the hell did you get into my apartment?" Camile asked focusing her puffy, red-rimmed eyes on the woman.

"Stopping you from making a big mistake, that's what!" The woman replied sharply. Her tone was like that of a teacher scolding a student for running with scissors.

"Well, it's a little late for that. What do you care anyway? No—forget that—who are you and what are you doing here?!" Camile asked, raising her voice significantly.

"*Who am I?!* Girl, you need to pay more attention. I'm Zareah, your new neighbor. I moved in a few weeks ago and I live in the apartment below yours. Do you have any idea how much noise you've been making tonight? I'm surprised the neighbors next door didn't beat me over here!"

She carefully removed the knife from Camile's hand and placed it on the far end of the table.

"Well, Zareah, the next time I try to kill myself, I'll try to keep it down!" Camile snapped.

Suddenly, Zareah smacked her clear across the face.

"What the—?" Camile began to yell in protest, but Zareah interrupted.

"Life's a very valuable gift. You shouldn't take it for granted. There are so many people who wish they could have a chance at a full life and look at you! You're wasting yours!"

Camile held her stinging cheek, shocked that a woman she'd just met had slapped her, almost into sobriety!

"You don't know anything about me or my life. So, who the hell are you to judge?! By the way, don't you *ever* hit me again! My *mother* doesn't even hit me!" Camile yelled, still holding her cheek.

"If I got here a few minutes later I'd be able to slap you as much as I wanted. Besides, you were about to do something much worse to yourself. If you can't respect yourself enough to preserve your own life, why should I respect you at all?" Zareah replied coolly, sitting in the chair across from Camile. "Anyway," she continued. "I bet if your mother knew what you were up to, she would've slapped you too. After all she went through just to bring you into this world, this is how you repay her? You're ultimately saying that all the pain she went through wasn't worth it!"

As much as Camile hated to admit it, she knew Zareah had a point.

"You still didn't answer my question. How'd you get in here?" Camile demanded.

"Well, when it became clear you weren't going to answer your door, I came through the window by the fire escape. I would tell you that you should keep it locked, but I guess it's a good thing you *didn't* lock it tonight. You're lucky my arthritis didn't slow me down. Well, I didn't come here to scold you." Zareah continued while regarding Camile with dark brown eyes. "I'm hoping I can help you."

"Don't waste your time, Miss." Camile said quietly as she waved. "No one can help me! I've done too many terrible things!"

"That's your opinion, but I think I know the best way to spend my time. Right now, this is it. Plus, I'm always up for new challenges." Zareah said with a faint smile.

Camile quietly regarded Zareah while considering the offer.

"You know my name. What's yours?" Zareah prompted.

"Camile."

"Well, Camile. Just try to talk things out with me for a little while. If you don't like the way things go, I'll leave you alone. What do you have to lose … other than your life?"

"Okay, but just for a few minutes." Camile replied and Zareah smiled reassuringly.

"That's all I ask." Zareah replied calmly. "So, can you tell me why you're so upset?"

"My mother's in the hospital. She was supposed to be released weeks ago, but then she saw that I … Well, let's just say that I upset her somehow. She got so upset that eventually, she just disconnected with everything and everyone. She's in a coma and it's all because of me!" Camile said as she began to sob anew.

Zareah removed a few tissues from the dispenser on the table and handed them to Camile.

"Camile, I'm so sorry to hear that. I can see that you're in a lot of pain, but I'm sure that you didn't upset her intentionally." Zareah replied. Camile shook her head.

"I didn't, but there was a part of me that was angry with her. She's been hiding things from me for years. Things about my childhood—things I desperately wanted to know. Then she realized that I found … certain things out on my own. It was purely accidental, I wasn't even looking for it, but I still discovered it nonetheless. When she realized that I …" Camile was too distraught to complete the sentence.

"Camile, in my experience, I've found that people sometimes shut themselves down in an attempt to protect themselves from something they fear or aren't equipped to handle at the moment." Zareah replied gently. "There's a chance that your mother will come out of this, but if and when she does will ultimately be up to her. I'm sure it would make it easier for her if you continued to visit with her, to let her know that you're there for her regardless. I know it'll be very difficult for you to do, but sometimes we have to help our parents walk again, just as they helped us to take our first steps when we were young. Camile, is there anyone in your family that you can talk to about this issue? It usually helps to share your concerns with a relative that understands and appreciates the complexity of your situation."

Camile shook her head.

"No. It's always been just me and my mother." She answered.

"Well, Camile. If you and your mother are the only family you've got, who would she have if she happened to get better and you were no longer alive? Did you consider that before you made your decision to … end it all?" Zareah asked gently.

"Oh my God! I'm so selfish! I didn't even think of it that way!" Camile exclaimed between sniffles.

"Unfortunately, people who commit suicide are usually so depressed and upset that they only see a small piece of the puzzle. They're usually so overwhelmed by the negative aspects of their situation that nothing else seems to exist—particularly hope. However, it's always there waiting to be discovered. We just need to learn to collect our thoughts and see how that one puzzle piece fits into the larger picture. If you kill yourself, you'll never find out the reasons why your mother did the things she did."

"But still, I just discovered that I'm responsible for a lot of people getting hurt and … and worse!"

"Really? How's that?" Zareah asked with a raised eyebrow.

Camile avoided going into specifics, fearing Zareah would alert the authorities. She wasn't afraid for herself, but she didn't want them to track down her mother.

"I really don't want to go into it. It's too painful." Camile dodged.

"I understand." Zareah replied before pausing for a moment. A somber look crossed her face. "Camile, a friend of mine was in a terrible car accident a few years back. She was driving down the road and before she knew it, a little boy ran in front of her car. He was trying to catch a ball that rolled into the street. It happened at the last possible moment. She did everything she could to avoid him, but the car just wouldn't stop in time. Unfortunately, the boy was hit and died instantly."

Camile solemnly shook her head as Zareah continued the story.

"My friend was absolutely devastated. She blamed herself for what happened. She couldn't live with the guilt and killed herself the very next day. She died just before it was discovered that her car was defective. If she would've waited, just a little longer, she would've learned the whole truth—that it wasn't her fault—and I would still have my friend today." Zareah explained with anguish in her eyes.

"That's terrible! I'm so sorry to hear that!" Camile said in little more than a whisper. She suddenly realized that Zareah had somehow talked her out of her self-destructive thinking. After a pregnant pause, she asked: "How did you know you'd be able to talk me out of this?"

"I didn't. I just took a chance—a chance you weren't willing to give yourself." Zareah replied with a sympathetic smile.

"I think you should be a therapist or something. You really helped me a lot."

"I'm glad to hear it. Actually, it's funny you should mention the word 'Therapist', that's technically what I am."

"What! So you've been shrinking me the whole time?!"

"I'm a *Therapist* not a Psychiatrist and I didn't come here on the clock, if that's what you're thinking. I just wanted to help. I understand that you're probably cautious. The world has gotten to be a very cold place. Not many people want to help someone if it doesn't hold the promise of personal gain. But I swear to you, that's not the reason why I came here."

Looking at Zareah's expression, Camile believed she was sincere.

"Camile, how are you feeling now?"

"Better, just embarrassed about what I was going to do. Well actually, I don't think I would've gone through with it—even if you didn't interrupt. I guess I just had a really weak moment there. Thanks for talking with me though."

"Don't mention it. Seeing you give life another chance is all the thanks I need. It's so easy to forget what the light looks like when you've been walking in the dark for so long, but it doesn't mean that the light is gone forever. There's always hope. *Always.*" Zareah replied, gently touching Camile's shoulder before handing her a business card. "Camile, whenever you want to talk, *as a friend*, feel free to call me or stop by any time. Don't worry. I won't bill you if that's what you're thinking." Zareah said with a brief, faint chuckle. "If you ever have any more thoughts of hurting yourself, please come to me first. Sometimes all you need is someone to listen to you. It's strange, but in a way, helping you seems therapeutic to me as well. I just wish I could've helped my friend the same way." She sighed before turning to walk towards the door.

"Zareah, if you don't mind. Could you stay a little longer? It's comforting to have you here."

"Sure, as I mentioned earlier I'm not charging you, so no worries." Zareah joked.

Camile walked over to the window. Zareah joined her as she stared for a moment.

"Who does your hair? It's very pretty." Zareah inquired with a faint smile.

"Oh, thanks." Camile replied, tucking her bang behind her ear. "My friend, Akalina, did it. She did my makeup too, but I cried so much I ruined it."

"Akalina?" Zareah asked softly, furrowing her brow as though searching her mind for a memory.

"Yeah, do you know her?"

There was a slight pause. Zareah briefly narrowed her eyes in thought before shaking her head.

"The name just sounds familiar." She answered. "I'm trying to think of where I've heard it before."

"Well, she's a really good stylist. Maybe you've heard her name by word of mouth. She works at the *Mane and Talons* salon on Spring Street."

"That must be it." Zareah replied, broadening her smile a bit. "I've been there a few times, but I usually just get my nails done. I don't really trust anyone with my hair anymore thanks to a traumatic haircut I received awhile back. But looking at how nicely your hair looks, I might change my mind."

The two spoke for another hour before concluding their conversation when Camile mentioned she was getting sleepy.

"Rest would probably do you good. Just remember that I'm just downstairs in 5A if you need me for anything." Zareah said as she exited.

Camile locked the door before going to the window and locking it as well. She walked over to the coffee table in the living room and paused for a moment, noticing the knife she'd intended to use as the instrument of her death. Exhaling a deep breath, she picked it up and returned it to the utensil drawer in the kitchen.

What was I thinking? She thought to herself.

Camile went into the bathroom to draw a bubble bath. As the tub filled with water, the relaxing fragrance of lavender filled the room. She went into her bedroom to put her hair into a twist, securing it with a clip before retrieving the nightgown she would change into after her bath. By the time she returned to the bathroom the tub was full of warm, fragrant and inviting water. She tossed the clothes she had been wearing into the hamper before stepping into the tub. The water was slightly hotter than she liked so she took a minute to adjust to the temperature before sitting completely. Once she got settled in, the warm water relaxed her tense muscles. Smiling gently, she rested her head on the wall behind her. As she looked down at the bubbles, she noticed that she had forgotten to remove the necklace.

"Oh well." She sighed lazily.

She closed her eyes, enjoying her soak. Suddenly, she was overcome by yet another memory. She was taken back to when she was six years old and at a public indoor swimming pool. The popular facility was bustling with the noise of young children and parents trying to keep them in line. However, it looked much different than the local pool she used to visit in Brooklyn. There were a bunch of rowdy teens debating over which sports team would win the finals. A few of them sported towels with the name 'Arizona' embroidered on it. Young Camile was walking along the swimming pool, but she wasn't alone. Someone was holding her hand and from what she could tell, the person was a female with a pristine manicure. However, Camile couldn't see the woman's face, but her voice was very familiar.

"Are you ready for your swimming lesson, Camile?" The woman asked.

"Uh-huh." Little Camile replied excitedly.

Camile played with her necklace as she walked with the woman along the poolside. She and the woman stopped walking when they arrived at the steps. For the first time, Camile turned to face her. It was a younger version of her mother, who was smiling endearingly at her.

"Camile, you'll need to take off the necklace before going in the water." Kylie said gently.

"No! I don't want to take it off. It's mine!" Camile exclaimed.

"I know, but you might lose it in the pool. If you give it to me I'll keep it safe for you."

Camile vigorously shook her head in protest and her mother suddenly became impatient.

"Camile give it to me!" She said sharply and then realized how harsh she sounded. "I'm sorry, Camile. I know how much you like your necklace, but how would you feel if you lost it in the water and couldn't get it back?"

"Don't worry, Mommy. I won't lose it. If the necklace comes off, Daddy will catch it for me."

Kylie sighed. Her face was the picture of frustration. As if on cue, Camile heard the tenor-pitched voice of a young man.

"Camile, did you come here to learn how to swim or to stand at the side of the pool?" The voice called from the water.

Camile turned to see a handsome, medium-built, man with piercing grey eyes. He was treading water as he smiled up at her.

"I'm here to swim, Daddy. I'm ready!" Camile exclaimed happily as she attempted to walk down the pool steps, but was stopped by her mother.

"Zephyr, she refuses to remove the necklace before going in the water." Kylie revealed.

"Camile, listen to your mother." He advised, but Camile refused. "Alright, I guess we'll just have to go with plan B then." He glanced at Kylie for a moment before returning his gaze to his daughter. "We'll have to have a long talk about this later, Camile. Go give your mother a hug before you come in the pool and make sure you apologize to her."

"Okay, Daddy!" Little Camile replied before she quickly apologized to Kylie, hugged her and ran down the pool steps.

"No running, Camile!" Kylie called but by the time she finished talking, Camile had already jumped into the water. Her father took hold of her waist to support her then began tickling her.

Camile laughed jubilantly as he hoisted her out of the water and spun her around. She continued to laugh as she waved to her mother, who was sitting poolside. For a split second, Camile barely noticed something—Kylie slipping a glowing object into her pocket. Camile thought nothing of it since she was having too much fun with her father. However, in retrospect, she realized that it was the necklace! Her mother had somehow removed it from her neck without her noticing. Camile's father began teaching her a few basic swimming strokes. Young Camile practiced them as he supported her in his large hands.

"Very good, Camile! You're learning fast! Now, I'm gonna let go so you can try it on your own okay?" He asked.

"Okay, Daddy." Camile replied happily as she splashed around.

She felt the pressure of her father's hands slowly release her midsection and she began to feel heavy in the water. The water covered her chin and mouth. She struggled to lift her head, but the harder she tried to stay above water the quicker she seemed to submerge. She succeeded in getting her head above the surface once or twice and even managed to call out for her father between gasps and coughs before completely submerging.

For a few moments, Camile could neither see nor hear anything. There was only the sickening smell of chlorine bombarding her senses. In the midst of her struggle, she became increasingly dizzy and her consciousness was rapidly fading. When her sense of sound finally returned, she could only hear the deep whooshing noise her limbs made as they thrashed around. Her backside made contact with the pool floor and she somehow managed to push herself up with her feet. Once she broke through to the surface she gasped for air.

"Daddy, help me!" She desperately cried out.

Searing pain ravaged her eyes and nasal passages. She looked around and was bemused to see that she wasn't drowning in a swimming pool, but in her own bathtub! Her hair was soaked and plastered to her head. A faint smell of chlorine seemed to linger. She continued to cough and struggled to catch her breath. She glanced down at her chest and was relieved to see that she was still wearing the necklace. Camile couldn't help but appreciate the immense irony of the situation. Just hours earlier, she was more than willing to take her own life and now she was fighting with great ferocity to stay alive!

Everything seemed to be happening so quickly. The memories were flooding back into her mind faster than she could process them. Camile was beginning to think Akalina was right and that perhaps ignorance truly was bliss. She felt that the magnitude of her memories was too much to handle since they caused even more questions to arise. It felt as if she were battling the mythical Hydra—for each question that was answered, others would spring up. She was faced with the shocking reality that her own mother had taken the necklace and convinced her that she had lost it. At the same time, Camile realized she knew her father, Zephyr much longer than her mother had indicated. It also appeared that she and her mother moved to New York *after* she was six years old—not three years old as she'd been told. What was the reason for such lies and deceit? Camile began to wonder what else her mother had lied about. Camile became even more disturbed as she pondered possible reasons for her mother's deception. She didn't know what to think anymore. Her memories were so undeniably real, so fresh in her mind that it seemed like it all happened yesterday.

After changing for bed, Camile no longer seemed to be as lethargic as she was before her latest flashback. She slipped into bed, but once again her mind was racing. As she stared at the ceiling, she traced her fingers over the stone medallion of her necklace. She tried to figure out a possible link between her two memories. She also wondered why they were coming to her seventeen years later. A wave of emotions came over her. Anger was the most prominent and it was clearly directed towards her mother. Then she remembered Kylie's condition and tried to set her negative thoughts aside. Despite all the lies her mother had told her, Camile wanted her to make a full recovery now more than ever. She wanted to hear Kylie's explanation of the whole mess. However, Camile knew it would be very difficult to continue her visits with the knowledge that her mother had repeatedly lied to her through the years.

What other parts of my life are based on lies? Camile wondered while pondering all the events that unfolded that day. Then suddenly, she remembered the envelope Nancy had given her.

Camile bolted into the corridor, opened the coat closet and retrieved the small violet envelope from her coat pocket. The envelope was slightly crinkled and tainted due to age. She slowly walked into the living room, switched on a light and sat on the sofa. Several moments elapsed as she stared at the envelope feeling pangs of anxiety and anticipation. Finally, she opened it carefully as though it were made of rice paper. As she unfolded the letter she swore—that for a brief instant—she could smell the sweet, gentle scent of her mother's perfume. Her eyes filled with tears as she began to read:

Dear Camile, If you're reading this it means that something serious has happened to me and that I'm no longer able to make my own decisions concerning my health. By now, you're probably aware that I've given my best friend, Nancy Miller, the responsibility of being my Medical Power of Attorney. You're probably wondering why I didn't leave that responsibility to you. Please know that I love you very much and that this choice in no way represents my trust in you. There are many reasons that have led me to make this very tough decision, reasons I can't include in this letter since there is no guarantee that it won't fall into the wrong hands.

There are just some things Nancy will be better equipped to handle if or when the time comes. I'm sure that someday, when you find out everything you need to know, you'll come to understand why. Please don't challenge Nancy's decisions regarding my condition, she knows my wishes. Camile, I know this situation won't be easy for you, but please try your best to be strong and have faith that things will turn out alright. I hope someday you'll understand why I had to do this. I'm truly sorry for whatever pain this might cause you. I hope someday you'll find it in your heart to forgive me for all the choices I've had to make, but please know that I've made them with your best interest at heart.

All my love to you always.

Your mother,

Kylie

After she finished reading the letter, Camile realized that her mother had fore-knowledge of whatever her mysterious illness was since the letter was dated about seventeen years ago. More and more questions arose giving Camile much to think about: *What sort of illness does my mother have? Is it hereditary? Do I have it too? Do the symptoms include delusions? Why would she mention the possibility of the letter falling into the wrong hands? Just whose hands are the 'wrong ones'?*

Camile's somber mood was unshakeable. Her sad eyes continued to gaze at the letter long after she was done reading, but they yielded no tears. She believed that she'd finally run out of them. However, her heart wept and her very soul seemed lost and hollow. She was faced with the reality that although she hadn't succeeded in taking her own life that night, her life—as she knew it—had indeed ended.

CHAPTER 12

▼

IDENTITY CRISIS

The following day, Camile awoke to the sound of crackling thunder and rain pounding against her window panes. It seemed to be an appropriate backdrop for her increasingly gloomy disposition. She realized that she had fallen asleep clutching her pillow while curled in a fetal position. As she sat up in her bed, there was another bright flash of lightning and a loud clap of thunder, which caused her to flinch. She exhaled a quick breath as she checked the time. It was 8:17 A.M. She walked over to the window and watched stray paper and loose trash being tossed along the street by the strong winds. She also saw a few people struggling to maintain control of their umbrellas.

Camile went into the kitchen, poured herself some juice and sat in the living room. She called her boss, Becky, and informed her that she wasn't feeling well enough to go into work. By the sound of Becky's voice, Camile could tell she wasn't pleased. However, Camile didn't care. She was dead tired and needed a break. After hanging up the phone, she watched the weather report to see when the messy rain would end. When she tuned in, there was a field reporter getting commentary from irate commuters. They were obviously more than aggravated with the weatherman's inaccurate forecast prediction.

"He said it was gonna be sunny today! It sure don't look sunny to me! Maybe that idiot should switch careers, like jumping out of planes to test defective parachutes or somethin'!" One shivering, drenched woman hissed angrily before climbing into a bus.

"Whoa! I guess she's angry!" The reporter exclaimed through an awkward chuckle.

Ordinarily, Camile would've found it funny, but given recent events, she was in no mood for humor. It just reminded her about how unreliable people could be. The program cut to the weatherman, who was in the process of explaining how a storm system suddenly developed over the area.

"According to our radar, this system should move out of the area within the next three to five hours. However, we can see as much as three inches of rain before the end of it. Flood warnings have been issued to all coastal areas and—"

Camile switched off the television and thought about how she would face her mother that day. Her contemplation was cut short by the ringing of the phone. It was Becky.

"Hi, Becky. Is something wrong?" Camile answered.

"I'm afraid so. I just got off a conference call with payroll and human resources. There seems to be a problem with cutting your check."

Oh, this is some bullshit! Of all the sneaky tactics to get me to come in! Camile thought, but instead asked: "Why is that?"

"Apparently, you're not in the system. Payroll thought that it might've been some sort of computer glitch, but after checking all the information we have in our paper trail, it appears you were never *in* the system. This has been under investigation for the past week and the company ordered a background check. Camile, according to the results, you have no valid identity whatsoever. Everything we have on file from your social security number to your driver's license can't be verified."

"What?! That's impossible. You've got to be shitting me!" Camile exclaimed.

It was the first time she'd ever used an expletive in a conversation with her manager. Becky seemed taken aback for a brief moment and there was a slight pause. However, she didn't seem to be offended.

"I shit you not, Camile. This is mind-boggling to us since you passed the first background check with flying colors and your previous work references all seem to check out. You might want to make a few phone calls to get this all straightened out right away."

'No kidding!' Camile wanted to yell, but instead she replied: "I sure will!"

"I'm afraid until you do, you can't work here anymore. For your sake, I hope this is just a big misunderstanding. If not, I'm afraid you're in deep shit."

I'm betting it's the latter! Camile thought bitterly, failing to come up with anything to say.

"I'm sorry, Camile. I know how badly you needed this job. I'll try to hold the position as long as I can in order to give you time to try and sort things out. If you do, please let us know. Hopefully, the position will still be open."

For the first time, Camile detected compassion in Becky's voice.

When the conversation ended, Camile found herself in a state of disorientation. She immediately began to mentally backtrack to the other jobs she's had. Her heart sank when she realized that every job she held up until that point was due to some type of intervention by her mother. She recalled a discussion she had with her mother before getting hired at her last job. Kylie persistently offered to help Camile in her job search. However, Camile wanted to go it alone.

"Mom, it's not that I don't appreciate your help, but I want to find my next job on my own. I'm twenty years old and I think it's well overdue for me to depend on myself for things like that."

"But Camile, you shouldn't have to struggle when you have a mother that has the connections to get you hired."

Camile, eventually lost that battle and her mother got her the job at the retail firm—a job she just lost.

After recalling the details of that conversation—and the particulars of every job she's ever held, she came to the chilling realization that her mother had manipulated her life more than she originally thought.

"What's going on?" Camile asked herself, not entirely sure if she was ready for the answer.

She knew she would only discover the truth if she looked for it herself. Therefore, she decided to begin with her latest mystery—the apparent disappearance of her very identity. She planned to start at the hospital's clinic where she received medical care since elementary school.

Due to the adverse weather, it took Camile nearly two hours to commute to the hospital. When she arrived at the hospital's clinic she noticed it was relatively empty, except for a few patients waiting to be seen. She was very familiar with one of the nurses, Marina, who was at the front desk. However, Camile had a strong suspicion that she was somehow involved with some of the mysterious events unfolding in her life. Therefore, Camile planned to announce herself to the other nurse once Marina walked away. It seemed to take forever before Marina finally stepped away from her post. Camile immediately made her move, approaching the other receptionist.

"Good morning. I don't have an appointment, but I need to see a doctor." Camile lied in her attempt to dig for information.

"Okay. What's bothering you?" The nurse asked.

"I have a stomach ache." Camile answered nervously, desperately hoping Marina wouldn't return anytime soon.

"Alright." The receptionist sighed lazily. "Name?"

"Camile Leon."

The nurse repeated the name—a little too loudly for Camile's taste—while she entered it in the computer. She scrunched her face in a curious manner when she saw the results.

"How do you spell your last name?" She asked.

"L-E-O-N" Camile spelled out as quietly as she could.

"Have you been here before?" The nurse asked.

"Yes, I've been coming here for years!" Camile quietly exclaimed.

"When was your last visit?"

"I don't know … about six months ago, but that was to see the dentist."

The nurse conducted another search on the computer and shook her head, clearly confused.

"Nothing's coming up in the system. I'll check our chart room."

Camile nodded and the nurse disappeared into the small file room next to the front desk. The process seemed to take forever. Camile was anxious and desperately hoped Marina wouldn't return before she received confirmation of her suspicions. Her heart skipped when she saw Marina approaching from the far end of the corridor. Suddenly, a doctor called her back to give her a chart to file.

"*Hurry up, lady!*" Camile whispered to herself. Not a moment too soon, the nurse reemerged from the file room with a perplexed look on her face.

"I'm sorry, Ms. Leon, but there's no record of you ever being at this clinic. Would you still like to see the doctor? If so, I'm afraid you'll need to fill out some forms."

"No. I'm good, thanks." Camile said before she all but ran out of the clinic into the elevator bank.

She furiously pushed both the up and down buttons in hopes that it would expedite the elevator's arrival. She felt the overwhelming need to get out of there. Her mind was spinning and it felt as though the entire world were closing in on her.

"Camile?" A familiar voice called from behind her.

After a silent sigh, Camile turned to face Marina, who was about 4' 11" with an olive complexion and short, straight brown hair.

"Hi, Marina. How are you?" Camile asked, trying her best to sound relaxed.

"I'm alright, but I think I should be asking *you* that question. What brings you here? Are you feeling alright?" Marina asked with a concerned expression.

"I'm fine. I just had an upset stomach, but it just turned out to be indigestion. I guess it must be from all the junk food I keep eating, but I'm fine now."

Camile quickly realized that she used the word 'fine' one time too many. Marina regarded her with slight skepticism in her eyes.

"It's not that busy today, but I could probably bump you in front of a few people if you're in a hurry. Oh, and don't worry about the new nurse not being able to find your records. It's been an absolute nightmare getting her acclimated to our filing system." Marina explained.

She didn't believe Marina for a minute. She felt nauseous as it became over-whelmingly clear that the deception in her life ran much deeper than she thought. She began to wonder just how many people were involved in covering it up. Camile made an attempt to keep her emotional chaos beneath the surface. Apparently, her attempt failed.

"Are you sure you're alright, Camile? You look really tense."

Camile thought for a moment before responding.

"I guess I'm still pretty shaken up about my mother still being in a coma."

"Oh, how stupid of me not to remember that! I'm so sorry, Camile. I've been meaning to contact you since I found out, but—"

The elevator door opened up as if on cue and Camile held it open, clinging to her route of escape.

"Don't worry about it. Speaking of which, I better get up there to see her now." She replied as casually as she could.

"Of course. Camile, if you need anything just let me know." Marina said delicately.

Camile nodded and quickly entered the elevator.

After the doors closed, Camile felt the urge to scream. It took everything in her power to resist the temptation to do so. Something incredibly strange was going on. The clinic where she had been going to for as long as she could remember had absolutely no record of her! Marina was clearly trying to conceal that fact. Camile was growing increasingly frustrated, angry and most of all afraid. It was doubtful, and highly unlikely, that both the digital and hardcopies of all of her medical files had been lost coincidentally. Had they been deliberately erased? If so, by whom and for what purpose? Camile breathed deeply in a vain attempt to calm herself, but her heart was pounding so hard it felt as though it would leap out of her chest. Upon exiting the elevator, she walked towards her mother's room, storming past Nancy in the hall.

"Camile!" Nancy called, but Camile ignored her and kept walking.

Nancy attempted to follow her, but was interrupted by a doctor instructing her to pull some charts and check on a patient. When Camile entered her mother's room, she was shocked to see Akalina all dressed in black and sitting by the window. The sight stopped her in her tracks and she had the eerie thought of the grim reaper coming to claim a soul. It sent a chill up her spine.

"Akalina, what are you doing here?" She asked warily.

"Hi, Camile. I came to see you, but saw that you were running late. So I decided to sit and wait awhile."

Camile felt slightly uneasy about Akalina being in the room alone with Kylie. There was something disturbing about her appearance in black clothes. Then Camile remembered that she was still in mourning for her mother, Holly.

"Yeah, the weather's pretty bad out there." Camile replied, making her way to Kylie's bedside.

"Camile, is there something wrong?" Akalina asked.

"It's just strange seeing you here alone with my mother like this."

"Hey, like I said, I came here to see you."

"Yeah, but suppose I wanted to be alone with my mother today? It's just a bit intrusive for you to show up unannounced like this."

There was an awkward pause before Akalina responded.

"Oh, I get it." Akalina smirked. "New hair, new makeup, new attitude huh?"

"What? No. It's not like that at all!" Camile exclaimed before expelling a deep breath. "Look, there have been some very crazy things going on with me lately. I just need some time to deal with them and sort everything out. Don't take it personally. I'm not trying to ditch you or anything."

Akalina looked at the floor before returning her teary gaze to Camile's eyes.

"Camile, I'm sorry. Now that I look at it from your point of view, I guess I would find it a bit strange if my friend made an unannounced visit to *my* mother. I've lost so much already. I don't want to lose the only best friend I've ever known. I guess I just got a little clingy. That probably sounds weird." Akalina said tremulously, glancing at the floor anew.

"It's doesn't sound weird. Just call me ahead of time to plan what time we'll meet each other. That way we'll avoid these awkward moments."

"Okay." Akalina sighed. "I never thought I'd turn out to be one of those needy types. Then again I thought my mother would live long enough to see me get married and have children."

"You? Marriage and children?" Camile asked with a smile.

"Yeah. Is that funny?"

"No, but you don't exactly strike me as the marriage and carriage type."

"Maybe not now, but I'd like to settle down eventually before I shrivel up into a prune!" Akalina replied with soft smile.

"I know what you mean." Camile replied while thinking her life was too screwed up to even *consider* the possibility of children.

"Have you figured out where you're going to have your mother transferred?" Akalina asked.

"I've been giving it a lot of thought. It's a really tough decision." Camile replied, not wanting to go into details.

"Wait a minute. You're not changing your mind about it, are you?"

Pressure was building in Camile's head and she felt a headache coming on.

Grimacing slightly, she asked: "Akalina, could we not talk about this right now?"

"Sorry for prying. I'm letting my own bad experience get in the way. Seems like I'm doing an awful lot of apologizing today. Do you have some salt and pepper to go with the colossal foot in my mouth?" Akalina joked in an attempt to lighten the heavy mood and Camile chuckled quietly.

"Finally, the sun rises again!" Akalina exclaimed with apparent relief.

Camile had an odd feeling of déjà vu after hearing Akalina's remark.

"What did you—?" She began to ask in order to ensure that she heard correctly. However, she was interrupted by a strong grip around her arm. When she looked down she saw that Kylie was staring directly at her with a perplexed look on her face.

"Mom! You're awake!" Camile exclaimed with great excitement. "You're at the hospital. You've been ... sleeping for a long time."

She didn't want to upset her mother by using the word 'coma'.

Kylie frowned, as though she didn't recognize her.

"Mom, it's me ... Camile! I just changed my hair and makeup that's all."

"Hi, Kylie. Your daughter was right, you *do* have pretty eyes." Akalina said with a broad smile before turning to Camile. "I'll get the nurse right away! She should know that your mother's finally awake."

Kylie's eyes remained fixed on Camile the entire time, almost entranced. After Akalina left the room, Camile continued her attempt to communicate as silent tears made tracks down her mother's cheeks.

"Mom, can you talk? What's wrong? Why are you crying?"

Kylie's eyes suddenly grew wide with fear as she shouted: "This can't be happening! I failed! I failed!"

"Mom, what are you talking about?"

Kylie violently shook her head before going into convulsions. Camile panicked.

"Nancy, come quick!" She called from the doorway.

Within seconds, Akalina returned with Nancy, who instantly began to work on stabilizing Kylie.

"Camile, what happened?" Nancy asked urgently.

"I … I don't—"

"Camile tell me what happened!" Nancy demanded sharply.

"I don't know!" Camile sobbed, shaking her head.

Akalina immediately hugged Camile while glowering at Nancy, who had successfully stabilized Kylie.

"Hey! Don't you yell at her! It's not helping!" Akalina chided.

Nancy stared at Akalina for a long moment as though she'd been slapped. Finally, she apologized to Camile.

"I'm sorry Camile. C—can you tell me what happened before her episode?" Nancy asked, her stare lingering on Akalina for a moment.

Camile walked to a chair at the foot of her mother's bed, afraid that if she got much closer, it would trigger another attack.

"She woke up, but she didn't recognize me. Akalina left to get you while I tried to get her to speak and she … started crying. When I asked her what was wrong, her face had such an extreme look of fear. I never saw her look so scared in my life! Then she yelled: *'This can't be happening! I failed! I failed!'* That's when she started shaking." Camile explained through her tears.

"Well, she's stable now, but she's unconscious again." Nancy said while reading the medical instruments. She glanced at Akalina before returning her attention to Camile. "We'll have to run additional tests to see if there were any significant changes in neural activity." Nancy continued.

"Here we go with the tests!" Akalina muttered under her breath.

Nancy was suddenly called out into the hallway by a doctor who urgently needed her assistance. Before she left, she told Camile that she would return as soon as she could. Camile stood there totally aghast as she stared at her mother.

"It's my fault … *again!*" She quietly declared.

"How can this *possibly* be your fault?" Akalina inquired.

"I was the only one in here when it happened. She just went nuts! She didn't even *recognize* me!"

"Camile, try to think rationally. This could've happened even if you weren't here. Plus she's been in a coma for awhile. She's bound to be disoriented, you know."

"I'm not sure. The reason why she's here in the first place is because I found this stupid necklace and ..." Camile looked down and realized that the necklace was once again exposed.

"Oh no! You see? She saw it again and now she's probably back in a coma because of me! Why didn't I just leave this stupid thing at home?!"

"Camile, come on. Don't beat yourself up over this." Akalina replied, a concerned expression crossing her features.

"Maybe I need to! I've been discovering things about my past that have made me very angry at my mother for feeding me lies all these years. Maybe subconsciously I wanted her to see the necklace again. Maybe part of me *wanted* this to happen! How could I be so wicked?!"

"Hey, stop it! Don't blame yourself for feeling angry about the lies she told you. I know as well as anyone how unfair life can be. I know what it's like to be mistreated, lied to and abandoned by friends, boyfriends and even my own parents! For a long time I wallowed in self pity but then one day I got tired—so tired of being weak, sad and vulnerable. Camile, feeling bitter about what happened to you doesn't mean you should condemn yourself, but you have to realize that there's a reason why all of this is happening. Just like I discovered that I went through hell and back for a reason. I believe my reason is to try to help others in their struggle and maybe even prevent those things from happening to other people. Camile, it can be *so* empowering. I'd like to help you find that empowerment in yourself ... if you let me." Akalina replied gently.

"I don't know. Sometimes I think I'm a lost cause." Camile sighed while looking at her mother—who appeared to be resting peacefully.

"Camile, are you underestimating me again? Remember, you didn't think I would do such a great job on improving your image either." Akalina said with a gentle smile.

"I know, but, a style change and a life change are two entirely different things."

Akalina shrugged before saying: "Come on, Camile. What do you say? Will you let me help you?"

"And just how do you plan on doing that?"

"Agree and I'll show you."

Camile though for a moment before she responded. "Okay, but I can't promise anything."

"Me either. Camile, this will be a leap of faith."

CHAPTER 13

▼

SHIFTING THE BALANCE

Over the course of the following week Camile avoided visiting with her mother altogether, but was always sure to check in with Nancy about her condition—which remained unchanged. Along with her recurring dreams, the necklace continued to show her various signs. Camile finally understood that they were working in tandem to instruct her to travel during the next half moon. However, there was never any indication of the destination, only the starting point—the Verrazano Bridge.

Camile often visited Zareah in her apartment. She was very impressed with how well Zareah's place was decorated. The living room was furnished with classic, yet ornate furniture. A curio full of knick-knacks stood in a well-lit corner. Zareah appeared to be a collector of the odd and unusual. Among them was a five-leaf clover in a crystal cube with the words *'A little extra luck never hurts'* etched across the bottom. Another item that caught Camile's attention was a multi-faceted, concave silver dish. It was about a foot in diameter with a mirrored finish and had a kaleidoscopic effect. As Camile leaned closer to inspect the details, her eyes were reflected dozens of times. It was like looking into the lenses of a fly's eye. The rest of the curio's contents consisted of African statuettes, small hand-painted glasses and dishes from various countries.

The sofa had fancy white cushions and was trimmed with mahogany. Upon seeing it, Camile doubted that Zareah was the type who entertained much—either that or she was fanatically tidy. During one particular visit, Camile noticed that there weren't any photographs. Unable to restrain herself, she inquired about Zareah's family. Initially, Zareah refused to answer. Her aging face reflected the emotions of a very hurt and lonely woman. It was a vulnerable side Camile had never seen before. She felt terribly for triggering such a reaction in her neighbor and new friend.

"I don't have any photos of my relatives because it's too painful to see something you no longer have. Years ago, I had a falling out with them. We all had our faults and unfortunately we let them get in the way of what really mattered. We allowed a few ill-spoken words and mistakes get in the way of the love we had for each other. Things escalated to a point where I'm not sure if forgiveness is even possible." Zareah explained.

"Have you tried talking it out with them?" Camile asked.

"We've been scattered for sometime. I've been trying my hardest to contact them though. I'm getting old. Each year that passes is another year lost, but I refuse to lose hope. It's all I have left—that and my career to keep me busy. I guess that's why I decided to go into therapy as a career. I guess I get gratification by helping others since I can't help myself. It's funny, my advice seems to work for everyone but me." Zareah said with a faint chuckle before furrowing her brow with a curious smile. "Hmm … I'm supposed to be helping *you* to sort things out and somehow you managed to flip the script on me!"

Zareah shifted the focus of the conversation to Camile. Although she found Zareah's company to be comforting, she was hesitant to discuss the details of her troubles and recurring dreams at length. The fact that Zareah was a therapist was a bit intimidating to Camile, who felt there was a chance of getting locked away if she ever divulged details of recent events.

During that same week, Camile also met with Akalina on several occasions. They compared stories about their unusual abilities. Akalina was always eager to demonstrate and Camile felt comforted by the fact that she finally had someone she could identify with. However, she couldn't help but feel a little jealous of how easily Akalina seemed to control her capabilities. On one particular day, they were sitting in a small Brooklyn café eating sandwiches and drinking coffee when they noticed a young man approaching their table.

"Camile, watch this. I'll make him leave us alone, but not before he pays for our lunch." Akalina whispered excitedly.

"Yeah, right!" Camile said with a doubtful smirk.

"Shh! He's coming." Akalina hushed.

The man was lean and well over six feet tall. His medium tanned skin and dark hair emphasized his emerald green eyes. He wore a wool trench coat that was left open, revealing the charcoal grey pinstriped suit he wore underneath. His appearance was odd in that he could be considered either handsome or average depending on one's perception.

"Good afternoon ladies!" He greeted. "My name's Bryce. I couldn't help but notice you from across the room."

Although he greeted both women, he was clearly more interested in Camile, looking only at her. Akalina glanced at Camile while making a funny face. She was obviously less than impressed with the man. Her sudden childish gesture incited Camile to chuckle. When Bryce looked at Akalina, she gave him her best innocent 'I didn't do anything' smile. He returned his attention to Camile. Akalina smirked as she fixed her gaze on him.

"So, you already know my name. What's y—?" Bryce began to say before he suddenly stopped talking and reached for his wallet.

Camile regarded her friend with shock and amazement.

"Sorry I disturbed you." Bryce told the women before turning to the waiter who was walking by. "Sir, add whatever they're having to my bill."

"In that case, I'll have a slice of cheesecake to go." Akalina said to the waiter. Camile was beginning to see how opportunistic she could be and found it a bit discomforting. It was a feeling that manifested itself in her furrowed brow. Akalina shrugged.

"What?" She asked almost defensively in a hushed whisper. "He's buying!"

"Have a nice day ladies." Bryce concluded before leaving to pay for the meals.

"How the hell did you do that?!" Camile asked before realizing her voice was just a little too loud.

"Hmph! That's what *I* wanna find out." said a middle aged woman at the next table. "I've been married for five years and still can't get my husband to pick up the tab!"

Akalina and Camile laughed, but the woman's husband was not at all amused. After finishing their lunch, they walked out of the café into the frigid weather.

"Whoo! It's *freezing* out here!" Camile shivered.

"You got that right!" Akalina said in agreement while adjusting her scarf.

"So, how did you do it?" Camile asked. "How could you think of something so specific and make him do it? How can you affect free will like that?"

"No, no, no." Akalina replied quickly. "I don't think it works like that. I don't think anyone can affect free will. Believe me there's been many times I wished I had that ability."

"Then how *did* you do it?"

"A magician never reveals their secrets." Akalina said with a wink. "Anyway, it's kind of hard to explain. I'm not sure if words can describe it. It's kind of like asking someone to teach you how to breathe."

Camile was disappointed that Akalina was either unable or unwilling to explain how she was able to control her powers so well.

"Oh. Well, I think I understand that." Camile lied, unable to mask the disappointment in her voice. "I just wish I knew how to control my powers as well as you control yours. I thought you said you were going to help me. How exactly are you doing that?"

"I'm leading by example!" Akalina exclaimed almost smugly. "Camile, I think you're being unfair to yourself by comparing our abilities. I've been practicing for years! You've only just discovered your powers. Give yourself time and cut yourself some slack for goodness sakes."

"I can't afford any slack. I'm afraid that if I don't get a grip on things soon, someone else may get hurt ... or worse!" Camile replied impatiently.

Akalina stopped walking. Camile noticed and turned to face her.

"Someone *else*? You mean someone has already gotten hurt because of your abilities?" Akalina asked.

"Well, yeah. My mother's in the hospital because of all this remember? And don't forget about Delilah."

"Oh. I *did* forget about poor Delilah. Camile, what do you think our abilities mean? Why do you think we have them?" Akalina asked in a manner which indicated that she thought she already knew the answer.

"I'm not exactly sure, but I wish I knew who I got them from so I could give them back!"

"Give them back?! Why would you wanna do a stupid thing like that?" Akalina asked, her voice laden with shock.

"I'm hurting people that's why."

"Yeah, but maybe that's our purpose. Think about it. Why else would we have the ability to only hurt people? Maybe we're *meant* to do it so they'll learn their lessons and stop hurting innocent people. Imagine all the good we could do if we stop them? I don't know about you, but I'm tired of hearing about good people suffering and bad people getting nothing more than a slap on the wrist—if even that! Aren't you tired of it too Camile?" Akalina said fervently.

"I see what you're getting at. It would make sense if I didn't make my mother end up in the hospital. She's not a bad person. Sure she's made bad choices, but I believe she did them with the best intentions."

"You know what they say; *'the road to hell is paved with good intentions.'*"

"Don't remind me. My mother's going through hell because of me."

"Okay, that's enough wallowing." Akalina said impatiently. "Snap out of it, Camile. You can't change the past. So what do you plan to do with your future? You need to start thinking about that. You and I have been given a great power to potentially shift the balance of what's going on in the world. Imagine how many others there are like us! We'll never have to get bent out of shape to fit into other people's molds again! But first you have to harness and refine that power of yours. You can't just sit on it and do nothing. It'll be a terrible waste. Besides, if you ignore your gifts, you'll probably only end up hurting more innocent people because you won't know how to control it."

Camile couldn't help but agree with what Akalina was telling her. She began to think that if she did nothing to control her powers she would never be able to see her mother again. If that were to happen, her endless questions would forever remain unanswered.

"I guess you're right." Camile replied almost reluctantly.

"Of course I'm right!" Akalina exclaimed with a smile.

"So how do you suggest I go about 'harnessing' my so-called gift? It's not exactly as simple as learning how to ride a bike." Camile replied.

"Well, it won't be with that attitude." Akalina chuckled slightly. "It'll be as difficult or as simple as you want it to be. Just like with anything else, practice makes perfect."

As they descended the subway steps, they were briefly hit by the unmistakable stench of pungent urine. Covering their noses, they increased their pace. When they got to the platform they noticed that there were only a small group of people—a clear indication that they had just missed the train. Camile sat on an empty bench. Akalina sat beside her after looking into the subway tunnel to see if there was an approaching train, but there were none in sight.

"Looks like it's gonna be awhile before the next one gets here." Akalina sighed.

The station was a bit on the chilly side, but still much warmer than the blustery temperatures outside. Camile wore a glum expression as she stared at the tracks.

"*Now* what's wrong?" Akalina asked, her tone slightly annoyed.

"I was just wondering when this nightmare is going to end." She answered, regarding Akalina with a weak smile.

Before Akalina could respond, the brief silence was shattered by the furious clacking of heels descending the stairway. It grabbed their attention and they looked in the direction of the sudden loud noise. A woman in her late twenties was running down the steps as fast as she could. The top two buttons of her coat were missing, her hair was disheveled and her eye makeup was smeared due to the fact that she'd been crying.

"Leave me alone!" The woman shrieked frantically. The fear in her voice sent shivers down Camile's spine.

Camile was shocked to see that the man who was chasing the woman was none other than Bryce—the same man that had just paid for their lunch.

"Allison, get your boney ass back here!" He bellowed angrily.

"No!" Allison shrieked as she ran down the platform in the direction of where Camile and Akalina were sitting.

Allison tripped, falling in front of them. Camile tried to help the woman to stand. Her heart skipped a beat when she realized that Bryce was rapidly approaching.

"Don't you *dare* help her! Stay out of this you little—" Bryce started to yell, but his voice softened when he recognized Camile's face. "I'm sorry. It's just that me and my ex-girlfriend have some unfinished business."

"Oh, it's finished alright!" Allison exclaimed as she backed up and stood behind Camile as though she were a shield. "It's over you lyin', cheatin', good-for-nothin' bastard!"

Bryce laughed, all the while gazing into Camile's eyes.

"*She's* the one who was cheating. She's just upset because I'm trying to take back everything I gave her." Bryce replied with a sly smile.

He reached out to caress Camile's face but she quickly backed away from his reach, stepping on Allison's feet in the process.

"Ow! Watch where you're steppin'!" Allison shrieked in pain.

Camile said nothing as she maintained her focus on avoiding Bryce.

"I didn't mean to scare you. It's just … so good to be in the presence of a *real* woman." He said to Camile, apparently aiming to get Allison jealous and even more upset. Based on the look on Allison's face it seemed his strategy was working.

"*Real woman?!* You wouldn't recognize a real woman if she punched you in the face, which is exactly what I'm about to do!" Allison yelled as she made an attempt to approach Bryce.

Camile held Allison back as Akalina approached the unfolding scene.

"Let me go, you stupid bitch! Mind your own business!"

"Well *excuse me!* She was just trying to help you out!" Akalina retorted defensively.

Allison broke away from Camile, but before she could attack Bryce, he smacked her with the back of his hand—knocking her out instantly. Camile watched in shock as Allison's unconscious body sprawled on the floor. Akalina leapt in front of Camile before Bryce could get any closer.

"Don't even think about it man!" Akalina sneered angrily.

Bryce chuckled to himself as he shot Akalina a sinister smile.

"And I suppose *you'll* stop me? I don't think so, babe!" He exclaimed as he pushed Akalina into a column, nearly knocking her out.

Camile was infuriated as Bryce continued his approach towards her. As angry as she was, she became increasingly fearful. She continued to back away from him as he stalked her—much like a lion stalks its prey.

"Don't worry. I won't hurt you. I like you. I really like you a lot." He said with a slick, creepy smile as he reached out for Camile. She tripped over the bench behind her forcing her to sit down.

"Get away from me! Somebody please help me!" Camile shrieked in a panic as she looked around at the other people at the station. They all simply pretended nothing was happening.

Camile was frozen with fear and intense anger. She shut her eyes when Bryce got within inches of her and she hoped that he would just leave her alone. After a few short moments, Camile heard screams from just about everyone in the station. She opened her eyes and saw that Bryce was no longer in front of her. Akalina slowly made her way over to Camile after helping Allison to stand up.

"Where'd he go?" Camile asked while glancing around with extreme caution.

Akalina shrugged her shoulders, indicating she had no clue where the menacing man had gone. A small group of people screamed hysterically while pointing to the subway tracks.

"Somebody, get him out of there!" Someone yelled while pointing to Bryce—who was lying on the train tracks waiting for the train to come.

"Leave me alone!" Bryce yelled. "I deserve to die!"

"Well, y'all heard the man!" Allison exclaimed to the crowd before speaking to Bryce. "For once we agree on somethin'!"

Akalina chuckled but immediately stopped when Camile glanced at her with mild disapproval.

"Sorry." Akalina mouthed.

Camile saw the light of an approaching train, which was just minutes from pulling into the station—and ending Bryce's life. She was at a total loss as to what she should do. She attempted to use her power to get him off the tracks.

Get off the tracks! Move! Don't kill yourself! Camile thought frantically in her mind as she focused her thoughts on Bryce.

Try as she might, it had no effect. Bryce continued to lay on the tracks as though he were sunbathing. Out of nowhere, a Good Samaritan leapt onto the tracks and dragged him out of harm's way just seconds before impact. The crowd cheered once they realized Bryce was saved, but Allison quickly made a run for it. Camile felt intense burning anger towards the crowd for ignoring her pleas for help and leaping to the rescue of her adversary. Once the train came to a complete stop, an intense bright light flooded the station. Camile and Akalina collapsed to the ground as they shielded their eyes from the painful glare. The train station was filled with terrifying screams and panic.

"Oh my God! Is it a bomb? What's going on? I can't see! I'm blind!" One woman screamed.

"Somebody help me! Please! I can't see!" A man yelled hysterically.

"Me either! What's going on? Please help me!" Another woman hollered.

The light faded away and it took some time for Camile's eyes to adjust. When they did, she was devastated by what she saw. The same people who refused to help her were crawling on the floor, crying—desperately trying to feel their way around. They all were hysterically screaming that they had been blinded. Camile took a moment to think about what happened and realized that she was somehow responsible.

"Oh no! It's happening again!" Camile exclaimed as she ran up the stairs and away from the platform. Akalina swiftly chased after her.

"Wait! What's happening again?" Akalina asked. "Hey, wait up!"

Camile ran quickly, nearly exiting the station, but Akalina grabbed her arm.

"Camile stop! What's going on and why are you freakin' out?"

"Did you *not* see what just happened down there? All those people are blind and it's my fault!" Camile exclaimed.

"How did you come to that conclusion?"

"I was so mad at those people for turning a blind eye when I screamed for their help then rescuing the man that was trying to attack me. Now they're all blind!"

"But how do you think you made them go blind?" Akalina asked.

"Just before that strange light filled the station, I was so mad about how rotten those people were! I thought that since they were pretending not to see anything, they may as well give their sight to someone who'd appreciate it!' The next thing I knew, they were all blind!"

"Wow, Camile!" Akalina exclaimed as her eyes lit up with amazement.

"Akalina, you say that like it's cool, but it's not! Don't you understand what's happening? I just—"

Camile was interrupted by the sound of a man, screaming at the top of his lungs. At first it sounded as if though he were in distress. When she and Akalina looked towards the direction of the voice they noticed an old man kneeling on the dirty floor, his hands outstretched toward the ceiling. He was crying with profuse joy. He'd been traveling with a large, black Seeing Eye dog—who, after circling the man repeatedly, nudged him in an attempt to help him off the ground.

"I can see! Thank the Lord! Praise be to God! I can finally see! For many years I've prayed for the return of the beautiful gift of sight and now I have it! Thank you! Thank you my sweet, merciful Lord! It's all so very beautiful!" The man exclaimed.

Camile and Akalina exchanged astonished glances before returning their attention to the old man, who embraced his confused dog, kissing him on the muzzle.

"And you, my good, loyal friend!" The man said to his canine companion. "You've helped take such good care of me all these years! Now I'll do my best to return the favor!"

The old man got up on his feet and danced out of the station while singing a spiritual hymn out loud and quite off-key as his dog followed him.

"See, Camile?! Look what you've done!" Akalina happily exclaimed. "Because of you that man can finally see! You're like a modern day Robin Hood or something!"

"Akalina stop it!" Camile exclaimed. "Don't make me out to be a hero when I'm not! Did you forget that because of me there's at least a half a dozen people who lost their sight?"

"Maybe they were meant to lose it. After all, they *did* ignore you when you needed their help. The least they could've done was call the police if they were too scared to get directly involved."

"That's not the point—"

"Camile, that's *exactly* the point! Face it, if they would've helped you they would still have their sight right now. The punishment fits their crime. They pretended not to see your troubles so now they see nothing at all. Justice was served and you helped someone receive a very special gift in the process. Who knows how many people that old man will help thanks to his new vision and new outlook on life? Didn't you see how incredibly happy he was and how *thankful* he was? Isn't that worth punishing a few ungrateful, ignorant people who refused to help you? For all they knew, Bryce was going to rape and/or kill you and they still did nothing! But as soon as his wicked life was in danger, they leapt to his rescue! So don't you *dare* feel guilty about them losing their eyesight!" Akalina lectured.

"I can't help but feel guilty. Whether people are bad or not it still feels terrible to hurt anybody." Camile admitted.

"Get over it! Do you think Bryce would've felt guilty if he got the chance to hurt you? Do you think any of those people down there would've given a damn if he *did* hurt you? I don't think so!"

Camile hated the fact that everything Akalina said seemed to make perfect sense.

"Yeah, well either way I still have to report this to the police." She replied.

"Not if I can help it!" Akalina exclaimed.

"Excuse me?" Asked Camile, her face contorted with shock.

"Camile, think for a minute! What are you going to tell the police?"

"The truth! I'll tell them how that wacko tried to attack me and—"

"That you used your necklace to blind nearly everyone on the subway platform?" Akalina interrupted.

"What?!" Camile exclaimed in a hushed whisper. "What are you talking about?"

"Okay, I get it. You're playing dumb. Don't pretend you didn't see that light coming from your necklace. I was looking right at you when it happened. It would've been beautiful if it didn't hurt my eyes so damn bad!"

"My necklace did all that?! I honestly didn't know where that light came from!" Camile whispered.

"Well, now you do. Where'd you say you got that thing?"

"My father ..." Camile's voice trailed off as she tried to figure out what was happening.

"Well, that's one hell of a gift if you ask me!" Akalina exclaimed as she leaned in to take a closer look. "It's not like anything I've ever seen before, that's for damn sure!"

"Akalina, you're right. Going to the police is out of the question. If I tell them what happened, they'll have me institutionalized for sure!" Camile stated. The fact that she had no valid identity further deterred her from alerting the authorities.

"You're damn right they will!" Akalina replied in agreement.

"There's just too much happening all at once!" Camile exclaimed. "I don't know what's happening to me. I have an opportunity to find out more about my past, but I'm not sure if I want to at this point."

"What opportunity?"

Camile instantly regretted her statement since she was now forced to dance around the issue. She really didn't want to go into too much detail with Akalina. Camile's trust in her was beginning to falter.

"It's kind of complicated. I've been having really strange dreams lately." She answered.

"And you think they have something to do with your past?"

"No, not really … well maybe. Never mind, this is too crazy for me to explain."

"Camile, take your time. You can tell me. I'll listen to you."

"Never mind. Don't worry about it. I'll be fine. I shouldn't have brought it up in the first place."

"Camile, why do you always start to tell me something and then change your mind? If you don't want to tell the whole story, why say anything at all?" Akalina asked, a frown emerging on her face.

"I'm sorry, it's a bad habit of mine—not thinking things through before I talk."

"Yeah, I noticed." Akalina said with a faint smile. "But seriously, it's quite clear that the more you pry into your past, the more misery it seems to bring you. I know what it's like to be so enraged about past family issues, my father in particular. For years I chased after a dream that maybe—*just maybe*—one day he would finally accept me and perhaps even grow to love me for who I was. Year after year I tortured myself with the hope that my elusive dream would come true—that I would no longer feel disregarded and irrelevant. One day, I finally realized I wasn't a little girl anymore, but a grown woman. I accepted the fact that it was time for me to finally abandon my obsession with my troubled past and look to my future. The day I realized I didn't have to plead for my father's acceptance was the day I also understood that I didn't need a father figure to validate who I was as a person. Camile, I'm not telling you what to do, but based on everything that's happened I just ask you to please be extremely careful before trying to dig any further. I nearly lost myself in all my family drama and I don't want that to happen to you. It's a very ugly place to be."

"So you think I shouldn't pursue it even if someone has given a clear indication that I should seek the information out?" Camile asked, instantly regretting it since Nancy specifically asked her not to mention it to anyone.

"Who told you that?" Akalina asked curiously, raising her eyebrows.

"I don't know. It was ... something I heard in a dream. I think it was probably a repressed memory." Camile lied in an awkward attempt to dance around the question.

"Well, in that case, no. Absolutely not. It might just be a scrap dream that's feeding on your desire to find out more about your past. Even if it wasn't a dream Camile, it's way too dangerous to go into something like that so blindly—no pun intended. Especially if you don't know who's feeding you the information." Akalina replied.

"Akalina, I don't know what this all means. Even though I have a slight idea of how my powers work, I still don't think I can control them. Until I know what's going on I can't visit my mother anymore. I can't risk hurting her more than I already have ... and I'll have to stay away from you too."

"Why?"

"You're my friend. I don't want to hurt you either." Camile said tearfully. The lonely feeling in her heart felt as though it would cause it to explode.

"Hey, shouldn't *I* have a say in this?! Anyway, I don't think you'll be able to hurt me."

"I thought the same thing about my mother and we both know how she ended up."

"But that's different. Your power won't work against me." Akalina blurted out.

"And just how do you know that for sure?"

There was a slight pause as a remorseful expression crossed Akalina's face.

"Shit!" Akalina muttered to herself before addressing Camile. "Well ... that night when we went to the bar I tried to use my power on you and it didn't work."

"What?! How could you?! What did you try to do?" Camile demanded.

"It's not something I'm proud of, but when I first saw your necklace I really wanted to see it up close. You put it in your shirt so fast and I became even more curious about why you were trying to hide it. So I tried to use my power to get you to show it to me, but it didn't work. I don't think we can use our power against other people like us."

"Akalina, how could you do that?" Camile asked, shocked.

"I was just curious that's all! I admit that my actions were stupid, but I swear they weren't mean-spirited in any way. I made a mistake and I'm really sorry. Please forgive me."

After much thought, she decided to forgive Akalina on the count of her honesty. However, Camile made a mental note that she'd be extra careful around her.

She found Akalina's increasingly unpredictable behavior to be unsettling. Nonetheless, Camile couldn't bear to sever the relationship after all they had been through.

"Alright, apology accepted, but just don't try it again." Camile replied sternly.

Emergency workers and police officers steadily poured into the station. The blinded people were being removed from the scene for transport to the hospital. They were becoming increasingly hysterical in the process. Camile felt claustrophobic. The hectic environment was beginning to take its toll on her.

"I've gotta get out of here." She said after feeling a slight wave of dizziness.

At that moment, there was an announcement of the suspension of subway service due to an investigation.

"Well, looks like we won't be going anywhere anytime soon unless we walk, take a bus or a cab." Akalina replied.

"It's too cold to walk and buses take forever, so I guess a cab is our best bet. Besides, anywhere's better than here." Camile replied.

"Agreed. Let's go." Akalina acquiesced.

They ascended the subway steps bracing themselves for the cold blast of air that awaited them on the street. Bryce walked ahead of them, winking at Camile on his way out of the station. She made an about-face to go to the police, but Akalina shook her head and took hold of her arm.

"Camile, don't." Akalina said almost pleadingly.

Camile paused for a second before turning around to resume her exit from the station. Once outside, they immediately attempted to hail a livery cab while walking up Joralemon Street. Several passed and one driver had the audacity to smile, waving back at them as he drove by—much to Akalina's chagrin. In response, she muttered obscenities and gestured rudely as the cab turned a corner.

They continued to walk, passing several busy courthouses along the way. Eventually, they ended up in the boisterous shopping area on Fulton Street. As they crossed the hectic streets, they were bombarded with the sounds of honking horns, scrambling pedestrians and the loud thumping bass of hip-hop music emanating from several vehicles. During their stroll, Camile and Akalina discussed their theories regarding their abilities. Akalina's outlook clearly illustrated her willingness to accept the 'gift' they possessed. She even went into detail about witnessing other people with similar abilities and how she planned to approach them. Camile felt strangely comforted by the fact that she and Akalina weren't alone, but was apprehensive about reaching out to others—especially since she wasn't exactly sure what they were dealing with. She voiced her concerns to Akalina, who agreed that they should probably learn more before advertising their special talents to others. After what seemed like a half-hour, they finally caught a cab.

Once in the cab, they spoke covertly, concerned the driver would overhear their unusual discussion. As they had done several times before, they tried to see if they had any common ties but failed to find any links. Akalina was born and raised in California, where she spent most of her life. She had never been to Arizona, but decided to move to New York after she turned twenty-one. Since Akalina's mother no longer had anything to hold onto in California, she decided to make the move as well. Camile and Akalina went over every detail they could possibly imagine, but still failed to find a common connection.

CHAPTER 14

▼

SECLUSION INTERRUPTED

Camile sulked at home over the next few days, obsessing over the subway incident. Akalina would occasionally try to coax her out of the apartment, but she repeatedly declined. Although she had forgiven Akalina for what she'd done, she wanted to keep her distance from the person who once tried to manipulate her. Camile's recurring dreams were a welcome distraction from her mounting guilt. Upon each waking, her necklace displayed the same images as it did on the night she discovered it. One evening, the necklace indicated that she needed to travel during the following night. However, the medallion only showed her some road signs and the Verrazano Bridge—the apparent starting point of her journey. She tried everything to get her mind off of the pending trip, especially since the idea made her feel uneasy.

Later that same evening, she had an experience that made her forget about the trip for a while, but it wasn't necessarily a welcome distraction. She couldn't see anything, but the sensations she felt were erotic and disturbingly real. Her body was being thoroughly explored by powerful hands hungrily traveling from her neck, over her breasts and down her torso. There was an overwhelming sensation of her naked body pressed tightly against another. Her lips were raided with lustful kisses and there was a distinct sensation of a tongue—not hers—probing her mouth. She was the dominant party in the encounter, sitting astride her partner—though she couldn't see who he was. Aggressively pushing his muscular chest, she forced him to lie flat. Her arousal climbed when her partner's energy filled her from the inside. She felt her buttocks being grasped as she rode the tumultuous waves of her lustful passion. Just as she was about to explode ...

Camile awoke in her own bed, fully clothed in her nightclothes. Her warm cheeks tingled with the residual arousal her dream left behind. It all seemed so real! She could still feel the lingering sensation of someone caressing her. She checked to see if there was anyone else in the room with her, but there was no one present. Upon inspecting her apartment, she found that all of her windows were securely locked, as was the entrance. She was all alone with nothing but her thoughts to keep her company. As she reflected on her dream, she couldn't help but realize how unusual it was. In actuality, Camile had never been the instigator in sexual matters in any of her previous relationships. Yet in the dream, she was clearly the initiator and was even a bit animalistic in fulfilling her lustful desires. She deduced that she had the dream due to the fact that she hadn't been in an intimate relationship in quite sometime. In addition, she figured her hormones were running amuck. She shamefully admitted to herself that although the dream was a bit unsettling, she enjoyed it on some level.

The next day, she checked in with Nancy regarding her mother. Camile was still too afraid to visit in person, fearing she would somehow aggravate her mother's condition. Later that morning, she watched an inspirational television program in an attempt to boost her morale. As soon as the show ended, there was an update on the elderly man in the subway who suddenly regained his sight. In addition, it was reported that at least five other blind people also miraculously received the gift of sight on the exact same day. Following that story was an update on the half-dozen people who had been blinded. Camile's guilt was threatening to rise and she figured enough was enough. She decided to finally leave the apartment if only to go to the grocery store.

After showering, she dressed in comfortable blue jeans and a thick, grey sweater. She secured the top half of her hair with a clip, leaving the bottom half to flow freely. Camile threw on her favorite winter coat and opened her door to exit. Much to her surprise, there was someone on the other side of it—someone she was completely unprepared to see. Horrified, her eyes widened while looking up into Bryce's smoldering emerald gaze! He was holding a large bouquet of flowers as he smiled seductively at her.

"Hey there, sexy!" He exclaimed casually, attempting to hand her the blooms. "These are for you, love."

Still in a state of shock, Camile gasped loudly and quickly attempted to shut the door. However, Bryce was quick to catch it with his free hand, forcing it open. There was no indication of anger, only a perplexed expression on his face.

"Camile, what's wrong? You're acting all weird! I thought we had a great time together last night." He stated before entering the apartment and attempting to kiss her.

"What are you doing? Get out! Get the hell away from me!" Camile demanded.

"Baby calm down. What's wrong?" Bryce asked softly.

"You! That's what! Now get out!" Camile ordered, trying to focus her energy on getting him to leave. It didn't work. Instead he took her hand, but she quickly snatched it away.

Camile was confused. His touch felt familiar—*too* familiar!

"Okay, what's the matter with you, Camile? You're starting to scare me." Bryce replied with sharp annoyance in his voice. "Last night you were all over me! You couldn't keep your hands off me and now you give me the cold shoulder? Did you forget that *you're* the one that asked me to come over here today? What are you bipolar or something?"

Camile was absolutely terrified, not because there was a strange man in her apartment, but because she had a strong sense that he was telling the truth! Once again, she feared that she had lost control of her mental faculties. She recalled the dream she had the previous night and began to doubt it was a dream at all. However, she refused to accept that possibility.

"No! You're the one with mental problems!" Camile yelled through her tears. "Nothing happened between us last night or any other night! I haven't seen you since the stunt you pulled in the subway and I sure as hell didn't invite you over here! Get the hell out of here *right now!* I'm calling the cops!"

Camile darted into the living room and frantically began dialing for help.

"Oh, no you're not! You're not calling anybody!" Bryce shouted in disgust, violently ripping the phone cord from the wall. "What kind of sick game are you playing with me?"

A sudden wave of anger came over Camile and she hit Bryce across the face with the receiver. He recoiled from the blow, blinking several times as though to process what had happened. His bloody brow furrowed with intense anger. Camile knew that if she didn't act quickly she was in for a world of trouble. She hit him two more times, cracking the receiver with her final blow. Bryce fell backward onto the floor and was out cold. Raising her watery gaze, she noticed Zareah standing in the doorway next to the building's superintendent, Mr. Nichols. They were both staring at Camile with shock in their eyes.

"I heard the noise and came up to help you, but it looks like you've got everything under control. Way to go, girl!" Zareah exclaimed.

Camile dropped the phone from her quivering hands and plopped on the sofa while attempting to catch her breath. A faint, relieved smile crossed her features.

"Are you alright Camile?" Mr. Nichols asked.

"I'm alright. Just a bit spooked." Camile answered.

"The police are on their way. They should be here any minute. You have some very good neighbors, Camile." Mr. Nichols said with a smile.

When the police and medical team arrived, Bryce was removed on a stretcher. Slowly regaining consciousness, he muttered expletives—clearly directed at Camile. The police asked her routine questions as they examined the scene. Prior to leaving, they gave her instructions on how to file for a restraining order if she decided to opt for one. Before long, only Camile, Zareah and Mr. Nichols remained in the apartment. Zareah crossed the room and peered out the window, watching as the emergency vehicles cleared away.

"Are you gonna be okay?" Mr. Nichols asked.

"I'll be fine. Besides, I have a good friend I can talk to." Camile replied, glancing at Zareah—who nodded with a smile.

"You better believe it!" Zareah exclaimed.

Mr. Nichols looked in Zareah's direction before turning his attention back to Camile, giving her a faint smile.

"That's good. You probably have a lot to get off your chest. Don't let me keep you. I would fix the phone for you today, but since you have the one in the other room, I'll be back to fix it tomorrow. How lucky are you to have super who used to work with the phone company, huh?" He asked with a warm smile, patting Camile's shoulder before walking to the door.

"Very lucky." She answered, while holding the door for him.

"Let me know if you need anything okay? And at least try to enjoy the rest of your day." Mr. Nichols concluded.

Upon watching him exit, Zareah appeared to remember something and walked swiftly towards the door.

"Wait! Mr. Nichols, my kitchen faucet is leaking again. Can you—?" She called, but he ignored her, quickly turning a corner.

"Well, I'll be damned!" Zareah exclaimed to Camile. "I'd call that age discrimination! Oh well, I guess I'll just have to deal with him later."

After Camile closed the door Zareah noticed that she looked as if she were about to cry.

"Camile, are you sure you're okay?" Zareah asked.

Camile began to tear up as she shook her head.

"No, Zareah. I'm not okay!" Camile sobbed.

"Oh, sweetie! It might not seem like it now, but you're going to be just fine." Zareah replied while hugging Camile.

"I'm not so sure about that. It seems like everything's falling apart, including what's left of my sanity. I'm not sure if I can deal with this anymore."

"I bet you weren't sure if you had the strength to beat the shit out of that man, but you did. Whoa! You really let him have it didn't you? I bet that boy saw all kinds of stars after the whoopin' you gave him!" Zareah exclaimed with a chuckle.

Camile laughed at Zareah's comment before ceasing the embrace.

"Now that's more like it." Zareah replied. "You should be proud. You're learning to stand up for yourself. It's a great sign of strength. You've come a long way since when we first met. You're much stronger now, whether you realize it or not. Sometimes, we all just need a little reminder."

"It wasn't easy. He was so much bigger than me."

"It never *is* easy, but size is not always the deciding factor in who triumphs and who fails—as you've just seen for yourself." Zareah replied with a wink.

Camile caught a chill, realizing how much Zareah reminded her of her mother. Suddenly, her thoughts shifted to her recurring dreams, messages from the medallion and her pending trip. She was within hours of departure, yet she still hadn't decided whether or not she would go. She was nearly lost in her thoughts when Zareah cut in.

"Penny for your thoughts?" She asked.

"What? Oh, I'm sorry. My mind's been drifting a lot lately."

"No need to apologize."

"I was just thinking about some messages I've been getting."

"Oh? What sort of messages?"

"It may sound silly, and it's probably risky saying this to a therapist—"

"Uh-uh, correction; I'm here as your friend." Zareah smiled softly.

"Well, I've been receiving ... certain messages." Camile began. "They all seemed urgent and hint that I have to take some sort of trip ... *tonight*. There was no clear sign of where the trip would lead me—only where it begins. I have a very strong feeling that it will lead me to the truth about my past, but I'm so scared to find out what it might be. Akalina suggested that I leave well enough alone. She's concerned that if I pursue the truth any further, I'll only end up doing more damage to my life in the process. Based on all that's happened so far, I'm afraid she might be right."

"Camile, it's noble of your friend to be worried about you, but in the end you have to do what's right for you. You're the one that'll have to live with the decision you'll make. What does *your heart* tell you to do?"

Camile gave serious thought to the question before answering.

"It's telling me that I should go. I feel in my heart that I *have* to go, but I'm so scared. I wish I wasn't. I don't even know exactly *where* I'm supposed to be going." She said with quiet helplessness.

"Camile, isn't that like almost every other journey in life? Isn't that like the very journey of life itself? We're all traveling on roads of the unknown. We can never be certain about where they lead. The scariest trips are often the ones we *must* take."

"So you're saying I should go?"

"No. That's a decision you'll have to make for yourself, but I get the feeling that you already have." Zareah replied. Camile nodded in response.

"So far I only know that I have to travel across the Verrazano Bridge tonight, but I'm not exactly sure how I'll manage to do that. If I ask a cab driver to drop me off on the bridge, he'll think I'm nuts!" Camile chortled faintly. "Buses are probably out of the question too."

Zareah regarded Camile for a moment, exhaling a deep breath.

"I don't generally do this for people, but I see how important this is for you." She said reluctantly. "You can borrow my car for your trip. You can drive, can't you?"

"Y—yeah, I can drive." Camile stammered with disbelief regarding her neighbor's generous offer.

"Are you a good driver?" Zareah asked, raising her brow.

"Well, it's been a while, but I think I'm—"

"I'm just bustin' your chops! My car is the first silver one to the right when you leave the building." Zareah explained, pulling the car keys and registration out of her purse, handing them to Camile.

"You're *really* lending me your car?"

"Yeah, don't make a big deal out of it before I change my mind. It took me a while to save up for that car. It's my baby. Please don't trash it."

Camile surprised Zareah with a quick hug. However, she felt guilty that she no longer had a valid identity—which automatically nullified her 'so-called' driver's license.

"Thank you! I promise to be very careful with it."

"Yeah, you'd better. Just make sure to fill 'er up when you get back."

"I'm surprised you're lending it to me, not just offering to drive me to wherever it is I have to go."

"What do I look like, a chauffeur? I'm too old to be shuffling people around like that." Zareah chortled. "Anyway, I figured this is a trip you would probably want to take on your own, given its sensitive nature. Just don't forget to take your cell phone and don't stop for any strangers."

"You sound like my mother, but I guess you're right about me wanting to do this alone. Whatever I'm about to find out is bound to be very emotional and you've already seen me fall apart so many times as it is. Thanks so much for everything, Zareah. I really do appreciate it. You're like my fairy godmother or something. You've done so much to help me, it feels like you're family." Camile said as tears rolled down her cheeks.

"Oh, don't mention it. No tears now, no tears!" Zareah quickly exclaimed as she waved her hand. For a very brief moment, it seemed as though she were fighting back a few tears of her own.

"Good luck, Camile. I hope you find what you're looking for. Be careful." Zareah softly cautioned before leaving.

Camile then called Akalina to explain the incident that had transpired with Bryce.

"What?!" Akalina nearly shrieked in response. "That lunatic actually came over to your place?! How did he get your address?!"

"I don't know. Do you think he followed us the other day? I mean, how else could he have figured out where I live?"

"I don't know, but he'd better not come over here. I'll make that bastard sorry he was ever born!"

"That won't be necessary. I knocked him out and the police came and got him."

"Really? Wow! Good for you, Camile! I hope it wasn't too late though. He didn't … *hurt* you or anything, did he?"

"No. I didn't wait long before I started swinging. He freaked out when I tried to call the cops, so I whacked him a few times with the phone."

"Camile, I'm proud of you. Most women would have frozen and become a victim, but I'm curious. Why didn't you use your powers instead of resorting to brut force?"

"I tried, but it didn't work on him. Wait a minute!"

"What?"

"Do you think he's … like us? I mean, do you think he has the same abilities as we do? Maybe that's why he's immune to them!"

There was a brief pause before Akalina responded.

"Whoa! I never thought of that, Camile! Do you think he knows about our powers? Do you think that's the reason why he's after us?"

"Akalina, I really wish I knew, but he seems to only be focused on me for some reason."

"Maybe it has something to do with your necklace."

"Maybe. I'm not sure. There's something even weirder though. When he came here, he swore that we ... slept together last night." Camile explained, lowering her voice while saying the last four words.

"Are you serious?! Gosh, he sounds like a real psycho!"

"You're telling me? Anyway, he really seemed to believe that something happened between us. It's creepy, but based on the vibe I got from him ... he was telling the truth. But it's impossible! I spent the past few days here. I don't recall ever leaving the apartment and I *certainly* don't remember letting anyone in. I *did* have a rather vivid dream of being with someone, but I didn't see who they were. It was just a dream though. I didn't actually do anything with anybody. I *couldn't* have!"

"Camile, that's really strange and downright creepy. I mean, you can't both be telling the truth!" Akalina exclaimed vigorously, inciting her to panic.

"I know! That's the part that's freaking me out! I have no clue what's happening here! I don't know what to make of the situation. Is he the crazy one or am I the one with the mental problems? After all, it's not like I haven't had problems with my memory before. I don't know how he figured out where I live or—or how come he honestly believes that we ..." Camile's voice trailed off as she began sobbing quietly. The very thought of the events nauseated her.

"Camile, don't cry. We'll get to the bottom of this."

"It's easy for you to tell me not to cry because this shit isn't happening to you!" Camile snapped. As soon as the words escaped her mouth, she immediately regretted it. "I'm sorry, Akalina. I didn't mean to yell at you like that."

"I know you didn't. Don't worry about it. It's not like you do it very often. You're understandably upset about what's going on in your life. Look, we haven't seen each other for a few days. Let's say we meet up for drinks tonight? It'll give you the chance to get some things off your chest, plus it'll do you some good to get out of that apartment. It sounds like you're suffocating in there." Akalina replied.

Camile thought about the trip she was planning to take that evening and instantly knew that Akalina's offer was out of the question. She decided that she wouldn't come out and tell her about the trip in case she would try to convince her not to go—especially after everything that had already happened.

"I'm sorry, Akalina. I just want to take it easy tonight. It's been a hectic day, you know?"

"Oh ... all right. How about tomorrow night then?"

"That sounds good. I know that creep was taken into custody, but there's no telling if or when he's getting out, so be careful."

"You too, Camile. Make sure you lock up before you go to sleep. Are you sure you're gonna be alright? I could come over to keep you company for a while."

"That's really nice of you, but I'll be okay. I just really need to get some rest. I haven't been sleeping too well lately."

"Alright then. I guess I'll see you tomorrow. Bye." Akalina replied, failing to mask the disappointment in her voice.

For the remainder of the day, Camile tried her best to distract herself from thinking about her latest disturbing encounter with Bryce. After checking in with the hospital about her mother's condition once more, she attempted to busy herself with mundane household chores. Although she knew she had to go on a mysterious trip, she somehow knew she had to wait for a signal from her medallion. Slowly but surely, the sun began to set in the late afternoon sky, generating a lovely collage of colors ranging from mild yellows to intense oranges, pinks and purples. Her mind quieted as she marveled at the serene view.

Glancing down at her necklace, she noticed it glowing. It displayed a symbol she'd never seen before, but she somehow understood that it was indicating for her to begin the journey. Her hands trembled with nervous excitement while grabbing her things. She had packed a bag containing a few days worth of clothes and other items since the exact destination and duration of her trip were unknown. Upon exiting the building, she saw the sleek silver sedan Zareah had described earlier.

"Nice!" She exclaimed to herself before climbing into the car.

Her heart raced with excitement as she drove off, following the symbols appearing on the medallion. The symbols indicated which roads she needed to take in order to get to the bridge. Once she reached the bridge, the necklace displayed the next road on which she needed to travel. That process continued until the sun completely dipped below the horizon.

CHAPTER 15

▼

THE JOURNEY TO NOWHERE

While traveling under the cover of night, Camile realized how precarious the trip was. The roads were very dark due to the lack of lighting, prompting her to use the car's high beams in order to navigate. All other road traffic had curiously dispersed. The trees on either side of the highway resembled skeletal hands reaching to close her path. She had never traveled so far on her own and was therefore a bit anxious. Figuring the radio would calm her nerves, she switched through several stations, but received nothing but static. Disappointed, she shut it off and was once again alone with her disturbing thoughts.

She began to regret going on the journey, but nevertheless felt compelled to continue. It was as though there were some sort of magnetic force pulling her in. It wouldn't have been so scary if she knew exactly where she was going. As she drove around a large hill, the silvery half-moon slowly emerged. The sky no longer seemed like a black void, but appeared to be a rich, dark velvety blue studded with countless dazzling stars. The hills and trees were silhouetted against the night sky and the reflection of the moon danced across the placid lake.

Camile was relieved to see a few lit cabins not far from the waters edge and several more in the distance. It was somewhat comforting to her. She wondered what the family in the cabin might have been doing at that very moment. Perhaps there was a mother and father telling stories to their children as they tucked them in for the night. Maybe the children were helping their parents prepare for the next day's plans. She felt a wave of sadness as she thought about how things turned out in her life. She thought that if her father had been present, perhaps her mother wouldn't have lost her mind. Maybe she wouldn't feel so hollow inside and maybe her life could've turned out differently. Suddenly, she was shaken by the thought that perhaps her father had committed suicide because of what she did in Arizona. It seemed disturbingly logical given all the events that had transpired.

Tears filled her eyes, blurring her vision. She noticed that her necklace began to glow once again, displaying yet another symbol. Try as she might, she couldn't continue driving while looking at the stone, so she pulled over to the shoulder of the road. As she cradled the medallion in her hands she noticed that the various shades of blue were shifting and rippling like the ocean. Beneath the ripples were a series of curved L-shaped designs and another zigzag shape intertwined in it.

She was fascinated and mesmerized as she analyzed the symbol. It was the same image which appeared on the rock in her recurring dreams, but what was it and what did it mean? Camile had a feeling that she would find the answers upon reaching her destination. She clearly wasn't going to get them by sitting on the side of an empty road. Just as she prepared to pull off, there was a loud bang on the driver's side door. Nearly jumping out of her skin at the sound, she quickly turned her attention to the window.

There was a tall lanky man in his late twenties peering in. His eyes were as black as tar pits and his dark hair was disheveled—as though he'd just rolled out of bed. It was a sharp contrast to the clean and neat clothing he was wearing. The man was ruggedly handsome, but seemed equally disturbing. Camile tried to resume normal breathing while addressing the stranger.

"What are you doing? I'm trying to pull off!" She said loudly through the closed window.

"Didn't mean to scare you, Miss. My name's Jeff. I'm lost and I've been wandering the woods all day trying to get back to my friend's cabin. Can you please give me a lift to the nearest gas station so I can call him? Or maybe I could borrow your cell phone if you have one?"

Camile's gut strongly objected to having anything to do with the guy. Something didn't feel quite right about him.

"Sorry, I can't. I really have to go. There might not be another station for miles, but I saw a few cabins about half a mile back. You can't miss them. Someone there can help you okay? Please move out my way. I'm already late and there are people expecting me." She replied hoping that the last line would deter any harmful intentions the man may have had.

"I know you must have very important things to do." The stranger replied calmly. "I know that people are waiting for you Camile … because I'm one of them."

Frozen with terror, Camile's hands tremulously clutched the steering wheel as her heart quaked violently in her chest. She felt prickly heat in her cheeks as blood rushed to her face.

"How—do you know—?" She attempted to ask.

"So you see, I can't move out of your way." He continued, his face bearing a menacing sneer as he leaned closer, fixing his eyes on Camile's medallion. You're not late. You're right on time."

She knew if she didn't leave something terrible would happen. Her fear inter-mixed with desperate anger.

"Move or I'll run your ass over! I swear I will!" She shouted.

Camile's mind was screaming at her to quit talking and get the hell out of there. Her mind was determined to slam on the gas and speed away. However, her body seemed paralyzed with unshakeable fear—except for her heart, which seemed to have a desire to leap out of her chest and escape the scene on its own.

The stranger's fixation on the necklace became more apparent with his next statement.

"Okay. I'll leave you alone. After I take this!" He exclaimed with a demented smile before balling his fist and punching through the window. Glass fragments sprayed across her face. With a startled shriek, she stomped on the gas before he could grab her. Tearing down the road at top speed, she looked through her rear-view mirror and saw the creepy man vanish into thin air. Her foot felt as though it were hugging the gas pedal for dear life.

"What the hell was that all about?!" She asked herself in vain, knowing she didn't have the answer.

How did he just disappear like that?! I'm so freaking stupid! I don't have a clue where I'm going! I never should've taken this crazy trip! I should've listened to Akalina! She thought frantically.

Camile briefly entertained the thought of turning around to go home, but was terrified of running into the strange man again. He was clearly out to get her, but why? To her knowledge she'd never met him before, but how did he know her name? She had and wanted nothing to do with him! Feeling she'd traveled a safe distance away from the madman, she slowly eased on the gas pedal. However, her heart still pounded as tears continued flowing from her weary eyes. Glowing once more, the medallion pulsated gently. Camile resisted the temptation to pull over a second time so she removed the necklace, holding it as she steered. She toggled her attention between the road and the necklace, noticing that the intricate curved L-shaped symbol was no longer visible. It had been replaced by another image. She couldn't devote her full attention to it since she was driving and hoped the symbol wouldn't disappear too quickly. Suddenly, the pulsation of the stone became increasingly urgent as its illumination intensified. It became so bright, Camile could no longer see the road or anything else for that matter. It was a lot like that day in the subway. She thought it was best to stop the car before she crashed, so she stepped on the brake. Without warning, the steering wheel jerked sharply to the right. She felt the car lose contact with the pavement and for a few moments, it seemed as though gravity ceased to exist.

Camile was briefly surrounded by an eerie, quiet calm. It was a stark contrast to the energetic pulsation of the necklace. Coming to a violent crash, the car tumbled down a rough embankment. The deafening sound of shattering glass and twisting metal created a bizarre symphony of destruction. After what seemed like forever, the car stopped rolling and landed on its roof. She was rendered unconscious for an unknown length of time before finally waking. Aside from a headache, lacerations on her hands, neck and face, Camile was relatively unscathed. Hanging upside down in the car, she expelled a long sigh.

Adrenaline is overrated. She thought before the realization of the accident finally sank in. *Oh shit! Zareah's gonna kill me!*

Unfastening her seat belt, she took care not to land on her head while adjusting her position to exit the car. None of the doors budged in her attempt to open them, so she climbed out of a shattered window on her hands and knees. Upon standing, Camile realized she was dizzy and disoriented from the tumble. She placed her left hand on the side of the car in order to gain stability.

"Whoa!" She exclaimed before taking a deep breath

Upon surveying the damage, she noticed steam coming from the car's radiator. After looking up to estimate how far she had fallen, she couldn't believe what her eyes were showing her. The guardrail the car had gone over no longer seemed to exist, neither did the road! There was nothing but foliage surrounding a very tall wall and what appeared to be a large hill beyond that. The wall was neither brick nor stone, yet it appeared to have properties of both. There was something oddly beautiful about the iridescence of the coarse material.

Camile was at a total loss as to what she should do next. She began weighing her options, one of which was to figure out a way to get back to the road. However, she was puzzled as to how she should go about the task since the road no longer seemed to exist. Another alternative was to wait it out until daylight—also not an appealing option since there were rodents roaming several feet away from her.

She considered screaming for help in hopes that someone would come to her rescue. She thought better of it when she realized that Jeff would probably be in the area by now and would likely hear her cries first. She was in an area she knew nothing about and it worked to her disadvantage. She didn't welcome the possibility of a dangerous stranger taking advantage of her vulnerable situation. She slid down to the ground, hugging her knees close to her chest. Then she wondered if the necklace could get her out of her dire situation. She felt at her neck before remembering she had removed it shortly before the crash.

With a jolt, she leapt up and crawled back into the mangled car to search for it. After combing through the wreckage, her heart dropped upon realizing the necklace was no longer in the vehicle. It had been ejected during the accident. Searching the perimeter, she found her purse, some of its scattered contents, her bag of clothes and her cell phone—all of which were strewn several feet from each other.

She picked up the cell phone, feeling optimistic that salvation was close at hand. However, her hopes were dashed when she discovered that the phone had been destroyed. The chilly night air made her shiver as she continued to look around. She eventually noticed a faint light about twenty feet away from where she was standing. It was her necklace! In spite of the violent accident it continued to pulsate very rapidly. Camile hadn't noticed it from her original position because it was hanging behind some foliage. As she made her way over to reclaim it, a dark, furry rodent-like creature emerged and blocked her path. It was about the size of an adult raccoon. Its dark eyes shimmered in the moonlight.

Kneeling slowly, Camile picked up an egg-sized rock and a small tree branch for reinforcement. She continued to advance towards the creature, which assumed an aggressive position when she got within five feet of it. Without warning it charged. She immediately threw the rock, catching the creature square on its nozzle. It let out a series of squealing whines while scurrying into the distance. Camile couldn't help but feel a little guilty since she was imposing on its territory after all.

She moved closer to the necklace before recoiling with a gasp. Until that moment, she had been completely unaware of a large, gaping hole that was masked by the surrounding foliage. The necklace was precariously dangling over it from a delicate twig. In order to reach it, she would have to stretch herself over the hole.

"This is unbelievable! Something's obviously out to get me tonight!" She exclaimed. "Wait a second. I wouldn't be in this mess in the first place if it weren't for you! You're trying to get me killed!" She yelled at the necklace. "Oh great! Now I'm *really* losing it! First I'm talking to a necklace and now I'm talking to myself!"

In an attempt to collect her thoughts and determine her next move, she sat on a large white rock and glanced up into the starry sky. The half moon was slowly drifting away as the sky brightened very slightly, hinting that the promise of daylight was just hours away. Something about the moon seemed somewhat different to Camile. She thought it looked more beautiful than ever. It felt as though she were looking at it for the first time.

From the corner of her eye, she noticed that the twig—from which the necklace dangled—was moving. There was a rodent, larger than the first, shaking the twig causing the necklace to swing. Camile stood up from the rock, taking her branch with her. When the necklace suddenly slipped from the twig, she quickly dove for it. She landed on her stomach with a thud, hanging over the hole from the waist up. She stretched out her hand and caught it just in the nick of time.

"Gotcha!" She proudly exclaimed while grasping the necklace securely.

Rising carefully to her feet, she cautiously glanced around to see if the creature was still in the immediate area. It was apparently scared off when she leapt for the necklace—which still pulsated while displaying the image of a tree. Moving away from the hole, Camile secured the chain around her neck. She walked forward, noticing that there were peculiar leaves falling around her like rain. She hadn't noticed them earlier, but they looked extremely familiar to her. She picked one up to take a closer look, holding it in front of her necklace to examine it in the delicate light. It was a beautiful red leaf. No. It wasn't quite a leaf, but more like a glittering, translucent flower petal. As the petals continued to fall around her, she gazed at the rock she had been sitting on earlier and realized that it wasn't a rock after all, but a very large root.

Camile slowly raised her gaze and saw an enormous tree with a white trunk and branches. The tree flourished with thousands of red leaf-like petals that glistened like gems in the delicate moonlight. Thousands of multicolored fireflies twinkled through the tree's plentiful petals. The necklace glowed steadily bathing the trunk with its beautiful blue light, which contributed to the tree's wondrous and mystical appearance.

The tree was very unusual. As one leaf fell another would immediately grow in its place. Each fallen leaf eventually dissolved into a fine, metallic shimmering powder that appeared to be readily absorbed into the soil and grass. Although

Camile was still filled with anxiety, she couldn't help but wonder how come she hadn't seen the majestic tree from the road. It was so massive she should've been able to see it from at least a mile away! Tears trickled down her cheeks as she realized she was standing before the very tree where she and her father had their photo taken many years ago!

"Oh my God! I'm here!" She exclaimed softly with tears in her eyes. "It's so beautiful!"

The tree was so large, all of it couldn't fit into her line of vision. Camile continued to step back, determined to take it all in. Overcome with emotion, she had completely forgotten about the hole behind her. She lost her footing and slid backwards into the dark pit, grasping for the foliage failing to get a solid grip. The excitement proved too much for her and she fainted shortly before impact.

When she awoke, she found herself lying on a thick pile of red, iridescent petals. They were slowly degrading into a metallic, powdery substance. Judging by the blanket of freshly fallen petals on top of her, she concluded that she must have been unconscious for quite some time. Standing up, she brushed the residual petals from her coat as she analyzed her surroundings. The blanket of petals quickly dissolved into the soil.

It didn't take long for Camile to realize she was in a dark tunnel. Luckily, her necklace was still emitting a soft light. She looked to her right, seeing what appeared to be a wall made entirely of plants forming a dead end. Climbing out of the tunnel wasn't a possibility since the walls were incredibly steep.

Camile had no choice but to navigate through the tunnel to her left. Therefore, she began walking cautiously through the passage. The necklace illuminated the vein-like roots that laced the walls. Each root began at a width of about a half-inch, gradually increasing in width as she progressed through the tunnel. She came to a point where there was a ten to twelve inch gap in the root pattern in the tunnel walls. When she came within two feet of the gap, a thick, heavy stone wall slammed down in front of her, blocking her path. Shrieking with fear, she instinctively jumped backward.

"No! I need to get out of here!" She exclaimed while furiously pounding on the wall before her. It accomplished nothing other than making her hands very sore.

Suddenly, she realized she was in the same tunnel from her recurring dream! After approaching the left wall, she realized that it housed the very recessed handprint that she'd seen in her dream. Much to her dismay, she found nothing but more soil. Camile leaned against the wall, sliding down to the ground in exhaustion. Looking from one dead end to the other she realized she wasn't getting out of there and wished she had never found the necklace. It seemed to have led her from one hazardous situation to the next. Now it seemed to have led Camile to her demise. She hugged her knees close to her chest, resting her head in her arms as she wept. A sickening mixture of rage, melancholy and defeat dominated her thoughts and feelings.

All of a sudden, she felt something else. There was a tickling sensation creeping down the nape of her neck. Thinking it was just her own hair, she reached her hand back to brush it aside. In doing so, she came to the disturbing realization that the itch was caused by a strange multi-legged insect nearly the same size as her hand. Camile immediately brushed it off. After standing up to analyze it, she was revolted by what she saw.

The insect looked like a scientific experiment that had gone terribly wrong. It resembled a cross-breed of a tarantula and a centipede. However, it had pincers in the front and a sharp, silvery stinger at the end. The stinger was slightly shorter than the length of a steak knife blade and was several times thicker than a hypothermic needle. The insect was very furry and had no less than twenty very long legs. The ghastly arachnid landed on the ground before rapidly approaching Camile. Lifting her foot, she prepared to stomp on it. A strange voice suddenly caught her attention.

"I wouldn't do that if I were you!" The voice urgently advised.

Startled, Camile lost her balance in her avoidance of killing the bug. She fell against the wall, causing at least a dozen more unusual arachnids to emerge. She quickly backed away from them before inspecting the area for the source of the voice.

"Who are you? Why can't I see you?" Camile inquired tremulously, frantically looking around the sealed tunnel.

Just when she thought she'd seen it all, a swarm of fireflies began streaming out of the hole she dug into the wall just moments earlier. Watching with a mixture of fear and astonishment, she backed into the adjacent wall taking care not to lean against it for very long. She watched in awe as scores of tiny fireflies traveled through the semi-translucent roots in the wall towards the hole from which they were emerging. It was an utterly amazing and electrical sight reminiscent of strings of holiday chase lights. Thousands of vibrant, multicolored fireflies continued to stream out of the wall, swarming in a rapid, circular motion in front of her.

For a moment, the light emanating from the fireflies was nearly blinding. Camile averted her gaze and looked at the ground. That's when she noticed they were forming familiar shapes like feet and legs! Shifting her gaze slowly upward, she witnessed the dazzling insects forming upper legs, arms, a torso, neck and head. At first, it was a simple silhouette, but with a final blast of light the details of the figure were finalized in an instant. Camile was absolutely stunned by the image standing before her and regarded it with teary eyes.

"*Dad?* Dad is that really you?!" She asked in little more than a whisper.

"Yes, Camile. It's me. I know you must have so many questions by now." Zephyr replied in a strangely garbled voice.

Camile wiped tears from her eyes while approaching the image of her father. The light from the fireflies allowed her to see the outline of the clothing he was wearing, but none of the details. She opened her mouth to speak, but no sound came out as she stared at her father's angelic image.

"Thanks for not destroying the little guy." He said, referring to the strange insect. "He was only trying to treat your injuries, but had you killed him, the others would have viciously attacked you. Let's just say, that wouldn't have been pleasant."

Camile suddenly felt tickling sensations on both of her arms and noticed that two of the large bugs were feverishly repairing the cuts on them. In the meantime, a smaller arachnid—presumably a baby—traveled along her face, repairing the lacerations. She cringed while resisting the urge to shake them off, but before long they were finished. Inspecting her hands with astonishment, she saw no evidence that any damage had taken place!

"How did they—?" She began to ask.

"I'm afraid that question will have to wait for another time. You see, time is something we don't have a lot of. Technically you weren't supposed to come here tonight, but I just had to see you before … Well, I can't tell you now, but you'll find out very soon."

Camile cautiously closed the distance between her and her father. She gently reached out to touch his face, but the fireflies that formed his head scattered briefly before rejoining formation. Weeping softly, she regarded his glowing image.

"Dad, so you're really dead after all. Is this all that's left of you, a ghost? Is that why can't I touch your face?" She asked quietly. Her heart seemed to swell inside her chest.

"Oh, Camile. I'm as alive as you need me to be." Zephyr replied somberly. "The point is that I'm able to contact you now, although I might be interfering …"

"Interfering with what?"

"Unfortunately, that's another thing I can't tell you." He sighed. "But you will find out what it is very soon. If I told you, I would be interfering with a very important process and it could effect your decisions. The consequences for that would be extreme. All I can tell you right now is that you are a part of something very important. Please remember that no matter what happens."

"Is it something so important that you left Mom and me?" Camile asked, her voice laced with a hint of bitterness. "Are you aware that she's in the hospital right now and do you know how it happened? I asked her about you and she just snapped! She lost her mind! What did you do to her?!" She was growing increasingly angry and raised her voice when asking the last question.

"Camile, I assure you, I've never mistreated your mother." Zephyr replied with a pained expression on his face.

"So why did you just abandon her like that? Was it because of what I did in Arizona? If so, that had nothing to do with her! She never gave up on you after all those years! Why are you talking to *me* right now instead of her? You're a ghost! Aren't you able to go wherever you want? Why don't you communicate with her? You owe it to her to at least—"

"Camile, it's doesn't work that way. It's not that simple!" He exclaimed, interrupting her relentless barrage of questions. The expression on his face plainly illustrated his internal struggle.

Camile knew it was pointless to argue with a ghost, but she needed to get everything off her chest. The questions and feelings she had harbored for well over a decade were finally being released. It felt somewhat liberating to her.

"It's never simple, is it? You just quit on her. You never even gave her a choice!"

"Neither of us had a choice, Camile!" Zephyr exclaimed, not with anger but irritation. The fireflies violently flickered in unison for a moment, but Camile was too distraught to pay attention to it.

"Then whose choice was it?" She asked.

"Everything will be explained to you ... but not yet. You have to do what's right when the time comes. Only then will you receive the answers you're looking for."

"What do you mean '*when the time comes*'? What's going on? You sound like a broken record. All you can tell me is that you can't tell me anything at all!"

Camile saw the frustrated expression on her father's face as he pursed his lips.

"I wish I *could* tell you more, but I just can't. I know it's unfair, Camile." He sighed, shaking his head in frustration before quietly asking himself: "Why did we have to agree to this?"

For the first time, Camile actually felt sorry for him. The story was clearly a lot deeper than she realized. At first, she considered subscribing to Akalina's theory about ignorance being blissful. She decided against it, figuring she'd ask her father to elaborate his last statement. Before she could inquire, he spoke again, but much more calmly.

"Camile, by now I guess you've noticed that you've always been different. You have a lot of potential. You see, there are people who are given the power and opportunity to do things that are demanding, dangerous, but very necessary. Damn it! I wish I could spell it out for you!" He hissed. The fireflies flickered in unison once again, but a bit more violently than the first time. Camile finally took notice.

"Dad. What's going on?" She asked, but he remained silent, staring blankly for a moment.

"Are you alright?" Camile asked nervously.

"Yes. I—I'm fine. I just need to be a little more careful that's all." He replied softly before humming a tune she didn't recognize.

"Dad? Are you sure you're—" She tried to ask, but was interrupted when her father began to sing, closing his eyes:

"Traveling the underground road,
can be perilous that's what I've been told.
I must travel before the path is forever closed,
I need to get home so I can grow old.
Now it seems I'm low on time,
at times I feel like I've lost my mind.
When faced with the impossible I'll open my mind,
Then finally the truth I will find—"

"Dad? What are you—?" Camile attempted to interrupt.

Zephyr silenced her with a vigorous wave of his hand. At that moment, her heart palpitated with excitement when she realized her father was singing her a riddle! With his eyes still closed, he continued:

"Toward my destiny I'll find a way,
I'll go at the end of tomorrow's day,
Listen carefully to what I say,
There will be barriers along the way.
It's very strange and quite bizarre,
I don't know who my foes really are,
Some are near and others are far,
but I will soon know who they are.

There'll be challenges, but no need for dismay,
Hands will help guide me along the way.
But in the end it will be up to me,
To embrace the warrior I was born to be."

Upon finishing the song, he smiled victoriously to himself. However, Camile was as confused as ever since nothing in the song made any sense to her.

"How am I supposed to remember all that?" She asked.

"*You'll* remember it … when it's time."

"Does it have something to do with this necklace? It's been showing me weird symbols, most of them led me here. I don't understand the rest though. What does it all mean?" Camile asked, but her father stood in somber silence while shaking his head.

"What's the use of asking questions? You're clearly not able to answer any of them." She sighed with frustration. Zephyr glumly nodded.

"Camile, you already have everything you need whether you realize it or not. Just remember that I've always loved your mother, despite how things have turned out. We always loved you and always will. You'll get the answers you've been looking for, I promise you that. Until then, I'm afraid you'll have to leave. Our time is up."

"But—but how will I know if any of this was real? How do I know that this whole thing wasn't a dream or a figment of my imagination?" She asked.

Zephyr appeared to think for a moment before nodding to one of the furry insects. It quickly made its way up Camile's leg, pausing after it wrapped itself around her right hand.

"What's it doing?" She asked anxiously as she cringed, resisting the urge to shake it off.

"I'm sorry, Camile, but this is necessary for you to know you weren't dreaming. Just remember not to hurt the creature. He doesn't want to do this, but only does it because there's no other way."

"Wait! He doesn't want to do what?" She asked uneasily.

As if on cue, the grotesque arachnid bit Camile just below her thumb. She immediately experienced a scalding sensation comparable to a wasp sting. She shrieked while fighting the impulse to kill the bug.

"Why did it do that?!" She exclaimed through gritted teeth.

"That wound will be a reminder of your visit. It's proof that you weren't dreaming. Don't worry, it'll heal in time." Zephyr calmly explained.

After cradling her aching hand, Camile analyzed the fresh scar. Then she noticed several petals blowing across the tunnel floor.

"Why not just give me one of those as proof?!" She asked with slight irritation, referring to the unusual petals.

"That's not possible." He explained. "You see, taking things from this place is forbidden."

"But I can take a bug bite scar, is that it?" She asked, almost bitterly.

"The scar belongs to you. It's part of your flesh."

"Or lack there of!" Camile exclaimed as she rubbed the stinging scar.

There was a moment of silence as they stared at one another.

"Dad, will I ever see you again?" She asked, tears filling her eyes once more.

"I'm sure you will … someday." Her father answered with a forced smile.

"It's strange. I barely knew you, but I know that I love you. Can't I just stay here and talk to you a while longer?"

"I wish you could, but unfortunately that's not the case. I'm glad the necklace led you here, but something's missing—something you have to find. Then and only then will you be able to—"

He shuddered sharply and the fireflies flickered intensely.

"Dad, what's wrong?"

"I can't explain. You have to leave … *now!*" He said urgently while glancing around. "I've already said too much. I shouldn't have signaled for you to come yet. You weren't supposed to come here alone, but it was so good to see you. I just had to see you before—"

Zephyr's statement was truncated. The swarm's illumination became erratic as he shuddered anew.

"Before what? Dad, I don't—"

Before Camile could finish her sentence, her father's image grew so intense, it caused her eyes extreme discomfort. It was like a flash grenade had gone off in slow motion. She shouted with surprise while forcing her eyes shut. Almost immediately thereafter, she heard the hectic, deafening buzz of the fireflies as the swarm broke formation. Upon reopening her eyes, she was stunned to find herself back in the car. Oddly enough, it was no longer crushed, but in pristine condition and back on the road. Her coat—which had become soiled and tattered in her escapade—was mysteriously clean and intact.

She sat up, shaking her head slightly as if to wake herself up. Peering out of the window and looking across the road, she no longer saw the gigantic tree. However, she noticed the end trail of a swarm of fireflies as they descended over the guardrail and down the embankment, returning to where they'd originated. Camile began to think she had imagined everything until she placed her hand on the steering wheel and saw the fresh scar just below her thumb.

CHAPTER 16

▼

THE REVELATION

Camile returned to her apartment early the next morning, her mind hanging on thoughts of her father. She was deeply saddened by the fact that she'd seen his ghost—confirmation of his death. However, she was elated that she was finally able to communicate with him, but as usual she was faced with the endless questions that whirled around in her head.

A strange feeling came over her as she looked around her apartment. Everything seemed so foreign. It was as though she had been gone for weeks, months or even years. It was an eerie feeling that she could neither shake nor explain. The odd silence in her bedroom made it seem as though she'd lost her hearing. Suddenly, the phone rang loudly, startling her. As her heart fluttered, she answered it.

"Camile, it's Nancy." A slightly nervous voice greeted from the other end.

"Nancy, is there something—?" Camile began to ask, but was interrupted.

"No need to worry. Your mother's condition is still stable. Actually, I'm not calling about her. I wanted to know if I could speak to you … in person if possible." Nancy asked.

"I'm afraid I can't come over right now, I'm exhausted. Can we just talk over the phone?" Camile asked after yawning quietly.

"Oh. Well … alright." Nancy replied with a note of disappointment in her voice.

"What's going on? Are you okay?"

"I'm fine, Camile. I was just wondering … about that lady you introduced me to."

"Who? Akalina? What about her?"

"Where exactly did you meet her?"

"I met her on the day my mother was supposed to be released from the hospital, just before the coma. Why do you ask?"

"Did she tell you why she was here?"

"Yeah. She was there to see her mother. My mother and hers shared the same room. Why do you ask?"

"Have you ever actually … *met* her mother, Camile?"

"No. Unfortunately she was always out for tests and procedures. She died before I had the chance to meet her. Nancy, why are you asking all these questions?" Camile asked impatiently.

"Camile, your mother had that room to herself ever since she was admitted. She never shared it with anyone."

Camile was utterly flabbergasted. Her heart sank as she was struck with a wave of nausea.

"What?!" She exclaimed in terror. "There must be some mistake! There was a nurse, her last name was Veena … Veeta … no, Vela! Nurse Vela talked to Akalina about her mother. She even—"

"Hold on." Nancy instructed. The sound of vigorous typing filled the brief silence before the conversation resumed. "Camile, there's no one at the hospital by that name. There's obviously something on Akalina's agenda. From the sound of things, she might not be working alone. You need to be very careful with her."

"What does she want? Why did she go through all that trouble just to be my friend?"

There was a slight pause before Nancy gave a chilling response.

"Maybe you have something she wants."

The first thing Camile thought of was the necklace.

"I can't believe this! I *trusted* her!" Camile exclaimed in quiet anger.

"Camile, if I were you I'd just—" Nancy's voice suddenly halted and was momentarily replaced with stark silence.

"Nancy? Hello?"

"Oh, I'm sorry. I—I really have to go now. I'll call you back in a little bit, okay?" Nancy quickly concluded.

"Nancy, wait. I—" Camile began, but stopped upon hearing the dial tone.

Rocked by the startling news of Akalina's fraudulence, she tried to think of ways to approach her. Nancy's advice seemed to indicate that she knew more than she was letting on—which scared Camile tremendously. That afternoon, Mr. Nichols came to the apartment to fix her phone jack. After inspecting the damage, he mentioned it wasn't as bad as it looked and that the repair would take less time than originally expected.

"Camile, how ya doin' today? Are you feelin' alright? You know … after what happened yesterday with that lunatic?" Mr. Nichols inquired.

"Yeah, I'm fine. Thanks for asking." She answered. On the contrary, she was far from fine. She was still preoccupied with the thought of Akalina's deception.

During a lengthy pause, Mr. Nichols worked on the repair. It gave her time to think about how to best approach Akalina about her lies. She was in a daze when the voice of Mr. Nichols suddenly cut into her thoughts.

"Camile!" He called, startling her.

"Yeah? What happened? Are you done already?"

"Nah. Not yet. Sorry I spooked ya there." He chortled, glancing at her for a moment before installing the new jack.

"I guess I got lost in my own thoughts for a moment there." She answered, forcing a chuckle.

"Ya know of anyone lookin' to rent an apartment?"

"No. I'm sorry, but I don't." Camile answered, still partially in a daze.

"Shit! Well, can't say I'm surprised with my luck! 5A has always been a pain in the ass to rent out! Anyway, ya phone's back in business." He replied after listening to the dial tone in the receiver and hanging it up.

"Excuse me?" Camile responded, jolted out of her semi-daydream. "What apartment did you say it was?"

"5A. Why? Ya think of someone?" He asked hopefully.

"No. Did—did Zareah move out or something?"

"Who's Zareah?"

"My friend. She moved in a couple months ago."

"Unless she's been living there illegally, I'm afraid it ain't so. That apartment's been vacant for nearly four months now!" Mr. Nichols explained just before his cell phone rang. "Yeah." He answered, his eyes growing wide as he heard the response. "What?! I'll be there right away. Throw plenty of towels on the floor or somethin' ya hear?"

Camile called after him as he made a mad dash for the door.

"Mr. Nichols, wait! What do you mean that the apartment has been—?"

"Sorry darlin', but there's a huge flood in the apartment above mine and I just got a new home theater system!"

"Wait! Mr. Nichols!" Camile called, but it was no use.

Once again, Camile was left with a plethora of unanswered questions and doubt in her mind. Thoroughly stunned, she feared she was becoming mentally unhinged and wondered if her mind was playing serious tricks on her. She distinctly remembered visiting Zareah in her apartment on more than one occasion. She clearly recalled how impressed she was at how nicely Zareah decorated the place.

She didn't have to wait long to approach Zareah about the situation since she paid a visit that very afternoon. In an attempt not to scare her off, Camile maintained a pleasant demeanor until she entered the apartment. They exchanged greetings while walking into the living room. After that, Camile wasted no time beginning the interrogation.

"Zareah, I'm gonna ask you something and you'd better answer me honestly." She demanded.

"Whoa! Camile are you—?"

"No, I'm *not* alright! Everyone's been lying to me *including you!*"

"What exactly are you talking about?" Zareah asked, raising an eyebrow.

"You know damn well what I'm talking about, Zareah! That's probably not even your real name! I spoke to Mr. Nichols today and guess what he told me? He mentioned that apartment 5A has been vacant for months! What's up with that, huh? No forget that, just tell me who you really are and what you want from me!" Camile snapped, pointing furiously.

Standing there with her mouth agape, Zareah was apparently speechless.

"Well, say something, damn it! I want answers! I'm sick and tired of everything in my life being such a big freakin' mystery! Who are you and what the hell do you want from me?!" Camile bellowed.

"Please calm down. I just want you to know that everything I did was for the best. I tried to protect you as much as I could. There are certain things that needed to be done. I just hope that you'll understand—"

"Cut the bullshit! I've heard this all before and frankly I'm *sick* of it! I'm tired of everyone feeling that it's their job to—!" Her tirade was interrupted by a knock on her door.

"Camile, open up! It's Akalina!" A voice called from the other side.

"Oh, look who's joining the party!" Camile sarcastically exclaimed, sprinting to the door and opening it.

"I came over here as soon as I got your message." Akalina replied urgently upon entering.

Camile found Akalina's statement to be odd since she had been way too preoccupied to contact her.

"What message? I didn't leave you any messages!" Camile replied angrily, her face scrunched with shock and disbelief.

"Okay Camile, so you didn't send a text message to my cell phone saying to come here right away and that you found out how the necklace works?" Akalina asked cynically.

"What?! No! I think I'd remember something like that!"

"Really? Maybe your memory's acting up again. Or maybe you just don't trust me enough to tell me what's *really* going on!" Akalina snorted angrily.

"What the hell's gotten into you? You're not making any sense whatsoever! But anyway, I'm glad you're here. We have *a lot* to talk about." Camile spat.

"Camile, stop playing games! You should've received all the signs by now so spit it out! What did it show you?!"

Camile was a bit frightened and bewildered, wondering how Akalina knew about the signs. She never mentioned the particulars about the medallion's special symbols to anyone other than her father.

"Signs? What do you know about the signs?" Camile asked.

They stared at each other for an intense moment. Anticipating Akalina's attack, she ran towards the kitchen in hopes of getting something to defend herself with. However, Akalina was right on her heels and shoved her into the refrigerator. She landed face down on the cold floor. Akalina turned her over and started choking her. Camile gasped for air while thrashing underneath Akalina's weight. She tried to pry Akalina's fingers from her neck, but her grip was just too tight. Her eyes widened with anger and the desperate need to breathe. Akalina smiled at her in a calm, sinister manner while attempting to wring the air out of her. Just as she began to see dots, Akalina slowly eased her grip, but continued pinning her to the floor.

"Camile, I really don't wanna have to kill you. You've suddenly become very important to me. We've been through so much together. That has to be worth something! So tell me, what did the necklace show you?" Akalina asked impatiently.

"I don't know … what you're talking about." Camile answered, struggling to catch her breath.

"Let's see if the necklace has any answers shall we?"

Before Camile had the chance to protect it, Akalina snatched the necklace. Camile sat helplessly on the floor, nearly depleted of energy. Neither she nor Akalina noticed Zareah slowly making her way into the kitchen.

"It's not doing anything! How does it work? Tell me!" Akalina demanded.

"I don't know, you stupid psycho!" Camile snapped.

"Oh, so now you *don't* know, huh?" Akalina crooned. "How convenient! Almost as convenient as the mysterious message you left me. On second thoughts, maybe you were trying to send the message to someone else, but accidentally dialed my number instead. Is that it? Well, I'll tell you what, if you don't start giving me answers in the next five seconds I'll show you just what a psycho I can *really* be!"

"I'm telling you the truth! I didn't send the damned message!"

"If you didn't, who did?!" Akalina hissed through gritted teeth.

"I did." Zareah answered calmly.

Whipping her head around, Akalina noticed Zareah standing in the kitchen entrance. Her silky, wavy, salt and pepper hair was up in a neat twist, gleaming in the fluorescent light. A satisfied smirk crossed her aging features.

"What?!" Camile and Akalina asked simultaneously.

"That's impossible, I … wait a minute. Who the hell are you?" Akalina demanded.

"I've been hearing that question a lot lately." Zareah muttered.

Akalina lunged at Zareah, who was prepared for the attack. Balling her fist, she punched Akalina in the face. The blow knocked her out instantly and she collapsed onto the floor next to Camile, who immediately got up. Zareah immediately began looking for something to tie her up with. She wound up using the very scarf Akalina was wearing. After sitting her in a chair, Zareah used the scarf to tie her arms behind it.

"Quick, I need something to tie her feet with!" She exclaimed, but Camile just stood there in shock. "Well hurry, unless you want her to finish choking the life out of you!" Zareah added.

Dashing into to the living room, Camile retrieved the damaged telephone cord that had been replaced earlier. Upon returning to the kitchen, she noticed Zareah admiring the necklace. Seeing this, she froze in her tracks, not knowing what to think, do or say next.

"This is very beautiful." Zareah smiled, placing the necklace in her hand. "You'd better keep it close."

Camile quickly slipped it around her neck while Zareah tied Akalina's legs to the chair. Akalina winced as some of the knots were tightly secured. Camile realized that she was alone in her apartment with two very dangerous women. She didn't want to delay in calling the cops. She stepped backwards and planned to quietly exit the kitchen while Zareah was busy. However, Zareah saw Camile before she was able to make her exit.

"Hey! You're not gonna to do anything stupid, are you girl?" Zareah asked sternly.

"Not unless you force me to." Camile replied sharply, trying to mask the fear in her voice.

"Is that the thanks I get for saving your life? *Again* I might add!"

"I'm tired, frustrated and I have a million questions! Like why did you leave Akalina that fraudulent message and why did you make her think I needed her help? How do you two know each other in the first place and—" Camile ranted.

"Okay, Camile. I know you're desperate for answers, but I can only give you one at a time. I left her that message in order for her to show you her true colors. Akalina possesses a level of deception that surpasses even my skills ... not that I'm vain or anything. I knew that the only thing that would make her blow her cover is if she felt that her one and only chance at ultimate power and freedom was about to slip away. She got so desperate that she let her guard down and *voila!*" Zareah explained as she gestured towards an unconscious Akalina.

"Power and freedom? Freedom from what?" Camile asked.

"I'm not entirely sure of that myself, but my guess is that it has something to do with that necklace."

"Who are you?" Camile asked pleadingly on the verge of tears. "Please, *just tell me!*"

"I'll get to that in time Camile. You already know that I'm not who I claim to be, but neither is she. I need to show you this before she wakes up. Those cords won't hold her in that chair for very long and when she's regains consciousness you might not get another chance to see who she really is. Camile, hold your necklace out in front of her!" Zareah said as she switched off the kitchen light.

The kitchen was in near total darkness. The only light came from the microwave display panel. The necklace remained dormant.

"Zareah, I can't make it work. It usually happens on its own." Camile replied.

"You underestimate yourself too much Camile. Try to focus. Concentrate your pure energy and desire on the necklace. Think of it as an extension of your heart and your mind. Block everything else out and *make* it work for you. Listen to yourself and follow your heart."

The silence was deafening. Camile tried her best to focus but no matter how hard she tried, it just didn't work. She felt like such an idiot. *What the hell is this supposed to prove anyway?* She thought. Exhaling a deep breath, she flicked the light back on.

"This is ridiculous. I can't do this!" She exclaimed.

"Fine, I guess you'll never get your answers then!" Zareah replied abruptly. "What is it with you? Do you get your kicks out of being a victim? No wonder Akalina tried to choke the living shit out of you! She was trying to do you a favor and put you out of your misery! Look at you. You still don't know what you want out of life. A few weeks ago you didn't even *want* your life! What would your parents think of you now?!"

Zareah's harsh words cut deep into her mind and burned her heart painfully.

"Shut up! You don't know my parents and you don't know me!"

"That seems to be the recurring theme these days." Zareah quipped flatly.

"Stop it!" Camile cried. "I love my parents! I'll make it up to them, I swear I will! So don't you dare judge me for my mistakes, I never claimed to be perfect! I didn't know any better! I didn't mean any harm!"

She was furious and pounded her fist on the counter to get her point across. Zareah was surprised the commotion didn't wake Akalina, but she smiled at Camile with admiration as she switched off the light once more.

"It sounds like you're finally starting to forgive yourself." She said with a soft smile, touching Camile gently on the shoulder. "Now try it again."

Almost as soon as Camile began to think, the necklace emitted the most beautiful glow she'd ever seen it produce. Her steely-grey eyes reflected the cool blue radiance of the medallion. The entire kitchen was engulfed by the brilliant blast of light as ocean like patterns rippled across the wall. She noticed that several large images zoomed across the ceiling for a few seconds, but quickly vanished before she could distinguish what they were. A single tear trailed from her right eye as she smiled with amazement.

"Look, Camile! It's happening!" Zareah exclaimed, pointing at Akalina, who was slowly regaining consciousness.

Akalina's head slumped over. Her face was completely covered with her highlighted hair, which mysteriously began turning jet black while becoming slightly shorter. Camile was amazed at what was happening. Akalina was transforming before her very eyes! She appeared to be growing taller, more muscular and the restraints were beginning to stretch and strain. Camile grew increasingly nervous and hoped they would be able to withstand the stress of the transformation.

Quite noticeably, Akalina's perfectly curvy figure became more masculine. Her breasts deflated and her shoulders broadened. Suddenly, the glow from the medallion decreased in intensity. The newly transformed Akalina moved her hanging head from side to side, but still appeared to be very groggy. Camile and Zareah cautiously leaned in to take a look at Akalina's new identity, but she was still looking downward.

With a jolt, the transformed figure suddenly jerked its head up to face Camile, whose face contorted as she screamed. Camile fell backwards to the floor. The shocking image she saw was that of a young man in his late twenties. His disheveled hair looked as though he'd just rolled out of bed. His eyes were as black as deep tar pits. It was none other than Jeff, the same madman who tried to attack her the night before!

"No! No!" Camile screamed hysterically, feverishly shaking her head. "Oh my God!"

"Well, hey there pretty lady!" He said in a raspy voice. He winked at Camile and licked his lips as he looked her up and down. "I *hoped* I'd see you again. Care to give me that lovely necklace now or do I have to pry it from your cold dead hands?" He said with a sneer and laughed menacingly.

He wriggled violently in an attempt to free himself from the chair. Zareah quickly elbowed him in the face. Jeff was stunned, but still awake. He growled at Zareah before she punched him, knocking him out. Afterwards, she shook her hand to relieve the sting.

"Oh my God!" Camile continued to shriek hysterically. She somehow managed to stumble onto her feet. She ran into the living to call the police. Receiver in hand, she began to dial the numbers, but Zareah snatched it out of her hand and hung it up.

"What are you doing?!" Camile yelled frantically. "That maniac tried to kill me last night!"

"Camile, there's more to this than you think. That's not Akalina's true identity. She's still trying to hide it from you, but she's still weak. If you want to know the truth we have to go back in there before she regains her full strength." Zareah replied urgently as she gestured towards the kitchen.

"Oh, screw that! There's no way in *hell* I'm going back in there! I've seen enough!"

"Don't be ignorant, Camile. This is important!" Zareah chided. "You're finally ready to see the truth you just don't know it yet. Quick, come on before she regains her strength!"

"Zareah don't make me go back in there! *Please* don't make me go back in there!" She begged tearfully.

"Stop being a victim and stand up for yourself for goodness sake! I know you've got the guts to do it, so come on!"

Zareah directed her towards the dark kitchen, but Camile didn't go easily. She fought like a condemned prisoner who was headed to the gallows. Zareah practically had to drag her back to the kitchen. Camile was amazed at how much strength the older woman had. Before Camile knew it, she was facing her demon afresh. Jeff was still unconscious and groaning quietly. Camile's necklace was still casting a faint, eerie glow on everything in the kitchen.

"Now what?" Camile asked.

The medallion's illumination increased significantly. Once again, the kitchen was flooded with aquatic blue light.

Camile repeatedly clenched her hands nervously at her sides as she watched Jeff intently. His hair began to grow longer, thicker and more luxurious as the color changed from pitch black to auburn. The length eventually stopped just past his shoulders and a long bang swept over his right eye. His height decreased as his body became more voluptuous and lady-like which looked much less awkward in women's clothing!

The figure was once again transformed. It threw its head back in exhaustion and faced the ceiling while gasping for air. When Camile saw the result of the figure's latest transformation, she was thoroughly convinced that she had finally and completely lost her mind. Her face froze in horror as she realized that the person who was tied to the chair now was a mirror image of herself! Zareah stood there immobilized with shock with a very perplexed look on her face.

"*Twins?!* But how ...?" Zareah's voice trailed off, she looked thoroughly puzzled as she tried to make sense of it all.

CHAPTER 17

▼

HOMEWARD BOUND

Camile felt as though her heart would burst out of her chest. As she struggled to breathe, she nearly hyperventilated. After backing into the wall behind her, she slid down to the floor. She felt a wave of nausea as she continued staring at her double who sat tied to the chair.

"Oh my God!" She said tremulously, tears streaming down her cheeks. "How is this even possible?! This has to be some kind of trick! This isn't happening!"

Akalina tossed her hair back with a flip of her head. Cocking her head to one side, she smiled sinisterly while looking down at Camile. After gliding her tongue across her top row of teeth and winking, Akalina laughed hysterically.

"Aw! *Come on,* sis. You should feel lucky to look as gorgeous as me, but I obviously have better powers. Not to mention better style." She said before shaking her head. The action caused her hair to revert in color and length until it was just past her chin—as it was before her disturbing transformations.

"Who *are* you?" Camile asked as she wept.

"*Who are you?*" Akalina mocked with a snarl while rolling her eyes. "Don't you recognize your own sister? Who would've thought I'd be related to such a punk! No wonder Mom slipped into a coma. It was probably her only way of getting some peace and quiet away from your whining!"

"Shut up!" Camile shouted.

We both know I can't do that, sis." Akalina shrugged. "It's the gift of gab we inherited from Mom—one of the few things we have in common."

Camile shook her head in disbelief. Her body trembled with a sickening mélange of confusion and angst. Her mind was plagued with questions and a desperate need for clarity. Finally, she turned her attention to Zareah—who still wore a perplexed expression.

"You mean to tell me that you didn't even *know* what her real identity was?" Camile asked.

"No." Zareah replied softly, shaking her head as she stared at Akalina. "I was only told that she's been masquerading as two people other than her true self. There was never any specification as to what the identities were. I certainly didn't expect her to be your *twin!*"

Camile was astounded that Akalina was able to shape-shift into other people. She wondered how that was possible and internally speculated the possibility of such abilities running in the family. However, the most frightening question that entered her mind was: *Who or what am I?*

"Well, Camile, I'm glad the truth is finally out in the open." Akalina casually admitted. "I was getting sick of pretending to be your friend anyway. You're boring, annoying and clueless. You should be grateful that I came into your life to spice things up a bit, but do you appreciate it? *No!* Well, at least Bryce didn't seem to mind." She giggled. "As a matter of fact, he *really* seemed to appreciate it."

A mischievous look crossed her face as she winked, playfully biting her lower lip. It immediately became evident to Camile that her erotic dream was actually a projection of Akalina's sordid interlude with Bryce.

"So it was you all along! *You're* the reason why that wacko was stalking me! You're a sick, twisted pervert! I thought I was losing my freakin' mind!" She shouted furiously. Never in her life had she been so angry.

"But sis! That was the *whole idea!* It was too easy for me to screw with your mind. I don't know how I managed to keep a straight face when you called crying to me. *Oh, boohoo!*" Akalina taunted with a wicked laugh. "You really should thank me for adding some zest to your reputation. Lord only knows when's the last time you've gotten any! Too bad Bryce gave you all the credit, but on the upside, *I* had all the fun. I was hoping that his stalking you would have been enough motivation for you to use the full extent of your powers—perhaps even kill him—but of course you're too much of a coward for that. It disgusts me that someone in my bloodline could be so … *spineless!*"

Camile was so astonished, all she could do was stand there, listening as her newlyfound relative ranted on.

"I can't believe you were actually dumb enough to think that our powers had no effect on Bryce." Akalina continued. "Did you forget that I *made* him pay for our lunch that day? And why did you think he tried to attack you in the subway in the first place? *I* made him attack you in order to get you to use your powers and it worked! It was so much fun … watching you struggle with your guilt about blinding those pathetic people. Sure it was a risk for me to let Bryce attack you since he could've actually killed you, but it was a risk worth taking. Ironically enough, it turns out that you're worth more alive … at least for now anyway."

Akalina clearly enjoyed berating and insulting Camile while highlighting her weaknesses. Zareah watched the heated exchange between the doubles in stunned silence.

"You set that whole thing up? Why? Why are you doing this? Do you want to steal my identity is that it?" Camile asked angrily while standing up. "You want to take my place?"

Akalina laughed cruelly before sucking her teeth.

"Take *your* place? Oh please! Don't flatter yourself! I'm just here to collect a very old debt from my over-privileged sister. You owe me and you owe me big time, girl! You can start by giving me that necklace!"

"What?!"

"Oh, so now you're deaf *and* dumb, huh?" Akalina asked with bitter sarcasm. "I know you heard what I said. Let's face it, you're a loser and you don't deserve it. You didn't even *want* your own life. You tried to kill yourself and couldn't even do that right!"

Camile was flabbergasted. Other than Zareah, she spoke of her suicide attempt to no one.

"Wait a minute! You *know* about that?" She asked.

"Yep! Wasn't that the reason why you were trying to call me that night? Did you honestly think I would try to talk you out of it? No way! Not after I worked so damn hard to put the idea in your head in the first place!" Akalina explained with a hearty chortle. "I was about to become one step closer to getting everything I wanted … until *she* ruined it all." She replied bluntly shifting her icy gaze to Zareah.

In hindsight, Camile realized that with each conversation she had with Akalina, she was slowly implanting suicidal thoughts in her head. She wondered how many other things she had done under the influence of her sister. As she stood speechless, Akalina and Zareah began arguing.

"I stopped her from making a mistake, and as for the—" Zareah attempted to explain.

"Who said it was a mistake?" Akalina asked. Her face wore a mask of faux innocence. "For all we know, maybe she *should've* died! Maybe that was her destiny, to do some good in the world by sparing it of her pathetic existence. Don't worry, Camile. There's still time. I'll be more than happy to help you fulfill that destiny."

"Like hell you will!" Zareah snapped while moving to hit Akalina.

Suddenly, Akalina's hand flew from behind her back, catching Zareah's arm in mid-swing. She hit Zareah on her temple, knocking her out instantly. Camile stared in horror as she watched Zareah sprawl onto the floor. She momentarily feared Akalina had just killed the older woman, but was relieved to see that Zareah was still breathing. With a single motion, Akalina effortlessly undid the binds on her legs and freed herself. Before Camile had the chance to lunge for her, Akalina knelt beside Zareah and held her in a choke hold.

"That's it Camile." Akalina beckoned. "Come closer. Give me a reason to snap her scrawny old neck like a freakin' twig!"

Camile stopped hopelessly in her tracks before turning to exit the kitchen.

"Nah, uh-uh." Akalina crooned. "If you leave, I'll *still* break her neck. Or maybe I'll do something a little more creative."

Camile exhaled a deep breath while turning to glower at Akalina—who smirked anew.

"Aw! Now, sis, don't give me those dirty looks." Akalina taunted.

"What do you want?!" Camile retorted.

Akalina quickly grabbed a knife from the counter behind her. She slowly traced the blade with her slender index finger while casting a menacing glare at Camile.

"Like I said, I'm just here to collect an old debt." She smirked.

Zareah regained consciousness, but was a bit groggy. She attempted to get up, but Akalina dug a heel into her back, painfully forcing her back onto the floor.

"Don't you *dare* move!" She snapped before turning her attention back to Camile. "Give me the necklace … *now!* Slide it over to me!"

Camile flinched before taking a step toward Akalina, whose eyes were wide with intense anger.

"Don't do it! She'll kill you anyway. Just take the necklace and go! Don't worry about me, please!" Zareah pleaded.

"Shut up you old bat!" Akalina shrieked through her gritted teeth as she kicked the elder woman.

Zareah cried out in extreme agony as she writhed on the floor.

"That's right, bitch! Squirm like the little worm you are! This is what you get for not minding your own freakin' business!"

Camile found herself at a crossroads. She wanted more than anything to get the hell out of there, but she felt it would be wrong to leave the person she once knew as her neighbor. Especially since she had saved her life again.

"Leave her alone! If your problem is with me then deal with me and leave her out of it!" Camile demanded forcefully while wondering why Akalina couldn't use her powers to *make* her give up the necklace. It was apparent that Akalina no longer had the ability to influence her mind. Something was different now.

"What's this? *Bravery?*" Akalina sneered. "Camile, it's grossly out of character for you and it isn't very convincing. Just do yourself a favor. Slide the necklace over to me and *maybe* the two of you will walk away unscathed. I'm not without mercy you know, I've shown it to Nancy and our sweet mother too."

"*You're* the reason why Mom's in the hospital? And Nancy? What did you do to them?" Camile demanded.

"Now, now, I can't take *all* the credit. I'm not the reason why Mom ended up in the hospital. That honor goes to you. But on the day of her seizure, she sensed my presence in the room. That's what triggered her attack. Poor Mom. I wonder if she'll ever come out of her coma this time. You have to admit it was a nice touch for me to let you blame it on yourself, huh? You were so wrapped up in your own stupid self-pity that you didn't even notice that I pulled the necklace from behind your shirt to make it *seem* like you triggered her seizure. It was almost too easy to convince you that it was your fault since you were always so willing to blame yourself for *everything*." Akalina giggled cruelly.

Camile took an aggressive step forward. Seeing this, Akalina dug her heel into Zareah's back causing her to wince painfully.

"You'd better keep your ass over there, sis!" Akalina exclaimed angrily, prompting Camile to stop in her tracks. "As for Ms. Nosy Nancy, she should've minded her freakin' business. I heard her warn you about me. I was at the hospital when she called you. She was getting in my way and I had to get rid of her, but she was stubborn. She simply wouldn't die so she ended up bunking with Mom instead. How cozy?!"

Knowing that she was taking a huge risk, Camile defiantly fastened the necklace around her own neck.

"You know what? You're a sadistic, manipulative bitch and you don't deserve this!" She said defiantly.

"What?! How dare you?! You don't take me very seriously do you? Well that's a *big* mistake, sis!"

Akalina plunged the knife deep into Zareah's shoulder. The elder woman's shriek pierced through Camile's ears.

"Camile, I swear if you don't give it to me now the next wound will be fatal! Do you want her death to be on your conscience?" Akalina hissed.

"No! Don't do it, Camile!" Zareah feebly exclaimed.

"Shut up! Don't you learn?!" Akalina yelled.

Smirking, Akalina pressed her foot down on Zareah's bleeding wound causing her to cry out in extreme agony. Camile grimaced sympathetically, pleading for Akalina to stop. The increasingly violent scene halted when an intense light radiated from the necklace and generated a crystal-clear projection of Zephyr in the center of the room. Although the trio could see him, he could only hear them.

"Dad!" Camile exclaimed.

"Dad?" Akalina asked, her voice full of confusion.

"Camile, Akalina, if you can see this it means you have found each other. Now you have no choice but to begin your journey home, the clock has been set."

"Home? But—" Camile began to ask.

"Don't interrupt him!" Akalina snapped.

"I know you have so many questions, but everything will be explained to you once you arrive here. However, it's very important that you arrive here together. The three of you must leave immediately. There isn't much time left and this will be the only chance for you to come home."

"The *three* of us?" Camile asked. "What does Zareah have to do with all of this?"

"Zareah's your guide. She, along with the necklace, will help lead you along the way." He answered.

"Good going on stabbing our guide Akalina! Kudos!" Camile snapped angrily.

Akalina said nothing while rolling her eyes and shrugging.

"Stabbed?! Zareah, are you alright?" Zephyr asked with fearful unease.

Akalina reluctantly released her grip and slowly backed away from Zareah, who staggered onto her feet.

"Yeah, I guess I'm okay. This girl has been a real pain in the … back!" She answered, glaring at Akalina.

She then reached into her pocket and pulled out a tiny vial containing a silvery liquid. Applying the solution to her shoulder, she moaned with relief as it took effect. Camile and Akalina watched with amazement as the thick liquid replicated the exact color, texture and consistency of Zareah's skin. Amazingly, the bleeding stopped and the wound instantly healed.

"You need to work as a team if you expect to get through this alive." Zephyr stated. "Getting home is not as simple as it may sound. Camile, Akalina, you only have a brief window to get here. If you don't make it in time, you will certainly die. It's imperative that you leave immediately! But remember, Zareah is only your guide. There will be things that you will have to figure out on your own." He said with great urgency before his image vanished. The necklace and the room went dark.

Camile, Akalina and Zareah stood in silence, staring at one other for what seemed like an entire minute. Zareah's subtle southern voice finally broke the hush in the room.

"Well, what are you waiting for? You heard him! We've got to get moving!" She said anxiously.

Once they got to the street, they noticed the ground was covered with about three inches of freshly fallen, powdery snow. The three women adjusted their coats to fend themselves against the chilly night air. There was something about the street that seemed oddly empty and isolated. They traveled down the softly illuminated street, their bodies casting eerie shadows on the smooth blanket of snow. Zareah instructed Camile to remove her necklace.

"Camile, hold it out in front of you and aim it towards the ground. Move it from side to side in a sweeping motion." She instructed.

They continued to walk slowly along the street for nearly two uneventful minutes. Camile had no clue what they were looking for. Ordinarily, she would have thought the request was ridiculous, but given the events that happened that evening, she knew otherwise.

"What are we looking—?" She began to ask, still moving the necklace in a sweeping motion as instructed.

"Shush!" Zareah interrupted. "I know it's here somewhere."

They were halfway across the street when the necklace suddenly projected an intense beam of light onto the ground. The light was erratic until it projected an odd, intricately shaped arrow on the snow coated ground. It acted as a bizarre compass, indicating which direction the women needed to travel. Eventually, it highlighted a spot in the middle of the desolate street. Once the women reached the area, the arrow transformed into another strange symbol. It lasted for only a split second, before the light flickered out.

"We lost it! Where are we supposed to go?" Camile asked.

"We didn't lose it." Zareah smiled calmly. "We're exactly where we need to be."

Kneeling carefully on the ground, she began clearing away the snow. Camile immediately joined in. After a moment, they raised their gaze to Akalina.

"What?" She asked harshly.

"Some help would be appreciated!" Camile sharply suggested.

"Alright! I just thought the two of you had it covered!" Akalina retorted.

Reluctantly, she assisted in clearing away some snow. When their combined efforts revealed nothing but the smooth pavement underneath, she eagerly expressed her aggravation.

"So this is what we're looking for? Asphalt?!" She asked disdainfully.

"Camile, hold your necklace over it." Zareah instructed, ignoring Akalina's ranting.

Camile held the necklace over the patch of exposed ground. It emitted a soft glow, revealing a metal seal that wasn't there before. It was slightly similar to a New York City manhole cover, but with significant variations in its size and construction. When Camile moved the medallion away, the seal vanished. Nothing but solid pavement remained. Moving the necklace over the ground once more, the metal seal reappeared. It contained a circular indentation in exactly the same size and shape of Camile's medallion.

"There!" Zareah exclaimed while pointing to the indentation. "Camile, place your necklace in there!"

After a moment of hesitation, Camile placed the necklace in the circular opening. It was a perfect fit! Almost immediately, the residual snow over the metal seal melted with a hissing sound. Vapor danced upward from the metal for a few seconds before dissipating into the cold air. The seal was revealed to be over four feet in diameter and had beautiful intricate carvings all over it. A sliver of light briefly escaped upward through the slight gap between the metal object and the pavement.

Camile exhaled a deep breath. She was finally starting to believe that her sanity hadn't abandoned her after all. For a brief moment, she was overcome with excitement as she realized she was on the verge of an important discovery. She finally understood that her prior worries were pointless. She used to stress about things like work, money, and material possessions—things she knew she couldn't take with her after expelling her last breath. Camile then remembered the foreshadowing of her potential demise and for a moment, the prospect of learning about her past became less and less alluring. In fact, she found it downright scary. However, she knew she had no other choice but to move forward.

Zareah stepped onto the seal and motioned for Camile and Akalina to join her. Camile joined her right away, but Akalina seemed to hesitate for a moment before following suit. As soon as all of their feet made contact with the metal surface, there was a subtle rumble as it created friction with the ground. It slowly rotated while descending. Zareah remained calm, but the twins exchanged apprehensive glances. Camile found it disturbing to see her likeness without the aid of a mirror. The trio looked up into the night sky. Light snow flurried down upon them as they continued their descent. With a thud, the metal seal reached the bottom of an underground tunnel system. After they stepped off of the metal platform, Camile removed the necklace from the slot.

Immediately upon removal, the platform floated upward towards its original position. The tunnel was damp, cold and dimly lit. It looked like something out of a horror movie. Small light fixtures were imbedded into the smooth tunnel walls at ten foot intervals. Camile tried her best to mask the chilling fear that gripped her, but quickly realized her attempt had failed.

"Camile, you poor thing. You look terrified!" Akalina taunted.

"You're delirious." She responded. "You must be the one who's scared. Don't pawn it off on me."

"Come on. Who are you kidding? You look like you've seen a ghost or something."

"Cut it out, both of you!" Zareah ordered sharply while walking ahead. "We don't have time for this nonsense!"

Camile and Akalina followed behind her. The trio wandered for what seemed like an hour. The grimy tunnel seemed endless, especially since there were dozens of huge rats. In addition to the filthy rodentia were hundreds of large water bugs—which occasionally drizzled upon the women.

"This is pointless. We're going in circles! I swear we've passed this section before!" Akalina hissed impatiently, cringing at the sight of a contorted dead rat.

"How can we possibly be going in circles? This is a sewer. All of the tunnels are bound to look alike!" Camile stammered before hastily brushing a cockroach off her sleeve.

Zareah suddenly halted.

"Why did you stop?" Camile asked, eyeing her curiously.

"Yeah." Akalina said in harsh agreement.

"What? Can't a woman rest for a moment?" Zareah asked, winking at Camile before leaning against the bug-infested wall.

"Ugh! What are you doing?" Camile asked with utter disgust etched on her features.

Camile and Akalina were unprepared for what they saw next. Zareah was swiftly covered with water bugs which formed a bizarre curtain with their leggy, entangled bodies. A little more than two seconds passed before the insects scattered once again, revealing the damp, grimy wall. Zareah was nowhere in sight. Gasping with shock, Camile ran to the very spot where the elder woman stood just seconds earlier.

"What happened? Did they eat her or something?" Akalina asked, but Camile didn't answer since she didn't know.

"Zareah!" She called. "Are you alright? Where are you?"

There was no response. She and Akalina regarded one another with stunned expressions. Camile found it very difficult to look at Akalina since she was still coming to grips with the fact that she had a twin. She cautiously traced her fingers along the wall, trying her best to avoid the bugs as they energetically scurried about.

"I don't get it. How could she just—?" Camile started to ask before realizing that her hand had disappeared into the wall. The swarm of cockroaches quickly scurried to the point of contact.

There were dozens of grotesque insects crawling over where her hand was extended. Cringing, Camile prepared herself for the disturbing sensation of their legs on her skin, but surprisingly she couldn't feel them. Somehow, they were unable to make contact with her flesh. Her eyes widened with awe before she yanked her hand away. In doing so, it carried at least five of the large, repulsive bugs, inciting her to shriek in disgust. After violently shaking them off, Camile aggressively rubbed her hand to relieve the itchy sensation. She breathed deeply while trying to tame her overwhelming fear and revulsion. Nevertheless, she felt compelled to travel through the wall.

"You really *are* stupid aren't you?!" Akalina snapped upon hearing her plan. "You don't even know if *she* survived! Anyway, if we needed to go in there, don't you think she would've said so?"

"Remember what Dad said. She's our *guide,* but she's not supposed to tell us everything. We have to figure out some things on our own. I don't like the idea anymore than you do, but I really feel like we *have* to go in there."

"But you don't even know where 'there' is! You could be walking to your own death for all you know!"

"Since when do you care?!" Camile snapped. "Anyway, from the way Dad sounded, we may have to face death either way. I don't know about you, but if I'm going to die, I rather die while fighting to survive … not while sitting around waiting for whatever it is to snuff me out."

After conveying her notion, she cringed before leaning against the wall just as Zareah had done moments earlier. She was quickly covered with the bugs and disappeared in a little over a second. Akalina was left standing alone, cursing in anger. It took her a moment to compose herself, but once she did, she also leaned on the wall. Stumbling backward, she fell hard on her backside before noticing Camile and Zareah standing over her. They offered a hand to help her up, but she stubbornly declined, snatching away from them as she got to her feet.

"You could've told us about this you know!" She lashed out at Zareah.

"Oh, you think I'm supposed to map *everything* out for you?" Zareah asked calmly. Akalina sucked her teeth while brushing the dirt off her coat.

"How come we were able to go through the wall, but the bugs couldn't?" Camile asked.

"What, do you miss them or something?" Akalina retorted. Camile rolled her eyes in response.

"That's just how it works." Zareah answered plainly.

The three women now stood in an entirely different tunnel system that had slick wet walls laced with many small pipes which were intricately intertwined. The subtle overhead lighting throughout the tunnel highlighted a continuous groove in the center of the floor. Camile, Akalina and Zareah were standing in front of a wall with a small crack at the bottom of it. Water continuously leaked out, streaming along the groove in the floor. The trio walked cautiously along the damp tunnel in silence for a short while, only exchanging occasional glances.

"Wait, I think I see something!" Camile called while gazing at the ground.

She noticed a similar round indentation to the one in the metal seal on which the trio descended. She knelt down to take a closer look, but couldn't make out any of the distinctive designs due to the light reflecting off the water flowing around it.

"What is it?" Asked Akalina, but Camile only shrugged. Zareah nodded knowingly while looking on.

Instinctively, Camile removed the medallion from around her neck before inserting it into the opening. A series of translucent planks immediately folded upward from the ground, throwing Akalina and Camile off balance, causing them to land painfully on their backs. Zareah was somehow able to leap out of the way just in time to avoid the unfolding planks. In a matter of seconds, they were all standing around what appeared to be a small translucent watercraft with three pairs of handles on the inside. Camile stared in awe as the craft's edges gleamed in the dim light. It looked as though it were made entirely of ice or crystal. Akalina was obviously less than impressed and began laughing.

"Oh, this is just rich!" She exclaimed through her amusement.

Zareah quickly sat in the back of the small watercraft and tightly gripped a pair of handles. The serious expression on her face was enough to convince Camile to do the same. She quickly sat in the front of the boat and held onto her set of handles. It wasn't until the wall behind them quaked that Akalina finally stopped laughing and sat between Camile and Zareah. The entire tunnel began quivering violently.

Camile's adrenaline level kicked into overdrive. When she looked behind the craft, she noticed that the crack in the wall was many times its original size. Cold water sprayed out with enormous pressure. The women cried out as the chilling water made contact, drenching their clothes. Camile noticed that Zareah appeared to be calm and that Akalina was shivering as she squeezed her eyes shut. Akalina held onto her handles so tightly that the knuckles on her caramel colored hands turned white.

Camile realized that she was also shivering, but couldn't tell if it was due to the cold or the intense fear she was feeling. She forced herself to look ahead into the darkness. Suddenly, there was a very loud crashing sound when a wave of water collided with the small watercraft. It was instantly propelled forward with a violent jolt. Camile screamed loudly as she temporarily lost grip with one of the handles, but quickly regained it. It was at that moment when she cursed herself for sitting in the front of the vessel. The watercraft traveled so fast, Camile had to occasionally turn her head sideways in order to breathe comfortably.

The vessel whipped around one sharp turn after another before heading directly towards an apparent dead end. Camile opened her mouth to scream, but no sound came out. However, Akalina was doing enough screaming for all three of them. The watercraft screeched, coming to a halt just inches from a stone wall. The three women sighed, relieved that they hadn't crashed. They glanced around to examine the location and to see if there was a way out.

Just as Camile started to release her grip from one of the handles, there was a loud thump as a trap door opened beneath the craft. The vessel immediately plunged down an unexpected, steep and dark decline. Camile felt as though all her internal organs had migrated to her throat forcing a scream out of her mouth. She gripped her set of handles so tightly that her nails were digging into her palms. She leaned back so far in her seat that her head was practically in Akalina's lap, yet it still felt as though she would fall out of the speeding craft.

When the descent was finally over, the vessel traveled in a new series of tunnels at extreme speeds. Several times, it raced along the tunnel walls forcing the three women to lean backwards in order to avoid hitting their heads on the overhead lighting. Their rate of travel made it seem as though there was one continuous stream of light along the ceiling. Camile heard laughter coming from behind her. She initially thought it was coming from Akalina until she heard her cursing at Zareah.

"What are you laughing at? This isn't funny!" Akalina yelled between expletives. "It's not funny you crazy old—" Her screams faded against the crashing sound of the furious waves.

Camile was too preoccupied with the intense fear in her heart to pay much attention to anything else. Suddenly the watercraft made another sharp turn before making its way along the tunnel floor once more. After what seemed like an eternity, it finally slowed down and came to a counter-climactic stop. Akalina promptly leaned over the side of the craft and vomited. Camile looked around and saw that the pipes along the tunnel walls were suddenly semi-translucent and were somehow pumping the water out from underneath the watercraft.

As the water quickly drained from the tunnel, it was pumped through the pipes, presumably to be carried back to where it originated. Before long, the bottom of the craft made contact with the tunnel floor. As the women stood up, the necklace shot up into the air. Camile and Akalina both attempted to grasp it, but Camile was quicker and more successful at catching it. Akalina scowled while stepping away from the boat. Zareah's long, salt and pepper hair had come undone and she took a moment to secure it in a ponytail. The eerie lighting in the tunnel seemed to emphasize the wrinkles on her face, but not enough to make her look haggardly. Since their coats were soaked with icy water and no longer effective in keeping them warm, the women discarded them. Luckily, the current tunnel wasn't nearly as drafty as the one they first entered. As soon as Camile and Zareah vacated the boat, it instantly liquefied and was immediately pumped into the pipes.

"How—?" Camile began to ask.

"No time to explain." Zareah immediately interrupted.

The three women stood in front of a slimy, corroded metal gate. They couldn't see beyond it since it was blocked by extremely lush foliage on the other side. It looked like something one might see outside of an abandoned graveyard. Camile caught a frightening chill, giving her goose bumps all over. She began having second thoughts about going on the journey. Based on the contorted look on Akalina's face, it seemed that she was reconsidering her participation as well. Camile quickly reminded herself that she basically had no choice but to move forward. She also motivated herself with the hope of finally receiving all the answers she'd been searching for. She and Akalina inspected the gate for a handle or even a keyhole, but there were neither.

"No keyhole? Maybe it's not locked." Camile guessed.

Akalina grabbed hold of the bars. She pushed and then pulled, but the gate wouldn't budge. She snarled with disgust as some black slime got onto her hands.

"Ugh! I certainly hope the so-called 'home' Dad's referring to isn't as filthy as this! Honestly, when was the last time anyone's done any cleaning around here?" Akalina snorted after wiping her soiled hands on the legs of her snug-fitting jeans.

Camile sighed with frustration while looking for another way to open the gate. There were no rocks to smash it with, nor was there anything she could use as leverage to pry it open. Akalina ranted fervently, cutting into Camile's concentration.

"Zareah, aren't you supposed to be helping us? You *are* our guide aren't you?" Akalina said impatiently.

"Yes. I'm here to guide you. I know my job, there's no need for you to remind me." Zareah answered plainly.

"Well, then help us get this stupid gate open!" Akalina retorted.

"You each have a pair of hands, I suggest you use them." Zareah replied. The tone of her voice indicated mild annoyance.

"Are you blind? I tried to yank it open and it wouldn't budge!"

"Maybe what Zareah means is that one person can't open this gate alone. It's too heavy!" Camile interjected.

Akalina stared Zareah down for a moment before joining Camile in front of the gate. Camile grimaced when she realized she would have to touch the slimy filth that enshrouded the metal bars. She counted to three before the two of them pushed with all of their might. The gate still wouldn't open. They then tried pulling with the same result. Akalina became infuriated.

"It's still not working! This is ridiculous! Why don't you help us? We can use another pair of hands!" She snapped at Zareah.

"No. You have all the hands you need. You don't need mine." Zareah replied coolly.

Akalina decided that she'd heard enough and quickly approached Zareah. Her intentions were clearly malevolent.

"Oh, is that right? So, I guess we don't really need you after all!" Akalina exclaimed.

"Wait! I think I understand!" Camile called out.

Akalina and Zareah turned and saw Camile holding her necklace out towards the gate.

"What are you doing? There's no keyhole, it's—" Akalina began to say but stopped when the necklace started glowing.

It revealed a handprint along the wide center of the gate. *"… you each have a pair of hands, I suggest you use them!"* Zareah's voice resonated in Camile's head. As she slowly moved the medallion from side to side, another handprint appeared as the previous one vanished. By the time Camile was done scanning the gate with her necklace, it revealed a total of two sets of handprints. She and Akalina regarded one another for a brief moment before turning their attention to their guide.

"You knew it the whole time didn't you?" Camile asked with a slight smile.

Zareah smiled almost humbly, but didn't answer.

"So why the hell did you let us make asses of ourselves by—?" Akalina screamed.

"She gave us a hint!" Camile interrupted. "Dad told us that she's only supposed to guide us, not tell us everything. We have to think for ourselves too you know!" Camile snapped.

Akalina glared at Camile. She obviously didn't enjoy being spoken to so harshly. It was apparently something she could obviously dish out, but couldn't take.

"That's right, Camile." Zareah replied. "But, there might be some things I'll need to help you with directly. The catch is that you'll have to figure out exactly when you'll need my help."

Without any further exchange of words, Camile and Akalina stood in front of the gate. Camile scanned it with the glowing medallion once more in order to reveal the hidden handprints. Once the first pair became visible, Akalina placed her hands on them. Camile secured the necklace around her neck and then walked over to Akalina's left to reveal the second pair. Taking a deep breath, she finally placed her hands on them. It instantly triggered a humming sound, causing the tunnel to vibrate slightly.

There was also the sound of metal gears turning as the gate slowly screeched open. Surprisingly, it didn't open inward or outward, but instead retracted into the tunnel's left wall. The thick foliage unraveled and stretched along the wall like a botanical web. Once the foliage cleared, it revealed a long path. There was a moment of hesitation before the three women walked slowly into the newly revealed section of tunnel.

As Camile walked, she analyzed the bizarre leafy, snake-like vines that laced the tunnel walls. After the women traveled approximately eight feet past the entrance, they heard the unmistakable sound of turning gears. They whipped around in time to see the gate close behind them with a loud clank. The foliage quickly slithered along the wall towards the sealed gate. It intertwined and formed an impenetrable barrier between the women and the entry point, sealing them in.

"No! What is this? Some kind of trap?" asked Akalina. Her voice reflected more fear than anger.

"I assure you, this is no trap." Zareah replied.

"Then what is it?!" Akalina asked urgently.

"You're about to find out." Zareah answered in a calm and somewhat ominous tone.

▼

CHAPTER 18

OBSTACLES AND PERIL
PART ONE

Akalina rolled her eyes knowing full well that any further attempts to gain information from Zareah would be futile. Other than the sound of their footsteps rustling the leaves on the ground as they walked, there was deafening silence. It wasn't until they noticed an eight-foot hole in the tunnel's ceiling that Camile realized they were in the exact same tunnel she had fallen into the night before.

However, the atmosphere was significantly different this time around. As she looked up through the opening, she was bathed in the silvery moonlight that streamed down from above. It looked as though Camile were standing in some sort of spotlight as petals drizzled down around her. She caught one in her hand expecting to see the same shimmering red color the petals had during her last visit. However, she was surprised to see that the color of all the petals was rapidly draining—an evident sign of life depletion. She caught another petal and the same thing occurred, but at a slightly slower rate. Feeling pangs of concern, she stepped out of the moonlight to rejoin the others.

"Too bad we can't climb up there." Akalina sighed, referring to the hole in the ceiling.

Camile continued analyzing the dying leaf in her hand. She wondered what could've possibly caused the petals to deteriorate so quickly. She walked beside Akalina and Zareah amid silence that was immediately broken.

"What's the matter with you? What are you looking at?" Akalina asked curiously in a tone that seemed to demand an answer.

Camile was becoming increasingly annoyed with Akalina. Before she could respond, the petal in her hand deteriorated at least twice as quickly as the others. It disintegrated into ash.

"It's a … It *was* a flower petal." Camile replied in a perplexed tone while staring at the residue in her hand.

"*A flower petal?* We've been told that our lives are at stake. Now we're stuck in some Godforsaken tunnel and all you can do is pick dead flowers? Are they for your grave or something?!" Akalina chided.

"I've been here before." Camile replied impatiently.

"Yeah, right! If you were here before why did the house of horrors back there scare you so much? You almost peed your pants!"

"I don't care if you believe me or not, but the last time I was here these petals were alive. Now they're dying very quickly."

"So?" Akalina asked rhetorically.

"I don't know, but I think it might be related to the reason why we're here."

"Whoa! *Now* I get it. I know why we're here! It just dawned on me!" Akalina exclaimed.

"Really? What is it?" Camile asked.

"We must be the new housekeepers! We have to water the plants, do the dusting and clean those *disgusting* gates back there!" Akalina replied with angry sarcasm.

"That's not funny!" Camile snapped angrily, but Akalina only shrugged carelessly.

"I agree. You should take this more seriously. Your lives depend on it." Zareah replied flatly, glaring at Akalina.

As they continued to walk slowly, Akalina commented on the wall.

"This looks really weird. These roots look a lot like … *veins!* Ugh!"

"Yeah, I thought it was strange the first time I … Wait a minute. They're different!" Camile exclaimed.

She noticed that the roots appeared more translucent than during her previous visit. They served as channels for some sort of liquid—presumably water. As the women continued to walk through the tunnel they noticed that the roots gradually decreased in opacity while increasing in thickness. The women were so mesmerized with the transition of the roots that they neglected to pay full attention to the path ahead of them. At one point, Camile nearly tripped on a small boulder.

"Hey, that's weird." Akalina said. "The roots look like they disappear into the wall just up there!"

She pointed to a section of the wall that was less than three feet ahead of them. Camile realized she was right. There was about a twelve inch gap in the root pattern in the tunnel wall. Camile's heart palpitated wildly. She was confronted with the memory of her dream and her visit to the tunnel the previous night. She immediately stopped in her tracks.

"STOP!" She commanded the others.

It was nearly too late. They were just inches from the heavy wall when it slammed down in front of them with a violent bang. Akalina nearly jumped out of her skin.

"This place is a freakin' death trap! How did you know that was gonna happen?!" She screamed.

"I *told* you, I was here before!" Camile replied just short of rubbing it in her face.

However, Camile was disturbed that she had become so distracted that she nearly forgot about the descending wall.

"Okay, so what other pleasant surprises should we expect?!" Akalina asked angrily.

"I don't know. This is as far as I got." Camile answered quietly.

"How convenient! You're playing this all out to your advantage, aren't you?" Akalina hissed accusingly.

"What are you talking about?! If I didn't yell for you to stop you would've been smashed to bits! And this is how you thank me?!"

"*Thank* you? You can't be serious! We probably wouldn't even be in this mess if it weren't for you!" Akalina sneered contemptuously.

"Oh, and I suppose *you* know why we're here?!"

"No, but knowing you, I'm sure that we're here to clean up some mess you've made."

"I can't *wait* until this is over! One way or the other at least I won't have to deal with your ass anymore. I can't stand you! You're a nightmare and you're getting on my last nerve!" Camile exclaimed with frustration.

"Well, *there's* a pot calling a kettle black!" Akalina replied as she laughed roguishly.

"Alright, that's enough. Shut up, both of you! I refuse to stand here and get killed because the two of you choose to act like children!" Zareah chided.

Camile was instantly ashamed of her behavior. She finally understood how siblings had a way of getting under each other's skin. She was embarrassed at how easy it was for Akalina to push her buttons. At one time Camile would have embraced the idea of having a brother or sister, but the way things were panning out, she greatly missed being an only child. She struggled for a moment to regain her focus as Akalina began searching the tunnel floor for something.

"If you're looking for something to pry it open with, don't bother." Camile said calmly.

"And why not?" Akalina asked snidely.

Camile walked over to the left tunnel wall and brushed away the thick collection of soil from the upper section. She was relieved when a recessed handprint was revealed, just like in her dream!

"Because this button is the only thing that can open it." Camile answered matter-of-factly. She pressed the button and received a nasty surprise when nothing happened. "I don't get it. It's supposed to open." Her face cringed in a perplexed manner.

"Well, it looks like your little button is broken. What's the matter, Camile? Batteries not included?" Akalina taunted.

Camile groaned while pondering possible reasons for the button's inactivity. Then she had an idea. "Okay, you try it." She said to Akalina before stepping aside.

Sucking her teeth, Akalina approached the button.

"What makes you think that it's gonna work now? The button will still be broken no matter *who* presses it!" She replied arrogantly.

"Humor me!" Camile said impatiently.

Akalina made a few dramatic, sarcastic movements before pressing the button, but once again nothing happened. She shot Camile a nonchalant expression as if to say: 'Well, what did you expect?'"

"I don't get it! That button is *supposed* to work. It worked in my dream!"

"Camile, sis, I hate to break it to you," Akalina said condescendingly, "but dreams rarely ever come true. Believe me, if they did I'd be a very rich and happy woman right now and *you* wouldn't be here!"

Taking several deep breaths, Camile was determined not to allow Akalina to get the best of her. Instead she tried to reason everything out in her head—which helped to block out Akalina's snide remarks. Suddenly, something Zareah mentioned earlier dawned on her '... *there may be one or more things I may need to help you with directly. The catch is that you'll have to figure out exactly when you'll need my help.*'

"Zareah." Camile called. "Why don't you try it?"

"What? But she's just our guide remember? And not a very good one at that!" Akalina said contemptuously, sneering at the elder woman.

Ignoring the statement, Zareah made her way over to the wall after Akalina reluctantly stepped aside. She smiled softly while stretching her body slightly upward to reach the button. Pausing for a brief moment, she looked at Camile.

"I thought you'd never ask." Zareah replied.

When she pressed the button, the entire tunnel trembled briefly. The thick wall began retracting slowly into the ceiling. The vibration caused small amounts of loose soil to rain down on the women. Camile and Akalina walked slowly towards the opening. The wall was almost fully retracted when Zareah released the button. She took a step to join the twins. With a loud bang, the heavy wall came down like a guillotine blade. A brief but violent rumble reverberated through the tunnel. The wind from the impact vigorously tousled the women's hair as they leapt backward, falling painfully on their backsides.

"What are you doing?!" Akalina shrieked hysterically. "What's wrong with you? Are you trying to get us killed or something?!"

"I—I didn't know I was supposed to keep holding the button. That wasn't supposed to happen. It's not supposed to be like this." Zareah stammered in bewilderment.

Akalina suddenly laughed while pointing at Zareah.

"Look at this! The blind's leading the blind! You don't even know what you're doing, do you? Oh, that makes me feel *really* safe now!" Akalina replied sarcastically.

Camile continued to catch her breath before rising to her feet and dusting herself off. Her heart was working overtime. Zareah grimaced while slowly getting to her feet, offering a hand to assist Akalina.

"I can pick myself up. I'm not an invalid!" Akalina said harshly.

The three women faced their next obstacle. They tried to figure out a way for all of them to safely enter the next tunnel segment. Zareah pressed the button once more and the heavy wall began retracting into the ceiling once again. Once the wall was completely out of view, she released the button. There was nearly a second of silence before the wall slammed down yet again. The tunnel quaked and even more soil fell down on the women.

"Clearly all three of us aren't meant to go beyond this point. Zareah, you have to hold it open for us. Apparently that's your job in this little adventure! I guess I was wrong, you're not *completely* useless after all." Akalina smirked.

"No! That's not right! I didn't come all this way just to hold a door open!" Zareah fervently declared.

"Well, you have no choice, so you might as well just accept it. Anyway, I'm tired of this dirt shower!" Akalina retorted while brushing the dirt off her shoulders and out of her hair.

"Deal with it." Zareah replied. She analyzed the divider wall before her. She then inspected the recessed button on the tunnel wall to her left.

Camile found it to be unnerving that their guide was beginning to exhibit such desperate behavior. It was like watching a flight attendant panic in mid-flight. It wasn't exactly reassuring.

"We're not going to leave her here, she'll be trapped!" Camile exclaimed. "Would you want someone to do that to you?"

"That's irrelevant since I'm not in that position at the moment." Akalina answered plainly while cleaning dirt from under her nails.

"There *has* to be some way we can all make it through." Zareah said almost to herself while pressing the button yet again. "Maybe if we move fast enough we can run through."

"Lady, are you senile?! Have you noticed how quickly this thing comes down? Not to mention the fact that you're no spring chicken!" Akalina said sharply while gesturing to the wall. "If you want to run through, you go right ahead, but try not to let your blood splatter all over my shirt. The soil stains I can deal with, but blood will be a bitch to get out."

"Give it a rest." Camile replied sharply, but Akalina chuckled coldly.

Once again, the wall had retracted completely into the ceiling.

"I'm not sure about the stability of this tunnel. If that wall keeps coming down, there could be a cave-in. We could get buried alive." Akalina pointed out.

"Zareah, I hate to admit it, but she has a point. You should keep pressing that button until we figure out a solution." Camile replied.

"Easier said than done. This isn't exactly a comfortable position for me, but being that our lives are at stake here ..." Zareah's voice trailed off.

"I think there's something we can do to get around this problem." Camile stated. "I noticed a large rock on the way over here. We can bring it and lodge it under the wall. Then maybe we could crawl under."

As she turned, she noticed that Akalina had crossed beyond the raised wall and into the next segment of the tunnel.

"Why crawl when you can walk?" Akalina asked with a sly smile.

"Akalina, come back! I need your help to get the rock over here, it looked really heavy!" Camile demanded.

"Too bad." Akalina replied as she continued to walk away.

"What a little ..." Zareah muttered angrily under her breath.

"Akalina, come back!" Camile called, but it was too late. Her twin walked along a bend in the tunnel and disappeared around it.

Camile groaned with frustration before turning her attention to the elder woman. She was visibly shaken and breathing heavily.

"Zareah, are you okay?" Camile asked with genuine concern.

"I don't know. I can't ..." Her voice trailed off as her eyes became glassy.

Camile was taken aback. She'd seen Zareah in many moods before, but had never seen her cry.

"Zareah, what's the matter?" She asked.

"I can't fail my mission! I went through so much just to get it. The penalty for failing my mission is too great and there's so much at stake!" She whispered as a few tears slowly began to fall.

"What's at stake?"

Zareah either didn't hear the question or simply ignored it.

"It's not supposed to be like this. I don't want to die, Camile! Not here. Not like this. This isn't dignified!" Zareah exclaimed.

"*Oh, boohoo, I don't wanna die!*" Akalina said mockingly upon her return.

Camile couldn't believe the level of cruelty she was capable of.

"Why can't you just grow up?! What the hell's wrong with you?!" Camile hissed angrily.

"Not a damn thing. It's just my style, take it or leave it, sis."

"Believe me, if I had a choice I would've left it a long time ago. But unfortunately we need each other in order to get through whatever this puzzle is! What made you come back here anyway?"

"There's another obstacle up ahead." Akalina answered bitterly.

"What kind of obstacle?"

"Wouldn't *you* like to know?!"

It was clear that Akalina had no intention of sharing that information.

"Oh, *real* mature!" Camile said with impatient sarcasm. "Whatever, come and help me with the rock."

Before they could walk away, Zareah grabbed Camile's arm with her free hand.

"Zareah, don't worry we'll be right back." Camile said reassuringly.

"No, it's not that." Zareah replied cautiously, glancing at Akalina—who was several steps ahead of Camile.

"Then what is it?" Camile asked.

"Camile, just be careful. *Please.*" Zareah whispered.

It was very clear that Zareah didn't trust Akalina. It was something Camile understood very well.

"Are you coming, or are you just gonna stand there holding her hand?" Akalina asked impatiently.

"It'll be fine. We'll be back soon. The rock isn't that far." Camile whispered to Zareah.

Camile joined Akalina and they began walking towards where the boulder was located.

"Please hurry! I don't know how much longer I can stay like this!" Zareah called out to them as they disappeared into the distance.

Camile remained extra vigilant during the walk. She noticed that Akalina's eyes were practically glued to the necklace, which made her a bit nervous. She would've tucked it into her shirt if it weren't their main source of lighting.

"Stop looking at me like I'm gonna mug you or something!" Akalina snarled with utter disgust.

As if by reflex, Camile immediately shifted her eyes to look ahead.

"So, why do *you* think we're here?" Akalina asked curiously.

"I honestly have no clue." Camile answered.

"Well, at least you're consistent. I think we're here to straighten everything out and give the necklace to its rightful owner … me!"

"I could see how a delusional person would think that." Camile said flatly.

"You're just in denial. Face the facts, Camile. I'm more powerful, stronger, smarter, prettier—"

"I guess 'modest' didn't make the cut on your list, huh?"

"Go on, try to insult me, but it doesn't change the fact that I should get the necklace and everything that comes with it. You'll see for yourself that Dad made a mistake by giving it to you. You're much too weak and pathetic. That's why it should go to me. I can't wait to see your face when you finally realize that I've been right about this all along."

"I don't get it. Why do you hate me so much? I didn't even know I had a sister until today! I never did a damn thing to you and I never deliberately set out to hurt anybody. Can you say the same about yourself?"

For a second, there appeared to be a flicker of remorse on Akalina's face, but it quickly disappeared.

"No, I can't." She shrugged. "But in life, it's either hurt or be hurt, kill or be killed."

"That's a dangerous mentality to have and I don't believe in it." Camile replied flatly.

They finally approached the rock, got behind it and started pushing. To Camile's surprise, it was easier to move than she expected. As they moved the rock across the ground, Akalina continued the discussion.

"Camile, in case you haven't noticed, I'm a very dangerous woman. Don't you forget it. That mentality is what's helped me to survive. If you don't believe in it then you're not fit to survive in this world. All the better for me though." She lectured with a faint chortle. "No, Camile, you'll never survive. Not with your weak, naive attitude. Weren't you the one who said the world is doomed and that humanity's imploding on itself?"

"I didn't say those exact words. Anyway, I never condoned hurting or killing anyone."

"Don't knock it 'til you've tried it, sis! Oh, wait a minute. *You have!*" Akalina exclaimed with sarcastic amusement. "Camile, you need to get off of that high horse of yours and stop thinking you're better than me. Don't forget, *you're* the one that put Mom in the hospital, not me! *You* made that rich little brat jump to her death. *You* blinded all of those pathetic fools in the subway. You even tried to off yourself! At least I have my priorities straight, I love myself way too much to try something so stupid."

"Shut up!"

"Oh, the truth hurts doesn't it, Camile? You're not the innocent little saint you thought you were. You should be *ashamed* of yourself for all of the heartache you've caused people. Hmph! And you have the nerve to call *me* a bitch?"

"You tricked me! You manipulated me! It wasn't fair and you made me think they were—" Camile screamed tearfully before she was suddenly overcome with dizziness.

"Face it, sis. I wouldn't have been able to convince you to hurt all those sorry saps if you didn't really want to do it." Akalina sneered before realizing Camile had ceased moving the boulder. "Why'd you stop pushing? Quit being a lazy ass! We don't have all night you know!"

Camile leaned against the wall, blinking several times as the dizziness slowly subsided.

"I just got dizzy. It happened out of nowhere." Camile explained.

"See? You just proved my point, you're weak." Akalina replied casually before they resumed pushing the rock.

Within minutes they approached Zareah—who was still holding the button. Based on the expression on her face, they arrived not a moment too soon.

"Please hurry. My arm is getting tired!" She pleaded.

"Stop your whining!" Akalina spat with impatient disgust.

She and Camile slid the rock in a position where they hoped it would prevent the wall from making contact with the ground. If everything were to go as planned, they would have about two feet of clearance to crawl under. Once the rock was in place, Camile and Akalina stood beside their guide.

"Okay, Zareah." Camile instructed. "Let go."

As soon as the button was released, the wall came down with incredible force and speed. Upon impact, the rock was instantly shattered. All that remained was a cloud of dust particles and a few small remnants. After shielding their eyes from the fragments, the women stood there in disbelief with open mouths. They realized that they had greatly underestimated the wall's destructive ability.

"If it could do that to such a big rock, imagine what it could do to flesh and bone." Camile said in quiet fear.

There was a moment of silence as they looked on—no doubt thinking about how dire the situation seemed.

"Well, any other bright ideas?" Akalina asked.

She received no answer to her question, but seemed to surprise herself as she had a thought.

"Wait a minute. What if we're going about this all wrong? Maybe there's another button." She suggested.

Akalina searched the tunnel wall parallel to the one housing the handprint button. She vigorously brushed aside some of the caked soil that was stuck to the wall. Camile and Zareah regarded each other for a moment before joining in the search. As they cleared away the soil, all they found were the same unusual plant roots they had seen on the opposing wall. Several small, peculiar bugs emerged as the women continued to clear away the soil. Seeing the insects, the women cringed in disgust. Camile knelt to see if there was a button in the ground but found nothing. She even scanned the entire area with her necklace, but with the same result.

"Now what?!" Camile exclaimed. Her frustration was both obvious and mutual.

She felt claustrophobic and the smell of the damp soil and mildew was making her nauseous. She was on the verge of panic, but somehow managed to calm herself to a point where she could at least function adequately.

"Okay ... okay." She said through deep breaths in an attempt to remain calm. She then began thinking externally. "In this part of the tunnel, there's only *one* button. It only works for Zareah. It's the only thing that can keep the wall open."

"I told you, Zareah's not meant to go any further. She has to hold it open in order for us to move on. We can't help her. Maybe her destiny is to die right here. She's kind of up there in age anyway. It's not like she hasn't exactly lived her life." Akalina replied brutally.

How can she be so damned heartless?! Camile thought to herself before coming up with an idea. "Akalina, I think you might be right about there being another button, but maybe we're looking in the wrong place."

"What are you talking about?" Akalina asked.

Before Camile could answer, the women were showered with more soil after the tunnel quaked slightly.

"I'll explain later." She replied quickly. "Zareah, quick! Press the button!"

"If that wall drops again we'll all be buried alive! We need to get out of here as soon as it opens up. We can't come back for her. If you wanna die trying to save her that's your business, but I'm getting my ass out of here!" Akalina exclaimed with great urgency.

"Don't leave me here!" Zareah said almost demandingly. "My work isn't finished and I'm not ready to die, not here!"

"Hey lady, that's *your* problem!" Akalina snapped.

"No Akalina, it's our problem! She's our guide, remember? We need her!" Camile said sharply.

"Hmph! Some guide she is! She can't even get herself out of this mess! She doesn't even know what the hell's going on here!" Akalina chuckled resentfully.

"Akalina, I think you're forgetting that I still have to open the wall in order for you to get out. I'd be a little nicer if I were you!" Zareah hissed.

"Are you threatening not to open the wall for us at all?" Akalina smirked as though she were hoping for some sort of provocation from Zareah. "If you are, you're even crazier than I thought."

The elder woman said nothing, but furiously stared at her. Chuckling menacingly, Akalina moved closer until their faces were just inches apart.

"Come on! We don't have time for this!" Camile shouted, trying to sound as authoritative as possible, but Akalina ignored her.

"Something tells me you don't need to be alive in order for this button to work, Zareah. I'm more than willing to find out if my assumption is right. I'm sure I could figure out some way to lodge your hand in place even after you're dead." Akalina hissed.

Without warning, she pulled out an unusual switchblade from her pocket and held it to Zareah's throat.

"Akalina, cut it out!" Camile shouted, immediately regretting her poor choice of words.

"Cut what out, Camile? Her heart ... her spleen? Maybe I'll start with her tongue!" Akalina hissed with a sadistic grin before turning her attention back to Zareah. "What's it gonna be, Zareah? The choice is yours."

After a brief moment of contemplation, Zareah pressed the button anew. The tunnel rumbled as the divider wall retracted into the ceiling yet again. Akalina stowed the knife and patted Zareah on the head—much like an owner pats their dog after catching a Frisbee.

"Good girl, Zareah. Good girl." Akalina smirked before walking into the adjacent tunnel segment. Camile approached Zareah and attempted to comfort her.

"Are you alright?" She asked.

"Yeah, I'm fine." Zareah answered in a defeated voice. "Camile, I was going to press the button. I wasn't going to leave you trapped in here. I just wanted her to sweat a little that's all. Who knows, that may have been my last chance to get even with her for stabbing me earlier."

"Something tells me you'll have other opportunities to set her straight. I have an idea. If it works, you'll be able to join us soon. But it's very important that you keep pressing that button until I figure it out, okay?"

Zareah nodded her acquiescence with a faint smile.

Camile joined her twin in the adjacent tunnel segment and searched for another button. The faint glow from the necklace illuminated the roots on the wall. They continued to gradually increase in width and were also becoming more translucent and reflective. Camile admired the beauty of the sparkling liquid flowing through them. She resisted distraction and continued with the search. She inspected the upper section of the left wall but found nothing.

She was so engrossed with the search that she didn't notice Akalina had stopped walking. Camile continued to side-step while inspecting the left wall of the tunnel. Suddenly, there was a sharp sound of metal grinding against metal. Thick, rusty blades protruded from the tunnel walls and formed a vertical circular barrier. Each blade had a wide base and tapered off as it curved to the right. Recoiling, Camile screamed fearfully. When she turned around, she saw Akalina standing there with a satisfied grin on her face.

"You knew that was going to happen didn't you? Why didn't you say anything? I could've lost my arm!" Camile shouted.

"What goes around comes around, Camile. Who am I to interfere with Karma?" Akalina replied smugly.

Camile was livid. She felt like choking the life out of Akalina, but quickly regained her focus on the task at hand.

"Just make yourself useful and help me find the button." Camile requested before moving to inspect the opposing wall.

Suddenly a strange expression crossed Akalina face as she resumed digging into the wall.

"Did you find something?" Camile asked.

"I think so, but it's weird, and that's saying something given the situation we're in!" Akalina exclaimed.

"Well, what is it?"

"I don't know, but this doesn't feel like a button. This feels like …" Akalina's voice trailed off as she cleared away some more soil. Suddenly, she screamed: "Get it off me! Get it off!"

A large, furry, multi-legged arachnid had latched onto her arm. It was the same type of insect Camile had encountered during her initial visit to the tunnel. However, the bug Akalina had just uncovered was a bit larger and had two dozen legs. Other than its plentiful appendages, bundles of glistening eyes and sharp silvery stinger, nothing else seemed to be included in its construction. Akalina hopped around hysterically. She slapped at her arm in an attempt to shake off the grotesque insect.

"Akalina wait. Calm down!" Camile exclaimed.

Akalina ignored her while continuing to slap at the bug to the tune of her hysterical screams. She finally managed to shake it off. When it fell to the ground, Akalina chased after it in revenge.

"Come here you ugly, furry little …" She yelled as it tried to scurry away from her stamping feet.

"Stop! Don't kill it! It'll only—" Camile tried to warn her, but it was too late.

Akalina stomped on the bug with a sickening squish. Thick, black and silvery liquid squirted out of its body. When Akalina lifted her foot, it revealed a mess of sprawled legs and fur that was matted with the insect's unusual blood.

"Ha! Gotcha! Didn't know who you were messin' with did you?!" Akalina shouted proudly. She dragged her foot across the ground to wipe the residual blood from the sole of her boot. "What *was* that thing? Ugh, and what's this stuff?!"

"Why did you do that? I told you not to …" Camile said, but was interrupted by Zareah's shouts.

"Something's coming!" She called frantically from the distance.

At first, Camile and Akalina heard nothing, but then noticed that there was a faint sound in the distance. It was comparable to a downpour of hail pounding on a tin roof. The noise was growing progressively louder.

"What the hell is that?" Akalina asked as her eyes widened.

"Your handiwork!" Camile snapped. "I told you not to kill that thing! Now we're *really* screwed! We need to get out of here or else we'll all die very painful deaths!"

The pair worked furiously to find a button to retract the bladed barrier. Akalina checked the floor as Camile finished checking the wall on the right.

"There's nothing here!" Akalina said in a furious panic. Meanwhile, the sound continued growing even louder and was accompanied by Zareah's desperate screams.

"Oh my God! They're getting closer!" She shouted hysterically.

"Zareah, let go of the button! You can seal them off with the wall! You have to sacrifice yourself for us or else we'll all die!" Akalina shouted over the noise.

"No, Zareah! Don't do it!" Camile yelled after finally finding a button on the lower portion of the wall. When she pressed it, nothing happened. The blades remained locked.

"Akalina, quick press this!" Camile said urgently as she gestured to the button.

Akalina walked over to the wall, crouched down, slipped her hand into the handprint. She pushed it and with a high-pitched screech, the bladed barrier quickly retracted into the wall.

"Zareah, run! Come on! Hurry!" Camile urgently called out, straining her voice against the deafening noise of approaching doom.

"I'm clear! I'm coming, but these … things are not far behind me at all!" Zareah breathlessly called to Camile, who had walked back just far enough to see her approaching. Seeing the elder woman uninjured, Camile smiled gently. However, it quickly faded when she saw the enormous sea of black, furry arachnids rapidly advancing behind her guide. Thousands of eyes glimmered from within the bizarre entanglement of thick hairy legs as they continued to swiftly approach. The creatures covered the tunnel floor, ceiling and walls as they came closer. Zareah ran with all her might, finally meeting up with Camile, who was consumed by intense fear while staring at the massive horde of arachnids. Their furry legs created waves and their stingers glinted in the dim light. The sight was like the mouth of a hellish monster about to swallow them whole. However, the women had one advantage; the creatures had yet to pass the heavy wall—which was still raised. Camile and Zareah regarded each other with baffled expressions for a brief moment before running to rejoin Akalina.

"Akalina, let go of the button!" Camile urgently ordered. "Let go!"

"But then we'll be trapped between—" Akalina contested.

"Do it! We have no choice! Trust me!"

"You've gotta be kidding!" Akalina replied, rolling her eyes before turning her attention away from Camile.

"Does it look like I'm joking? Let go of the damn button!" Camile demanded, pushing her twin's hand away. The action was so aggressive, Akalina lost her balance and landed on her butt. Aggravated, she immediately got up and began approaching Camile.

Before she could do anything more, the tunnel quaked. The three women heard the divider wall in the previous segment come crashing down a final time. It slightly muffled the sound the creature's legs made against the tunnel walls. Simultaneously, the blades screeched as they protruded from the wall and re-formed the barrier in front of the women. Akalina continued to glower at Camile, but before she had the chance to say or do anything, Zareah spoke.

"You did it!" Zareah exclaimed gratefully, still struggling to catch her breath. "Thank you!"

At that moment, the tunnel trembled once again, but a bit more violently. A loud rumble was followed by an intense high-pitched shriek from the creatures. The noise was so powerful that Camile and Akalina fell to their knees. They clutched their ears in an attempt to muffle the agonizing sound. There was no immediate relief as the noise continued for about ten seconds before it finally ceased. Silence filled the air and for a moment, Camile though she had lost her hearing. She and Akalina got to their feet.

"Are you okay?" Zareah asked.

"I think so. The sound was awful! Didn't you hear it?" Camile asked.

"No. I didn't hear anything." Zareah answered while shaking her head. A puzzled expression crossed her dark brown features.

"How *couldn't* you hear it?! It was terrible! Noises like that could raise the dead!" Akalina exclaimed.

"The two of you possess the gift of advanced hearing. That's a luxury I don't have." Zareah answered.

"Why not?" Camile asked.

"Ah, I know what it is! Those who can't do, teach." Akalina snorted.

"Something like that." Zareah replied with a broken smile. Camile was surprised at her slack reaction to the snide remark.

Akalina spotted something dull and grey protruding from the ground just a few inches in front of the blades. It was apparently something she and Camile had overlooked earlier.

"What's this?" She asked, clearing away the soil that was covering the item.

Camile and Zareah assisted in uncovering the object. They were unpleasantly surprised when their combined efforts revealed the lower half of a human skeleton. Camile and Akalina gasped while lurching backward, whereas Zareah grimaced and shook her head at the sight. Akalina shook her hands vigorously as though to shake the eerie feeling out of her system.

"I don't think we need to wonder where the other half is." Camile muttered glumly.

Upon analyzing the barrier more closely, they saw what appeared to be dried blood at the point where the blades converged.

"Well one thing's for sure, if we try anything stupid we'll be half the people we used to be!" Akalina joked.

Camile and Zareah groaned.

"Oh, come on!" Akalina exclaimed as she nudged the skeleton's leg with her foot. "Ol' Stumpy doesn't seem to mind my jokes! At least he still has a funny bone."

"You're sick. Do you know that?" Camile rhetorically asked with disgust.

Akalina said nothing because she was too busy laughing.

"Okay, just press the button." Camile said flatly.

Akalina suddenly stopped laughing and her expression became serious.

"Yeah, that reminds me ..." She said as she approached Camile until their faces were just inches apart. Camile's lack of comfort around Akalina wasn't getting any better. It felt as though she were walking around with a maniacal interactive mirror.

"... the next time you push me, you'll end up like Ol' Stumpy here. Do I make myself clear?" She murmured, poking Camile in the shoulder.

Not wanting to antagonize Akalina, Camile decided to peacefully concur, albeit reluctantly. After all, to intentionally irritate her made about as much sense as playing Russian roulette with a bullet in the chamber.

"Crystal clear." Camile replied flatly, displaying almost no sign of emotion.

Although she presented an unshakable calm on the exterior, on the inside she was absolutely terrified of Akalina and her unpredictable behavior. That fear was accompanied by seething anger. Camile almost literally had to bite her tongue in order to restrain herself.

"I thought so." Akalina smiled arrogantly before crouching down next to the button and pressing it afresh.

The friction of the blades made a sharp, grinding sound as they retracted into the wall. It sounded like knives being sharpened. The three women craned their necks to look as far as they could into the subsequent tunnel segment without actually entering.

"Well? What are you two waiting for? Go see what else we have to put up with in this hell hole!" Akalina demanded.

Camile and Zareah regarded one another for a moment before walking towards the opening. However, when they came within inches of the open barrier, Akalina suddenly released the button, forcing the blades to quickly protrude in front of them. Camile and Zareah shrieked with surprise while leaping back. It was an action that amused Akalina greatly.

"You should've seen yourselves!" She said through her hilarity. "You're a couple of punks!"

Camile and Zareah were obviously not amused and they both looked as though they wanted to throttle her.

"There's something seriously wrong with you! Another step and you could've killed us!" Camile shouted.

"Well, just be thankful that you're a couple of slowpokes too then." Akalina answered with nonchalance.

"Akalina, one day you'll get your just desserts!" Zareah said sternly.

"Well, until then I suggest you watch your back ... and your front for that matter." Akalina retorted with a wink.

Once again, Akalina triggered the retraction of the barrier. However, Camile and Zareah weren't so quick in their attempt to cross it the second time. They remained where they stood while attempting to gauge Akalina's intentions.

"What?" She asked, her voice projecting a false innocence. She waved her free hand as an indication that it was safe for Camile and Zareah to proceed. "I promise I won't do it again. After all, I might actually need the two of you in order to get out of this death trap!" She said with a sly smile.

After a moment of hesitation, Camile and Zareah crossed the area where the blade barrier had been just moments earlier. They stepped over the partially covered upper half of the skeleton on other side of the barrier. It was laying face-down. They traveled through a brief stretch of tunnel which led them around a bend and into a large, dimly-lit room. Upon entering, they realized the room was sealed off. There was nowhere to go but back. It was an apparent dead end.

CHAPTER 19

▼

OBSTACLES AND PERIL
PART TWO

As Camile and Zareah stepped further into the strange room, they gagged when they were hit with the unmistakable stench of putrid death. A short time later, they noticed the mummified remains of five of the tunnel's previous challengers. Two of them had several broken ribs and one suffered a shattered leg. Another was decapitated and one apparently had been attacked by one of the arachnids. Although the insect appeared dead, its stinger was still lodged between the skeleton's ribs. Camile was terrified and very concerned for her life. She wondered what force was capable of causing such horrible devastation. She also wondered where it was at that very instant. Was it dead? Or was it quietly lurking in some dark shadow waiting for the opportune moment to attack?

"Zareah, what is this place? What did all this?" Camile asked quietly as though trying not to wake a sleeping beast.

"I wish I knew." Zareah replied before looking at the one of skeletons, whose face was contorted in extreme perpetual agony. "On second thoughts, I *don't* want to find out." She said in retraction to her previous statement while grimacing.

Camile observed the wall and noticed four massive translucent pipes. They ran vertically along the wall in which they were partially encased. They appeared to come out from the floor and continue up into and beyond the ceiling. Each pipe had a diameter of about four feet. Camile stared in awe. Never before had she seen such pipes! She watched in amazement as they carried clear liquid in an upward motion. The fluid was converted from a silvery metallic substance. It appeared to be the same substance she had seen flow out of the hideous looking arachnid Akalina had killed earlier. There was clearly another level above the room in which they stood, but there was no indication as to how they could reach it.

"Zareah, maybe we could find keyholes similar to the ones in the other obstacles." Camile suggested.

They searched the walls and found nothing at first, but Zareah saw something behind one of the bodies. After hesitating for a moment, she grabbed the cadaver by the ankles, dragging it away from the wall. In doing so, a portion of a handprint was revealed. She rolled up her sleeves and began brushing away the soil. Camile immediately walked over and helped her remove the dirt that was covering the rest of the print.

"Care to do the honors?" She asked.

Zareah placed her hand into the print and pressed. They both looked around before realizing that nothing happened.

"Akalina!" Camile called. "Did anything happen over there?"

"No! Why? What's going on over there?" Akalina asked.

The tunnel caused their voices to echo in such an eerie manner, Camile couldn't recognize hers.

"We found another button, but it doesn't seem to do anything!" Camile answered. "Just keep pressing yours and we'll let you know when we find something!"

"You better not try to leave me back here. I swear I'll track your asses down!" Akalina threatened in response.

"Tempting thought though, isn't it?" Camile whispered to Zareah, who smiled in response.

"Don't worry, Akalina. I wouldn't dare leave my darling sister behind!" Camile responded sarcastically.

Camile expected the usual threats, ranting and raving from her twin, but there was only silence.

"Akalina?" She called.

"Yeah?" She answered, sounding annoyed and a little groggy.

"Are you alright?" Camile asked.

There was a slight pause before Akalina finally answered.

"I'm fine, just a little sleepy. I'm getting tired of this death trap!" She responded, her voice faint.

"Are you sure you're okay?" Camile asked.

"Just hurry up so I can get the hell out of here!" Akalina snapped.

"I'd say she's fine. Well, for *her* anyway!" Zareah muttered.

"Well, apparently that button is defective." Camile deduced while pointing to the handprint on the wall. "There has to be another one."

They continued to search opposite walls. Suddenly, Camile felt a wave of weakness, surrendering to the urge to sit on the floor. Breathing deeply, she watched Zareah continue to search the side of the room.

"There's nothing over here either." Zareah said before noticing her on the floor. "What's wrong?!"

"I don't know." Camile replied faintly while panting for air. "I suddenly got very dizzy. It happened before … when I went for the rock. What's happening, Zareah? Am I gonna die? Is this my punishment for all the terrible things I've done?"

"No, Camile. You're not dying. Do you know why?" Zareah asked to which Camile shook her head. "Because I won't let you. I didn't drag my arthritic ass all the way out here just to fail my mission now! Besides, my job is on the line here!" She smiled gently.

Camile chuckled softly for a moment, but stopped as she looked at one of the skeletons. She noticed the arachnid was no longer there. She alerted Zareah and they both glanced around the room in an attempt to spot it, but it was nowhere to be seen. Where did it go? Camile would've felt much more comfortable if she were able to see exactly where it was. Suddenly, she spotted something and was filled with a burst of energy.

"Zareah, look! Another handprint!" She exclaimed.

"Are you guys quite done yet?!" Akalina inquired impatiently from the previous tunnel segment.

"Be patient! You got a date or something?!" Zareah retorted grumpily.

She and Camile uncovered the dirt from the handprint that was recessed into the ground. Camile put her hand into the print and pressed down. Once again, they glanced around noticing no change or any sound to indicate that anything else had occurred. Exhaling a sigh of desperation, Camile closed her eyes in disbelief.

"Akalina, did anything change over there now?" She asked, her eyes still closed as though she already knew the answer.

"Yeah!" Akalina shouted.

Camile's eyes flickered open as a smile spread across her face. Zareah's face also exhibited a sign of relief.

"What happened?" Camile asked excitedly.

"My patience has completely run out!" Akalina yelled angrily.

Camile plopped against the wall in defeat as she looked at Zareah.

"We're not getting out of here are we?" Camile asked. "There's no way out and we're running out of air."

"There's a way out, we just haven't found it yet." Zareah said in an attempt to rebuild Camile's shattered motivation.

"But we've looked everywhere. There's obviously no exit! We only found two buttons that don't even work! Now we're gonna suffocate or get killed by one of those things!"

Zareah knelt before Camile, smiling gently.

"How can you smile at a time like this?" Camile asked glumly.

"Camile, it's never hopeless, but sometimes you have to let go of the past in order to move forward. We haven't looked *everywhere*. You just need to remember that things don't always work the way we expect them to." Zareah replied calmly. "You'll find the answer, Camile. You just need to keep your head up."

Camile was a little disoriented, so it took her a minute to process what the guide said. Then she realized it was a clue! She slowly raised her gaze to the arched ceiling and noticed an empty slot the same size and shape of her medallion! Surrounding the slot were intricate carvings similar to the ones on the metal disc that had lowered the women into the tunnel system. Once back on her feet, she walked to the center of the room so she could get a better look. The sight was astonishingly beautiful, yet intimidating all at once.

Camile knew she needed to use her necklace as a key, but was curious about how to gain access to the slot. The ceiling was well over twenty feet high! The walls in that portion of the tunnel were very smooth and slippery. Climbing was clearly not an option. Her head ached as she struggled to figure out what she needed to do next. She found herself reflecting on part of Zareah's statement: '... *sometimes you have to let go of the past in order to move forward ...*' It seemed to echo inside her head. She gasped softly when she finally understood.

"Akalina!" She called.

"What? Did you finally find something?" Akalina asked. Her voice was laden with impatience and boredom.

"Sort of. I need you to let go of your button for a minute. I think that'll activate the ones over here!"

"This isn't some kind of trick, is it?" Akalina asked suspiciously.

"No! It's not a trick! Look, we're running out of air down here and this could be our only chance to get out!"

"What about me?! I'll be trapped here!"

Camile hadn't exactly thought that part through, but came up with an idea.

"Akalina, just let go of the button so we can have enough power to activate the ones over here. Once we see that they're working, we'll let you know and you can reopen the barrier." Camile explained.

There was no response. Akalina was apparently thinking about the proposed idea.

"Akalina, it's obvious that all three of us will need to cooperate in order to get out of this." Camile said almost pleadingly, her voice growing hoarse from shouting to her twin in the distance. "There are two buttons and a keyhole over here! We'll need you to help us with this so we wouldn't dare leave you trapped over there!"

There was another slight pause before Akalina finally responded: "Okay, but hurry up. The air is getting thin over here!"

After hearing the unmistakable sound of the metal barrier screeching shut, Camile and Zareah sprang into action. Camile walked over to the button in the wall and Zareah crouched next to the one on the floor. They pushed their respective buttons, but to no avail.

"Let's switch places." Camile suggested and they changed positions.

Zareah pressed the button on the wall. Much to Camile's pleasant surprise, it triggered a humming sound which filled the room. The sound was similar to that of an electric generator.

"Akalina!" She called. "Press your button now!"

Camile smiled faintly when she heard the distinctive sound of the opening barrier. What had been the sound of uncertainty just moments earlier was now the sound of progress. However, her smile faded when she heard the sound of the blades almost immediately closing again.

"Akalina? What happened?" She asked before she heard the barrier open once more.

"How am I supposed to get out of here?" Her twin shouted. "As soon as I let go of the button, this ... *thing* snaps shut!"

Camile thought about the previous tunnel segments and immediately knew what had to be done.

"Akalina, keep holding the button!" Camile called.

"Hurry! I can't breathe over here!" Akalina yelled.

"Zareah press the button again. Only this time, hold it down." Camile instructed.

Zareah proceeded as suggested.

"Akalina, let your button go and see what happens! If the barrier doesn't move, you can come out!" Camile advised.

There was no response from Akalina.

"Akalina! Can you hear me?" Camile called, but there was still no response.

"Zareah, keep holding the button. I'm going over there." She said urgently before swiftly walking towards the metal barrier.

The light from her necklace grew extremely faint, limiting her range of vision to just a few feet. Turning a corner, she bumped into her twin. Both women screamed hysterically.

"Why the hell are you sneaking up on people?" Akalina snapped before smoothing back her golden, chin-length hair.

"*Sneaking?* I came to check on you. Didn't you hear me call you?" Camile asked.

"Sorry." Akalina replied almost drunkenly. "But I was a little preoccupied with staying conscious!"

They slowly walked towards the tunnel's 'dead end' and shortly reunited with Zareah. She was still holding the button but released it upon their arrival. They heard the metal barrier close anew. Camile and Zareah glanced at Akalina—who was quickly recuperating from oxygen deprivation.

"I see Ol' Stumpy has friends!" Akalina exclaimed, referring to the skeletons. Then she caught a whiff of the stench. "Whew! Boy does it stink in here!"

Camile and Zareah groaned and looked as if they regretted helping Akalina.

"What's this?" Akalina asked with marked disappointment. "A dead end? After all we went through?!"

"It's not a dead end. I think another passage will open up. First, I have to figure out how to get up there." Camile explained, pointing to the high ceiling.

"The two of you could lift me on your shoulders and *I* could insert the stone." Akalina replied sarcastically.

"Even if the three of us were somehow able to stand on each other's shoulders we still wouldn't be able to reach it." Camile answered before realizing her twin was joking.

"Way to go, shorty!" Akalina chuckled at Zareah.

"You really should learn to respect your elders!" Their guide chided in response.

"What's that humming sound?" Akalina asked.

"I don't know, but it started when Zareah pressed the button on that wall." Camile explained.

Akalina walked over to the handprint on the floor and knelt beside it.

"And what's this one do?" She asked while pressing it.

Camile started to say 'nothing' but paused when she heard a heavy mechanical clank. The twins looked at each other as though expecting an answer from the other.

"Look! Something's happening!" Zareah exclaimed, pointing to the ceiling.

The three of them watched with amazement as two bizarre handles protruded from the ceiling, one on each side of the keyhole.

"What the hell are those for?" Akalina asked.

"They're for me." Camile reluctantly answered. "It's clear that you and Zareah have done your parts here. Now it's my turn."

"But how are you gonna do that? You can't even *reach* those things!"

Before Camile could respond to her twin, a thick, horizontal, translucent beam descended from the ceiling in a circular motion like that of a Ferris wheel. The beam was white in color with a tinge of blue and had a ghostly appearance. It was roughly a foot in diameter and its lowest point of motion was about four inches from the floor. It headed straight for the three women, who were all standing side by side.

"Jump!" Camile commanded.

After leaping clear of the beam, they turned around to watch as it disappeared into the ceiling.

"What … was that?!" Akalina sharply inquired, looking to their guide for the answer.

Zareah only shook her head.

"They're not exactly rolling out the welcome mat for us here!" Akalina snapped.

Camile continued to stare upward while wondering what the beam was and how it managed to fuse into the ceiling without a trace.

"Camile, look out!" Zareah yelled.

When Camile turned around, everything went dark. The next thing she knew, she was lying flat on her back with Zareah and Akalina looking down at her. Zareah was frantically tapping her cheeks.

"Camile, you have to get up! Another one of those things is about to come out!" She said urgently.

Slightly dazed, Camile stood up with some assistance. That's when she felt warm liquid gush from her nose. It wasn't until she wiped it with her hand that she realized that it was bleeding and broken. She shrieked as her hand triggered extreme pain. It felt as though her nose was full of broken glass.

"Nice nose job!" Akalina replied with a cruel laugh.

"Akalina, do you have *any* compassion whatsoever?" Zareah asked harshly.

"Just a little bit, but I keep it for myself." Akalina replied apathetically.

There was no time for arguments since another beam was approaching. It was the same as the first and only one Camile had actually seen. Just as before, the three women stood in a row and jumped over it.

"I don't get it." Akalina said. "These things almost look *holographic!*"

"As you can see they're all too real!" Camile snapped angrily as she indicated her broken nose.

"But still … How is it that they can pass through those pipes and the walls without damaging them?" Akalina inquired.

Before anyone had a chance to speculate, another beam approached the trio. It was much higher than the first and advanced at head-level. Camile deduced that it was the same beam that had whacked her in the face. She felt somewhat vengeful towards it.

"Camile, you'll need to duck for this one." Zareah instructed.

"Yeah." Akalina chuckled. "Try to duck instead of hugging it with your face!"

"Oh, shut up!" Camile managed to grumble before they all ducked.

"Can't we just run back to where we came from?" She asked once they were all upright and on high alert.

"I already tried that. There's some sort of invisible barrier trapping us in here!" Akalina grunted. "Those things are starting to move faster!" She exclaimed. "Camile, you better do something quick to get us out of this blender!"

Suddenly, the first beam switched direction and approached them from behind, knocking them all to the ground.

"The direction's changing!" Camile exclaimed.

"I can see that!" Akalina snarled snappily.

They were barely on their feet when the higher beam approached, prompting them to duck quickly. As soon as they recovered from ducking, they had to jump over another low beam. Camile was able to see a pattern emerge in the sequence. She was also able to locate a point where the two beams crossed over each other.

"I think I know what I have to do." Camile stated.

"Well, it's about damn time!" Akalina bellowed.

Camile stood between Akalina and Zareah. When the next beam approached, everyone jumped over it—except for Camile, who jumped on top of it. She struggled to maintain her balance as it traveled toward the higher beam that was approaching.

When the two beams got close to each other, she leapt for the higher one but slipped off. Muttering with angry frustration, she quickly returned to her starting position to make another attempt. The beams were now moving even faster. Akalina and Zareah had a difficult time keeping up with the changing sequence. At the speed the beams were traveling, they could not afford a misstep since it would likely cost them a limb, if not their lives.

Camile knew she had to be successful in her next attempt if they were to survive. When the next low beam approached, she jumped onto it. By the time she caught her balance, it was time for her to jump to the higher beam. The impact nearly knocked the wind out of her when it collided with her stomach. She knew that if she held onto the beam too long, it would crush her against the ceiling.

Taking a deep breath, she quickly adjusted herself and squatted on the beam. She was in a position that made her look like a frog perched on a log. Camile knew that in order to reach the handles in the ceiling, she would have to jump at the last possible moment. She was also aware that doing so would bring her dangerously close to the ceiling. If she missed the handles or slipped from them she would fall ... most likely to her death.

Balancing carefully, she constantly monitored her distance from the ceiling. When she came within a few feet of it, she pushed her feet and hands hard against the beam, leaping out towards the handles. In the brief time her body took flight, her mind was bombarded with a multitude of thoughts. She thought of all the things she'd never get to do if she were to fail her attempt. She'd never get to discover the truth or tell her mother she loved her. She wouldn't be able to protect her from her angry sister, who was clearly out for revenge. Camile seemed to hang suspended in time as these thoughts coursed through her head. However, the beams continued to move in a circular path around her. She finally arrived at the pivotal point of their Ferris wheel-like motion. As her hands grabbed the handles, her mind was jolted back to real time.

Her left hand took hold of one handle, but her right hand failed to grasp the other. Her left arm strained and trembled as she swung herself to grab the other handle. Panting for air, she looked down underneath her right arm. Akalina and Zareah were struggling to keep up with the beam sequence, which continued to vary in speed and randomization. Zareah was sweating profusely while gasping for air. Akalina seemed to be fairing slightly better, but only just.

"Camile!" She exclaimed breathlessly. "What are you doing? Hurry up!"

"I'm just hanging out up here! I'm in no rush, you know!" Camile answered sarcastically.

Akalina and Zareah were too busy leaping and ducking for their lives to respond. Camile released her right hand and removed the medallion from around her neck. While extending her arm to hold the stone towards the keyhole in the ceiling, it nearly slipped from her hand. She quickly tightened her grip around the chain to prevent it from falling. Camile knew it would be necessary to hold the stone in her fingertips so she could accurately place it in the slot. However, she didn't want to take chances adjusting her grip with one hand. She feared she'd drop it.

Holding the necklace in her mouth, she properly adjusted the stone in her fingers. Stretching out her arm, she slid the stone into the slot and held it in place until she was certain that it wouldn't fall out. After an instant, the medallion glowed intensely, flooded the room with a beautiful blue light while simulating aquatic waves on the walls. She squinted until her eyes adjusted to the brilliant glow.

"We're not gonna make it!" Akalina screamed from below. Her voice trembled with panic-stricken fear.

Looking down, Camile noticed the high and low beams were moving in a unidirectional motion, parallel to each another. The beams were also closer to each other, allowing no way for them to duck under or jump over them. Camile watched in helpless horror from above as the beams swiftly advanced toward the pair. Akalina and Zareah both closed their eyes as they braced for impact and certain death. Camile couldn't believe her eyes as she witnessed the beams pass through their bodies before disappearing. The two women continued to stand with their eyes closed long after the beams had vanished.

"You're okay! The beams just went right through you!" Camile finally exclaimed after a moment of speechlessness.

It took a moment for Akalina and Zareah to realize that they were still alive. They both smiled with great relief while observing the glowing medallion with astonishment.

"Well, now what?" Akalina asked.

As if on cue, there was a sudden sound of blades whooshing through the air. The sound seemed to multiply and the three women regarded each other with exhaustion.

"Oh, you just *had* to ask!" Camile exclaimed angrily.

Gazing at the far wall their eyes grew wide with horror. Several large pendulums were slowly emerging. Moving in a crisscross motion parallel to the floor, the blades glinted in the radiant light. There was absolutely no way over, under or around the swinging razor-sharp blades.

"Well, now we know how that guy lost his head!" Akalina remarked while pointing to the headless carcass across the room.

Camile noticed she was hanging directly in the path of the approaching blades. She couldn't jump down because it was too steep a drop, but if she just hung there, she would undoubtedly be slowly sliced into pieces. Leaning her head back in defeat, tears escaped her closed eyes. The muscles in her arms and shoulders screamed with intense, burning pain. She opened her eyes and squinted as she trained her gaze on the ceiling.

A small section of the arched ceiling caved in, forming a handprint just below the medallion. It was another button! She gathered enough strength to release her right hand from the handle she'd been clutching and placed it into the handprint. The ceiling felt very cold to the touch and her hand fit perfectly into the recessed print. She pressed it, but there was no result. She noticed Akalina and Zareah backing away from the blades towards the wall behind them. The pendulums were just a few feet away from Camile when she called to them.

"The buttons! I think we all have to push them at the same time!" She yelled.

Zareah ran over to the wall on her left. After a second of hesitation, Akalina crouched down on the floor next to the button she pressed earlier. Her button happened to be the closest to the approaching blades.

"Now!" Camile yelled.

All three women pressed their respective buttons, but not before one of the pendulums took a slice out of Akalina's arm. She shrieked painfully as she was cut, but she didn't let it stop her from holding the button. There was a loud popping sound like that of a gunshot as the medallion generated a quick but powerful burst of light. Just as quickly as they had appeared, the pendulums vanished into nothingness. The room's lighting returned to its original state and all the chaos had been swallowed by complete silence.

Cradling her wound, Akalina grimaced as she watched the blood seep down her arm. A tear trickled down her cheek as she bit her bottom lip to offset the pain. The handles Camile had been holding onto disappeared as a platform materialized beneath her feet. It had the same consistency as the beam that had broken her nose. The unusual platform lowered her to the ground before disappearing. As soon as her feet touched the ground, she rotated her arms and shoulders in an attempt to relieve the pain of her strained muscles. Akalina, still holding her wounded arm, leapt to her feet and stormed towards her, but Zareah quickly stood between them.

"Move out of my way lady!" Akalina demanded.

"Akalina, when are you gonna realize that—?"

"I said move, bitch!" Akalina spat interrupting Zareah's question.

Nudging Zareah aside, she made her way over to Camile and looked her in the eye.

"Look what happened! I got cut because *you* were too slow!" She snapped.

There was a brief moment of awkward silence as the twins stared each other down. Finally, Akalina cracked a slight smirk.

"It would've been a lot worse had you not finally used your little brain. Let's hope it's not a rare occurrence." She said harshly before gazing at the medallion in the ceiling.

Camile was convinced that Akalina's statement was the closest thing to a *'Thank you'* she would ever receive from her. As she followed Akalina's gaze, she realized the stone was still in the slot. She had no way of retrieving it.

"Looks like you're not getting it back. I knew it would get taken away from you. It's only a matter of time before it goes to me!" Akalina exclaimed with a broad smile.

Camile sighed hopelessly before noticing a change in the large tubular pipes in the wall to her left. Three of the four pipes had completely drained of liquid and an opening materialized on each one. Each empty tube also appeared to glow with the same light that had filled the room moments earlier. At that moment, words escaped Camile, so she pointed to the pipes instead. Akalina gasped quietly and Zareah cracked a slight smile. The trio cautiously approached the empty pipes and noticed that inside each one was a flat platform at the base.

"You mean, we're supposed to go in *there?!*" Akalina asked with disbelief.

"That's what it looks like." Camile answered, looking to her twin on her right, then Zareah on her left.

"Alright. Then, you go first!" Akalina exclaimed.

"Such a coward!" Camile muttered under her breath while slowly entering the tubular structure, stepping onto the platform.

"What's that, Camile? I didn't quite catch that." Her twin said in an attempt to instigate a fight, but she ignored it.

A long moment passed before they all realized that nothing was going to happen until they all got into their respective tubes. Zareah silently entered the tube to Camile's right. Akalina followed suit on her left. A translucent door slid down in front of Camile and snapped shut, sealing her in. All evidence of a door ever having been present had instantly vanished. When she saw Akalina pounding on her tube attempting to get out, she realized that the same had happened there.

She then looked over at Zareah. Her eyes were closed and her face was tilted upwards. She had an eerie, gentle smile on her face. Apparently Zareah knew what was about to happen.

The next thing Camile knew, Akalina was going ballistic! She went into a fit of intense screaming and panic as she looked upwards. Her face contorted with horror as she waved her hand to shoo something away. Camile craned her neck in an attempt to see what was going on, but only managed to bump her head on the inside of her own tube. She didn't have to wait long to realize what was happening. Soon, she saw one of the large arachnids climbing down into Akalina's tube, its long, furry legs moving at an agonizingly slow pace. Its stinger occasionally tapped against the glass tube. Camile was amazed at how agile the creature was on the smooth surface.

"No! Make it go away!" Akalina hollered.

Camile wanted to tell her to calm down and that the strange bug meant no harm, but after remembering that Akalina had killed one of the creatures, she wasn't so sure of its intentions. The bug suddenly jumped on Akalina, landing on her injured arm. She continued to scream hysterically while swinging at it, but before she could land a decent hit, the bug thrust its sharp, silvery stinger into her arm. Camile gasped at the disturbing sight. Akalina stopped moving in mid-scream. She appeared to be permanently muted and frozen with fear.

"Akalina!" Camile called out, but there was no response. Her twin's wide, lifeless eyes continued to gaze at the bug. Her mouth appeared to be fixed in a silent, perpetual scream.

Seeing her twin in such a lifeless state sent chills up Camile's spine. She watched helplessly as the insect tore away Akalina's sleeve, exposing her flesh. It then wrapped itself around her injured arm, covering the entire wound—which was still bleeding, albeit not as severely. After a few minutes, the arachnid leapt onto Akalina's inanimate face, staring deeply into her eyes. Camile noticed that in the arachnid's bundles of eyes, each one moved independently. The sight was nauseating. She fearfully wondered if she would soon face the same fate as her twin. Satisfied with its work, the insect sprang onto the glass and quickly scurried out of the tube. Helpless tears fell from Camile's eyes after she looked at the top of her own pipe. A massive arachnid was descending towards her. She looked over at Zareah and watched as the insect in her tube quickly inspected her before scurrying out, leaving her untouched.

"Zareah! One of those things just killed Akalina! What's happening?" Camile asked.

"Camile, don't fight it. It's okay." Zareah replied with a soft smile.

"Just what part of this is supposed to be okay?!" Camile yelled. "Akalina's dead and ..."

Camile stopped in mid-sentence when she looked into Akalina's tube. She noticed that her arm had been completely healed, although she was still paralyzed. Camile exhaled a tremulous sigh of relief. Upon turning her head, she came face-to-face with the furry, multi-legged insect. Gasping hard, she sharply recoiled, hitting the back of her head in the process.

Before she could recover, the huge arachnid leapt onto her chest and looked up at her face. She tried to turn away, but the arachnid's large pincers took hold of her chin and shifted her head, forcing her to face forward. The insect's fur irritated Camile's face. She raised her right hand towards the creature in an attempt to alleviate the disturbing sensation. The arachnid apparently didn't like her sudden response and raised its sharp stinger to her neck to defend itself.

Camile slowly lowered her hand to peacefully surrender. Without moving her head, she strained her eyes to glance down carefully. She caught a glimpse of the gleaming silvery stinger as the bug continued to hold it up to her neck. After a few seconds, the bug lowered the stinger and quickly jumped onto her face, prompting Camile to gasp. The creature hugged her head tightly, its legs digging into the sides of her face in order to maintain its grip. Camile felt something hard and flexible shoot into each of her nostrils. For a few long seconds, she endured a burning, crushing, unbearable pain. She shrieked loudly until her voice failed her. She came close to fainting—or so she hoped—but her nose eventually became numb to the agony. However, she was forced to breathe though her mouth since her nostrils were completely obstructed. The air she took in was laced with the bitter taste of soil from the creature's belly.

Although she no longer felt any pain, she experienced extreme pressure. She also heard the sickening sounds of clicking and the suction of liquid as the insect performed some sort of operation in her nasal cavity. The whole process took a matter of minutes, but to Camile, it felt like an eternity. The insect finally released Camile's face and crawled over the rest her body, inspecting it for further damage. Since the bug found nothing more, it leapt onto the tube and made a swift exit. Camile cautiously touched her nose. She was relieved that it was no longer broken or bleeding. She turned to look at Zareah—who wore a tranquil smile.

"See? I told you it would be fine." Zareah softly replied.

Before Camile could respond, she noticed that her feet suddenly felt cold. When she looked down, she noticed that silvery liquid was beginning to fill the tube. She noticed the other tubes were filling with the liquid as well. Camile attempted to jump up to see if she could somehow climb out of the pipe, but her feet seemed to be glued into place. All she could do was wriggle around in vain.

The cold, thick liquid soon reached her chin. She stretched her neck up as much as she possibly could—which wasn't very far. Just before the liquid covered her mouth, Camile took a deep breath. Within a matter of seconds the strange silvery solution covered her nose and finally her eyes—which she managed to close at the last moment.

As soon as Camile was completely submerged in the strange fluid, she immediately wished that she had taken a deeper breath, but it was already too late. A few seconds went by before she felt a slight sudden release of the pressure that had built up around her head. However, she continued to hold her breath and kept her eyes tightly closed. Suddenly she felt a brief, yet slightly painful increase in pressure around her midsection. All of the air she had been holding in her lungs was instantly forced out. She panicked and gave in to her natural reaction to take another breath. Much to her surprise the air went in and out effortlessly. Camile was beyond relieved when she realized that she was able to breathe!

CHAPTER 20

▼

THE GATHERING

The pressure around Camile's midsection quickly vanished. She carefully opened her eyes and saw her own reflection. Her head was in a mirror-like bubble which slowly elongated downward until her entire body appeared to be encased in it. She turned in place, noticing her entire body reflected all around her. It reminded her of the mirror she'd seen in one of her dreams. The reflection was slightly warped since it was in liquid form. It faded as the silvery substance became diluted with a clear liquid. Gradually, Camile was once again able to see out of her own tube. Looking into the pipes Akalina and Zareah were encased in, she was in absolute awe as she watched the clear liquid encircling them just as it was with her.

The fluid drained upward from the tubes in a cyclonic motion. Amazingly she, Akalina and Zareah were completely dry. Each tube lit up even brighter with the same, hauntingly beautiful light that had emanated from the stone in the ceiling awhile earlier. Camile felt a wonderful warm sensation as the platform began rising. All of her senses seemed to relax. Akalina—who was still unconscious—and Zareah were also being guided upward by the platforms in their respective tubes.

Camile blacked out during her brief wave of euphoria. When she finally came to, she was standing between Akalina and Zareah. However, the three of them were no longer encased in the pipes. They were standing about ten feet to the left of them in a very large corridor. Camile had no recollection of exiting the tubes or walking to the location where she was standing.

Almost immediately, she noticed that her medallion was once again hanging around her neck. Instinctively, she tucked it into her shirt before looking at Akalina, who still resembled a terrified mannequin. It was obvious that she was still in a state of suspended animation. Just as Camile lifted a foot to approach her, she suddenly sprang back to life—still experiencing the terror of her encounter with the arachnid. Akalina's sudden reanimation startled Camile.

"Get it off me! Get it—" Akalina shrieked wildly while slapping at her arm, but was surprised to see nothing on it.

Turning in place, Akalina frantically looked around and noticed that she was no longer in the tube, but in a different location altogether.

"What happened?" she asked excitedly.

"It fixed your arm. I guess you were freaking out so much it had to put you to sleep before it … well … *operated.*" Camile answered.

"What? That *thing* fixed my arm?!"

"And my nose." Camile added.

"Okay, now I've heard it all."

"*You?* Watching you morph into my twin sister wasn't exactly a picnic you know!"

"Alright, Camile!" Akalina exclaimed impatiently with a dismissive wave of her hand. "We can compare traumatic experiences some other time, but right now we have to focus on getting out of this place. Where are we anyway?"

For the first time since she regained consciousness, Camile was able to fully observe the details of their current location. It was remarkably different from the dark, ominous tunnels that they had traveled through. Instead, they stood in a large, warm, immaculate corridor that was well-lit. It was a stark contrast to everything they had seen and been through thus far. The three women cautiously moved along the corridor, keeping a watchful eye for any other unwelcome surprises. Looking up at the high ceiling, Camile noticed intricate light fixtures that seemed to be made entirely of multi-faceted crystal.

As they walked along the passageway, Camile saw a series of pipes and plant roots of varied sizes, but none were larger than the four tubes that led the three women to the corridor in which they currently traveled. All of the smaller pipes were carrying various fluids, some were clear and others were silvery. However, Camile took particular interest in the very large pipes to her right, which had an awfully familiar curve.

In order to see the full effect, she stepped back approximately fifteen paces. Her eyes enlarged and her jaw dropped when she noticed the four massive pipes were curved into the same L-shape design she had seen in her dreams and on her necklace. There was a medium sized plant root that was interwoven with the pipes. The plant root sprouted many other smaller roots that sprawled across the wall like lace. At that moment, she was struck by a strong memory. She was six years old, running up and down the same spacious corridor in which she now stood. She enjoyed climbing up the curve of the pipe before sliding down. Little Camile knew that if her mother saw her, she'd be in big trouble since she'd been forbidden from playing in that area. However, her mother, Kylie was preoccupied in serious conversation.

In the distance, Camile saw her mother speaking to an older man with somewhat spiky, silvery hair. She couldn't see his face since his back was turned. Besides, she was too busy trying to climb the bend of the massive pipes, grasping roots in order to do so. At one point, young Camile checked to make sure her mother couldn't see her. That's when she noticed her mother was so upset she was very close to tears. One of the roots wasn't sturdy enough to support Camile's weight and snapped, spilling a black tar-like substance onto the floor. Almost instantly, several arachnids emerged from behind the pipes in a threatening manner. Little Camile let out a startled shriek, prompting Kylie to spot her.

"Camile!"

"Camile!" Akalina shouted, jolting her out of her memories.

"Whoa!" Was all Camile could utter.

"What do you mean 'Whoa'?" Akalina probed.

"The shape of these pipes appeared to me as a symbol a few times, but I had no idea that …" Camile paused a moment. She thought better of telling Akalina the full story since she knew it would result in more chiding and contempt. "… it was referring to something so huge!"

"That's it?" Akalina snorted before walking forward. Camile and Zareah soon followed.

As they continued to move along, the women noticed a vivid, spacious room at the end of the corridor. It was so bright that any details within the room were undistinguishable from their vantage point. As they got within eight feet of the entrance, a tall man walked into view. It took Camile a minute before she realized that it was her father, Zephyr, in the flesh! He wore what appeared to be some sort of uniform. The top was slate grey in color—which accentuated his eyes— and was like nothing Camile had seen before. He wore black pants, which matched the trimming of his tunic-like top.

"Dad, you're ... *alive?!*" Camile exclaimed in utter disbelief.

"Well if it isn't dear old Dad!" Akalina snorted angrily. "What's your problem making me go through all that crap back there? Do you know that you almost killed me?!"

"It wasn't my choice. If I had my way, things would have been much, much different." He said with a glum expression.

"Dad, those spider things fixed my broken nose. They might be able to help Mom too! If I brought one to her, maybe it could—" Camile said excitedly.

"Camile, I'm afraid I can't allow them to be removed from the premises." He interrupted.

"You don't understand. I can't bring Mom here. She'll die if she leaves the hospital. You have to let me take one to her!"

"Camile, calm down. Your mother's in very good hands—"

"With who? Nancy? That ship has sailed! Nancy can't even help herself since she's in a coma too thanks to this ..." Camile snapped, referring to Akalina—who smiled with immense pride, but she refrained from cursing in the presence of her father.

"Zephyr, surely there must be some way you can let her—" Zareah said in appeal.

"Zareah, you know the rules as well as anyone. You know very well that I can't break them." He said sharply.

"Rules?!" Camile shouted. "You're gonna let my mother die on the count of some stupid rules? Do you *want* her to die? How—?"

"Camile, that's enough." A firm but gentle voice interrupted.

Camile was perplexed as a second figure took its place by her father's side. When the form stepped into the light and turned to face the three women, Camile was absolutely dumbfounded.

"Mom? You're okay?" Camile asked with a mixture of confusion and delirious happiness.

"I'm fine, Camile." Kylie responded with a loving smile and gentle nod.

Kylie wore a beautiful light-grey, flowing tunic and matching loose-fitting pants. She looked almost angelic. Her hair glinted in the radiant light of the room in which she stood.

"Mom, how did you get here and why didn't you tell me about Akalina? Why didn't you tell me that I had a twin?" Camile asked somberly as she slowly approached. She maintained caution since she wasn't sure if there were any other obstacles or booby traps around.

"Camile, it was time for me to return here. Your father and I always wanted to tell you the truth about Akalina, but there were other complicated factors involved. We did what we had to do, but please know that we had nothing but the best of intentions for you." Kylie answered.

"For her?!" Akalina exploded with great ferocity. "What about me? Do you have any idea of the hell I've been through over the years? Do you even give a damn?!"

"Akalina, of course we care. But there were things we were forced to do. We fought as best we could to keep you both, but the conditions were that we each could only choose one of you to raise and—" Kylie tried to explain.

"So Mom, you chose poor, innocent, saintly Camile over me!" Akalina shouted through her angry tears. "You chose to give her a chance at having a life where everyone didn't look at her like she was a walking plague or a curse. You decided to leave me—the reject—here to be constantly shunned for something I couldn't even control?" Akalina snapped viciously.

"No! That's not how it was at all!"

"Whatever … *Mom!*" Akalina shouted with disregard. "*You* made your choice and *I've* had to live with it, so why do you need me now? You were obviously able to cope very well without me for what … *seventeen years!*"

"Akalina, if you think my life was easy, you're—" Camile started to explain.

"Shut up, Camile! Just shut the hell up!" Akalina snapped viciously as she dismissively waved her hand.

"Please, if you would just give us a chance to explain, I—" Kylie replied, but was interrupted by Akalina.

"I don't need your sorry explanations now! You've had many years to explain and you blew it. The truth is all too clear. You obviously thought that … *Camile* was the better daughter but you were wrong. All these years you've been banking all your dreams on this … pathetic loser!" Akalina replied harshly as she pointed at Camile. "You think leaving me here to live with Dad and visiting me every once in a while made things okay but it didn't. I needed my mother! I've had to fight everyday of my life to defend myself against just about everybody, until finally I had enough and decided to run away. That's when I finally learned the truth. It's a damn shame that I had to learn it from strangers instead of my own parents. Camile's had everything handed to her including the necklace! I have superior power and it should've gone to me. If I couldn't have your love, you should've at least given me that! But *noooo!* What did I get? What did I *ever* get?!" Akalina ranted.

"Wait, you lived with Dad?" Camile asked with marked disbelief. "So that little story you told me about your so-called aunts wasn't true was it?"

"No! Don't you get it, you stupid bitch?! I did what I *had* to in order to get you to feel sorry for me." Akalina explained. "I knew that the only way I would get you to do that was if you believed my life was more pathetic than yours. I couldn't actually tell you the truth and blow my cover now could I? I wanted to see for myself whose shadow I've been living in all these years. Once I found you, believe me, I was not at all impressed. I couldn't believe that you were the reason why I almost never got to see my own mother. I couldn't believe that someone so pathetic could be the cause of so much misery. As for Dad, yeah he raised me until I turned sixteen—when I finally got the sense to run away. I just couldn't take the lies and silent ridicule anymore. I'm sure Dad was relieved that I ran away just as I'm sure Mom was happy that she didn't have to inconvenience herself to come see me anymore, especially since she had her sweet, perfect Camile!"

"That's not true!" Her parents exclaimed in near-perfect unison.

"Akalina, your mother and I love you both very much. We never took joy in seeing either of you suffer." Their father replied.

"Well you sure have a hell of a way of showing it!" Akalina interrupted angrily. "What about the house of hell down there, huh?" She asked referring to the hurdles that she, Camile and Zareah had encountered.

"The specific details of the obstacles weren't revealed to us. We were only told that they were necessary in order to—" Kylie replied.

"Necessary?!" Camile asked quietly. "How in the world is nearly killing us a necessary thing? And what about Zareah? She's just *our guide* for goodness sake! Why risk her life too?"

"Zareah was well aware of the risks when she was selected for the task of bringing you here." Zephyr answered.

"Okay, so why *are* we here?" Camile asked.

"You'll find out momentarily, but first there is one final task."

Akalina became outraged.

"Are you serious?!" She shouted furiously. "No! Screw this! I'm sick and tired of these stupid tasks!"

Akalina walked swiftly towards the room and Camile quickly followed. As the twins attempted to enter, they were violently thrown a few feet away from the entrance, landing hard on their tailbones. The impact knocked the wind out of both of them. After taking a moment to recover, they picked themselves up off the ground. They realized there was an invisible barrier which prevented them from entering. Although they could see clearly into the room, there was a distortion that resembled water ripples. The distortion faded after a few seconds. Before Camile or Akalina could ask any questions, their mother briefly and tearfully explained the reason for the occurrence.

"Camile, Akalina … I'm afraid only one can enter. You have to … choose amongst yourselves who it will be." Kylie said, choking back tears. "Zareah, you've successfully completed your task. You may enter whenever you wish."

"What the hell is that supposed to mean!" Akalina screamed furiously. "You brought the two of us all the way out here for one of us to die? And you want us to mutually decide? What kind of sick, twisted parents are you?!"

Camile was suddenly overcome with yet another wave of dizziness and she staggered to lean on one of the pipes for support.

"Are you okay, Camile?" Zareah asked as she touched Camile gently on the shoulder.

Just as Zareah finished her question, Akalina also became woozy and leaned on a wall to prevent herself from falling over.

"The air is getting too thin!" Camile said after she gasped. "We need to get in that room!"

"You need to make your decision soon or else you'll die!" Zephyr pressed urgently.

Kylie said nothing as she wept silently. Just as suddenly as it came, the wave of dizziness faded. Camile and Akalina stood up once again. Zareah looked at their parents before bursting into tears.

"No! I didn't go through all that stuff for nothing! Let one of them take my place! That way they could both live and no one has to die!" She pleaded.

"Zareah, it's very noble of you to offer your place, but you know you can't sacrifice yourself. You can't abandon your responsibilities." Zephyr explained.

"To hell with my responsibilities! You're asking me to do nothing while someone dies. I can't do it. Especially since I worked so hard to get them here in the first place! I refuse …"

"Zareah, don't forget your place! Don't misunderstand us, we're not happy about the sacrifices that must be made, but this is the only way." He replied sternly.

"You don't get it! I can't return to my duties. If I fail, they'll be no duties left! I wish I could take everything back, I'm so sorry!" Zareah sobbed as she violently shook her head.

Camile and Akalina's parents looked at one another with puzzled expressions before returning their gaze to Zareah.

"The old lady's finally going to snap!" Akalina said to Camile with a wicked chuckle. "Maybe she'll have a coronary."

Camile ignored Akalina with contempt and focused her attention on the unfolding scene.

"Zareah, what do you mean? You've done everything that was expected of you. You've brought them here. You should be very proud of your accomplishments." He replied faintly.

"No, you don't understand. I messed up. I've done something I shouldn't have and I need your forgiveness!" Zareah explained as she sobbed uncontrollably.

"Zareah, what do you need our forgiveness for?" Kylie asked with concern.

"I can't tell you, you might not forgive me if I do. Tell me that you forgive me first and then I'll let you know what I've done. *Please,* I just need to hear you say it!" Zareah said pleadingly. The mask of desperation on her face seemed to emphasize her age.

"Zareah, I forgive you." Kylie replied after a moment of hesitation. She wore a very perplexed look on her face.

"I forgive you too." The twins' father replied, looking equally confused.

Zareah closed her eyes and sighed as silent tears rolled down her cheeks.

"Thank you!" She whispered.

"What—?" Zephyr began to ask but stopped when he saw her turn to face Camile.

She then stated gently: "I need your forgiveness too."

"Why? What did you ever do to me?" Camile asked cautiously. "I mean ... I know you lied to me but that was only because you had to ... right?"

"It's not that simple. I hope you'll understand. I know it's strange, but right now I just need you to forgive me first. *Please.*" Zareah replied with a note of desperation.

"Zareah, I don't understand ..." Camile began to protest but then reconsidered. "Okay, Zareah. I forgive you."

Zareah laughed gently through her tears and smiled at Camile.

"You've come a long way. I'm ... proud of you." Zareah replied with great relief.

"Hey! Don't you need my forgiveness too?" Akalina asked crudely.

"No, because the things I did didn't affect you." Zareah replied flatly before turning away to walk towards the entrance.

"Zareah, wait. You didn't explain why …" Camile began to say as she grasped Zareah's left arm. She was extremely confused and appalled at what she saw when she looked down.

There was a long vertical scar along the inside Zareah's left arm and the skin lightened to a caramel color.

"Zareah, what's this? What happened to your … OH MY GOD!" Camile screamed hysterically before collapsing onto the floor. She simultaneously clutched her mouth and chest after seeing Zareah's face. Zareah was no longer a feisty, older woman. In fact, Zareah no longer existed. Camile had come face-to-face with her own ghost!

Camile sobbed inconsolably and shivered with unbearable fear, sadness and disbelief.

Her parents were also extremely shocked and devastated.

"Camile!" Kylie exclaimed in a tremulous soft voice before nearly fainting.

Zephyr caught Kylie, preventing her collapse. Tears flowed from his eyes as he too had been traumatized and dismayed by the revelation. For the first time, Akalina was too stunned for words. Her face contorted with severe uneasiness as she looked on.

"Remember when you told me that had I not shown up to your apartment that night, you might not have killed yourself after all? Well … I know for a fact that you would've succeeded in your attempt … because you already did." Camile's ghost replied in a gentle voice that cracked with sorrow.

Camile hugged her knees and tried to rock the fear and the pain away.

"No! No! This can't be happening! I didn't kill myself! I didn't! It's a mistake! It's a mistake!" She screamed hysterically through her gut-wrenching sobs as she tried to convince herself. Camile repeated those three words as if trying to reprogram her brain and alter the past.

"You're right, it was a *terrible* mistake—one that I was sent back to correct." Camile's ghost somberly explained.

Akalina finally managed to verbalize her thoughts.

"Does this mean I have a ghost out there somewhere too?" She asked with genuine concern.

"Akalina, I don't know, but I sure hope not. One of you is bad enough." Camile's ghost replied softly.

Camile's ghost offered Camile a hand to help her off the floor. Camile quickly moved away.

"No! *Please* don't touch me!" She shouted hysterically as she stumbled onto her feet and was suddenly struck with another wave of dizziness.

Akalina took advantage of the moment and attempted to enter the room. She was instantly thrown to the floor and landed on her back with a thud. She grimaced with pain as she stood up and angrily faced her parents. Still sobbing, Camile slowly approached the entrance, but instead of trying to go in, she tested it to see if she could get her arm to go through first. As she extended her arm, it was thrown back by a powerful force. It was evident that she couldn't enter either.

"What's this?! You said only one can enter?! Akalina shouted. "What are we supposed to do?!"

Their parents sadly looked on without a word. Frustrated, Akalina found a small rock and hurled it at them. The rock struck the invisible barrier and nearly hit Camile as it ricocheted in her direction.

"Say something! You owe me at least that!" Akalina bellowed angrily, but her parents remained silent—with the exception of Kylie's hysterical sobs. Zephyr tried his best to remain strong as he held her in his arms.

"Stop it! This solves nothing!" Camile replied through her sobs.

Akalina exhaled a frustrated breath as she stopped to think. Suddenly a cold, sinister grin emerged on her face. It clearly expressed that there were dark, demented thoughts in progress.

"Camile, you're absolutely right. Arguing with them solves nothing ... but killing you does!" She said in a low creepy voice. "Clearly it's not meant for both of us to live through this and I refuse to be the one to die! It should be easy for you, since technically you already have experience with death!"

Before Camile could react, Akalina attacked her with all her might, knocking her to the ground. Their parents watched helplessly as they watched them scuffle. Tears continued to flow down their mother's face as their father put an arm around her in comfort. Camile's ghost tried to separate Camile and Akalina, but was surprised when her arms phased through them. She tried to grab hold of Akalina, but once again her arm passed through her. The ghost no longer had solid form.

"Stop it! Don't do this!" Camile's ghost yelled desperately.

The twins rolled across the ground as they viciously punched, clawed, scratched, bit and kicked at one another. The scuffle didn't last very long before Camile and Akalina both felt another wave of intense dizziness. Helplessly prostrate on the ground, they attempted to catch their breath.

"Akalina," Camile panted faintly, "we're going about this the wrong way."

"You're only saying that because you're losing!" Akalina said between labored breaths.

"Think what you want, but I'm done fighting! I don't know about you, but I refuse to spend my last moments fighting for something I'll probably never understand." Camile replied.

"So you're just going to let yourself die right here. Is that it?"

"I guess so." Camile said with a slight giggle. "It wouldn't be the first time I've been dead!"

"Camile, don't do it! Don't give up! Please!" Her ghost exclaimed desperately.

"Sorry you came all this way to save me for nothing." Camile replied to her ghost. "At least we know there's life after death. Maybe there's a chance I can come back again."

"No! Don't give up! Please! You don't understand! This is our *only* chance!" The ghost cried desperately.

As Camile's ghost wept, Akalina limped to the entrance and was shocked to discover that she still couldn't enter. She cursed furiously before collapsing at her twin's side once again.

"You're still here?" Camile asked.

"Apparently we're both … meant to die!" Akalina spat angrily yet breathlessly, casting a spiteful glare at her parents. "Some parents we have huh? Sentencing their … own children to death!"

Camile's ghost refused to give up, continuing her attempts to persuade her living counterpart to persevere.

"Don't give up! You're stronger than you give yourself credit for!" The ghost fervently exclaimed.

Suddenly, Camile remembered something her mother used to tell her when she was a teenager. Then she gasped softly while recalling the final line of her father's song. The past words of her parents resonated in her head and tears streamed down her face as she struggled to accept what she now knew she needed to do.

"Akalina, I—I know we've had our … differences. Despite the fact that you've done terrible things and that you even … tried to kill me, I … accept you for who you are, even though I might not like it." Camile replied as she wheezed for air.

"Accept *me?* What's wrong with you! *You're* the one that should be begging for *my* acceptance." Akalina exclaimed angrily before wincing. "Wait a minute! What are you doing? Stop messing with my head!"

"This is … not for you, Akalina. I'm doing it for myself. But you can't deny that we both want the same thing right now. There's no ignoring the fact that …"

"No! Stop it! You don't know what you're talking about! What are you doing?" Akalina shouted with a look of terror on her face as Camile approached her.

Akalina moved to strike, but for the first time, Camile was much too quick for her. Camile blocked her strikes before quickly wrapping her arms around Akalina—who became frozen with shock.

"I accept you." Camile whispered while hugging her twin. Tears flowed from her eyes since she had no clue of what was about to happen.

After a brief moment, Akalina reluctantly returned the gesture. The pair embraced each other while preparing for the end. Suddenly, an intense blast of energy surrounded each of them. Camile was engulfed by a cool blue glow and Akalina by a fiery red illumination. Their parents and Camile's ghost looked on with sheer amazement and apprehension. After a moment, both energies became intermixed and the radiance intensified as its color transformed into a remarkable shade of violet. Their parents strained their eyes against the intense glare in an attempt to catch a glimpse of what was happening, but their efforts were in vain.

"Camile!" The ghost called frantically. "Where are you? What's happening?"

Kylie and Zephyr called out for their daughters, but there was no answer.

The light eventually faded away, forcing Kylie, Zephyr and Camile's ghost to adjust their eyes. They looked at the spot where the twins had been embracing just moments earlier and saw a single woman standing before them with closed eyes. At first, it was indistinguishable whether it was Akalina or Camile, but the dark, layered hairstyle gave an indication that it was the latter.

"Camile?" Kylie asked almost cautiously. "Is that you?"

"Mom, it's me." Camile answered quietly.

"Where's Akalina?" Her ghost asked as she cautiously looked around.

"I was somehow able to convince her that we needed each other in order to live … or maybe it was her that convinced me. I don't understand exactly how it happened or why, but we somehow … *merged* with each other. Now we're one … and only *one* can enter, right?" Camile said with a dazed expression on her face. Her parents nodded with happy tears in their eyes.

"What?!" Camile's ghost exclaimed with unbridled shock. "But … How …?"

"Come in. We're finally able to explain everything now. It's long overdue." Zephyr replied.

"No kidding!" Camile and her ghost replied in unison before awkwardly regarding one another.

She and her ghost walked slowly towards the entrance and were relieved to find they were able to enter the room. The space was quite large, about the size of half a football field and was warmly lit. The room was completely circular and had beautiful light fixtures on the wall—equidistant to each other. There also appeared to be five other corridors that led to the room. It seemed like some sort of common meeting area within the large structure. It looked awkwardly empty since Camile, her parents and her ghost were the only ones present in the large room.

As Camile looked up at the ceiling, she noticed a huge skylight. It looked exactly like her medallion, but on a much grander scale. Although it was night-time, she could see the calm ripples of the water above and saw within the starry sky beyond a few wispy clouds. Her breath was taken away by the sheer beauty of it. Upon entering, Camile immediately ran to her parents, who embraced her tenderly as her ghost watched with a tearful smile.

"Well, I guess I've completed my mission. Now yours can continue." The ghost gently said to her living counterpart.

"What? You're leaving now?" Camile asked.

"My work here is done. Besides, there can't very well be two of us now can there?" The ghost chuckled slightly with a wink.

"If you asked me that yesterday I would've said that was impossible. Now, I'm not so sure." Camile replied. "Anyway, don't you want to find out the answers to all our questions?"

The ghost thought for a brief moment before regarding her living counterpart with a warm smile.

"Don't worry. I'll … *we'll* get the answers." The ghost answered with a wink. "Don't forget, we're not dead … not anymore anyway."

As the ghost watched Camile tearfully embrace her parents, she seemed to be in a state of extreme joy. Happy tears trickled down her cheeks. Camile's ghost tilted her head back and outstretched her arms. It seemed as though she were mentally hugging her parents before fading away. After a few moments, Camile gently ceased her embrace and looked at her parents.

"So, I guess we have a lot to catch up on. Where would you like to start?" She asked.

CHAPTER 21

▼

THE TRUTH & THE PAST

Camile's parents led her to the center of the large room and sat with her at a cozy table. They were visibly ecstatic to reunite with their daughter. Camile couldn't help but stare into the skylight and admire the spectacular view. She compared it with her necklace several times before fixing her gaze upward, staring up through the water and into the starry sky with wondrous amazement. She was wide-eyed with bewilderment while admiring the silhouettes of several large fish swimming peacefully overhead. It looked as though they were soaring across the star-studded sky.

"Wow!" She whispered.

"Stunning isn't it? You should see how beautiful it looks during meteor showers!" Zephyr replied with a smile.

"So, this place ... is underwater?" Camile asked.

"This structure is located underneath a very large lake." He explained after nodding.

Although Camile was very happy to see her parents alive and together, she couldn't help but feel sorely about all the lies and pain she endured over the years. Her bitterness became clear to her parents as she regarded them with a glum expression. Suddenly, she became aware that she now shared Akalina's thoughts, feelings and desires. It was a realization she found most disturbing.

"I don't blame you for being angry at us, but when you hear what we have to say I think you'll realize that we did the best we could with the gravity of the situation we faced." Kylie replied.

"Why was it necessary for me to risk my life going through that … *maze?*" Camile asked with a hint of bitterness in her voice.

"We had to be sure that it was you. Over the years, several imposters have tried to make their way through it—some of which I'm sure you've encountered." Zephyr replied, slightly raising his brow.

Camile shuddered as she recalled the skeletons she came across just a short while earlier.

"Why would they pretend to be me?" She asked.

"They were apparently under the impression that if they completed the maze, as you call it, that they would obtain a very valuable reward. Little did they know the obstacles were specifically built for you to complete."

"Why me? What's so special about me?"

"You're about to find out, but first there's a lot to explain." Her mother replied.

"Mom, how could you lie to me all those years?" Camile passionately blurted out. "How could you let me believe Dad was dead?"

"Camile, I tried to give you hope that he was still alive, but you didn't believe me—" Kylie attempted to explain.

"Well can you blame me? There was no evidence that he was still alive and all I had to cling to was a picture!"

"There's no need for arguments." Zephyr said softly. "Please, just give us a chance to explain."

"But Zephyr, there's so much to explain! Where do we even start?" Kylie exclaimed.

"At the beginning of course." He replied with a half smile. "Camile, you might find this hard to believe, but your special abilities come from my side of the family."

"What's so hard to believe about that?" She asked.

"Well, I'm not sure how to tell you this so I'll just say it. I'm not from the same world as your mother."

"Wait, are you trying to tell me that you're an alien or something?!" Camile chortled sarcastically. "So, what's the name of your home planet?"

"No, Camile. It's not like that. He's not an alien." Her mother replied.

"Camile, I *am* from Earth, just from a different dimension of it." Zephyr explained. "Right now you're not in the same dimension as the one you've grown accustomed to. Right now, you're on a separate dimensional layer from the life you once knew. We call this dimension the *Transcendent World*. The dimension you grew up in is called the *Coexistent World*. I'm a *Transcendent Human* and your mother's a *Coexistent Human*. As you may have guessed, you're half of each. We've discovered that the *Coexistent World* is slowly but surely losing stability due to the increasingly destructive and careless ways of the humans there. Over the centuries, our people have been sending teams there. The sole purpose of these teams is to attempt to rectify the situation by introducing new methods and ideas to help remedy the problem. With each attempt, the *Coexistent Humans* initially show great improvement and progress, but they eventually revert to their destructive ways."

"What does all this have to do with me?" Camile asked.

"There was a prediction; a child would be born half of this world and half of the other. That child would grow to potentially help us to succeed in our mission of salvaging and repairing these worlds. It has been said that this child could possibly grow to initiate the pivotal point of a remarkable change."

"But there was a flipside to the prediction." Kylie added. "It foresaw another child, a nemesis that would have the capability of generating unimaginable turmoil, heartache and terrible destruction. For the most part, people disregarded the predictions since they began to lose faith in certain things. But then there where hints that these predictions were more accurate than people were willing to admit. When the council realized that you possessed powers far beyond anything we'd ever seen and that you seemed to be using it only to hurt people, they passed an order. That order was for you to be … destroyed before you had the chance to go on a destructive rampage."

"*Destroyed?* They thought I was this … nemesis? And they arranged to kill me?" Camile asked with quiet disbelief.

"I'm afraid it's true." Zephyr explained sadly. "The council became divided between those who thought you were innocent and those who believed you were the dark prophecy incarnate. The latter would eventually come to be known by many names—most of which are too vulgar to repeat, but they are most commonly known as *The Rebels*."

"I still can't believe how easily they rationalized the idea of killing a child." Kylie glumly replied. "But we later discovered that their decision was based on exaggerated speculation from certain council members who were threatened by— and even jealous of—your existence. We fought as much as we could. We tried to convince them that you could be taught to control your powers. When that didn't work, we attempted to run away with you one night, but we were caught.

The guards ripped you from my arms and took you away. We knew our last chance of saving your life was to suggest an unorthodox solution of having them perform a procedure to separate your positive and negative powers. It was done in hopes that your negative powers could be contained. It's usually a procedure reserved for violent delinquents and is rarely ever performed on children, but it was certainly better than the alternative of watching our only child die!" She explained as she broke into sobs.

"Little did we know that it would be that very action that would fulfill the darker half of the prediction." Camile's father explained. "You see, Camile, Akalina was never your twin. She's your other half, your darker half ... your nemesis."

Camile struggled to wrap her head around all of the information being thrown at her. Her thirst for the truth was finally being quenched, but it was happening so quickly she feared she would drown in it. There were so many questions enshrouding her mind and she tried to force herself to make sense of the whole thing, but simply couldn't.

"I—I don't understand. How is that possible?" She asked, clearly baffled with the latest revelation.

"Akalina was the result of something that went terribly wrong during the procedure." Zephyr explained. "Although you were only a six year old child, you fought against the separation harder than people five times that age. Your mother and I witnessed the incident first hand. It—it's something we both wished we'd never seen, our only child being torn apart in front of our very eyes." His voice cracked with sorrow as tears trickled from his eyes.

Kylie's tears flowed freely as she held his hand which helped him to continue.

"The technician who conducted the procedure suddenly went insane after a strange explosion in the lab. When everything cleared, we were stunned to see that your negative side had become unhinged from your positive and had somehow taken physical form. It was too risky to attempt fusing your two halves together again, so the council ruled that the two halves never know about each other." He explained.

"In order for that to happen," Kylie added, "most of your memory had to be altered. The council then ordered that I raise you in the *Coexistent World* while your father raised Akalina here. Your father and I had biological transmitters implanted in our brains to ensure we wouldn't reveal anything that happened to you. But, you were so persuasive and so determined to hear the truth about your past that you were almost able to get me to tell you everything. It nearly overloaded the transmitters. The reason why I went into a coma was because the transmitters needed to use more of my energy than usual in order to continue working. It turns out that they needed *a lot* of energy to resist your persuasion. The transmitters were the reasons why my CT scan *appeared* to indicate tumors. Nancy had been instructed in advance that in the event something like that happened, she would immediately switch the slides, with the ones I had taken prior to the implants, before anyone got the chance to see them. Somehow Dr. Kline got a hold of the *real* slides and Nancy was forced to bring him here to have his memory altered. If any doctor from our world were to attempt to biopsy or operate on the so-called tumors, it most likely would've been fatal since *Coexistent Humans* haven't advanced to such technology."

"But Nancy showed the same symptoms as you when I began to push her for answers. Did she have those things implanted in her head too?" Camile asked.

"Yes, she did. So did everyone who was directly involved with your case."

"Akalina attacked Nancy. Is she okay?"

"Nancy's fine. She's resting comfortably." Kylie answered. Camile exhaled a sigh of relief.

"Well, although we were ordered to raise you and Akalina separately, I was allowed to come up to visit her on occasion. But there was one condition, I couldn't mention that I was her mother so I posed as a family friend. Over time she discovered the truth of my identity from somebody, but I never found out who they were—although I've had suspicions. Unfortunately your father was restricted from leaving this dimension to see you and it was quite clear that you couldn't come here to see him being that Akalina was here."

"Whoa!" Camile exclaimed silently and there was a slight pause before she asked her next question. "In the … other world, I've had jobs, visited doctors and even had a driver's license, but nothing was in the system. Were my records erased?"

"In actuality, you never had any *official* records since you're technically not of that world. Your mother was instrumental in coordinating the illusion of your identity in the *Coexistent World*. She helped strategize everything from your medical appointments to your employment." Zephyr clarified.

"Everything was going smoothly until I ended up in the hospital." Kylie added. "Someone slipped up after that, but everything worked out for the best."

"But how were you able to falsify so many records? Wouldn't the authorities have caught on? If you had that much power, why didn't you make it so we were rich?"

"It was very important that you were exposed to all facets of humanity in the coexisting world." Zephyr answered. "That might not have been the case if you were rich and didn't have to work. Every aspect of your life, no matter how mundane it may have seemed, has shaped you into the person you need to be. As for your records, we've had many people in place to handle the mundane details and to make sure everything went smoothly. I can't go into specifics since I've been sworn to secrecy."

"But why was it necessary to do all that stuff?"

"For precautionary measures. Camile, although most of the humans in both dimensions look very similar on the outside, on the inside we have different physiological structures. Nothing too extreme, but different enough to raise a few flags in the *Coexistent World*. Had they discovered the unique qualities of your internal structure, they would've been curious and most likely would've wanted to poke, prod and operate to 'correct' certain 'problems'. It's happened to our kind in the past and ... Well, it was devastating."

Camile's face expressed mild fear and anxiety about the current subject.

"J—Just how different is my 'internal structure'?" She asked somewhat reluctantly.

"We'll get to that in time, Camile. There's just so much to cover." Kylie gently interjected.

Glancing down with slight impatience, Camile caught sight of her necklace, which prompted her next question.

"I'm curious. How does the necklace fit into all this? Is it the source of my power?" She asked, stroking the stone with her fingers. "Why did you flip out when you realized I found it and why did you take it from me in the first place?"

"The necklace is a talisman." Her mother answered with a faint smile. "Many people here have them. Although it helps you to *channel* your power, it's not the source of it by any means. Over time I'm sure you will be able to use your powers quite efficiently without it. I took it away from you only because I had to. It was believed that the separation procedure wouldn't have worked if you were wearing it. Your father and I requested for it to be destroyed in order to eliminate any chance of you or Akalina finding it ... or each other. That's why when I saw you walk into the hospital wearing it I was a bit shocked."

"After I found the necklace, I met Akalina at the hospital, but I didn't have a clue who she was. She had the ability to ... change into other people." Camile replied.

"When you found the necklace it enabled her to track you." Zephyr explained. "As for her ability to morph her appearance it's not exactly an unusual gift among our kind, but it's something that usually takes years to master."

"Although she changed her appearance I still sensed her presence at the hospital." Kylie explained. "When I saw that you had changed your hair and makeup to the same exact way she used to wear hers, I panicked. I thought she had already reintegrated with you and had taken over."

"So she did it on purpose!" Camile exclaimed angrily, almost to herself. "That's why she was so focused on having me change my look! She must've known how you'd react."

Camile thought for a moment before asking her next question.

"You mentioned that Akalina is my negative half, but I noticed that even though I disagreed with the things she did, I was also tempted by anger and hatred. What does that mean?" She asked.

"It means that although you were separated, you left a bit of yourselves imprinted on the other. That's how come Akalina seemed so accepting of you before you reintegrated. The two of you accepting each other was the one thing that saved your life. That was the whole point of you having to overcome all those obstacles. In order to accept your future tasks it was critical that you accept yourself first. We didn't know about Zareah, she was ... a bit of a surprise." Zephyr said. His face wore an expression of sad uneasiness that was mirrored by Kylie.

Feeling awkward, Camile decided to avoid the subject of her ghost.

"But if Akalina was capable of such terrible things and now she's a part of me, won't I be capable of those things too? Isn't there a chance I'll have urges to hurt people?" She asked with concern in her eyes.

"Yes, but that's something that we all struggle with. All people struggle to recognize negative behavior and learn how to control it. You're just more aware of that battle now."

Camile took a moment to admire the beautiful skylight once again, realizing the sky was becoming brighter—an indication that a new day would soon be dawning.

"The council recognized that they were misled and they greatly regret their decision about ordering your execution." Camile's father replied. "It turns out that *The Rebels* exaggerated certain incidents and twisted the details to make it seem that executing you was the only viable solution to protect our people as well as the positive side of the prediction. *The Rebels* were afraid since the prediction also stated that the same child who possessed remarkable potential would initiate a complete reform of the council and expose lurking treachery. They were obviously uncomfortable with any changes since it would reveal their corruption.

Ironically, it was their own actions that led to their exposure, which in turn brought about the beginning of the council's reformation."

"Who exactly are *The Rebels?*"

"They're *Transcendent Humans*—most of whom were members of the council. *The Rebels* objected to the council's decision to aid the *Coexistent Humans* instead of dominating and even destroying them. They also strongly disagreed with the council's decision to allow you to live after the mishaps that took place." He explained.

"Why do *The Rebels* want the humans in the other dimension to be destroyed?" Camile asked while frowning.

"The *Coexistent Humans* are losing compassion and respect for one another and the world in which they live. It seems that they have become so obsessed with material possessions, money, greed and appearances that not much else seems to matter. They are becoming increasingly self-absorbed and superficial for the most part and it will ultimately result in their undoing. That sort of careless and reckless behavior is not only affecting the humans there, but their environment as well. We continually attempt to rectify the situation by introducing reconstructive ideas such as environmental programs and behavioral alternatives that encourage less destructive behavior. However, I'm afraid that it will only delay the expected. Their destruction is inevitable ... unless they change their attitudes towards each other. That's where the prophecy comes in, that's where you come in. However, *The Rebels* feel that it's an impossible feat to work with and educate the *Coexistent Humans*. They believe that the humans there will simply never learn and that our people should take matters into our own hands and take complete control of their world."

"So, why are the Trans ...?"

"*Transcendent Humans.*"

"Yeah. Why do they want to intervene anyway? It's not like what happens in the other dimension affects this one."

"I wish that were true, but it simply isn't. It's ironic, the things that seem to be the most separated are often the most connected. There are ways that the damage in one dimension can be transferred into the next, albeit perhaps not in the same way. With each war and each catastrophic event that takes place in that dimension, it sends a ripple of devastation into ours and vice versa. So I guess you can't blame us for feeling so passionate about helping the *Coexistent Humans* to repair the damage of their ways before matters get worse. You and many others will be instrumental in that process, Camile."

CHAPTER 22

▼

DAWN OF THE FUTURE

A long pause ensued as Camile tried her best to come to grips with the information she was receiving.

"Wow! What a trip!" She exclaimed. "So you're saying that unless we do something, that entire dimension will be destroyed? That all the humans there will die?"

"Not in the way you might think. They'll still remain alive physically, but only just. If they continue to progress on such a destructive course, their emotional connection with each other will continue to deteriorate. They'll become emotionally inept and completely isolated from each other. In a sense, they will die internally, which will make them very vulnerable prey." Zephyr clarified.

"Vulnerable to who? *The Rebels*?" Camile asked.

"Yes, among other things." He sadly answered.

"Things like what?"

"I'm afraid it's a little too soon for me to go into that. You already have a lot of information to digest as it is. Besides, there are some things you will need to be properly prepared for."

Camile was desperate to learn more, but realized that Zephyr was right. She'd already been through a lot and needed time to process the information she'd already been given.

"So I'm destined to single-handedly save the world? Is that it?" Camile asked with a note of skepticism in her voice.

"No one can single-handedly save an entire world." Zephyr chuckled. "That's just an idea that's often romanticized in books and movies. Truth is, it takes more than just one person to do that. *Much more.* But, one person can start a new chain of events. You're the pivotal person who can help start such a chain. You have the power to remind people about what's really important and that they shouldn't allow things like jealousy, material things, anger or ill-will to rule them. You have the ability to remind them about their connection and that there's still hope. If you're able to do all that, you'll help them to win the first phase of the *Invisible War.* You'll learn more about this later. However, your powers alone might not be enough to help you in that mission, but you will have something special to guide you."

Camile held her necklace's stone in her hand and gazed at it for a moment.

"This thing doesn't always seem to work for me." She replied.

"Your father's not talking about the necklace, Camile." Kylie explained. "It's only a tool. He was referring to your heart and the genuine sensitivity, kindness, love and strength that it possesses."

Raising an eyebrow, Camile regarded her father, who nodded in acquiescence.

"*Strength?* I think you're confusing me with Akalina!" Camile chortled.

"Just because you can't see beyond your own pain and sensitivity doesn't mean that your strength doesn't exist. You wouldn't *be* here right now if it wasn't for your strength and determination. Sometimes sensitivity can be a form of strength in itself." Kylie stated.

"I still don't get it. Even with this power, how am I supposed to accomplish all those things? Why should I even bother to try? Most of people in the *Coexistent World* only seem to value money and how much they can make of it. I've seen people walk over each other, steal and turn their backs on each other when they were in desperate need of help. There's nothing on the news that doesn't have something to do with murder, hate, terrorism, war, corruption—"

"Camile," Kylie interrupted, "just because the positive isn't advertised as often as the negative doesn't mean that it's not there. It just needs to be magnified."

"But Mom, there are a lot of *really evil* people out there! How can I *possibly* reach all those people and get them to understand me? I can't even get people to *listen* to me! How can I possibly get everyone to care about anything other than themselves?!" She asked with a note of frustration in her voice.

"You'll have help. You won't be able to do this all on your own. But Camile, you're forgetting that you've just received the power of your other half." Her father explained. "Believe it or not, you can make it work to your advantage."

Camile and Zephyr stared at each other for a brief moment before she finally got the idea.

"You've got to be joking! You're suggesting that I tap into my newfound evil side?"

"I know it sounds strange, but yes. It will be necessary at times. It will help you to understand how certain people think and will allow you to relate to them on a certain level and then when they're ready—if they're ready—you can help them to realize that there's a better way to live. In turn, it will start a chain reaction as those people will help others to understand that there is a better way—a more balanced way—to live. That process will give humanity a greater chance of survival." He explained.

"And if they're *not* ready? What then? What if they get mad and try to kill me or something?" Camile asked.

"Camile, we don't expect you to be able to reach *all* people. That would be impossible. I'm sure that there will be many people who will reject your help. But I think you'll be able to reach enough people to restore the natural balance of things. However, there are many people out there who won't want you to succeed—mainly *The Rebels*—but I imagine that you will also encounter *Coexistent Humans* who have grown so accustomed to living in the emotional misery they call home. As strange as it may seem, they will likely lash out to protect what they have become familiar with even though it's bad for them. Camile, I'm afraid that when the next phase of the *Invisible War* begins, you *will* have even more enemies. You have the power to defend yourself and even … to destroy, but only if it becomes absolutely necessary. You might need to use that to your defense if your life is ever in danger."

"No! I *won't* kill anyone!" Camile exclaimed loudly, her voice echoed throughout the empty room.

"Camile, right now this is all theoretical. Hopefully you will never have to use your powers in that way. For the most part, our civilization is very peaceful and we believe that the loss of any kind of life is tragic. However, regrettably there are times when violence becomes quite necessary in order to defend ourselves. Especially in times of war—which is exactly what's coming."

'*… in life it's either hurt or be hurt, kill or be killed.*' Akalina's voice resounded inside Camile's head.

She tried to shake the thought as she looked at her parents, sighed nervously and wondered what was next.

"Camile, do you remember when people would claim that you seemed to appear out of thin air?" Kylie asked.

"Yeah, but what does that have to do with this?"

"Everything. On each of those occasions you were daydreaming weren't you?"

"Yeah, why?" asked Camile.

"Was there something specific you would see in those daydreams?"

Camile shook her head while trying to recall. After a few long moments she gasped when she realized that before each incident of her apparent 'disappearing acts' she had daydreamed about the enormous, beautiful tree that flourished outside of the structure in which they were sitting. She never paid much attention to the subject of her daydreams until that very moment.

"The tree!" She whispered.

"Do you get it now, Camileon? Technically you didn't disappear, but you have the ability to blend in with your surrounding energy. Not only that, but you can also shift beyond the realm of perception of the people in the *Coexistent Dimension*. You're able to do the same thing here too." Zephyr explained.

"*Camileon?*" She inquired.

"That was our nickname for you. We came up with it when we noticed your ability to ... *blend in*. When your mother was about seven months pregnant with you, something weird started happening. When she went to her checkups, the equipment no longer registered her as being pregnant. They couldn't find your heartbeat, couldn't detect you through the sonogram, nothing. Needless to say your mother was hysterical since she could still feel you move on occasion. Thankfully, everything turned out alright. In retrospect we realize that you were blending in with your mother's energy."

"How is this possible? How could I possibly shift between dimensions *and* blend in with energy?" Camile asked with puzzled disbelief.

"That's what everyone wants to know, particularly *The Rebels*. So far, the only way to travel between dimensions is through rifts or portals. We have known this to be true for many years. In order to prevent a stream of people and creatures traveling into the other dimension, we guard those openings. Try to think of it as inter-dimensional border patrol."

"Camile, that's what your father does. He's in charge of an organization that monitors and controls inter-dimensional travel. He was chasing rebels in his shuttle when he unexpectedly traveled through a rift and crashed into our dimension. The rift quickly resealed itself and he had no way of getting back to his own world so he decided to take his chances and walked to the hospital where I treated him. However, I noticed something very strange about his physiological structure. Over time, he eventually trusted me enough to tell me the truth about who he was." Kylie replied.

"Love can make a person do strange things—no matter which world they're from." Zephyr said with a soft smile before continuing his explanation. "*The Rebels* can't travel between dimensions without being detected by our guards … for the most part anyway. Somehow, you're able to travel between dimensions without using the portals. That's why *The Rebels* are so determined to get to you. If they're able to find out how you do it, we'll have no power over them. The *Coexistent Humans* will be defenseless since most of them can't see things that originate outside of their world. Hell, these days, they can barely see each other. The few *Coexistent Humans* who can see, hear or sense *Transcendent* beings, often confuse them with ghosts. Some of them dismiss the sounds and/or visions as hallucinations or paranoia. The people who accept what they see and hear, are usually classified as over-imaginative, drunks, addicts or mentally ill. Unfortunately, this all plays out to the advantage of *The Rebels*. Once they slip through our defenses and into the *Coexistent World*, they have free range to wreak havoc. Even in their most private moments, the humans there are under constant scrutiny. *The Rebels* are proving to be one of their most stealthy enemies. *The Rebels* are constantly stalking their prey, evaluating their weaknesses as the *Coexistent Humans* work, sleep, enjoy leisure activities, totally oblivious to the silent, seemingly invisible enemy just inches away, waiting to snuff them out. From the looks of things, *The Rebels* are stepping up their game and I'm afraid it'll only get worse. That's why guarding the portals is no longer enough to help protect the *Coexistent World*."

"Wait a minute. I remember seeing two ghosts on a train once, but I thought it was a dream or something. They caused a fight on the train that day. Were they from this world?"

Camile's father thought for a moment as a perplexed expression crossed his face.

"I wasn't aware you were on the train that day." He replied with a baffled expression. "But yes, they're delinquent *Transcendent Humans*—not ghosts. They didn't have clearance to travel into the coexisting world and we've been chasing them for quite awhile. They're now in custody and we're trying to determine if they are linked to *The Rebels*."

"Mom. Does this mean that I *really did* make Barry disappear when I was a teenager?" Camile asked.

"Well, you didn't exactly make him disappear, but you accidentally projected such a strong image of the tree that he felt compelled to come here. He made it to the embankment and tried to jump over into this dimension, but the guardians caught him in time before he entered. However, he still had the image of the tree and the knowledge of where the portal was, so we had no choice but to remove it from his memory. Then we masked the event with a cover story claiming he was hit by lightning." Kylie answered.

"But, *I* didn't even remember anything about this place! How could I make him go somewhere I didn't even remember existed?" Camile asked with pain in her eyes, but felt slightly proud, which disturbed her.

"Deep inside, the memories were still there. They weren't erased, just deeply repressed. Camile, have you figured out how your powers work?"

She attempted to think for a moment before shaking her head.

"I think I have an idea." She answered.

"Do you remember what happened at *Arizona General Hospital?*"

"Yeah. It's ironic, the things I want to forget I seem to easily remember and the things I want to remember seem lost." Camile said hopelessly.

"Well, after that incident, your father and I asked you about what you were feeling at the time. It took us some time to piece it together but once we did ..."

"Piece what together?"

"In addition to your other powers, you possess the ability to somehow merge your thoughts, feelings and desires into other people. Apparently, on the day of the incident you incorporated intense feelings of rage, sorrow as well as a powerful desire to get those children to pay for what they had done to you."

"I made them do those horrible things to themselves?" Camile replied with despair, coupled with the disturbing thought that *they deserved it.*

"Camile, their actions were their own. Those people couldn't handle the intensity of the feelings you evoked in them, so they dealt with it the best way they knew how. They figured that if they punished themselves for what they had done and how they treated you that perhaps the hurt and the pain would go away. You provided them with your feelings, what they did with them was their own decision." Zephyr glumly explained.

"How do you know all this? Did they tell you?" Camile asked.

"Yes. The council did a complete investigation on the matter and spoke to the ... victims." He appeared to feel awkward saying the word since the situation was caused by his daughter.

"It's okay, they *were* victims after all." Camile solemnly admitted.

"They were all completely unaware that the feelings were not initially their own and some of them became so devastated that they even contemplated taking their own lives."

"Well, that sounds awfully familiar." Camile muttered under her breath.

"Camile, this is the most powerful of all the gifts you possess." He explained. "It's very unusual and it has the potential to become more destructive than any manmade weapon, but can also bring about understanding and great peace if handled carefully. That's why it's very important that *The Rebels* don't get to you before you learn to fully control your powers. That's the reason why they're after you, Camile. They want to use your powers to do their bidding and they will stop at nothing to get it."

"But how can you trust me to make the right decision to use my powers to help people when I've already used them to hurt so many? Some people at *Arizona General* even died as a result!" Camile asked tearfully.

Her parents exchanged apprehensive glances before regarding her with compassionate expressions.

"Camile, you should focus on learning how to trust yourself. That's the most important thing you have to accomplish at this time. You need to have confidence and faith in yourself in order to become the warrior you're supposed to be. There's a war coming. We call it the *Invisible War* because at first, the *Coexistent Humans* won't even realize that it's taking place. Actually, the first phase of the war has been in the process of being fought for centuries. It's the struggle to choose between positive and negative. *The Rebels* have begun to upset the process of how the *Coexistent Humans* make their decisions. As you've undoubtedly seen in news reports, it's had dire consequences—people blowing each other up, killing and tormenting each other without a second thought to anything other than themselves or finances." Zephyr replied grimly.

"So, now I'm supposed to be a warrior, huh?" Camile asked softly after a brief pause. "And just what is it I'm supposed to fight against?"

"You will undoubtedly have to fight against many things—most of which we'll prepare you for in time—but the main question you should ask yourself is: *What are you supposed to fight for?*" He answered.

"Which is?"

"Compassion, peace, love, understanding ... in a sense, humanity itself. You will be one of many who will help to restore the balance in the *Invisible War*. In doing so, you'll help protect something very precious. I'll explain more about that when the time is right." He answered.

He cleared his throat before he spoke again.

"Camile, I think it's time for you to see just how different this dimension really is from the coexisting one."

Kylie and Zephyr rose from their seats. Camile regarded them cautiously before joining them.

"Come, there are some things you must be shown, not told." Zephyr said.

Camile's parents led her down a long corridor. As they walked, they passed by several people dressed in similar attire to her parents'. She felt as though she were back in high school as she observed the behavior of the citizens. Some pretended not to see her and others stared with either astonishment or apprehension. At the end of the corridor was a spacious room with a series of large transparent tubular lifts. Each lift could accommodate up to twenty people.

As soon as Camile and her parents entered, a transparent capsule-like pod formed around them and sealed shut before steadily escalating through the ceiling. Camile was astounded when she saw that they were traveling upward through the lake. She saw a wonderful array of colorful marine creatures swimming around the tube which contained the pod. It was the kind of aquatic life she never dreamed existed. Suddenly, Camile's view was obstructed when the capsule traveled through a rocky wall.

Her parents regarded Camile with proud, loving smiles as the pod came to a gentle halt. The pod door opened to reveal an even terrain path that stretched between the large rocky walls on each side. Camile gazed at her parents as if asking for permission to exit and they gestured warmly for her to do so. As they walked along the path together, the walls gradually decreased in height. She stopped in her tracks when she heard frightening, thunderous and unfamiliar sounds which caused the ground to shake violently for a few moments.

"Camile, it's alright. Go ahead." Kylie reassured.

As they continued to walk, Camile noticed that the path began to curve around the rightmost wall. When she and her parents turned the corner, the path suddenly grew wide and revealed that they were high on a mountain. The sun was just beginning to peak over the horizon as the moon and stars slowly began to fade into the morning light. The sky seemed to be painted with the most spectacular combination of colors she had ever seen. Lovely shades of intense blues, violets and pinks harmoniously played across the heavens. A few stray shooting stars faintly streamed in the distance. The fresh, cool air filled her lungs but carried with it the unmistakably pungent smell of wildlife. As she shifted her attention downward from the fading stars, her eyes grew wide with amazement and disbelief as she saw the most bizarre, spectacular variety of animals.

There were dozens of flying creatures—including very odd, large insects such as dragonflies with wingspans that exceeded two feet. There were also huge winged creatures, like flying bird-like reptiles—most of which had people riding on their backs. Among the unusual flying creatures were several strange, oddly-shaped aircraft. Below, were enormous creatures that were being utilized to assist with the construction of buildings. Camile also noticed groups of people being carried across the large lake by gigantic sea turtles the size of small boats. It was so much for her to take in that she stumbled backward. Her father helped her to catch her balance.

"This part of the *Transcendent World* is known as *Arvaina*. Beautiful isn't it? This dimension, for the most part, is a harmonious marriage between man, technology and nature." He proudly replied.

"For the *most part?*" Camile asked with a raised eyebrow.

"Well, nothing's perfect. There are some things we have to work on, even in this world, but we're making progress."

"So this dimension is in the past … right?" Camile asked breathlessly.

"No, believe it or not, both dimensions occupy the same space and time, but are usually invisible and intangible to each other."

"How's that possible? So many of these creatures are extinct!"

"Yes, you're right. They *are* extinct … in the *Coexistent Dimension.*"

At that moment, a freakishly large dragonfly zoomed past them, startling Camile. She noticed it was carrying something, but the insect traveled too fast for her to distinguish what is was.

"Don't worry, they won't hurt you." Zephyr assured.

"Just please do me a favor, wherever the mosquitoes are, just keep them away from me." Camile replied as she continued to catch her breath. She looked around with wide eyes, determined to soak in the unusual scene.

Her parents glanced at one another before smiling at her.

"Camile, mosquitoes have been extinct from this dimension for centuries now." Zephyr explained. "There are many creatures that presently exist in the other dimension that are currently extinct in ours and vice-versa. The reason for these dimensional variations is simply due to the different paths each dimension took during the evolutionary process. That's why some of the humans here look a little different and have a slightly different biological structures but nothing so extreme that we're incompatible, as you may have guessed by now."

After he finished his explanation, Camile's parents smiled affectionately at one another as Camile marveled at the astonishing sight before her.

"I can understand why you don't want any of these things crossing over into the other dimension!" Camile exclaimed.

"Camile, these creatures are the absolute *least* we have to worry about making it over to the other world! There are some downright terrifying things residing in this realm. We manage to coexist with them quite effectively here, but if they managed to cross into the other dimension the results would be ... cataclysmic to say the least!" Zephyr exclaimed.

He saw the uneasy look on Camile's face and placed his hand on her shoulder while Kylie wrapped an arm around her waist.

"Have you ever wondered why myths and ghost tales never seem to fade? Have you ever thought about why so many children have imaginary friends or why they see things that others can't?

Camile nodded.

"Well, you're about to find out, my dear." Zephyr chuckled warmly. "Don't worry Camile. You'll be taught everything you need to know. In time, you'll be ready."

"I sure hope so!" Camile exclaimed with an uncertain sigh.

"Let's just hope the *Coexistent World* will be ready for what's coming." Kylie replied earnestly.

As Camile stood between her parents and looked into the new world before her, she felt a sense of wonder and achievement. She reflected on the perilous journey she took to get to this moment of the truth. She also pondered the uncertainty of the long road ahead of her.

However, in the midst of all the turmoil and fear in her mind, something else began to emerge. For the first time, in a very long time, there was a glimmer of hope that radiated from within her heart. As Camile's parents continued to embrace her, she felt comforted by the fact that the pieces to the puzzle that was her life were at last beginning to come together. As strange as the *Transcendent World* seemed to Camile, she realized that she was finally beginning to see something she always wanted. The truth, her destiny and her place in life.

Stay tuned for the next installment of the saga:
CAMILEON: Beyond the Veil

978-0-595-48607-6
0-595-48607-X

Printed in the United States
203399BV00003B/112-144/P